THE FAMILY RECIPE

ANDERSON CREEK #2

K.T. EGAN

Emma,
Thank you for the copy of
"The Guest"! I hope you enjoy
this piece of my heart!
Congratulations on all
your success!

K.T.

Supervising Editor: Emily Oliver
Associate Editors: Allison Macdonald, Alexandria Boykin
Internal Formatting: Allison Macdonald
Cover by: L. Austen Johnson, www.allaboutbookcovers.com

ISBN (eBook): 978-1-952919-27-5
ISBN (paperback): 978-1-952919-28-2

GenZPublishing.org
Aberdeen, NJ

For my grandfather, my first best pal, my biggest fan, and my guardian angel. Thank you for all the cherry tomatoes and the laughs.

THE ANDERSON CREEK KIDS

Maverick Sterling

Roxanne Wortham

Cheyenne Anderson

Wesley Carmody

Connor Carmody

Silas Montgomery

PROLOGUE

AUGUST 2001

A soft ray of evening sunlight raced across the front porch of the Retirement House and blessed the toes of Caleb Anderson's loafers, turning the dark brown leather into something even richer. He braced himself on the porch railing, a glass of sun tea sweating by his left hand and a half-finished cigarette hanging from the corner of his mouth, and looked out over his side yard. His granddaughter, Cheyenne, ran around the wooden playset—his late wife had insisted they build it when Cheyenne's brothers were young—laughing as she chased her best friend. Her other friends tried their best to run foot races from the corner of the set to the first bend of the half-mile-long driveway.

Caleb put the cigarette out on the pink and orange stone Celeste had painted specifically for his nicotine habit and put the butt in a weather-worn Folgers can. In his youth, his father would put similar butts into it, burned even deeper inside. The tin was a relic of the year

1950, and if one squinted hard enough, the yellow 'Mountain Grown' could still be seen in the evening light. Caleb straightened, feeling the leftover nicotine coating his teeth, and took a long gulp of tea before he stepped off the porch toward the gleefully loud children.

Their voices carried like music in the early evening air, filling the cleared two acres of land with a sense of life and joy. Cheyenne darted around Silas Montgomery, while her curly-haired friend, Roxanne, all but plowed into Connor, the younger Carmody boy, the two of them tumbling into a heap. Caleb started to laugh and moved to help the kids up.

Connor jutted out his lower lip, fighting off tears that the older boys would only mock him for. When Roxanne ran off to catch up with the others, who had abandoned their own individual amusements to look at something Maverick had found on the tree line, Caleb helped Connor brush off his shirt. "Don't let it bug you," Caleb told the boy. "Someday you're gonna be bigger than... at least the girls."

Connor sniffed and rubbed the back of his hand across his eyes. "Someday I'm gonna be bigger than all of them," he swore.

Caleb grinned and let out a sharp whistle, calling attention to the rest of the kids. "It's time to get going, guys. It's gonna be dark pretty soon and we all know how Ms. Sterling"—at the mention of his grandmother, Maverick's ears turned hot pink—"feels about little boys and girls being out past dark."

Mention of Greta Sterling made the rest of the congregation of kids more than willing to escape, lest they get a lecture on all the evil things that existed once the sun went down. Fifteen minutes, a round of heartfelt, slightly over-dramatic goodbyes, and a solemn promise between Cheyenne and Roxanne to call before bed, and the five kids that did not belong to Caleb shuffled to their bikes. Cheyenne and Caleb stood behind his red Ford pickup, his hand resting on his granddaughter's sleek fire-colored hair, and waved until the group had disappeared down the driveway.

Cheyenne turned to beam up at her grandfather, her dark eyes winking at him in the way that reminded him so much of his wife. "Dinner time?" she asked in a sweet, childlike chirp.

"Come sit with me for a few minutes, Pal? The meat-loaf's almost done."

"Sure, Gramps." She hooked her arm around his lower back and leaned into him. "Can Roxanne sleep over tomorrow night? Her parents have to go to Philadelphia for a wedding and she doesn't wanna go."

Caleb squeezed her shoulders. "I'll talk to Ralph in the morning."

That appeased her. She beamed at him as they sat down on one of the stone benches in the large garden of the Retirement House. The garden, a pet project of his sweet Celeste, was in full bloom. It surrounded them with the perfume of a warm, late summer day in the middle of one of the quietest places in the country.

Caleb handed her a book wrapped in wax paper, a trinket he'd put on the bench before going for his last cigarette of the day, and leaned against the bench's bank to watch her open it. His bones creaked as he moved on the stone, reminding him of his age.

Cheyenne beamed at Caleb after uncovering the lavender-covered recipe book. Her small fingers brushed across her grandmother's looping calligraphy, tracing each individual line of '*Recipes 1987.*' "Is this for me?" she breathed out in awe.

"It was your Gram's." He was pleased at the pure happiness that filled her face. "She had a whole collection of them. I found the trunk in the attic this morning."

"I can keep it?" she asked, unsure.

Caleb smoothed her hair back from her face and grinned. "You can keep them all." Caleb had gotten Cheyenne an Easy Bake Oven for Christmas the year before and had been amazed with how quickly she caught on to the toy. By that January, she had given up on the pre-packaged snack mixes and had started to come up with her own recipes for cookies, cakes, and even savory snacks. "If you want them."

Cheyenne jumped to her feet and wrapped her arms around her grandfather's neck, squeezing it with everything her slender arms could manage. "I love it! Thank you, thank you, thank you! I have to tell Mom!"

"You can call them after dinner." Her delighted face, the brilliant eyes that gazed up at him like he was the greatest thing in the world, made his old heart settle. He held her against him while she flipped through the pages of recipes, written in his wife's elegant script. His Pal, his beautiful granddaughter. Giving her the book, a piece of the grandmother who had loved her but had passed on before they could have met, filled him with a sense of peace he didn't know he needed.

Behind them, in its little hollow on the hill, the Retirement House settled as well—as much at peace as its proud owner.

1

*P*ennDot had taken that spring off. There had been no official government shutdown or press release on Pennsylvania Department of Transportation's state of affairs; the only indication that PennDot had given up on their designated duties since the snow had started to thaw was the lackluster job performance by the hundreds of people in their employ. As Cheyenne navigated the backroads she'd learned to drive on—two-lane, tree-lined roads that she had raced up and down on bikes and skinned her knees on a million times, ones she'd also navigated in her grandfather's red Ford— she found herself stewing over thoughts she'd been trying to neglect. When she passed the four-way intersection where Richard had died, Cheyenne found her stomach bottoming out as the grief, and the dread of what was to come, settled in.

On a particularly bad pothole, which had her gritting her teeth in panic over what it was doing to the bottom of her car, Cheyenne let out a snarling cuss and pleaded internally for a fast return to New York.

Of course, if she hadn't been running late, she wouldn't have had to drive as fast as she was. Speed definitely made the potholes and hairpin turns more annoying—and even worse for her Jeep. She scolded herself out loud, again, as she made a sharp turn onto Anderson Creek Road. The clock on her car's dash read well past when she'd wanted to be at the house—which was already two hours later than her mother had asked her to arrive. Logically, she reminded herself for the tenth time, if she hadn't delivered the Caprises' son's birthday cake herself that morning, she would have been mostly on time. Because kids—and their parents—were really, truly annoying about birthday cakes.

"Are you sure that's the right shade of green?" Marin Caprise had asked four times when Cheyenne dropped off the Hulk-themed cake for his eighth birthday bash. "I think he's supposed to be greener."

Cheyenne had smiled, enough to show even her back teeth, and told Marin that yes, in fact, the cake was the right color green. As they had discussed in their third concept meeting the week before, the cake was modeled after Mark Ruffalo's Hulk and, thus, was a different shade of green than the green streamers his parents had picked out. Sure, she could have chalked it up to the entitled way his parents let him rule the house (she'd known the Caprises since she moved to Albany, and they definitely catered to their only son a little too much), but she was more inclined to blame it on his age. And his kid-ness. Because, as she'd learned in her twenty-six years of life, kids were just plain wild. They were loud, they didn't agree with anything (even themselves), and quite honestly, they didn't listen to reason.

The cake, in no fewer words, had been a headache Cheyenne should not have dealt with on this day and at this point in her life. She had left the Caprises' house two hours later than she'd wanted to, with icing on her white t-shirt (thanks to Marin shoving the cake back at her and demanding it be greener) and a check nearly twice the size it should have been in her pocket. She was also running behind by nearly three hours by the time she made it home to change and got on the road, and the check did not make up for that.

By the time she'd turned onto the driveway leading up to her grandfather's house, Cheyenne's nerves were frayed. Between the road, replaying the encounter with Marin, and the knowledge that she was going to have to deal with her brothers being inevitably angry with each other the entire weekend, she was definitely going to need a stiff drink, or five, when she made it to the house.

It was the thought of dealing with CJ and Chester's arguing that made her cut the engine of the Cherokee abruptly and climb out of the vehicle. After bracing herself against the side of the car and muttering profanities under her breath, the kind that would have made her Sunday school teacher cringe, she got on her hands and knees and checked the Jeep's tires and underbelly for five minutes. Once she was sure her tires were in good shape and the frame hadn't suffered any permanent damage, Cheyenne patted the hood affectionately. Her temper back in check, and her sacred car in one piece, Cheyenne climbed back into the 4x4.

Instead of turning the car on and continuing up her journey, she laid her head back against the headrest and closed her eyes. In the shady hollow at the bottom of the driveway, with her wide-open windows, she could hear squirrels playing in the woods and the shouts of her nieces and nephews playing in the distance. The symphony of the early Northeast Pennsylvania summer washed over her; it smelled like her childhood—fresh-cut grass and moist earth, sticky tree bark and impending summer storms. If she sniffed hard enough, she could even taste coppery blood on her tongue from the parade of fat lips and loose teeth that came with being friends with pre-teen boys. She was reminded of all of the things her summers with her grandfather had promised her, had provided her, and found herself slipping again into the anger and the grief that had been ruling her life for the last two weeks.

Cheyenne eventually turned the key and started up the quarter-mile drive that led to the three-story farmhouse. As she took the last turn into the half-acre clearing that the house was situated in, she was engulfed in a wealth of emotion. The hairs on the back of her arms stood up and she felt her pulse pick up in her neck. She let the Jeep roll to a stop behind her brother's Tacoma and cut the engine as quickly as possible so as not to garner any extra attention from the half-dozen children running around on the other side of the hill.

The farmhouse loomed over the dirt drive, casting a shadow on the sea of cars that sat in its wake. Caleb had retired in 1986 from a successful career as a stockbroker and relocated his wife to the northeast tip of Pennsylvania, to the same sleepy town where they had used to vacation when their kids were young. They had purchased back a significant amount of the land that had been sold away when Caleb's family had moved out of the area eighty years before. The road they had purchased on was named after his family, a relic of the early days of Northeastern Pennsylvania, and Caleb and Celeste had fallen in love with it immediately. Celeste had hired an architect from the city, who had plans drawn up to model the feel of an older farmhouse but with enough room for their expansive family. The house was nestled in the middle of a wide clearing. Its back half overlooked the creek that cut through the corner of the clearing and traced the whole property.

Their home had been finished in 1988 and had been the place where Celeste had lived peacefully until she passed away in 1990, a month short of Cheyenne's being born.

Along with ten bedrooms—so that children and grandchildren could visit at will—and a kitchen that could seat twenty, the house was surrounded by a large garden and a full-size playground. From her seat at the bottom of the hill leading up to the house, Cheyenne could see her nieces and nephews playing on the large wooden structure.

At that distance, she could still make out each of their smiling faces. Unaffected by the events that had brought them together, the six children enjoyed the last reaches of the August sun. If she hurried, she could make it to the house without any of them noticing her. If she hurried. And if she was lucky.

Cheyenne left her purse and suitcase in the Cherokee and slipped between the Tacoma and her oldest brother's silver Pontiac, moving covertly. She loved the kids—had even taken the oldest two for a week each in June—but small doses of them were preferred.

Luck was on her side. She made it to the front door without being noticed and managed to slip inside just as her oldest nephew, twelve-year-old Allen, came running across the front yard. The door closed behind her softly, drowned out by the sounds of her brothers yelling in the kitchen. Cheyenne sagged against the front door and waited a minute or two to catch her bearings and drown out the sea of sadness that filled her once she was inside the house.

"You're a freaking moron," CJ was yelling from the kitchen, breaking Cheyenne's momentary relief. She had escaped the six actual children only to have to deal with another two.

Her brothers were standing chest-to-chest, scowling at each other as if they were the same age as their children outside. CJ's face was a violent shade of pink that matched the polka dots on his wife's t-shirt and clashed with his carrot-colored hair, and Chester's whole body was heaving with the same anger. Cheyenne was used to the scene. Chester's wife, Anya, clapped her hands to try and catch the attention of the two men. Both women were ignored as the brothers struggled to catch the upper hand in the inch of height that separated them.

Cheyenne stopped next to the chair the very pregnant Anya was sitting on. "What's, uh. What's going on here?"

Anya put her hand over Cheyenne's on her shoulder and snorted. "They're fighting over the flower arrangements for Sunday."

"Flowers. Arrangements?"

"It started out with the will reading and just ended up here," Riley offered with a roll of her eyes. CJ's wife was sitting on the opposite side of the table, leafing through a magazine while she half-listened to the two men bickering in front of them. When Cheyenne had spoken, she'd picked her head up and given her a quick wink before turning the page to the catalogue and circling a child's jacket with a black marker.

The two women looked exhausted. Anya, in her third trimester with her second child, was leaning heavily against the back of the chair. Riley's face sported more bags than a kindergarten teacher's. Cheyenne rubbed at the back of her neck as they looked at her, asking for help.

"Riley, go sit on the porch. The kids are playing, and they won't bother you. Anya, why don't you go take a bath in the claw foot tub in the master bath? I know for a fact I left some eucalyptus bubble bath solution under the sink." Cheyenne helped her sister-in-law stand. "Go on. I've got them."

Riley kissed her cheek as she walked past, a silent 'thank you' written all over her face. Once her sisters-in-law had left the kitchen, Cheyenne closed the sliding doors that separated the dining area from the rest of the house and slammed her hands down on the table. "You two. Sit down. Right. Now." By the sixth word both of her brothers had dropped down into two vacant seats at the head of the table, looking sullen. Her voice had reached an octave that had helped her decide she was never going to have children—the same voice that had been mediating fights between the two men for over two and a half decades.

She had been an afterthought, not quite an accident but not quite the planned arrival that Chester and CJ had been. She'd been born in '90, to her father and his second wife, when CJ had been twelve and Chester had barely turned ten. Her mother, who was considered 'too old' to conceive, had been beyond amazed and in awe of the miracle that had somehow been bestowed upon her and her new husband, and her father had been just as enamored. In spite of the relatively messy divorce between Caleb Jr. and her brothers' mother, Nora, her brothers' mother had also been quite taken by Cheyenne's big dark eyes and chubby cheeks.

Cheyenne grew up like an only child, despite the only ten-year age gap between her and Chester. She'd spent most of her childhood as a shared pet between her mother, father, and Nora, and most of her teenage years as a mediator at the holidays. She broke up fights between her brothers every time they were all together. She even kept Nora and her father from killing each other. Politics were off the table when Cheyenne was around, and so were paint colors. Chester had to stop bringing up his college career and CJ wasn't allowed to talk about how he could have done so much better in another field.

Cheyenne got to pick and choose what topics were safe for the dinner table, and that seemed to go best for everyone. The last time she had pulled back, had allowed topic of conversation to flow naturally through and through, had been at CJ's wedding. In response to the alcohol, and the downpour of the night, she'd had to drag an intoxicated Chester away from the stage in the middle of his best man speech as he babbled about Gambian politics and some obscure joke from CJ's bachelor party.

"Hey, what is going on?" She used the same tone now as she had back then. "Where is Dad?"

CJ sighed dramatically and used his hand to prop his head up. "Your brother is an idiot."

Chester, knuckling the table, shook his head and snorted at CJ's words. "We agreed to split the funeral costs fifty-fifty and he's saying he already paid for the service. Meaning that I get no say whatsoever."

"In return, instead of doing the split, I asked him to pay the caterer, but no. That's asking too much of His Royal Highness."

"Where is Dad?" she asked, calling their attention back to her before the argument turned into a full-out brawl.

"Dad, Mom, and Lisa are with the lawyers right now." CJ rubbed at his eyelids. "Please tell Chester to take some responsi—"

"He was my grandfather too! He already had all the things he wanted written down in the will, and you are making this way too complicated. Christ."

"Enough. Please," Cheyenne begged, her voice cracking with a soft emotion.

The men looked at each other, alarmed. Neither knew how to deal with their sister when she got soft-spoken. It made them nervous. CJ looked at Chester, who shrugged his shoulders and looked blandly back at him. "We'll figure out a way to make it run smoothly," the oldest said meekly.

"Thank you." Her head had started to ache, pulsing behind her eyes. "Let's just take a few minutes, and then we'll figure it out together."

"I'm going to go check on Anya." Chester hugged his sister quickly before he headed up the stairs.

CJ shook his head at their brother's back and stood up. "Coffee?"

"Please."

He grabbed two mugs and the old flower-decorated pot and sank into the chair closest to her right. "How was the drive?"

Cheyenne snorted while mixing a spoonful of sugar into the dark liquid. "The roads are awful." Their eyes, duplicate honey pairs that winked at each other over their coffee cups, met and they both laughed quietly. "I was in tears by the time I got off of Route 6."

"I'm not surprised. They're just getting worse by the day, and it hasn't helped that it's rained more days than it hasn't for the last couple of months." He took a drink of his coffee as he surveyed his sister. "You look exhausted."

"It's been… a long week. Between work and… well…"

"Mhmmm. I feel that."

Cheyenne nodded and puckered her lips. They sat in silence, her drawing shapes on the table and him staring down at his milk-lightened cup. When she sighed, he jerked his head up. "Rox told me that she and Maverick will be there tomorrow. For the reading." She filled the space with conversation that felt safe, if slightly strained.

"Yeah. Yeah, you know how Grandpa felt about keeping the will in the family. Well." CJ's brow furrowed. "I guess Rick's family now."

Cheyenne couldn't help but grin at her brother. "Amazingly." The wedding had been her favorite topic of conversation lately.

When her face clouded over, CJ set his cup down and knocked against the table's surface. "So, they're really getting married, huh? Rick and Rox?"

"Yeah." Cheyenne wiped underneath her eyes and finished her coffee. She was contemplating taking another mug. A few straggling rays of sunlight peeking in through the dining room window kept her from reaching for the pot again—she'd need to sleep at some point before the reading in the morning. "January fourteenth."

"Bless 'em both. We got the invitation in the mail, and I didn't believe it when Riley called me at work." He chuckled. When all Cheyenne did was nod and sigh, CJ seemed to lose steam. He played with the quarter sitting on the table in front of him for a few minutes before knocking down the elephant in the room. "How… how are you doing?"

"It… I…" Her lips furrowed. "It hasn't hit me yet. I… I was just here three weeks ago, and he was fine. Making jokes about the weather." A tear raced down her cheek to drip off her chin, and she stifled a sob.

Her brother opened his mouth and then closed it. Since they got the call that Caleb had passed away, since his handyman and friend found him on the ground outside the house, conversation had been falling short—and failing often—for the three Anderson siblings. It'd been hard for Cheyenne to vocalize what they had lost. What she had lost. It made her feel powerless because, while they all knew that Caleb had loved the three of them equally, Cheyenne had had the closest relationship with him.

CJ stared at Cheyenne, his eyes filled with grief, until she forced her gaze away and looked out the window, past the children playing in her line of sight to the tire swing that was attached to a piece of faded and yellowed rope.

Cheyenne could see herself as a child, playing on the fixture while Caleb watched from a few feet away, urging her to try to go higher, faster. His laugh and the broadness of his smile, salt-and-pepper hair with a speck of paprika left at the tips and the front roots. In his blue work jeans and the soft flannels that she had come into possession of when he passed away.

"I'm going to get my bags." She stood up, clearing the moisture from her throat. Before her brother could respond, Cheyenne escaped his pitiful gaze, a sob working in her throat.

2

$\mathcal{C}$heyenne slipped out the back door just off the kitchen as stealthily as possible with the hope that the kids wouldn't see her just yet. Instead of turning toward the driveway, she made a detour to give her a chance to clear her head. She picked her way down the dirt path that led around the house in search of her favorite spot on the property.

The garden had been Celeste Anderson's retirement project in the same way that the expansive house behind the garden had been Caleb's. The garden took up over three hundred feet of passion from the grandmother she had never met and reminded Cheyenne of every summer, holiday, and extended weekend of her sunny childhood. Walking through it, Cheyenne felt the loss of her grandfather settle in. A sadness crept through her gut that she couldn't put words to if she tried.

She lowered herself onto her favorite bench, their favorite bench, and felt pain in her chest that almost took her breath away. The bench sat between two flush butterfly bushes and provided enough of a curtain to hide her, and her tears, from the rest of her family. She and her grandfather had sat there for hours at a time, watching the sun set on hot, sticky nights with iced tea in their hands and conversation floating easily between them. Caleb would tell her stories about Celeste and their globe-trotting years, about her father and uncle as kids, about the adult world she would someday be a part of. In return, Cheyenne would exchange stories with him about her friends, her books, and school. Many hours had passed in the quiet thrum of conversation and companionship.

At the base of the water fountain, an angel held a basin of water that had been the site of bird play for her entire life. Its cherubic face was upturned toward the sky, wings spread wide. The narrowed eyes stared up at the sun, as if blinking out the sunset that slowly blanketed the ground. Because of the way the shadow of the sun sat on its face, it looked like it was crying. Cheyenne put her face in her hands and felt the sadness come in one hard wave before she swallowed it back down. There had been plenty of time to fall apart already, and there would be plenty more time to come apart at the seams after the weekend was over.

Cheyenne forced her eyes closed again and leaned her head against the back of the bench. She could see her grandfather on the bench beside her, still active in his old age, only a year before. His wrinkled hand held a tiger lily, and he was telling her about the last time he saw her grandmother dance. Or about the time her father had nearly set the whole house on fire trying to make a s'more for CJ while holding her on his shoulders. Or was it the moment he asked her grandmother to marry him, in a sunlit cove off the Atlantic Ocean in 1946?

All of the memories felt like weights on her ribcage, crushing her until she could hardly breathe. In her mind's eye, she could hear his mischievous laughter and the way he talked about how her grandmother had always hated roses and how she would sing while she cooked. He sang while he cooked too.

Her sniffles, the silent vigil, were interrupted by her second-oldest nephew, Kyle, calling her name from the front entrance of the garden. Cheyenne jerked her head up, wiped the warmth under her eyes, and shakily climbed to her feet. She took one last look at the angel, a promise to come back and lament more with its stone façade, before she started toward the other side. "Coming!"

She found Kyle standing with CJ and Chester on the front of the wraparound porch. Her brothers were having a conversation with a man she just barely recognized while her nephew stood waiting.

He was tall, taller than either of her brothers, and was dressed in a loose gray t-shirt and worn jeans. His long arms, like his clothes, were covered in bits of grass clippings and dirt. Even his ball cap, which was turned around so that the bill dipped down the back of his head, was sporting a fine layer of grime. When CJ said something, he laughed in response and flashed a set of mostly white teeth that turned his hard face into something soft and agreeable.

Cheyenne stood staring at him for what was definitely too long. Kyle caught on to the fact that she was standing there and beamed in her direction, big blue eyes filling most of his face, before he bowled into her. "Hi!"

"Oh!" Cheyenne staggered back, her arms reflexively wrapping around the pre-teen. "Hi."

"Kyle," CJ reprimanded him before he cleared his throat. "Jesse, this is my sister, Cheyenne. Chey, this is Jesse Kaiser. Jesse's been working for Gramps for the last couple of years. Doing odds and ends to help with the house upkeep."

"Yeah. I think I've seen you around." Cheyenne held her hand out to his. "It's nice to meet you."

"You too." The tall man's hand engulfed hers. It was strong under her grip but calloused enough to tickle her palms. Jesse grinned at her, quick and warm. His whole face was transformed with the simple act, and Cheyenne felt the pit of her stomach contract. "I'm so sorry for your loss." He squeezed her fingers before dropping her hand and adjusting the brim of his hat.

Cheyenne nearly snatched her hand back as soon as he let her fingers go. She wrapped her fingers, still warm from his hand, around the silver pendant hanging around her neck. No words formed on her lips, and she shot a panicked glance at her brother, afraid the dampness building underneath her lower lid would give her away.

"He's been here helping the last couple of days while we've been trying to get things in order," Chester added, clearly oblivious to the panicked look Cheyenne was leveling at CJ. "He's been very helpful."

"Well, if he's been helpful." Cheyenne cleared her throat and brushed her hands on her jean legs. "I've got to go grab my bags out of the car."

"I'll walk down with you." Jesse shook hands with her brothers and gave Kyle a fist bump before the two of them made their way down the driveway's slight slope.

Cheyenne stuffed her hands in the front pockets of her jeans and walked quietly next to him, the crunch of their footsteps the only thing making noise between them. Jesse walked her to the Jeep and opened the door for her with another quick grin. "Your grandfather was a good man." He leaned against the door, his arm propped over its window, and watched her fish her suitcase out of the backseat.

"I know." Cheyenne swallowed back the small snap and forced a teeth-baring smile. "Thank you."

Jesse rubbed his hands on his thighs as if he didn't know what to do with them. "He and I were friends."

"He was easy to be friends with." Cheyenne forced herself to soften her smile. It was so hard speaking about her grandfather, thinking about him and that friendly smile that drew people to him like flies. She turned away from the man to slam her door closed, shaking her head at herself.

When she looked up again, the man had made his way down the hill to the black truck parked in front of her father's toolshed. He turned, right before he opened the truck door, to give her a short wave. Cheyenne found herself waving back, kicking herself in the butt for the slight twinge of attraction she felt when he grinned up at her. He climbed into his truck and turned the engine on.

3

---

*J*esse took the last turn a little too hard, too fast, and felt the truck shudder underneath him in protest. He hated being late; he also hated the way the truck groaned at his efforts to make it on time, but he hated being late even more. Being late made his skin crawl no matter where he was supposed to be—church, home, work, he always felt guilty if he didn't arrive at least on time. Early was preferable, but on time at least made him feel like he wasn't a complete waste of space. His parents had raised him with a set inner clock and the knowledge that being punctual made a good man, and he desired to be a good man more than anything else. While being late made him crazy, the being late for one thing in particular made him crazy. And somehow, he was always late to it.

He bumped down the patched road to his in-laws', watching the minutes tick away on the truck's dashboard. His daughter was going to be furious with him for being late, never mind the cause. Never mind that he'd spent the last three hours helping to set up the Anderson House for the will reading tomorrow, or the fact that he was covered in dirt and grass and was in desperate need of a cold beer. Never mind the fact that he had lost a good friend. Being eleven wasn't quite old enough, at least in his opinion, to wrap your head around these concepts.

The white farmhouse sat on the outside of Penn Ridge, surrounded by sixty acres of wheat and corn fields and marked by a wooden plaque stuck to the driveway entrance's fading arch. It read 'Heinley's Orchard' in white and referred to a woman he'd never met but knew the world about. By the time he could see the plaque clearly, he was two minutes over an hour late.

Jesse pulled up in front of the farmhouse, muttering curses and cramming the truck into park. He ducked his head apologetically to the scrawny brown-haired girl that was standing on the wraparound porch with her arms folded over her chest. He climbed out of the truck with a loud sigh and started to hike through the dusty drive, his hands held up in surrender.

"Melia." He tried not to sound defeated.

The tween rolled her eyes and turned around, stomping back into the house. Jesse made it to the bottom of the porch just as the screen door slammed shut. He groaned and pried off his work boots, using the wire brush to scrape off as many layers of dirt and grass clippings as he could. Through the screen door, he could see his six-year-old son standing on a chair at the kitchen table. His blue checkered shirt was covered in flour, and he was rolling out some sort of pastry dough with a roller that was almost as big as he was. Jesse's mother-in-law mixed something in a Formica bowl across the table from him, wearing the paisley apron that his son had picked out for Christmas.

Through the screen door, he could smell coffee brewing and his mother-in-law's meatloaf baking in the oven. He could hear the radio playing songs from the 1980s. His son's happy chatter and Carol's warm responses filled out the picture. Jesse finished shaking the dust and dirt off of his clothes, smiling at the scene on the other side of the door, before he let himself into the farmhouse. He stopped just shy of the kitchen threshold to smile at the framed picture of his wife that hung on the doorway between the entry and the hub of the house. It hung opposite Carol's beloved wedding crucifix and showed Mara, a beaming woman of thirty-two, in front of the farmhouse's white exterior, holding Amelia on her hip.

Jesse gave himself a moment to smile at the picture, despite his anxiety over being late, before he announced his presence to his son and mother-in-law. "I know, I know I'm late. Things ran a little long at Caleb's."

Carol looked up from her mixing bowl, tenseness in her eyes. She still offered him a smile of greeting but shook her head in her signal for *all is not well in the sweet-smelling kitchen*. "Not a problem, Jess."

Miles dropped the rolling pin and all but knocked the chair, and Jesse, over when he flung himself at his father's legs. The six-year-old wrapped his arms around his father's neck once Jesse hoisted him up and beamed. "Hi! We're making pie!"

He announced it so gloriously that Jesse had to laugh.

"Pie! That's awesome, buddy. What kind of pie?" Jesse wiped a smudge of flour off his son's cheek.

The child looked at his grandmother for confirmation. Carol smiled and leaned across the table to exchange a 'hello' peck on the cheek with her son-in-law. "Blueberry. We picked them ourselves today," she informed him. "Miles did a lot of the picking himself."

"Daaaaad." Miles whined. "I gotta get back to work!"

"Work?"

"I'm making the pie crust! It's a big job."

Jesse laughed and set his son on his chair. He plucked a blueberry out of the plastic bowl in the center of the table and headed for the smell of fresh coffee coming from the counter by the sink. "You picked blueberries this morning? Beautiful day to do it." With the summer rolling out slowly, the days had only begun to get residually warmer. "How's his roll and pick coming?"

Carol rolled her eyes up toward the ceiling, fighting a smile. The Heinleys had been growing blueberries every summer since Mitch's father had bought the land, back in the early 1920s. The Orchard, which was the proud home of apple trees, berry bushes, and a whole vegetable garden that supplied half the farmer's market from August until November, had been built on the premise of the perfect blueberry roll and pick. It was an art. One that Carol and Mitch had taught their daughter and had made sure Jesse learned before the two got married.

"Mara learned how to do it by the time she was four," Carol said with an affectionate sigh as she ruffled her grandson's hair, "but we're getting there."

"He's got my clubbed fingers." Jesse sprinkled a little

sugar in his coffee cup. "How were they, Ma?" He leaned against the counter and massaged the kink out of the back of his neck. He felt the muscles stiffen in his ribcage and neck when he saw the look on Carol's face. He worked to gulp down as much coffee as he could. The daily report always gave him acid reflux.

"Miles has been a busy bee all day." Carol smiled at her grandson. "After the berries, we went grocery shopping, and then he got to help Lou at the market shuck Indian corn."

"Uh-huh." The six-year-old nodded briskly as he helped Carol drape the crust into the greased pie dish.

"Oh yeah? Did anything else exciting happen?" Jesse plopped another blueberry into his mouth.

"Melia and Grandpa got into a fight today." Miles' big brown eyes gazed up at his father, wide and innocent and the kind of concerned that a small child could easily adapt. "Big fight."

Jesse's head snapped back to Carol's face. "'Big fight'?"

"Mhmm." Carol nodded. "Mitch hasn't come in from the shop since Miles and I got back from the market. And she hasn't said a word to me. Not a word." Carol's hazel eyes clouded.

"Great." Jesse pinched the bridge of his nose. "Why don't I go talk to him?" He turned and grabbed a mug from the cabinet over his head. After filling his mug and its matching orange companion, he kissed his son on the head and nodded at Carol. She gave him a face that clearly wished him luck.

He stopped at the back door to awkwardly slide on his calf-high rubber farm boots. He spilled hot coffee over his fingers as he sloshed the mugs around and was still stomping the boots into place while he ran down the steps of the back porch. Jesse found his father-in-law underneath the truck he'd been restoring for the last five years, cursing and grunting while he tinkered with the undercarriage.

Jesse set the mugs down on Mitch's oil-stained workbench and crouched by the tail end of the truck to peek underneath. "What's wrong?"

"Oil line snapped." Mitch grunted and rolled himself out from underneath the truck.

"Rusted through?" Jesse handed him a rag for his oil-stained fingers.

Mitch grunted again as he wiped the grease off. "No. I dropped the truck off the ramps and somehow the damn line snapped." Mitch sniffed, the scent of coffee catching up with him. Jesse saw the look of excitement on the man's lined face and chuckled before handing him the orange mug. "Care make this fresh?"

"It'd just finished perking when I got in."

"God bless her." Mitch used the stained rag to wipe the sweat and grime from his forehead before he got to his feet and shook the dirt off his jean legs. "How was it?" Mitch's grim eyes and furrowed brow met Jesse's and made it clear that, to get an answer, Jesse was going to have to offer some information of his own.

"It was okay." Jesse sipped his coffee, staring out the shop's open door to the farm's property. "Caleb's got one big family."

"Cal in town yet?" Mitch and Cal Anderson had spent their childhood summers as fast friends. The kind of friends that stayed friends throughout life, through school and marriage and kids. The kind of friends that hurt for each other when they lost parents and who, at the end of it all, felt like they shared those parents in some regard. Jesse would have put money on Mitch's grief having something to do with the fight he and Amelia had gotten into.

"He got in last night. I met his wife and his ex-wife today." Jesse and Mitch moved together outside of the shop. Instead of heading toward the house, the two men marched down behind the barn-turned-autobody-shop toward the vegetable garden. "CJ and Chester don't get along too well."

"They don't?" Mitch stopped to check on the sunflowers that grew outside the fence to the vegetables. He didn't sound surprised. "I bet they're like their father." Mitch grinned at Jesse before his mouth slipped. "How is Cal doing?"

"I only saw him for a few minutes. He looked really tired." Jesse finished his coffee and set it on the post holding the gate lock. "Were they close? He and Caleb?"

"Caleb didn't agree with Cal marrying Lisa after he and the boys' mom got divorced, so it was a little hairy for a while." Mitch was inspecting tomatoes. "Are you going back?"

"Yeah. There's the will reading on Saturday, and CJ asked me to come by tomorrow after I work on the Beckin house to help set up stuff for the wake." Jesse stopped by the pumpkin patch and crouched to pull a few weeds. "Are you going to the funeral on Sunday?"

"I told Cal I'd be there." Mitch gave Jesse a grim smile. "I should go over there tonight."

"I think that would be good." Jesse plucked weeds out from between two pumpkins and tossed them in the growing pile of discarded growth by his heel. After letting his father-in-law work for a few minutes in silence, taking in the warm afternoon breeze and the even sounds of the man's breathing, Jesse cleared his throat. "Ma said you and Melia got into a fight?"

The older man grunted as he clambered to his feet. "Girl's got no respect." He shot his son-in-law a look that was returned with a blank stare. "She mouthed off while her grandmother was out and expected me to not say anything."

"About what?" Jesse felt a tidal wave of dread roll into the pit of his stomach and take residence in the coffee he'd gulped down. The last time Amelia and Mitch had gotten into it, he'd had to ground the eleven-year-old for a week. That had gone over about as well as the time he told her she couldn't dye her hair pink; both incidents had resulted in Jesse and Miles hiding in the den while Amelia raved and ranted in her bedroom for hours.

"She slammed the screen door and almost knocked her grandmother's cross off the wall. When I told her to be careful, she took great offense."

"I'll talk to her." Jesse shoved his hand through his hair out of frustration and sent a withering look at the farmhouse. No one had told him that having a pre-teen daughter would require so many lessons on manners.

Mitch clapped a hand on his shoulder. "Mara was the

same way when she reached that age. Always had an attitude with her mother and me. Thought she knew best."

Jesse chuckled. Mara had always believed she knew what was best; it had been one of the things that had brought them together in the college biology class where they met. "I'll talk to her," he repeated.

"You do that. Let me know how it goes." Mitch's laugh was the one of a man who'd been in Jesse's footsteps before. And had lost. "C'mon. Dinner should be just about done by now."

IT TOOK four books to get Miles down that night, not the all-time high but not the three books and then bed that he and his father had negotiated after the six-year-old's bath. Jesse had held fast at the end of *One Fish, Two Fish* and had almost escaped the racecar bed when the child had called out that his nightlight was dimmer than usual. That could lead to nightmares, which would lead to small hands shaking Jesse awake in the middle of the night. So, Jesse had half-begrudgingly read another Dr. Seuss classic to his son and then hummed a lullaby until Miles was sound asleep, nestled underneath his left arm.

After checking the nightlight and the locked windows, and making sure the closet door was firmly closed, Jesse slipped out of the bedroom and meandered into the kitchen. Amelia was sitting at the kitchen table with a sheet of math practice problems in front of her and a half-finished glass of milk at her elbow. She looked a little like her mother, her lips nestled in a small pout and her eyebrows furrowed in the same way Mara would concentrate on just about anything. Jesse smiled and crossed the room to grab the pint of chocolate ice cream out of the freezer.

"Can you take a break?" he asked while he fished two spoons out of the dishwasher.

His daughter huffed dramatically, but he heard the paper and pencil scrape against the table as she shoved it away from her. "I'm done for the night," she announced.

"Good. You and me gotta have a little talk." He dropped down in the chair next to hers and offered her a spoon. "I heard you and Grandpa got into a fight today?"

Amelia's brown eyes narrowed suspiciously at the corners. She plucked the spoon from his fingers and took a bite of ice cream. "He fought."

"Amelia."

"He told me that I was being disrespectful. The door closes loudly. That's not my fault."

"Melia. You've got to stop being so rude to your grandfather." Jesse watched his daughter stab another spoon's worth of ice cream out of the container. "You and I can go back and forth and bicker and fight as much as we want to, but you giving them a hard time isn't going to do anything but hurt them. And they're not going to be around forever." His voice softened on the last thought as he watched her face go from 'ready to fight' to 'ready to cry.'

"They treat me like I'm a baby," she said after a second,

her spoonful of ice cream forgotten in the tub between them.

Jesse put his hand over hers and squeezed it gently. "You are a baby. To them, and to me, you are always going to be a baby. Our baby." She looked up at him with her big brown eyes, so like her mother's, and Jesse had to fight the urge to remind her of the resemblance she had to her grandparents' only daughter. "Cut them some slack and watch your mouth. Please?"

Amelia blew a breath of air out at him and picked her spoon up. "I'll see what I can do." She gave him an impish smile. "Can Lilly come over next weekend if I'm really good?"

"We'll see how good you are this week. With me and with the grandparents." Jesse found himself grinning back at his daughter. "You're gonna have to spend all day tomorrow with Grandma and Grandpa again."

"More stuff to do at Mr. Anderson's?" She scraped at the cardboard container with the tip of her spoon. "Is his family really sad?" His daughter looked up at him, curiosity lacing the concentration in her eyes. She'd been so young the last time someone close to her had passed away that the notion of Caleb Anderson's death was still sinking in. She knew that her father and grandparents were affected by his passing, but death was still synonymous with her mother in her mind, and Jesse hadn't been able to move her past that fact.

"Melia." Jesse sighed when she batted her eyelashes at him. "Everyone is really sad. But it will be okay."

"Grandma said there's going to be a funeral on Sunday. Do Miles and I have to go? I mean, I know he gave us all those cookies and we got to play on his jungle gym, but do we have to?"

"No, sweetie. You and Miles aren't going."

"Good." She frowned at her father, trying to cover the momentary panic that had crossed her face when it occurred to her that they might have to go to the service. "It probably would have made Miles really upset to go."

"Probably." Jesse smiled and ruffled his daughter's hair. "Let's take this ice cream party into the den. I think there's an episode or two recorded of that hospital show you like so much." Even though she smiled at him, Jesse could see the panic, and the sadness, still lingering in his daughter's eyes. It broke his heart, as it always did when anything but joy sat in her chocolate-colored gaze.

Amelia hopped up, unaffected by the sad look on her father's face. "I'll go grab the fluffy pillows from my bed!" She beamed up at him and sped out of the kitchen.

4

"The lawyer is going to be here in a few minutes, and people will start to show up shortly after. I think it'd be best if we were done before he shows up." CJ Anderson's slight panic caused his normally deep voice to rise a couple of octaves.

Jesse rubbed the back of his neck and forced a smile for CJ's sake. The older man, older by only three years, was starting to look more and more like Jesse's father. Wrinkles were setting around his face, lining his cheeks and supporting the corners of his eyes, and he looked like he hadn't slept in a week. It made sense. Jesse himself remembered the loss-induced insomnia that had taken him over after Mara had passed away. The man needed all of the sympathy, and all of the help, Jesse could muster. Even if they had been dragging around boards and cleaning up the porch (and all the children's toys) for the last hour.

He crouched to wedge the hammer hanging in his belt

loop into Caleb's teal toolbox. "I'll stuff this in the tool shed and get going, then?"

CJ nodded gratefully at the offer and scooped up the bucket of Tonka trucks he'd set on the porch railing. "I appreciate all the time you've been putting in here. We all do."

Jesse waved him off. "Is there anything else I can do to help set up for the service tomorrow?"

"I don't think so."

Chester popped out of the house's front door, his hair falling over his forehead in a copper wave.

He and his brother weren't necessarily handy, but they had proven to be good enough in the friend department that Jesse didn't mind the extra work, and the long hours, that he'd spent at the house since the proper Anderson horde had all finally shown up. He'd done everything from putting together cots for extra cousins to reattaching pieces to the swing set in the back after Kyle and Nathan had gotten into a brawl over the good tire swing. It was good work Jesse was doing— and part of the agreement he'd had with Caleb that he would work on the house's general upkeep for as long as he was able, should something happen to the eldest Anderson.

Chester was fidgeting with the wreath that his wife, Anya, had fixed to the door. His mouth was twitching with a suppressed laugh and he looked between CJ and Jesse with a wry look in his eyes. "Gramps would be rolling his eyes like crazy at all this perfectionist stuff." He gestured to the other flower wreaths that decorated the front porch, all sent from friends of the family with condolences and anecdotes of their late grandfather.

"Tell me about it." At Jesse's raised eyebrows, CJ grinned. "Ri, Anya, and Chey have been cleaning and cooking and moving shit for the last two days. You're lucky you haven't had the misfortune of stepping foot inside."

"Funerals." Jesse snorted while packing up the leftover nails. "They bring out the neat freaks in all of us." He could picture, clear as day, his mother-in-law obsessively cleaning—before the funeral and after it—the little house he and Mara had set up shop in. "When my wife passed, my mother-in-law rearranged the same vase of flowers six times a day for weeks. Always put fresh flowers in and then couldn't decide where she wanted it. It made her feel… useful. Like she was in control of something." Carol had also rearranged his furniture, refolded all of the clothes in his and the kids' dressers, and almost bought them a dog. Her franticness had made Jesse feel displaced, but he'd had a one-year-old and a six-year-old to take care of, so he'd let her do what she needed.

"Between the nesting and the funeral arrangements, Anya's been a mess." Chester smiled fondly before paling when his wife yelled his name.

"Go. I'll grab the tools off the side porch." Jesse chuckled as the other man ducked his head in thanks and disappeared inside the house. He might not have had much patience for the Anderson brothers' upkeep skills, but he was going to miss their company, he decided, as he wandered around to the side porch. He stopped to pick up a few random screws and pieces of trash that came across his path.

In the side yard, the biggest stretch of grass without a

slope, he could see Cheyenne, the youngest Anderson grandchild, dragging around white-topped folding tables. She was wearing a black dress that hugged her figure. It was a nice figure, he thought while he watched her move; fit but not slim, with a definitive, feminine curve to it. He stopped at the corner of the porch to watch her work, enjoying the way the dress moved with her body as she struggled to pull the table. His eyes traveled down from her shoulders, taking in the entirety of her body in its knee-length sheath, until he realized that she wasn't wearing shoes.

It took her all of five seconds from the time he realized she wasn't wearing shoes for her to stub her toe on a rock.

Jesse tried not to laugh at the way her face turned red, almost as red as her hair, while he jogged off the steps of the porch and through the yard. "Need some help?" he called out while she hunched over to hold her foot.

"I'm good," she shouted back before she wrapped her hands around the legs of the table and started to tug it backwards again.

"You're going to break your ankle," he scolded before grabbing the other end of the table she was dragging and helping her to lift it. "Where's this going?"

"Over there. In front of that one." She jerked her chin to her left.

"I thought your brother was taking care of this." Jesse waited until she lowered her half of the table before he let go of his.

Cheyenne rolled her eyes and marched toward the next table, situated under the big pine tree at the corner of the yard. "He and the kids did. And now all these tables, which are supposed to be for eating on tomorrow, have pine needles all over them."

Jesse chuckled. "You're moving the tables to save them from the pine trees?" They lifted the table and carried it back toward the other two.

The redhead sent him a look that could have injured a lesser man. "I am making food for just about a hundred people for tomorrow. Do you know how long that takes?" When Jesse shrugged at her, she continued her diatribe, dropping her end of the table in a huff. "Six hours of peeling potatoes this morning and rolling meatballs and baking cookies. And I am not going to have my food get all sticky and pine needle-y."

Jesse laughed but let her guide him, and the subsequent couple of tables, into position. The duo worked quietly, the only conversation coming when Cheyenne ordered him to move a table one way instead of the other or when he picked up his end faster than she was prepared for. She seemed preoccupied, leaving Jesse with the perfect vantage point to enjoy her face. Her nice figure was matched by an equally nice face; it was made up of soft cheekbones and a dimpled chin, framed by several inches of fiery red hair and specked with freckles that were various shades of brown. Her eyes were a soft shade of hazel and, even as distracted as they were, had a warmth to them that Jesse had never seen before.

Cheyenne stepped back from the last rental table they moved and cocked her head to the side before whipping around to follow the sound of a car that raced by the property. She started to play with the silver four-leafed clover that hung from a thin chain around her neck, her slender fingers fiddling with the charm as a soft breeze wafted some of her hair around her round face. Jesse couldn't make out what the car was through the trees, but it was headed toward town. He watched her face relax when the crunch of the car's tires disappeared.

"It's a shame." She sighed without looking away from the road. "The house is abandoned now. It'll probably be boarded up or sold in a few days." It was said in such a way that Jesse knew it didn't need an answer, but he felt compelled to speak.

He ran his hand through his hair and thought of the most comforting thing he could come up with. "Your grandfather loved this house. He was always puttering around in it, asking for help with little things. I'm sure he figured out a way to keep it in the family."

"Are you staying for the will reading?" The redhead looked at Jesse sharply, resurfacing from wherever her mind had been when the last table was lined up neatly with the other dozen they had moved.

"No—I have to go pick my kids up from my in-laws." Jesse was caught off guard by the question. "But I'll be at the funeral tomorrow. In-laws in hand. My father-in-law and your father are friends. Mitch Heinley."

Cheyenne smiled a little, a fraction at the corners of her pouty lips. "Mr. Heinley. He came by last night and it cheered Dad up a little. It was nice." The woman rubbed her upper arms as if she were cold, her gaze landing on the slope of the driveway. "The lawyer who's doing the reading is a good friend of mine. One of my best friends," she spoke softly. Jesse inclined his head toward her to hear her better and caught a whiff of her perfume. It was sweet, but he couldn't put a finger on what it reminded him of. "Family, really. This whole damn thing is such a family affair." The redhead's voice broke in a watery whimper.

Jesse was at a loss. The anger from the tables had transformed, almost imperceptibly, into the waxing shakes of a woman who was lost. Jesse knew it well; he saw Carol sport the same expression from time to time even now, and it had been years since Mara had passed away. "Family's good to have with you at times like this."

"Yeah. Yeah, I guess." She picked up the black heels she'd slipped off before moving toward Jesse. "You ever held a funeral?"

"One." Jesse offered his arm for her to leverage herself against and she gripped his bicep as she slipped on her shoes. "Can't say it was much fun."

"Ha." She snorted and he felt accomplished. "That was almost funny."

"That's me. Almost funny, all the time." They walked across the yard to the porch. Jesse collected his toolbox while Cheyenne fixed her skirt and kicked the dirt off her shoes. "You should hear the zingers I've got for muffins."

Cheyenne let out a soft, tired laugh. "I'd love to hear them." She stiffened, the laugh fading away, at the sound of tires on the driveway. "I'll have to take a rain check."

"Absolutely." Jesse reached out and plucked a pine needle from her hair. "I'll hold you to that." They exchanged a smile, and Jesse was struck by how much it lit up the redhead's face.

She was so small. Jesse was absolutely astounded by just how small she was. He had to nearly bend down just to continuously make eye contact with her, and her head was tilted completely back in the afternoon sun. She was small and looked wonderful in the fitted black dress she wore, and Jesse nearly kicked himself.

The woman was wearing black, for crying out loud. They were about to read her grandfather's will and here he was, like a schmuck, thinking about how nice she looked. "I should get going," he heard himself saying. He dropped his hands to his side and took a big step back. "I've gotta go pick up my kids."

"I should go see who just pulled up." Cheyenne jerked her thumb over her head at the driveway, her own face turning pink around the edges. "It's, um… probably my friends." She laughed a little and turned like a soldier, marching to the porch and its two rocking chairs.

She was intercepted near the front door by a slim brunette with curly hair who nearly plowed her over in an embrace. The two women clung to each other in silence, while the brunette's companion slipped past them with a pat on Cheyenne's shoulder. Jesse and the man exchanged a brief nod before he slipped into the house and escaped off the porch. He didn't like lawyers, and the shorter man, even though his hair was grown out past his ears, had the aura of a lawyer. It made his skin crawl.

Jesse caught Cheyenne's eye before she was led in to the house by the brunette woman. She gave him a half-hearted smile and he offered a short wave before ducking into the truck's cab.

5

*C*heyenne stared at the back of Maverick's head while he talked to her brothers and father, Silas standing beside him acting as a silent chorus, and tried to stop herself from imagining what it would be like to cut off the little mahogany-colored curls that had formed at the base of his head. For every new set of footsteps she heard enter the living room, she imagined snipping off another curl. In her mind's eye, it was done with her grandmother's metal sewing shears, the ones with the long handles that Cheyenne had never been allowed to touch as a child.

Each snip made her feel a little better, a little more in control. A little more grounded. Just like Roxanne's fingers, wrapped around her own, kept her feeling grounded to the couch where they were crowded with Silas's wife, Nancy, and Cheyenne's second cousin, Madeline. Roxanne's engagement ring was digging into her fingers; the stones on the side around its opal face were definitely going to leave a mark on her pale skin.

Cheyenne didn't care much. Every time Roxanne tried to relax her hand, and the pressure she was putting on Cheyenne's, Cheyenne gripped back harder. She couldn't bear to be without Roxanne's presence, their thighs touching and their fingers intertwined.

"What do you think they're talking about?" Roxanne asked her, trying to pull her back from the depths of her own mind.

"Probably about the will. Dad said that it's really long. And there were a few things that, when Gramps put them in, Dad didn't agree with. Sort of convoluted. Dad's hoping some things got omitted after he looked at it. You know how Gramps is. Was." Cheyenne swallowed thickly. "I'm sure Rick's trying not to step on anyone's toes. But he'll definitely make sure it reads the same way Gramps would have wanted it to."

Roxanne nodded and tucked a piece of hair behind Cheyenne's ear. "Probably. He was really nervous about being the one to do the reading. Personally, I think he'd rather be sitting here holding your hand right now."

Cheyenne blinked at her best friend of nearly two decades and tried to smile. "Rick is family," she started, and then paused, thinking of what the handyman had said. "I'm glad he's the one doing it. Family's good to have with you at times like this."

Roxanne gave her fingers another sure squeeze and rested her head on Cheyenne's shoulder. "Of course. Of course."

"Do you think he would let me cut his hair?" Cheyenne squeezed Roxanne's hand back.

"Who? Rick?" The other woman pursed her lips

thoughtfully and looked at her fiancé for a moment before smiling at her friend. "I'm sure if you asked him after this is over with, he'd let you shave his head. And pierce his ear."

Cheyenne giggled and felt her shoulders untense, if only for a second. "I'd settle for him just letting me cut it shorter."

Nancy, her small, round stomach—sporting a second baby for the Montgomery lineage—keeping her from leaning forward enough to be fully in the conversation, let out a soft giggle. "I would pay to see that." She patted Cheyenne's knee affectionately. "I'll sit on him if you need help holding him down. With all this extra weight, it wouldn't be that much of an issue." Her hand rested on the swell of her stomach and it brought a soft, if slightly uncomfortable, smile to Cheyenne's face.

"That can be arranged. Without any extraordinary measures." Roxanne shot Nancy a smirk before setting her head back down on Cheyenne's shoulder. "I'm seriously hoping he'll cut it before the wedding."

"He will," Nancy piped up, sending a look at Silas. "Do you remember that awful crew cut Si got right before the wedding?" All three women laughed.

It felt good to laugh—too good, Cheyenne thought with a pang of guilt. She stopped her soft giggles and swallowed down a gulp of air, her lips trembling a little. "He will," she confirmed for Roxanne while she cracked the knuckles on her free hand. Her eyes drifted back to Maverick, his head of awkwardly long curls, and the silky strands of Silas' own head, which he kept a little long but styled in a peak at the front of his forehead. "The crew cut wasn't that bad," she murmured to Nancy, her brain doing its best to wander back to the mounds of food waiting in the kitchen and the packet of papers in Maverick's hands. Cheyenne forced herself to think about Maverick's hair—about cutting it. With those damned scissors.

At the front of the room, Cheyenne's father and brothers exchanged a round of handshaking with the young lawyer and accountant and dispersed for the row of chairs closest to the fireplace, where Maverick had set up shop. Silas and Maverick exchanged a quick hug before the accountant took his seat with the remaining Anderson men at the front of the room.

Maverick took a sip of water at the makeshift podium before his eyes drifted to his fiancée and friend. Those dark eyes grinned at them, a half-loving, half-paternal grin that made both women smile for very different reasons. Cheyenne was comforted, as comforted as she thought she could be, at least for the moment. She settled back against the couch, her hip jamming even more securely between Nancy's and Roxanne's thighs. Their warmth would be the only thing getting her through the next hour of her life. She knew that, took strength from that, as Maverick cleared his throat and the soft chatter in the room became overwhelmingly silent.

"All right, everyone," Maverick started, nodding at her father and mothers. "I think we're all set here. I'd like to get started." He looked to Cheyenne and then her father for permission. Out of respect for the family, he didn't continue until both the favorite grandchild and the only surviving son gave him their permission. "As you all can see, Caleb sure gave us a lot of last words to go through.

After the will is finished, I have a couple of contracts that I need the beneficiaries to sign, and Cheyenne put out a spread of snacks and coffee in the kitchen. Please take some."

Cheyenne smiled while an awkward chuckle ran through the surrounding people.

"*'Hello,'*" Maverick started to read. "*'If you are hearing this, my family, my closest friends, then I regret to inform you that I have moved on to the other side.'*"

It was all too much to bear. The piece of paper that Maverick was reading off of, the packet of papers in his hand, just made it real. Real in ways that Cheyenne wasn't sure she was able to handle. So, in a grasp at self-preservation, she tuned out Maverick's voice, instead focusing her attention on the crowd who had crammed into the Retirement House's spacious living room. Second cousins from all corners of the country, and one from Wales; old friends of her grandfather's and those who had known her grandmother back when the couple lived in the city; her nieces and nephews who couldn't sit still but had enough respect to try. Her grandfather had lived a full life. A full life that he willingly, and sarcastically, willed away.

Maverick carefully, clearly, and with some obvious hurt himself, amounted the entirety of her grandfather's existence into a handful of phrases. Caleb had outlined in his will absolutely everything he owned, from the apartment in New York City—which was supposed to be sold and the apartment separated by a handful of second cousins—to the bank assets that were split equally between her brothers. Cheyenne watched Maverick's mouth move and vaguely heard him dissect her grandfather's possessions but couldn't focus enough to process who got what or what the will stipulated was done with the remainder.

"Chey."

Cheyenne tuned back in from her inspection of her Aunt Sarah, who had had to fan her face to stop a flow of tears that sprouted up after hearing that Caleb had left her a couple of antique pieces of china, when Roxanne whispered her name. Her head whipped around until her nose was nearly touching her friend's, and she had to blink bag the fog of tears in her eyes. "Mhm?"

Roxanne jerked her head to the front of the room where Maverick was waiting, his eyes on the two women. Cheyenne glanced at him and realized that everyone's eyes were on them. "I'm sorry?" She'd missed something, obviously something important. "Could you...?"

"Uh." Maverick coughed and glanced back down at the page open in front of him. "Ah. *'To my granddaughter, the spitting image of my late wife and the best pal a guy could have'*"—Cheyenne's eyes watered—*"'I leave my Penn Ridge estate, including the Retirement House and all its contents not bequeathed in the preceding pages, for her to live in, to grow in, to start her family in and to make her own memories in. By stipulation of this last will and testament, Cheyenne will live in the house for a total of two years before she may, if she so chooses, sell the property.'"*

Cheyenne's jaw went slack. In all the commotion of the funeral and the will reading, the hours of cooking to keep her mind and hands busy, it had never occurred to her that Caleb would have left the house to anyone but her father. In fact, the house had never come up at all. In none of the conversations she'd had with her brothers since she arrived had any of them even speculated as to what would happen to the house. It had seemed impossible for anyone to own it other than Caleb. Least of all Cheyenne.

Maverick's voice wavered out again as Cheyenne thought about the house. Her favorite childhood memories had been spent on its premises; it was the kind of house she'd imagined having one day, long after the bakery had closed and she'd left Albany for someplace more remote. But she'd never intended to move into the Retirement House, or to Penn Ridge.

Cheyenne got up, dropped the hands of the two women that had clutched at her when the announcement was first made, and walked out of the living room with all eyes on her. She made it out of the house and almost to her Jeep before her stomach bottomed out. She emptied its contents by the back bumper of the Cherokee; coffee and the half bagel she'd managed to swallow down that morning mixed with stomach bile and the tears that rolled down her face.

Once her stomach was sufficiently empty, Cheyenne sank to her knees and leaned back against the back-driver side tire. He'd left her the house. She couldn't wrap her head around it. He'd left her the house. The whole house. The house and the responsibility, the sense of stability, and the sense of a center—it all belonged to her. Cheyenne's hands trembled and her stomach rolled, threatening to empty itself again as she started to process. He wanted her to live in the house. The house that he'd built for her grandmother, and for the life he'd hoped they would have for the future.

Cheyenne almost got sick again thinking about her grandfather and the pleased look on his face when he'd watch her drag her suitcases into the house as a kid. He'd always joke when she left that, one day, she wouldn't have to drag them back out, with a hug and a wink and a promise that they'd see each other again soon. That felt like a whole other lifetime.

Cheyenne got sick again, her grandfather's smile seared into the back of her mind.

6

*R*oxanne stood and half-listened to Cheyenne's mother, Lisa, talk about flower arrangements with Maverick and Silas while she scanned the room for Cheyenne. Her favorite redhead was nowhere to be seen, even though the room had started to thin with mourners heading back to their lives. Lisa continued to talk about lilacs, obviously fixating on anything other than her daughter's disappearance or the atmosphere of loss lingering around them. Maverick was doing a good job at keeping her occupied, taking verbal notes from her nervous speaking to prompt questions later on.

Roxanne kissed Maverick's cheek before she escaped the conversation and ducked out of the room in search of her best friend.

She found Cheyenne sitting on the bench in her grandmother's garden near the water fountain that they had made wishes on as little girls. She was hugging her knees to her chest, her heels discarded by a flowerbed, staring vacantly out into the trees. There were black smudges running down her face and a dampness around her lips that didn't look like it was from crying. Roxanne settled down on the bench beside her and put her arm around the redhead's shoulders, pressing her face into the other woman's hair.

"He left me the house," Cheyenne sobbed, her voice cracking. "He left me the goddamn house, Rox."

"He knew how much you loved it." Roxanne held her tighter.

"He left me the house."

"He also left you all the furniture. Which is good, 'cause trying to furnish this monster would have sucked. Big time." Cheyenne sniffled, looking at her. Roxanne rubbed her arm and tried to smile. "And I don't know about you, but watching Rick put together furniture is only entertaining for about an hour." When Cheyenne almost smiled, Roxanne grinned and squeezed her tighter. "Although you should see the desk he built me. It's beautiful."

"My bakery. My apartment." Cheyenne rubbed her eyes with her palms, streaking her half pound of makeup even more. Roxanne offered the sleeve of her dress for her friend to use. "My whole life is in Albany."

"We'll help you get your affairs in order. I could use a break from Rick for a few days."

"I can't take care of this entire house by myself."

"Your gramps thought about that. Rick said that there's been money set aside to pay Jesse Kaiser to keep up the maintenance and landscaping." Roxanne dried a few of Cheyenne's black tears with the pad of her thumb. "And Rick and I are living in the Ridge again.

Wes and Silas aren't that far away. It's not like you'll be alone."

"But the house. This house." Cheyenne flung her arm out toward the Retirement House and sniffled. "I've never owned a house before."

Maverick walked out of the sliding door, holding a case of beers under his arm and loosening the knot of his tie with his free hand. Roxanne smiled when she saw him, a gesture full of love. Behind him, Silas shut the door with a snap and shot the girls a half-hearted grin.

"We haven't, either. It's a learning experience, through and through. But we're going to tackle it together." She held her hand out to Cheyenne as she stood and toed off her black shoes.

Cheyenne frowned up at her but took her hand. "Where are we going?"

"You'll see."

A HINT of rain blew through the little clearing by Anderson Creek where Cheyenne, Maverick, Roxanne, and Silas sat around the circular stone that they had once held court at as kids. On Maverick's cellphone, which sat in the center of the stone with its screen skyward, the two Carmody brothers bickered on their own separate lines. Cheyenne smiled while she listened to the brothers fight, her eyes bloodshot and sore but still able to light up at the familiarity. It felt good to be away from the house, from the family and the friends who had all stared at her like she'd lost her mind. And it felt even better to be with the people that Cheyenne had been able to lean on for comfort, support, and a laugh for as long as she could remember.

"If you two are done," Maverick called out eventually, causing the argument to settle on the other end of the line.

Cheyenne watched him stand up and set the six-pack of beers on the round stone table. "Why are we out here?" She tugged the sleeves of her sweater down to cover her fingers and looked between the couple. "Rox?"

"Well, Wes will be here in the morning," Connor called out from the phone where he sat, in a rather empty room, FaceTiming with them. "I can't get off base, Chey. I tried like hell but Gramps wasn't actually blood family." The younger man sounded pained, but he looked chipper—for her benefit, she was sure. "But we wanted to do this tonight."

"Do what?"

Maverick handed her a beer can. "Remember when your gramps caught us sneaking beers out here in tenth grade?"

Cheyenne laughed in spite of herself and shoved her hand through her hair. "Yeah. He sat down right where you're standing and made us finish an entire twelve-pack."

"And it was disgusting." Roxanne giggled from beside her as she popped open her can.

"I didn't think it was that bad," Silas piped up while he

loosened his tie, "but it was the first beer any of us ever had. And Gramps didn't yell at us—didn't give us a hard time. He just sat here while we all got sick and then made sure we ate."

"And drank enough water," Connor added.

Wesley nodded vigorously and raised his beer can serendipitously. "And now we can't get enough of this stuff." To make his point, he took another swallow.

Cheyenne nodded and popped her can open. "This is for Gramps?"

Maverick nodded and held his can up. "And for you. To your new house-owner status."

On the phone screen, Wesley raised a bottle of beer toward the ceiling and Connor toasted with a bottle of water. Cheyenne raised her beer and clinked it to the cans that Roxanne, Silas, and Maverick held out to her. "To Gramps," she mumbled softly and took a careful sip of the lukewarm alcohol.

"To Gramps," her five closest friends all cheered her grandfather. Cheyenne closed her eyes and took another, longer pull of the beer.

For the first time since she heard about her grandfather's passing, Cheyenne felt like she was on even ground. She still didn't know what she was going to do with the house, other than move to Pennsylvania, but she could figure the rest of that out in time. Right there, in that moment, Cheyenne felt like she could breathe.

7

"*I* can't believe you're leaving."

Cheyenne looked up from the order form she was going through, her eyebrows furrowing together as she and Margo made eye contact over the counter. They'd had the same conversation daily since she'd gotten back from Pennsylvania, to varying degrees of success for each participant. Cheyenne's decision to move to Penn Ridge in the first week of June had settled poorly with her friend and assistant and had made Cheyenne's heart ache.

"It's not like I'm moving to a different country," Cheyenne said with a tired sigh. She capped her pen and stood from the wooden table that she'd been squatting at for the last hour, trying to get ahead on bills and paperwork so that she wouldn't have to drive up to Albany until August. She'd need the free time to get settled—and to figure out what she was going to do once she got to Penn Ridge.

"But you won't be here. What if we burn it down? What if I forget how to make shortbread?" Margo's gray eyes widened with panic. "What if I mess up the blueberry glaze? Or mess up an order? You know Liam only likes to work with you when it comes to the fruit truck."

Cheyenne leaned over the counter to put her hands on Margo's shoulders and give them a fond squeeze. "You're going to be okay. You won't forget how to make the shortbread. The recipe is in the book—just like all of my other recipes. You know how to make the blueberry glaze." She squeezed the skinny girl's arms before letting her hands drop to her sides. "I talked to Liam. He will be fine. You will be fine."

Margo looked doubtful, her lips still pointed in a pout. "You don't have to go."

Cheyenne sighed. "I do have to go. We talked about this already, too." At Margo's blank look, she pitched her hands through her hair and leaned against the counter. "In my grandfather's will, it specifically says that I have to move into the house or we have to sell it. No one else can move in and take my place."

"Which seems really weird, if you ask me."

"Oh, yeah. Completely bonkers. But that was my Gramps." He'd always wanted her to take the house; he'd told her so many times as she got older. But to back her into taking the house, to force her to uproot her entire life without a conversation (not that there was room for conversation now), was bonkers even for him. "And I can't let him down. He loved that house. My Gram died in that house. We're all pretty sure my mom got pregnant with me in that house. I couldn't just let it go to some cold-ass realtor or to some snooty weekend warrior couple who wouldn't appreciate it."

"But you have a life here. You have the bakery. You have William."

"Had William." There was still an unanswered voicemail on her landline, back in her pretty little apartment, to prove that she had once had—but was now left without—William. "He didn't take the news about me moving to another state very well."

"It is a lot to digest. I'm sure if you guys talked about it—"

"Mar, please. There is no talking about it." Cheyenne pinched the bridge of her nose. There was definitely no talking about it. Not when he'd left her apartment the night before and slammed the door so hard that it now sat a little crooked on its hinges. Not when he'd told her that she was putting their relationship on the back burner because she 'wanted to leave everything behind.' It made her head hurt to think about it. "Did you check the order for the Osgoods' anniversary party?"

The segue didn't do anything to lessen the concern in Margo's eyes. She still stiffened her upper lip and pulled the order book out from underneath the register counter. "It's four dozen cupcakes. Chocolate Triage and Strawberry Delight. Allen and I will drop them off Friday morning with their daughter, Sydney. Did they pay already?"

"Nope. Syd will pay you when you drop them off. Make sure you garnish them with the little sugar candy O's and L's that we made. Each cupcake needs an O and an L."

"Of course." Margo made a note in the margins of the order book. "Anything else?"

"Jonathan has to stack the flour sacks when he gets in this afternoon. And I have an interview around one for an assistant baker." Cheyenne navigated around the corner and patted Margo's head affectionately. "Now go take your break."

Her smile slipped away once Margo disappeared behind the revolving door that led to the back of the shop —a quirky addition that had been installed on a whim right after Cheyenne had opened and had turned into a minor headache she was too stubborn to cure. It had been hard, coming back from Penn Ridge and sitting Margo, Ella, and Jonathan down to tell them that she was leaving.

Ella, the only high schooler that Cheyenne had ever truly liked—she'd even been uncomfortable around them when she herself was a teen—had actually cried. Fat tears and loud, panicked sobs that had nearly brought Cheyenne to the brink. Jonathan had looked nervous; he'd worked for Cheyenne since he was a freshman in college, and when he graduated, instead of leaving for some big-time gig, he had taken up her other full-time position. She now had a nice website, a thriving 'indie' scene thanks to the addition of mood candles, worn books, and vegan options that he'd helped her make popular. She'd seen the look on his face and had felt nauseous. Margo had kept them both solid while she'd laid out the entire plan, her own panic residually falling away into sadness that her friend of four years was leaving.

Cheyenne scribbled notes down in the order book, trying to focus on the optimism that Margo had used to perk up her two younger employees. They would be just fine without her. The bakery, her bakery, was going to be just fine. Or… as close to fine as she could hope for.

She looked up, still mulling over the bakery's impending fineness, when the Cramer twins charged into the shop, followed by their perpetually exhausted-looking mother. Cheyenne smiled and dropped her pen on the counter. "Alison, hi."

The Cramers were some of her best customers—and her biggest headaches. Suzy, the younger twin, darted straight for the display counter. She pressed her hands, palms undoubtedly sticky and damp, and her face to the glass to peer in at the fresh-baked treats that Cheyenne had arranged meticulously inside an hour before. Cheyenne could see the fingerprints, and the faint trail of snot and puff of fog from the child's face as she breathed against the glass, and she had to suppress a shudder. On the other side of the shop, Nathan, older than Suzy by four minutes and with eons of pre-teen sass condensed into a three-year-old package, was pulling books off the narrow bookshelves that she and Jonathan had spent months filling. The wrinkle of paper and the sound of hardcovers scraping against the tile on the floor, combined with Suzy's heavy, damp breathing against the display case, made Cheyenne's shoulders tense.

"Hi, Cheyenne." Alison tucked her short blonde bob behind her ears. She was, as always, unaffected by the noise and mess that her children were making of the shop. "I heard the funniest thing from Mary this morning, when we were dropping the kids off at their Gymboree class. It was Nadia's turn to stay with them while we grabbed the coffees. You know Nadia? Patrick, cute as a button, glasses, poor kid. Right. Well, Mary and I were running to get the coffees and Mary said that you were leaving for some hick town in Pennsylvania! Well, I was just like 'No way!' and had to come down here to find out for myself. But then Nathan wanted to go see that new cartoon movie, that one with the talking babies—can you imagine babies that talked? Oh! There would be no peace!

"Anyways." Her talking, flitting through the shop, barely masked the sounds of her son pulling more and more and more books down—or her daughter drawing smiling faces in her breath fog on the glass. Cheyenne's eyebrow twitched, as it usually did when the Cramers came in, but she swallowed back her irritation in favor of keeping good business in the shop. Alison stopped talking for the briefest of moments and looked around the shop. "It doesn't look like you're leaving!"

"I, uh, I am leaving," Cheyenne said after a moment, her brain trying to catch up to the incessant babbling of the other woman while also trying to keep her eye on both toddlers. She liked them fine, especially when they were with their parents who were going to spend money in her shop, but Suzy and Nathan had a bad habit of trashing the place.

"But everything is still here! Mary said you were leaving tomorrow! You can't possibly pack all of this up in a day. It took me two months to pack up our condo when we got pregnant. Two months! Of course, if Bill had offered to help instead of working all the time, it wouldn't have taken nearly that long, but still." Alison fluttered her fingers at Cheyenne with a roll of her eyes that read 'men.'

Cheyenne took a deep breath and had to force herself

not to play with the charm around her neck. The necklace, a gift from Roxanne almost two decades before, was her favorite stress toy. And Alison, with her two miniature human hurricanes, always made her stressed. Behind Alison's shoulder, she could see Nathan doing his best to fold the pages of the book he was flipping through. Suzy had moved on from the display case to the coffee bar, where she was tugging wooden stirring sticks out of their metal bin, one by one. She could feel her eye starting to twitch.

"I am moving to Pennsylvania for a little while. Margo, Jonathan, and Ella are going to keep the shop operating up here. I'll be back every couple weeks to check on things, do the books, check on you and Mary."

Alison fluttered again. "Oh, that's wonderful!" She turned to look for her son. "What did you find, Natey?" she crooned, and the kid beamed, holding up the leatherbound copy of *A Study in Scarlet*, its gorgeous red cover glinting under the fluorescent lights. "Oooh, pretty. Well, you be nice to Ms. Cheyenne's books, okay? Suzy! Suzy, do not put the sticks up your nose."

The no-nose order left Suzy despondent for a second before she got the idea that the stirring sticks needed to be put methodically into sugar and sweetener packets. Little white crystals spilled all over the floor in front of the coffee bar. She giggled in joy and continued to try to spear packets.

"Aren't they darling?" Alison beamed at Cheyenne. "So inquisitive."

"Every day's a new experience when you're three." Cheyenne said with her best forced smile. "Listen, Alison,

I appreciate you coming to check on me, but I have a lot to get done before I leave tonight. Did you want to order anything, or…?"

Alison huffed. "Okay, okay. Ummm. How about a half dozen caramel mocha cupcakes and four pistachio biscotti. Suze, Natey, do you guys wanna come pick out a snack from Ms. Cheyenne's counter?"

Sugar packets, coffee stirring sticks, abused books, and one sad toy car that was bound to be forgotten were abandoned in lieu of something sweet. Another fifteen minutes, and a substantial amount of crying from Suzy when she learned she couldn't have all eight strawberry cake pops that were situated in the display case (she got all eight when the sobbing didn't stop), and Cheyenne was ushering the twins and their mother out of the shop.

Once they were gone and far enough down the sidewalk that Cheyenne couldn't see the bobbing blond heads of the twins, Cheyenne rushed into the kitchen and practically ripped the bottle of glass cleaner out of the cabinet. Margo, who was in the middle of stuffing a piece of bread in her mouth, looked up with wide eyes. Cheyenne laughed, a little at herself and a little at the chunk that fell out of Margo's plump lips onto the counter she was standing over.

"The Cramers came in," Cheyenne said by way of explanation, tugging a few paper towels off of the roll. "I'm going to go scrub down the display case."

"I've got the books." Margo groaned and stuffed the rest of her bread and fruit plate in the second fridge.

The two women braced themselves with a playful shrug at each other before they stepped back into the hub of the shop. Cheyenne's books lay in disarray on the floor and one picture book, a particular favorite of the shop's owner, lay in near tatters right next to the door. Cheyenne stifled a groan and shot her assistant, soon-to-be-head baker a long-suffering stare.

"I know, I know. You don't *hate* them," Margo said with a teasing smile as she bent to retrieve it.

"I don't! I just don't know what to do with them! And they make a mess of things. Like, every time Alison comes in with those two kids, they just make a mess. And what am I supposed to do? Deal with it?" Cheyenne wiped down the bottom right pane of glass on the display case.

"Yes. With a smile and a 'Hey, cutie,' like you've been doing. The Cramers are good business, and their referrals have helped us." Margo recited the same speech Cheyenne had given her after the first time the tornado twins came in almost a year ago. They went through the same routine every time the kids came in, the extent of which was usually synonymous with the amount of time the family spent in the shop.

"Good business, but Alison is such a busybody. 'Oh, I heard you were leaving. How can you leave?'" Cheyenne wheezed in a high-pitched voice, earning a dirty look from Margo. "I still have to finish packing."

"Jonathan will be here in a little bit. Then you can leave and finish packing. And call William?"

Cheyenne tossed a wad of dirty, damp paper towels at the back of Margo's head. "Hmph." She grunted when Margo just beamed at her and hunkered down to finish scrubbing the case.

CHEYENNE CALLED William on the way home. The brisk walk uphill to her apartment at the end of a long day was always the loneliest part of her day. Not that she was lonely. Cheyenne committed over a hundred hours a week to the business, sometimes getting there before four and staying until close at eight in the evening. She didn't have the time to be lonely. She just… wanted someone to come home to when her ankles were swollen from being on her feet and she smelled sickly sweet.

Still, as she walked past people dining in crowded clusters under sun catching umbrellas, enjoying the small restaurants she'd come to love or basking in the leftovers of the late June day, Cheyenne couldn't help but feel a little lonely.

Most of the men she'd dated since graduating from CIA and moving to Albany just hadn't stuck. Right after graduating, with a little seed money from her grandfather, Cheyenne had bought the little corner bakery and turned what had been a crumbling business into a staple of the community. The old owners of the shop had given her a good deal on the property and, with a lot of passion for sweets and the recipes of her grandmother's heart, Cheyenne had raised it from the ashes. By the time she'd turned twenty-three, she'd been able to repay her grandfather, with interest, and was making A Taste of Celeste dry goods mixes that were making their way all the way up to Maine. Business had been steady enough for her to hire Margo, and then Jonathan, and eventually Ella. It helped her put some aside for an expansion of the brand.

She'd already been planning to open another shop and had money set aside for just that purpose. Now, it'd have to be in a small corner of Pennsylvania—a place that she did have a lot of emotional ties with, but that she wasn't sure if she'd have picked as a site for the new shop.

Cheyenne had put everything in her into the bakery for five and a half years. Enough of herself that she'd had a string of possibly suitable relationships that had all ended with her eating a pint of ice cream, rewatching all seven seasons of *Gilmore Girls* in a week, and then reinvigorating her commitment to being single. Until she met a new guy and started all over again.

When she first moved, and the bakery was just getting off the ground, Cheyenne had had a relationship with an older man who'd wanted to get married. Allen had been convinced she'd leave the bakery behind, because it was just getting on its feet and was going to be a lot of work, for a penthouse in New York City, a kid, and a nanny. They'd had fun and had been able to dodge the subject for six months before Cheyenne had made it clear that she wasn't going to throw the bakery away for him or anyone else.

After Allen, there had been Matt. He was a guitarist who was gone more than he was around, and that had worked because neither of them had normal work, sleeping, or eating schedules. That had blown up when Matt had cheated on her while out on a six-show tour with his buddies. Cheyenne, while she couldn't have held him entirely accountable for that flop of a relationship, had packed all of the things he'd left at her apartment into a neat little box and left them on his front step the night he got home. And that had been that.

There'd been a few others, none of any real significance, until she'd met William a little under a year before. William was a financial consultant who spent his weeks in New York City but had made time to come on the weekends, and Tuesdays, to spend time with her. They'd met while she was out with Margo and Roxanne at a local bar that had easily been one of their favorite haunts when they were together.

For nearly a year, they'd made it work—Cheyenne dedicated to the bakery first and their budding, possible future second.

Until she'd told him she was moving to Pennsylvania.

She called him on her walk home and got his voicemail, its short greeting much more friendly than their terrible parting the night before. Cheyenne stopped, waiting for a crossing signal to let her make her way toward her block, and took a deep breath. "Hey, William," she started and bit her lip. "I just… I'm leaving tomorrow. But you know that. I was just… I don't know. Calling to say hi." Cheyenne licked her lips. "Call me back if you want to." Even as she said the words, she knew he wasn't going to call. She also didn't think, not when she stopped to put thought into it, that she wanted him to call.

So, she called Roxanne instead.

Her best friend answered on the first ring, as she had been doing lately out of concern. "Hey, how's the packing going?" Roxanne chirped at her.

Cheyenne smiled at the sound of her voice. She

unlocked the front door of her apartment building, an old, renovated Victorian with three floors of apartments fit for possibly five inhabitants. Cheyenne loved her studio on the third floor in the back of the building and had gotten permission from the property owners to paint the room a vibrant shade of lavender that always greeted her, and lit up her spirits, when she walked through the doors. The effect was dampened by the moving boxes in the center of the room, and the remnants of her bed—the mattress she had someone picking up in the morning—tucked neatly into the corner furthest from the door.

"It's going," she mumbled and dropped her keys on a box.

Roxanne didn't say anything right away. Cheyenne could hear Maverick in the background, yelling at something. "I'm so excited for you to be here," she told Cheyenne with a sigh.

Cheyenne got a bottle of water from her fridge and sat cross-legged on the floor by her half-packed bookshelf. "I'll be there tomorrow afternoon," Cheyenne said with half a laugh. She looked around the practically empty apartment and heaved a sigh. "I'll be there tomorrow afternoon," she said again, mostly to herself.

8

*C*heyenne pulled into the Retirement House's driveway the next afternoon, unsurprised to see Maverick's little black car parked beside her grandfather's truck. She supposed she'd need to find something to do with the old Chevy, which sat in the heavy afternoon sunlight, its orange-yellow paint matching the golden rays peeking over the roof of the house. Cheyenne climbed out of the Cherokee and gave the truck a pat. Maybe, she thought glumly, maybe keeping the truck for a little bit longer wouldn't be the worst thing that could happen.

Cheyenne wiped the stray tears rolling down her cheeks in slow progression with her free hand and cracked her neck. She'd cried more tears in the last three weeks than she had in her entire life, all twenty-six years under the sun. Now there would be no more tears; no more tears for the moment, anyway. She had her entire Jeep to unpack and a house full of stuff to sort through.

"Hey."

She looked up to see Maverick striding toward the

three cars. He was wearing a white t-shirt and blue jeans and still had a slight limp in his left leg. The movement looked painful, but he was grinning so broadly that it made up for the pain.

"What are you doing here?" she asked as she climbed out of the Jeep and yanked open the back door.

"Rox didn't want you to get here and be alone. She's been working on this article for, like, six hours now. It's due tomorrow and it's making her very, very angry."

"So, she sent you?" Cheyenne guessed with a smirk and pulled out the small suitcase she'd balanced against the driver's head rest.

"I offered, thank you very much." Maverick walked toward her. She'd noticed the change in his usually confident walk a while ago, but it always struck her as odd how much his movement had been altered by the accident he'd been in almost a year before. "I didn't think you should be alone when you brought all your stuff in."

"Aww, thanks." Cheyenne kissed his cheek.

Maverick grumbled her kiss off and peered over her head into the Jeep. "Where's the rest of it?"

"This is all of it." Cheyenne frowned at the packed vehicle. Several suitcases, four crammed-full boxes, two totes, and several stacks of loose books. It had taken her most of the morning to pack. "I sold off a lot of stuff since the house is fully furnished and all. And you signed for my kitchen boxes, right?"

"They got here two days ago. We even opened each box to make sure everything came in one piece." Maverick pulled out her large black suitcase. "Who knew that mixers were so heavy. Where is the rest of your clothes?"

"This is all of it, Rick." Cheyenne laughed.

Maverick looked perplexed, the shadows from the house only enhancing the confusion on his face. "It took two U-hauls to move Roxanne in, and most of that was her clothes."

Cheyenne shook her head and set her suitcase down long enough to strangle her hair back with an auburn elastic band. "Yeah, but that's Roxanne. I've got maybe three suitcases of clothes. And most of it's jeans and t-shirts that I've had since college." At Maverick's face, she sent him a dark look. "I have a degree, Maverick. Don't you start."

Maverick shrugged in his own defense and tugged out another bag. "Whatever you say."

The two of them were relatively quiet as they unloaded the Jeep and piled Cheyenne's measly belongings into the front foyer. Maverick's usual annoyingly cheeky banter seemed muffled by the underlying weight of their situation and Cheyenne, her own grief and frustration and anger too commingled to satiate his quietness, met it head-on. The silence was unusual. Their entire friendship had been built around the understanding that if Cheyenne wasn't talking, then Maverick was. Even with Roxanne and the guys around, they had always dominated the conversation. And gone head-to-head to overwhelm each other's voices when they were battling it out.

Their silence was understood as companionable, if a little uneven. Cheyenne's frustration steeped as she made trips back and forth from the Jeep to the house, her anger slipping away with the overwhelming realization that she wasn't unpacking her car for a long stay at the Retirement

House. Her grandfather wasn't in the kitchen making their evening cup of tea while she brought her things in from the car. That one stung to remember.

Maverick gave her space, helpful but quiet, so she could ruminate in her thoughts. His presence was more helpful than anything he could have said to her, and they both knew it. While she brought things in and stacked them in the foyer, Maverick brought the heavier bags inside and largely stayed out of her way.

Cheyenne brought in the last box, packed full of her collection of books and shelf decorations that she'd convinced herself to keep in the mad packing frenzy, and set it down in the foyer. She put it next to the little mail table, full of sympathy cards and the dying remains of a vase of flowers—leftovers from the overwhelming sadness that had filled the house, and the property, post-funeral. Cheyenne eased her hair out of the tight tail she'd pulled it up into and ran her fingers through it. It fell in a curtain around her face while she looked up at the tin-backed mirror over the table. The woman staring back at her had big hazel eyes, a little more deep-set than usual, and slinky, straight red hair that was in desperate need of a trim. There'd been no time to get it cut before the funeral, and even less time after. She'd have to fix that.

Cheyenne turned away from the mirror and peered down the hall toward the kitchen and dining room. Both rooms were clean, lit up with the yellow lightbulbs that Caleb could never be convinced to switch for something more energy efficient. They were also entirely empty, just like the rest of the house. The three-story house that was now Cheyenne's.

To her left sat the large living room, filled with the furniture that Celeste and Caleb had chosen almost twenty years before. The only new things in the room were gauzy white curtains that framed the six large windows and the large TV that sat against the far wall. CJ had gotten Caleb the flat screen a year and a half ago for his birthday. Caleb had adored it. Men and their toys, after all. Cheyenne strode into the room and ran her fingers over the arm of Caleb's favorite brown armchair. It had been one of the few things not moved in the commotion of the will reading, the funeral, and the kids who had run around the house in between. On the small table to the arm's right sat a little blue shaded lamp and one of her grandfather's mystery novels, the bookmark still in it.

She picked up the paperback and pressed her nose to the cover. It smelled like cloves and cinnamon, like her grandfather. It hadn't been moved in the fray of the activities surrounding her last visit to the house, out of respect for her grandfather and his adoration of all things Patterson, Clark, and Christie. Cheyenne cracked the book open, the well-worn spine easily falling open to the pages where the antique map-looking bookmark lay. She swallowed back a sniffle. The words on the top of the left page were underlined in blue ink, although she had no idea which read-through the mark belonged to, and the right page had a very large coffee stain in the middle of it. The book was well worn, and very much loved.

It struck her as she ran her fingers over the underlined print that these very well might have been the last words that Caleb ever read. What she didn't know, but she would learn later on, was that the DVD player next to the TV contained the last movie Caleb had ever seen, another favorite of his—*The Fifth Element*—which he had been listening to while reading on the morning he died. Cheyenne knew, from what CJ had gotten from Jesse, that the movie had been paused and the book had sat open on his chair when Caleb had made his last journey outside to the garden. His favorite place on the property. For the last time.

"He loved these," Cheyenne said glumly when she heard Maverick's footsteps behind her. "I don't think I ever met as big a James Patterson fan as Gramps."

"Rox had the new J.D. Robb book pre-ordered for him because he couldn't figure out Amazon. She won't cancel it," Maverick said softly as he put an arm around her shoulders. "We have a huge box of yard sale finds in the basement that she was slowly bringing over here."

"'Cause she wanted him to get out more." Cheyenne sniffled, cursing the silent stream of tears that poured down her cheeks. "And I just kept buying him books and mailing them."

"And he ran right through them." Maverick squeezed her shoulders and rested his head against hers. "We're going to keep the books."

"All the books," Cheyenne agreed, wiping her cheeks with the sleeve of her sweater. "I think he has the entire *Alex Cross* series somewhere in the library. Maybe I'll even start reading them."

Maverick chuckled and took the book from her. "Not tonight, though, okay? I don't think murder and mystery goes well with mascara stains and teardrops."

Cheyenne gave a watery laugh and pressed her face into Maverick's collarbone. "It just… it still just doesn't feel real. Not real at all."

He wrapped his other arm around her. Cheyenne and Maverick had hugged more in the last four weeks than they had in the whole twenty-two years they'd known each other, but it still felt… weird. She pondered over the weirdness of their embrace while she sniffled and hiccupped against his chest, using the thought to break her from the thoughts and feelings of her grandfather and the empty house. Caleb was always going to be gone now. She was going to have to adjust.

"He left me the house," she said after a few watery moments, shoving her hands between them to rub at her eyes. "He fucking died, and he left me the house. This whole house. I am one person and he left me the whole house?"

"He'd be happy you're here," Maverick said over her head, his hand awkwardly patting her upper back.

"He knew how much I'd be giving up by moving here. What was he thinking?" More tears trailed down her cheeks and dripped off of her chin. By now, Maverick's entire shirtfront was a mess of tears, snot, and trails of mascara.

"That you can run a bakery here just as well as you can in Albany," he offered, stepping back to pat her cheeks. "That you would appreciate the house much more than either of your brothers. Or, and this one is probably the closest to what Caleb was thinking, that he loved you, loved this place, and thought that you would be happy here."

"This whole house is mine." Cheyenne sighed and shoved her hands through her hair. She stepped back from Maverick with a half-hysterical laugh. "I own a house. Is this how you felt when you bought the house?"

His cheeks flashed a slight pink. "I mean, I bought the house in a frenzy to get my life in order, so there hasn't been a lot of 'I bought a house' panic. Definitely some 'I'm about to get married' panic, though. Does that kind of count?"

She laughed and slugged him in the arm playfully. "No, it does not count. Two totally different kinds of panic."

"Well, damn." He grinned at the smile that it brought to her face. "I'll have to tell Rox. You know how much she likes to compete."

"I mean, her panic about the house and the marriage probably equates to me owning a house?"

"Possibly. We'll tell her that. It'll make her feel better." He clapped his hands together and looked around the living room. "Do you have any crushing need to unpack all of your crap tonight?"

"Uh... not really. I guess I have time. A lot of time." She sniffed. "Why?"

"Because I only brought one beer. And there is absolutely no food in this house. Let's go find my fiancée and get some pizza."

LORENZO'S HADN'T CHANGED a bit. It amazed Cheyenne that the pastel orange booths and awkwardly brown tables, which had seemed ancient and out of place when she was a kid, still filled the back dining room in their cheerfully outdated manner. The side game room was full of kids, and most of the tables around them were crammed with families, small children, and elderly grandparents who were arguing politics or television shows. Cheyenne took it all in while they waited for their appetizer sampler.

It was nice, sitting in Lorenzo's on a Sunday night. Those were the nights she and her grandfather, usually with at least Roxanne in tow, would come into town and sit in a similar-looking booth to be a part of the buzz. Across the table from her, Maverick and Roxanne were bickering over last-minute changes to the seating arrangements and how much longer they should wait for RSVPs. Roxanne kept bringing up internet etiquette tips she'd picked up while searching for inane rules that would, or would not, apply to them.

"I think that you're good to wait another month," Cheyenne chimed in after a grateful smile at the waiter when a tray of piping hot mozzarella sticks were set down in front of them. "Just don't put me anywhere near your Aunt Patsy. She smells like mothballs. Always."

"Oh, don't worry. Mom's got Patsy down on the other end of the reception hall from the bridal table," Roxanne said as she split a mozzarella stick in half and dipped it in the marinara sauce. "I'm worried about Cynthia. Baby number three is going to be coming in real close to the wedding. If I put her too close to the front and she pops then it'd be a catastrophe, but she *is* in the wedding party. We put her too close to the back and not at the bridal table, and she's never going to talk to me again."

"Maybe you'll get lucky and she'll go into labor before the ceremony. Then she's not an issue," Cheyenne offered around a mouthful of hot cheese.

Roxanne groaned and sunk her teeth into her mozzarella stick in response.

"I said the same thing last week and Rhea told me I was going to Hell." Maverick smirked and raised his beer glass. "This is what happens when you get pregnant with your third child when your cousin is engaged." Roxanne swatted him in the chest, and he chuckled.

"This is what happens when you get pregnant in general," Cheyenne grumbled.

"Changing the subject now!" Roxanne giggled.

Cheyenne screwed up her nose and closed her lips to chew. "Do you think he's ever going to redecorate in here?" Cheyenne segued and shifted around on the vinyl.

"Probably not." Roxanne shrugged and rested her head against Maverick's arm. "Mom said that it's looked like this since she was a kid. In fact, I think Mom and Dad had their first kiss in this. Very. Booth." She jabbed her finger emphatically against the orange vinyl. "Or was it that one over there?"

"You'd think Lorenzo would put a plaque on every booth where a couple had their first kiss." Maverick chuckled at the way Roxanne's face lit up. "I mean, a ton of them have got to be married still."

"It would be weird if he hunted down all of those people who've had their first date here over the years."

Cheyenne craned her neck to look at the 'Established 1961' sign that sat above the doorway linking the back dining room to the front of the restaurant. "That's gotta be, what, a couple hundred couples?"

"I'm sure Lorenzo Senior would know." Maverick shrugged and popped a piece of jalapeño popper in his mouth. "For a man in his mid-eighties, he's smart as a whip. And picky as hell. His will could rival your grandfather's."

Roxanne shot him a dark look over the rim of her wine glass and took a sip of the cheap boxed wine they kept in the back by the gallon. "Anyway." She turned her attention back to Cheyenne. "Have you put any thought into what your next move is?"

"Rox, she just got here." Maverick kissed his fiancée's head and shook his own. "I'm going to run to the bathroom." He stood and kissed Roxanne, slow and soft, his hands cradling her face. Cheyenne mock gagged and wagged her fingers at his back as he walked away.

Once he was gone, Roxanne turned her startling blue eyes on Cheyenne and beamed. "So? What happens now, girlfriend?"

Cheyenne's smile fizzled into a prim line, and she made herself busy adjusting her paper napkin on her lap. When all Roxanne did was stare, she shifted around uncomfortably and shrugged. She hadn't put too much thought into what came after moving to Penn Ridge. Her last couple of weeks had been filled with just getting her affairs in order to get there. "I guess… I guess I'll open another bakery."

Roxanne pitched an eyebrow up toward her hairline. "Another bakery?"

"I wanted to open a second location anyway. And I have the collateral all set aside, all of my ducks in a row, so to speak. Now that I, myself, am in a totally new location, I might as well open a new shop." Cheyenne shrugged and swirled her wine around in her glass. "I guess that'll be the next step."

"That'd be nice. The nearest bakery is in Easton, which is a twenty-minute drive on a good day."

"Oh, I know. Gramps calls—" Cheyenne's face froze, the fond smile on her mouth stiffening into a grimace. Roxanne cleared her throat and Cheyenne shrugged it off. "Called me all the time to complain. I think he just liked the ginger snaps I would mail to him after one of those phone calls." Her fondness, tinged with sadness, fell off of her lips.

Roxanne reached across the table and squeezed Cheyenne's hands. "He loved your ginger snaps," she said with a sweet smile, her eyes winking. "Almost as much as he loved when you'd come to visit."

"He also loved when you moved back."

The girls beamed at each other and were still holding hands across the table when Maverick came back with their waiter and the large everything pizza steaming behind him. He dropped into his seat and served the girls each a large slice, piled full of meat and vegetables and the extra cheese Cheyenne had ordered. Roxanne's slice, at least fifteen percent bigger than Cheyenne's, disappeared quickly, while Cheyenne enjoyed every slow bite of hers. The slender woman's metabolism had been a thing of envy between the two of them since puberty, easily matched by the fact that Roxanne had been jealous of Cheyenne's straight hair until they turned twenty. But even then, Cheyenne watched her relish her slice of pizza with a little pink in her cheeks and thought about the way that she filled out the blue jeans she was wearing.

Her silent comparison was interrupted by a warm, if slightly out of nowhere, voice calling her name. She blinked a handful of times before looking up and to the left where Jesse stood, his hand anchored by a little boy with a wild flop of sand-colored hair and an Avengers t-shirt that was a size too big. He stood tall over their table, blocking out some of the yellow light coming from the sconces above their heads. He wore a pair of faded blue jeans and a long-sleeve black shirt. His wide grin, easy and warm, erased the metabolism jealousy away.

"Jesse. Hi." She awkwardly stood up and shoved her hands through her hair, the silky strands tangling around her knuckles.

"Hey."

She'd thought about him frequently since she'd left after the funeral. Not in the creepy, going-to-lick-whipped-cream-off-of-him-in-a-steamy-kitchen kind of way. But in the 'there's going to be a reliable man around to help me figure out this house crap' way that had made the move, and the catastrophic fight with William, seem the tiniest bit less difficult. Of course, it didn't hurt that his mile-long legs looked really good in blue jeans. "Hi." She coughed again and gestured to the table where Maverick and Roxanne were watching, both of them working on mouthfuls of pizza. "This is my best friend

Roxanne and her fiancé—I mean he's my friend too but they're getting married so, um—Maverick."

Jesse shook Maverick's hand and then Roxanne's while the little boy eyed their appetizer plate. "We met at the funeral," he said with a sigh as the little boy tugged on his free hand. He crouched and held his ear out to listen to the little boy whispering. His grin broadened as he stood, this time hauling the kid up to sit on his hip. "This is Miles."

The little boy waved with one arm, the other wrapped around the back of his father's neck. "Hi!" His grin was bigger than his father's and full of slightly crooked teeth, one of which was missing in the front. "I'm six!"

"Six? Really?" Roxanne eyed him playfully. "You are much too big for six," she half cooed, which totally delighted the child.

He kicked his feet joyfully and beamed up at his father. That one was sure to be the hit of the next week.

Cheyenne looked at the child in his father's arms, her own eyebrows twitching in bemusement. She found it amazing how the handyman had gone from looking delicious in his blue jeans and long sleeve shirt to a tired father, the kind she'd help pick out a birthday cake at the bakery. It didn't bother her. If anything, he looked even more attractive than he had before.

"He's six. I have the paperwork to prove it." Jesse squeezed his son before glancing back at Cheyenne. She hoped desperately that he couldn't read the thoughts that slipped through her mind. "You got in today, right? How was the drive?"

Cheyenne tucked her hair behind her ears with a slight

smile, still standing by the table. "It was good. Long but good. Barely any traffic. Everyone was going back into the city, not heading away from it."

Jesse nodded and puffed out his cheeks, as if at a loss for words. Miles, who was already bored of the conversation, sighed and dramatically rolled his eyes. "Can we go eat pizza now?"

"Yes. Yes. Pizza." Jesse readjusted the child and held his hand out to Cheyenne. "I'm going to stop by tomorrow morning and check on a few things. Is ten okay?"

"Ten is perfect," Cheyenne said quickly, awkwardly shaking his hand. "I'll see you then."

Jesse said a quick goodbye to Roxanne and Maverick before he and his son made their way to the counter of the pizzeria.

She turned back to Roxanne's smirk and Maverick's raised eyebrows and waved them off, unsure of herself and the feelings in her chest. "Who's ready for a second slice?"

9

*J*esse pulled up to the Retirement House at a quarter to ten Monday morning, a fresh cup of coffee on the console beside him and a little bit of satisfaction sitting in his shoulders. He had two fresh cashier's checks from the Martin rebuild burning a hole in his wallet and a happy crew that was definitely going to get their Christmas bonuses this year. The rebuild was coming along nicely and was going to put the small construction (and landscaping) company way in the black. Tim was going to go off the hook when he saw all of the zeroes they'd be adding to their business bank account.

He'd left the crew behind to finish some trim around the inside of the house, with Tim to supervise, and had taken the detour to Caleb's place himself. It had become a little pet project for him the summer he moved to Penn Ridge, partially because he and Caleb had gotten along really well and partially because he loved the garden that Celeste had left him. He and Caleb had put in a white fence around it the year before thanks to a particularly annoying deer influx. He made a mental note to add fence repairs to the short list of things that he knew had to be fixed. The attic door and the second story stairs were his biggest concerns at the moment, but the fence, and the garden, were definitely top priority.

Before he announced his presence to Cheyenne, he decided to take a walk through the crammed garden. With his toolbox in the truck and his cellphone tucked securely in his back pocket, he strode across the yard and let himself into the garden. Most of the flowers were shriveled up, the beds of butterfly bushes and tulips drooping to the ground. The large beds of roses, daisies, and sunflowers had definitely seen warmer days. Jesse crouched to scoop up a handful of dirt to check its moisture and added a note to the list to water it, because there was no rain coming for a few days. He couldn't help but wonder if Cheyenne knew how to take care of the garden or if she was even going to maintain it. He hadn't spent a lot of time talking to Caleb about his granddaughter, other than to know that she was smart and a baker, and Caleb's entire world.

After his garden tour, which saw re-grouting the fountain and possibly replacing the paver stones added to his list, Jesse took the back steps up onto the porch and tapped on the glass sliding door that peeked into the living room. Cheyenne was curled up on the brown leather lounger, her nose buried in a book, looking as comfortable as he'd ever seen her. Her hair was piled on the top of her head, and from what he could tell, she was wearing lounge pants and a college sweatshirt. With her glasses on, and her face completely void of makeup, she looked more like sixteen than twenty-six. So much like Caleb that Jesse felt, for a moment, like the world was off-kilter.

He missed the old man. They had become great friends in the time that Jesse had worked for him, sharing a love for mystery novels, chocolate cake, and the fact that they were both devoted family men. They both had war stories of chemotherapy and snarky doctors that had kept them on the back porch with a cold glass of iced tea more nights than Jesse had ever spent with another client before. It'd been a month since he'd found Caleb unconscious in the garden, his lips blue from lack of oxygen and his skin almost too cold to touch. A month since he'd ridden in the ambulance with the man to the hospital in Easton and had waited until Cal and his wife, Lisa, had arrived. A month since he'd left the hospital numbly and driven straight to his in-laws', having to pull over on the side of the road to shed a few tears of disbelief and heartache.

Cheyenne looked up at his tapping and smiled, getting to her feet. "Are you early?" she asked as she yanked the door open. Jesse noticed that she'd had to plant her feet and give it a solid tug. He added it to the list.

Jesse checked his watch. It was fifteen after ten already. "Uh. No, I think I'm late." He scratched the back of his neck and met her frowning gaze. "I got here a half hour ago, but I was puttering in the garden. I, uh, I hope that's okay. Your gramps didn't mind me wandering around and all." His face felt hot and the neck scratching had gotten even more intense.

Cheyenne looked up at him with wide hazel eyes and frowned a little in perplexed kindness. "That's okay. You're probably going to be better in that than I am," she said with a little laugh. "That garden's always been more for enjoyment than work for me."

Jesse nodded and forced himself to drop his hand before he made the back of his neck raw. "Your lettuce is about ready to pick. The sooner the better. It tastes better when the leaves are plump." He inhaled to fill the silence and took in the sweet aromas of whatever Cheyenne had baking in the kitchen. It filled the house with warmth and the slightest hint of vanilla. It was absolutely wonderful.

She nodded and stepped back so that he could enter the house. "I'll keep that in mind." She pushed her glasses back up her nose and padded ahead of him into the kitchen.

Jesse followed her and skirted around a pile of untouched suitcases in the foyer. The dining room was littered with packing boxes that had been cracked open, showing gleaming silver pans and pots, a few glass dishes, and—from what he could tell—an ice cream maker. Jesse liked the clutter. It reminded him of his house, lived-in and full—fuller than Caleb had ever been able to make it on his own. He supposed it was because Cheyenne had more life in her than Caleb had had, or at least more energy.

"Do you like chocolate chip cookies?" she asked as she pulled a large, cookie-laden tray out of the oven and placed it on top. On the counter by the sink, there were two cooling trays full of cookies, all perfectly round and smelling delicious. "Or cranberries and oranges?"

"Yes to the chocolate. No to the oranges." He screwed up his nose when she looked at him. "My mother was big on the 'orange juice kills all sickness' train. Anytime my brother or I caught a cold or got the flu, we'd have to suck down a gallon of the stuff a day. I haven't been able to touch it since I turned eighteen and moved out of the house."

Cheyenne laughed and turned off the oven. "I love it. My mom and my dad's ex-wife are both big fans of hot tea and vapor rub when you're sick. I still like tea, though." She wiped her hands on a purple polka-dotted hand towel. "Do your kids like cookies?"

"They wouldn't eat the fruit ones. It would weird them out." He leaned against the island and watched her take hot cookies and place them on a cooling rack. "Amelia, my daughter, might try one, but I'd have to eat it first, and I would be weirded out 'cause oranges, so."

Her giggle was music to his ears. "Okay, okay. I'll send you home with some of the chocolate chip and some peanut butter? No nut allergies, right?"

"You don't have to send me home with any—" Her piercing look made him flush again. "No nut allergies," he confirmed.

"Good. Now, I'm sorry, but I don't know what kind of arrangement you had with Gramps, so I'm not entirely sure why you're here?" She said it with a cheeky smile as she pulled a long plastic container out of a bottom cabinet.

"Because things need to be fixed?"

"What things? The house looks fine to me. Do you get paid by the hour, or…?"

"Your grandfather left me a certain amount of money per year for the next, oh, I don't know, decade or so for me to work on the house as it needs to be worked on. That's all settled. You don't have to worry about me or paying me."

Jesse had agreed to the awkward lump sum that came out of the house's trust. He knew that the property taxes, as well as a few other odds and ends, were set up through a trust to go through the house and the law office that had handled his will. Jesse saw a monthly check show up from the trust, from money he didn't understand how Caleb had, and he didn't ask questions. He just knew the second landing stairs and the attic doors needed to be fixed soon, and that there was going to be more work on the horizon.

He reiterated his understanding of the house's financial holding to Cheyenne and added, emphatically, that the stairs needed to be fixed. "I won't show up when you're not here if you're not comfortable with that, but I do stop by every other week with my partner, Tim—he was at the funeral—and two of our guys to work on the landscaping. During the winter, that changes to driveway plowing and path shoveling, along with icicle removal. Your grandfather hated how they would hang off the gutters."

Cheyenne took it all in with a few nods and a murmur of agreement at his awe over the amount of money that had gone into trust for the house. "I'm not surprised. He was a smart man. He'd want this place taken care of."

"Well, I'm going to go fix the stairs. And then I have to fix the attic door. Depending on time, I'll get to work on the fence." Jesse eased away from the island and gave her what he hoped was a reassuring smile. Her skeptical face, sculpted out of soft features and hazel eyes that you could swim in, needed to relax. He'd give anything to hear her laugh again.

"Sounds good. Do you drink coffee?"

"Religiously."

"Well, if you do a good job with the stairs, maybe I'll make you some coffee." She went back to piling cookies in plastic containers, her shoulders hunched in tension.

Jesse rolled his eyes at the back of her head and wandered back out to the truck to grab his toolbox.

CHEYENNE FOUND herself fidgety while Jesse was in the house. She'd spent the morning alone, in quiet discomfort because she'd only spent a couple of hours in the empty house before. That quiet discomfort had turned into pure laziness when she saw the first *In Death* book on her grandfather's bookshelf, and she curled up in his recliner and lost herself in it while the cookies she'd popped in the oven baked. Then she found herself getting up to rotate baking sheets of cookies and rushing back to the book. She had completely lost track of time.

Now that Jesse was in the house, she was unsettled. She could hear someone else bumping around in the otherwise quiet house and didn't know what to think about it. By the time she'd gotten home the night before, she'd been too tired to worry about the quiet house or the fact that she wasn't sure which bedroom was hers. She'd passed out on the couch, suitcases and boxes be damned, and had slept solidly until the sun nearly burned her eyelids when dawn broke.

Maverick, when he'd dragged her big suitcase full of clothes in the house, had dropped it off in her grandfather's—in the master—bedroom on the second floor. The bed had been stripped by one of the sisters-in-law and fresh lavender sheets had been tugged tightly over its queen-sized mattress. A fresh bed set had also been draped across the bed, soft tones of gray and purple that matched the wooden four-poster bed better than anything Cheyenne would have picked out. Roxanne had bought the sheets and comforter set and had only told her the bed in the master had been made after she'd done it. Making the room, by anyone's choice but her own, hers.

Cheyenne stood in the doorway and took in the purple bed set and the fresh vase of lavender that Roxanne had dropped on the long, low dresser that sat on the wall opposite the bed. Her grandfather's reading lamp on the bedside table had been replaced with her modern white and silver fixture, and her suitcases were waiting expectantly for her in front of the closet. She tugged on the collar of her t-shirt while she looked around the room, taking it all in.

"Guess I should unpack," she said around the lump in her throat, and she ran her fingers over her face, trying to catch a couple of tears. The idea of unpacking was so daunting, so hard for her to wrap her head around. This was her room now. There would be no more morning coffees had over a laugh and a muffin in her grandfather's sitting chairs, no more lying on the old four-poster while her grandfather puttered in the closet, no more of Gramps' laughter bouncing off the worn wall paper. There was… no more Gramps.

Cheyenne was on the brink of tears, twisting her fingers in the ends of her hair, when Jesse started to hammer on something. Cheyenne braced herself against the foot of the bed and took a deep breath, trying to calm her thundering heartbeat. Once she'd stopped sniffling and stopped her hands shaking, she straightened up and decided that going to check on what Jesse was doing was much better than crying in her new bedroom.

She padded back out of the room and down the hall to check on Jesse's progress. He was sitting on the fourth step up with a mouthful of nails and a hammer poised in his left hand. "Do you care if I listen to music?" Under normal circumstances, she wouldn't have asked the handyman if he liked music before she turned it on. Then again, the handyman in her building back in Albany was usually only around late at night when the shower was out of hot water or during the day when she wasn't around. She wasn't sure what the etiquette was when it came to the basically built-in, hotter-than-hell handyman who was sitting on the stairs staring at her.

Jesse shook his head and went back to his hammering. He used each nail that was perched between his lips and seemed very content to just be sitting there, working in the unnerving silence.

She shook her head and padded back to the bedroom. She left both of the double doors open and opened her phone. With some heavy alternative rock turned on full blast and her mind escaping into the lyrics, she ripped open the first suitcase and dumped its contents onto the bed. A rainbow of soft greens, vibrant purples, deep blues, and more jeans than she'd realized she'd owned met her head-on.

It took her nearly two hours to unload the majority of the clothes and get them situated in the closet and drawers. Most of her clothes were easy to fold and pack away, with only a few sweaters and two dresses that took up closet space. Her shoes would be another story—a different argument between herself and the limited storage space in the closet. She'd have to ask Jesse to build in a few shelves to hold her shoes, and a towel rack in the en suite bathroom.

Her en suite bathroom. Her small closet. The spacious bedroom, with a sitting chair in the corner and a small bookshelf, that once belonged to Gramps and was now hers. Even with her clothes put away neatly, in drawers or hanging in the closet, and the lavender blanket and flowers that brightened up the otherwise brown room, it didn't feel like hers. She was seriously wondering if it would ever truly feel like hers.

"I'll make do," she said dryly to herself and smoothed her hands on the fabric of her sweatpants. She felt grubby and in desperate need of a shower, but the faint hammering she could hear behind the music was a constant reminder that she wasn't alone.

She was covered in dust, and a little sweaty from all the unpacking, so she decided after a disgruntled look in the mirror that she couldn't wait for Jesse to leave. Her skin was starting to crawl in the filth, and she managed to convince herself that he was preoccupied enough that he might not even notice her complete disappearance.

Cheyenne made sure the bathroom door was locked before she hopped into the shower to rinse off. Her music was still playing, and the sound of Jesse's hammer made a nice backdrop to the loud music that was pounding out of the speakers of her cellphone. Cheyenne lost herself in the sounds of the music, singing and swaying her hips as she rinsed soap off her body and out of the fiery tangle of her hair. For a few minutes, she forgot that Jesse was even in the house.

He still wasn't on her mind when she climbed out of the shower and wrapped herself in a towel. The bathroom faucet dripped excitedly as she toweled her hair a little and padded out of the small bathroom and into the hub of the bedroom. A bedroom of which the door was wide open.

Jesse was wiping sweat from his forehead and leaning against the attic doorjamb, his eyes unfocused and directed toward the open bedroom door. Cheyenne didn't notice at first, and frankly neither did he, that his glazed-over eyes were landing directly on her in her thin pink towel until the song she had been singing along to ended and they were shrouded in the quiet of her run-out playlist. She picked her head up and her eyes locked with Jesse's. Both of them turned red. She slipped back into the bathroom and slammed the door shut, her heart hammering in her chest.

When she got over her upset enough to get dressed and exit the bathroom, he was standing underneath the staircase where the door that led up to the attic was situated, his back pointedly turned toward the still-open door. She swallowed, hoping that he hadn't seen too much of her exposed skin, and padded out of the bedroom to see what he was working on. There was no part of her that hadn't felt a small thrill at the way his eyes had run over her in her towel, or how shocked he'd looked when she'd slammed the bathroom door shut behind her. It was enough of a look that Cheyenne felt hot, from the tips of her toes to the top of her head, as she stared at his well-defined back. It was also enough of a look to tell Cheyenne that she had never felt its intent before; not its intensity, per se, but the way he'd studied her like she was something exotic that he had never seen before and could, quite possibly, never get enough of. No one had ever looked at her like that before. Not even William, who had called her again the night before and whose voice was waiting for her in her voicemail box.

"Fighting with the door?" Cheyenne asked, keeping a few feet away.

Jesse turned with a sheepish smile and shrugged. "Your grandfather kept insisting this damned door was okay, but it hasn't closed right in a year." When he looked at her, his eyes didn't betray anything near their quiet intensity from before. That bothered her for reasons she would never be sure of, but she moved past it, convinced that what had happened only a few minutes before had been more her imagination and little of anything else.

"Yeah, I know." She smiled while her face struggled to stop being its hot pink hue. "You don't have to fix it, you know. I don't plan on going up there that often."

"It's been on my list for the last eight months."

"Your list, huh?"

"You gotta follow the list, especially when you do a thousand and five things like I do. Or things never get done." He turned back to the attic door.

"I'm amazed that he wouldn't let you fix it. Did he ever have a reason for it?" Cheyenne rubbed her hands together and yawned. "Coffee break?"

Jesse frowned at the door but dropped his hammer into his toolbox. "I'll take a cup of coffee." He drummed his fingers on his thigh. "I'm not sure. Whenever I asked him, he'd change the subject, or just start telling me some story about when he was my age."

"Those were his favorite." Cheyenne smiled fondly.

Jesse tapped his knuckle on the counter after a few beats of silence. "So… I'll probably have to come back and finish the door later this week. If that's okay?"

Cheyenne led him down the stairs and into the kitchen, shaking her head. "How many times a week do you usually come to the house?"

Jesse leaned against the counter and watched her intently while she made coffee. "Two or three times. Depending on what needs to be done. Hell, there would be weeks where I'd stop by and we'd just sit on the porch and drink iced tea. He loved iced tea."

She noticed the sad glint in his eyes, and it made her stomach do a weird gooey lurch. "You spent a lot of time with him?"

He nodded and looked at his hands. "He was a cool guy. My father-in-law and your dad were friends as kids, so he knew who I was and the kind of people I come from. We had a lot in common." He made a soft coughing sound, as if something were stuck in his throat, and took a sudden interest in the turnip-shaped salt shaker that sat in the center of the island.

"Gramps was easy to have a lot in common with. The man did just about everything." Her own throat felt a little mucky, and a little dry, and the two of them made eye contact for the briefest moment. His brown eyes bored into her own and she smiled weakly, tucking a loose strand of hair behind her ear. "I keep thinking we must've run into each other while I was visiting, but I just don't know."

"Maybe in town, but never here. Your grandfather always made it a point to schedule my appointments here for when you weren't going to be in." Jesse shrugged. "It made sense to just let him have it because, well, he didn't want you to think he couldn't get on here by himself."

She snorted and handed him a cup of steaming coffee. "Milk? Sugar? I might have some heavy cream."

"Just a splash of milk." Jesse took the mug and the little carton of milk she held out to him with a small grin. "You know who has good coffee? The Harvest Bean in town. Jeff and Pat roast their own beans and grind them. Good stuff."

"I have an appointment with a realtor in town tomorrow. I'll check it out."

"Who are you meeting with?"

"Some woman named Sam."

Jesse shook his head with a snort. "Let me know how that goes."

"What?" Cheyenne frowned at him.

Jesse shook his head. "You'd have better luck with my mother-in-law. She knows everyone in town. I'm sure she'd be able to find you something suited to what you need."

Cheyenne took a sip of coffee, looking out the window over the sink. "I'll let you know how it goes."

He grinned and raised his mug to her.

10
---

*C*heyenne stood staring at the empty storefront, her arms folded over her chest and her lips twisted into an ugly scowl that did not become her. This was not what she'd had in mind when she'd hastily made that Ridge Reality appointment right before moving to Penn Ridge. She'd told them that she needed to purchase a storefront as soon as possible. Sam, her real estate agent, stood beside her, giving her the rundown of how the storefront they were standing in front of was the 'perfect' space for her new bakery.

It was anything but. She resisted the urge to whirl on the bubbly blonde next to her and give her a passionate, and very aggressive, diatribe on how the shop was not perfect or even moderately good. It definitely was not worth the price tag. Cheyenne turned to the woman, who reeked of Avon perfume, and cut her off mid-thought with a dry look and two narrowed eyes.

"I don't think this is going to work for me," she said carefully, trying to think of how Roxanne would handle the situation. Her friend would definitely be a lot calmer about the conversation. Channeling her inner Roxanne, Cheyenne took a deep breath before continuing. "I'm not a big fan of yellow." The entire exterior of the building was a sickly yellow, painted over brick that kind of reminded her of snot. "And it's too small on the inside."

"But you said you didn't want anything too big." The blonde actually whined this out.

Her eye almost twitched. "Yes, but not this small." She rolled her eyes and gestured to the tiny storefront in front of her. "And… and the door is turquoise. The building is yellow, and the door is turquoise?"

Sam looked at her blankly. "I'm sure we could negotiate fresh paint in the lease."

"I wanted to buy," Cheyenne interjected with a sigh, "and the place doesn't even have kitchen space in it." The migraine that was sprouting behind her right eye was starting to make her nauseous, and she just needed the woman to stop.

The real estate agent did stop and looked at Cheyenne, her eyebrows knitting together. "Excuse me?"

Cheyenne gestured to the storefront. The off-green door, yellow awning, and orange-yellow bricks didn't seem to fit anywhere into the scheme of Orchard Street, in between the aged brick buildings with tasteful ornamentation and the trees that were changing leaves. Sam followed her hand. Her perfectly groomed eyebrows pinched together, and she pursed her lips. "How is it 'perfect'?" Cheyenne pressed.

"You could always put a kitchen in," the blonde offered, her clueless face beaming at the prospect.

Not a solution. Her perfume was really starting to make Cheyenne feel sick to her stomach. "Do you know how much it would cost to put in an industrial kitchen? I asked for two things. A really nice view and an industrial kitchen." Which, she thought grumpily while sending a dark look at the singular window with the yellow awning, this one did not have. "Well, three, I guess. 'Cause I was looking to buy."

Sam floundered while searching for an answer, her lips too red for her pale complexion. "I can go back to the office and see what's open, but not many spaces are for sale, per se. Many of the landlords in the business district prefer to lease out the spaces."

"A lease works too," Cheyenne said weakly, wondering if she could work around the realtor and find a storefront for sale. She'd have to make nice with some locals really fast in order for that one to happen. Of course, there was always Jesse's offer. Cheyenne found it more tempting by the minute as she stared at Sam, frustrated. "I just need a lease that I can renovate under." She wasn't going to find a building that had the kitchen space, counters, and ovens necessary to match the glorious New York building that her first bakery resided in. But as a bakery, having a kitchen was kind of a necessity, and she'd have thought that Sam would see the need for one as well. "I showed you the pictures of my original location, didn't I?"

"Yes, I have them saved on my desktop." Sam made a soft puff of air that sounded like a sigh and a giggle mixed into one. She kicked at the curb with the heel of her leather boot. "I'll go back to the office and take a look at what we've got available. You'll have to understand that Penn Ridge is a sweet hamlet with—"

"'Limited, valuable property options,' yes, I know." Cheyenne huffed and adjusted her purse strap. "But"—she refrained from reiterating that the real estate agent would 'have to understand' herself—"I need a place that I can renovate to my needs."

It wasn't hard to understand. Cheyenne was sure of that fact; she needed a space with a large kitchen area, a nice front, and room for tables and a coffee bar. She'd even gone so far as to design the storefront and kitchen space herself, with a little help from the interior designer who had set about creating what she knew and loved as "Taste of Celeste" when she bought the original building in Albany. All she needed was the space to turn the building into reality.

"I could always try to find something in another town —you know, places with more available property." And other realtors. Hopefully ones who didn't bathe in bad-smelling perfume.

Sam blinked in surprise and Cheyenne watched her smile slip when it dawned that she'd meant going to a different realtor. "No, no. I'm sure there's something, maybe on Church? Yeah. Let me see what we have open on Church Street."

Church Street would work for Cheyenne; she'd been driving down it the day before, on her way to the florist with Roxanne, and had seen a couple of empty storefronts that she really liked. "If you could find one as soon as possible," Cheyenne said around gritted teeth, "that would be great."

Cheyenne was itching to get in a kitchen again. She missed her shop, her employees—her regular customers who had become friends. She even missed the fact that the front door of her apartment never unlocked right away, or that she'd had to hike through snow to get to the bakery in the middle of the winter because driving the Jeep was too much work. Her hope was that being back in the kitchen would make time pass more easily.

"I'll have a few options for you by morning, Ms. Anderson." Sam held out her prim, red-manicured hand.

Cheyenne shook her hand briskly and heaved a sigh of relief when the other woman took off toward her car. Rather than backtracking to the Cherokee to spend another aimless day in the Retirement House, Cheyenne looked around before stepping off of the curb and crossing the street. Hands stuffed in the front pockets of her jeans, Cheyenne meandered to the corner of Orchard and Main and looked around. She loved summer in Penn Ridge—even if this particular summer felt a little cooler than most. Instead of climbing back in the Jeep, Cheyenne slipped through the buildings around her and turned onto Main Street, determined to explore for a while.

In all her childhood summers spent in the Ridge, she hadn't spent much face time in the town itself. Even when driving through, she hardly did more than stop for gas in town or do the grocery shopping at the local market. Of course, she and Gramps would get ice cream occasionally from the parlor and bowling alley. There was Lorenzo's, where the best pizza in town could be found and where she'd spent weekend nights with Gramps and Roxanne as often as possible. They would even venture into every shop on Main Street at least once on her vacation trips, and he always sent her gifts from the jewelry boutique on the corner. But she couldn't remember the last time she'd just wandered down the adorable, cluttered streets and taken in the cute, tourist-loving hamlet that her heritage dwelled in.

Her adventure took her all the way to what she understood was the end of Main Street, where the route that cut through it became Route 15 again. She crossed the street in front of a darling yellow-painted mansion—with a summer harvest's worth of vegetable banners, wreaths, and red and orange fairy lights lifting its fading paint into the twenty first century—and restarted her trek.

It'd taken forty-five minutes to get from her starting point to Route 15 and a half hour for her to get back to the car. Over the small town, which was bustling with people who all smiled and either called hello or gave a friendly wave when she passed them, the summer evening was coming in full force. A soft, amber glow from the setting sun had settled over the brick buildings, and the breeze that picked up Cheyenne's carrot hair and whipped the loose strands around her face put a chill in her bones. In another twenty feet, a beautiful, red building made out of different toned bricks sported a sign that read 'Fresh Coffee' in an elegant script.

The idea of stopping for a cup of coffee before returning to the house, even if it meant just another fifteen minutes out, was too appealing for her to pass up. Cheyenne checked the time on her watch and then the Jeep's doors to make sure they were still locked before she stiffened her shoulders and marched toward the coffee shop. To get there, she had to pass the funeral home where her grandfather had been put on display before the church service. It was painted a pistachio green, and the large sign in the front lawn declared it was a 'family establishment,' to which Cheyenne snorted. It didn't look like a family establishment; in fact, in the light of day it was just dreary. Dreary enough that she would have to tell Roxanne that Rupert, the hero in her published novel, should start his third level of soul searching in a similar place.

The funeral parlor shared its parking lot with the coffee shop that Jesse had mentioned to her the day before, her final destination, and she couldn't help but cock her head to the side in amusement. That'd be another conversation she'd have to have with the author and her fiancé; an inquiry into why the little hamlet's only genuine coffee shop shared its customer parking with the only funeral parlor for miles. "Life in small-town America," she mumbled with a soft, cheeky grin. These were all things she'd have to get used to, or at least find out why they belonged.

The Harvest Bean, aptly named for its warm decorations and small corner of the baby hamlet where it thrived, was crowded when Cheyenne slipped in its doorway. The small shop had three plush, tan leather couches, four easy chairs that had seen better days, and a handful of scuffed coffee tables that were piled high with magazines and worn leather-bound books. There were two high-topped tables and a bookshelf with more books and a dozen or so board games from someone's childhood past. Cheyenne walked into the shop's warm, eclectic vibe and the drum of conversation between patrons and felt comforted for the first time since she'd left the house that morning.

Stepping up to the counter, Cheyenne sifted her hand over her hair and smiled at the man on the other side. He fit the vibe of the shop, with a grizzled beard and salt-and-pepper hair that sat piled on his head in a nicer-looking messy bun than Cheyenne could ever hope to accomplish.

"How can I help you?" He grinned at her in hello—the smile made the corners of his eyes wrinkle. His eyes were a warm, deep blue, and extremely friendly. Cheyenne decided she liked him instantly.

"Um, a latte, please. With…" Her eyes flickered over the menu quickly. "Oat milk." At least in the small recesses of Northeast Pennsylvania she wouldn't have to forgo her favorite treats in favor of less healthy alternatives.

"Sure thing." The man stepped back from the register and started to press buttons on the espresso machine near the register. "Just passing through?" he called over its tepid hum while Cheyenne took in the shop.

"Oh? Oh. No. I just moved to Penn Ridge." She blinked as she said it. It had been the first time since before she'd moved that she'd told anyone she'd moved to the small town. When the words came out, she was surprised— surprised enough that her toes curled a little inside her boots and her palms felt a little sweaty.

"Just moved here, huh?" The man grinned and held his hand out over the register. "Jeffrey. Jeffrey Morgan. This is my establishment."

"Cheyenne Anderson." Cheyenne shook his wrinkled hand with a friendly smile.

"You're Caleb Anderson's granddaughter, ain'tcha?" His eyes grinned at her even as his tired mouth moved into a sad smile. Cheyenne saw in it kinship, someone who had loved Caleb as well and was still missing his presence.

Her throat felt tight and she tugged at her hair. Jeffrey moved back from the counter to make her drink without another word, as if he caught what she was feeling. "It's a beautiful little coffee shop," she said as he steamed her milk. Some sort of small talk to make the air feel a little less anxious. "I'm looking to open a business in the area myself."

"Oh? What kind of business do you dabble in?" Jeffrey's blue eyes winked at her.

"A bakery." Cheyenne smiled at the older man. "I own one back in Albany, and I figured I'd open a second one here."

"Carol Heinley mentioned that you own a bakery. She's a little bit of a gossip, but she means no harm." It was said kindly, as if Cheyenne's face gave away her uneasy feeling on the woman. "Most of the Ladies Auxiliary are a bunch of gossips, don't take it personally. Your Gramps was really liked around here." The kindness, the affection for her grandfather, was warm in his eyes.

"I was fond of him, too," Cheyenne said dryly. The conversation had dived too far into topics she wasn't comfortable covering. Her eyes roamed over the menu board behind Jeffrey's head again. "You sell your own grinds?"

"We roast the coffee here ourselves." Jeffrey fished out a small bag of blond roast from underneath the counter and pushed it toward her with her cardboard cup. "Try this. On me. My partner, Pat, he's the one who comes up with the roasting combinations, and this is one of our most popular blends."

Cheyenne paused, her fingers wrapped around her wallet in her purse. "Um. Thank you." The small act of kindness, something she'd heard of when talking to Maverick and Roxanne about their life in the Ridge, was unheard of before in her sum total years of adulthood. Cheyenne took the small pouch of coffee grinds and stuffed them into the brown leather sack that hung over her shoulder. "Can I at least pay you for the latte?"

Jeffrey chuckled. "How about this? Pat and I, well we've been thinking about expanding the assortment of baked goods we sell." He gestured to the small jar of cookies, with a "1 Dollar" sign attached, a sheepish look churning in his eyes. "If you get the itch to do some baking before you open shop, you come back and we'll talk. Commission-based sales, of course, to make up for the latte."

Cheyenne's lips twitched, but she kept her face as straight as possible. "Sure. Here." The wallet came out then, and she handed him one of her business cards. They still sported the "A Taste of Celeste" logo with the Albany location in pretty, periwinkle font over a background of cupcakes. "The address is wrong, but my number is still the same. And my email address."

"'A Taste of Celeste.' I like it." Jeffrey took the card and slipped it into his pants pocket. "For your grandmother?"

At her look, he grinned. "I knew Celeste. We met her a couple of times before she passed away. She was a fascinating woman."

"Uh, yeah. Yeah." Cheyenne had only met a handful of people in her entire life who remembered her grandmother outside of their immediate family. It always threw her off. "It seemed like a good name."

Jeffrey reached over the counter to shake her hand. "It was nice to meet you, Cheyenne. I'll talk to Pat and we'll get back to you tonight. Be prepared for an order."

"I look forward to it." Cheyenne held the latte up in a salute to the coffee shop owner. "Thanks, Jeffrey." She smiled, genuine and wide, thinking about the food in the fridge back home. An order would be a good way to keep her hands, and her mind, busy for a while. "Hey," she said when Jeffrey started to turn away, "do you think I could leave a couple of cards here? Just to… I don't know… give me something to do?" Cheyenne fished a few more out of her bag and held them out to the older man.

Jeffrey took them with a knowing smile. "I'll talk to you soon, Cheyenne."

Cheyenne turned, feeling a little more at home in the small town than she had a few hours before, only to come in contact with someone's chest. She collided with him hard, her coffee cup dropping with a loud 'sploosh' on the hardwood floor. Cheyenne heard the sad exclamation that slipped out of her mouth, muffled by the fabric of the dust covered t-shirt she'd come face to face with. A ropey arm tucked around her waist to keep her from following the cup to the ground.

In her bad temper over the loss of her latte, Cheyenne

almost didn't catch the quiet chuckle from Jesse as he stepped back and let her go. "Are you okay?"

She watched him scoop up a handful of napkins from the table nearest him and crouch down to mop up her spilled latte. Her stomach bottomed out at the sight of him in the long sleeve shirt and faded soft gray jeans. His grin, the hazel in his eyes that lit up when they made eye contact, made her flush around the chin. "I'm... okay." Her eyes darted to the remains of her latte and she felt a whole new wave of grief wash over her.

"Sorry about that. I was waiting to talk to you and you whipped around really fast." Jesse stood and dumped the wet napkins in a trash can by the fixing bar. "Hey Jeff, two lattes." He shot a look at Cheyenne, her shoulders raised with a flash of panic in her eyes, and wrinkled his nose. "I guess one of them will probably need to not have dairy in it." The addition made Cheyenne's shoulders relax.

"Thank you," Cheyenne said with a slight smile. "You were waiting to talk to me?"

Jesse grinned sheepishly and stepped around her to pay for their lattes. He led her to a recently vacated couch by the front windows of the shop, holding her cardboard cup hostage, and waited for her to sit before he handed it to her. "I wanted to check in with you—see if you were able to find a store?"

Cheyenne let out a pained whine and took an aggressive sip of her hot latte. "She is a very nice woman," she said diplomatically while trying to cool her aching tongue.

Jesse laughed so hard he sloshed coffee out of the lip of

his cup and down the front of his hand. "Do you want me to let Carol know that you're looking?"

"I don't want to bother her. It's not her problem." Cheyenne tapped her foot against the floor, the toes of her shoe tapping audibly with her frustration.

"Carol knows a little bit about everything and everyone in town. She'll be able to find you something faster than any realtor, and it'll probably fit what you're looking for a lot better."

She sighed in defeat, and he smiled in triumph before she was able to speak. "If you wouldn't mind."

"It's no bother at all," Jesse said, with only a hint of smugness.

Cheyenne shifted around in her seat, her jeans scratching against the cushion. Jesse didn't seem bothered by the lack of words, or the unnerving silence of the coffee shop around them. She didn't like the quiet, had never really enjoyed quiet, and the way he looked at her with his big brown eyes and his contented smile had her feeling a little unnerved.

"So…" Cheyenne kicked her foot.

Jesse quirked an eyebrow and ran a hand over his forehead, knocking his hat back to show a tuft of dark hair that stood straight up underneath it. "So?"

"How are the kids?" Cheyenne blurted after searching the recesses of her brain for something else to talk about. Talking about his kids was good, safe, but way out of her comfort zone.

It seemed to be the right thing to ask about, though. Jesse let out a pained groan and pitched forward, putting his head in his hands with an apathetic almost-whimper. "Don't get me started," he said good-naturedly.

"I mean…" Cheyenne blinked. Usually, when you asked someone about their kids, they were all too happy to ramble about them, much to Cheyenne's disgruntlement. It was the thing you asked when you knew someone had kids, and she was eager to keep the conversation going with Jesse. "I'm sorry for asking?" She took an unsure sip of her coffee.

"I really just don't want to complain," Jesse mumbled into his hands.

"Yeah." Cheyenne could feel herself smiling behind her coffee cup. She shrugged. "I'm a champion complainer. Try me."

"It's just… my daughter," he said with a grunt. "She's eleven." The groan that formed when he said it was hilarious coming out of his mouth. "Who would have ever thought that the hardest part of my life would be when she turned eleven."

Cheyenne made a soft, noncommittal sound in the back of her throat. "My nephews just made the transition to pre-teen as well," she offered after an awkward second. "They're driving my sisters-in-law crazy."

Jesse snorted. "It's awful, actually. Like, Melia went from being this great, sweet-mannered kid to being this crazy, moody… thing. My kid's wearing black. A year ago, she wouldn't even wear black shoes. She's fighting with her grandparents. Fighting with me. Fighting with her brother." He ran his hands through his hair, the hat lost completely to the cushions on the couch. "My kid hates me."

Cheyenne was moved. She reached over and put her hand on his arm in the same gesture she'd seen Roxanne do to guys thousands of times before, even if she'd never seen the reason to do it to a man herself. "It's hard to raise teenagers," Cheyenne said quietly. "Teenage girls are actually the worst. When I was a teenager, I was a complete ass. Roxanne wasn't much better. It just comes with the territory."

"I can't call my eleven-year-old an ass"—Jesse shook his head, a small grin forming—"now can I?"

Cheyenne smiled back at him. "You can to me if you feel like you need to. I promise I won't tell."

The man chuckled. "It's just so hard to raise her."

"Tell me about it." Cheyenne beamed. "I am much closer to my teenage years than you are, and I had the benefit of being raised by three parents." She'd been raised by a whole village. A wonderful, smart, headstrong village that had been able to help her navigate her aspirations, her downfalls, and all the issues that came with being a teenage girl. It'd been a weird village, but it had been full of people who had really loved her and had helped shape the woman she had become.

Her smile soured, thinking about her grandfather, the chieftain of her village. She cleared her throat. "Amelia is really lucky to have you," Cheyenne told him, her voice feeling watery. She got to her feet and gave him a tight grin. "I've got to go unpack."

Jesse stood too and scooped his hat up off the couch. "Yeah. I've gotta get back to work." His face told her he saw the flood gates threatening to burst and was entirely unsure of how—or even if—he could help. "Hey, Cheyenne," he said as she turned away.

Cheyenne turned back, blinking back the onslaught of water in her eyes. "Yeah?"

Jesse's face was soft. He cleared his throat and forced a grin. "I'll come over tomorrow… to finish the attic door and touch up the hedges."

"Thanks, Jesse."

The tears didn't come, thankfully, until she'd locked herself in the Cherokee and was able to press her face into the steering wheel so that nobody could see the depth of her pain.

11

*C*heyenne woke up on her third Saturday in a state of contented comfort. It was the end of the third full week of June and she'd been in the house for nearly three entire weeks, which meant she'd had three full Saturdays to revel in the warmth of her sheets and the feeling of absolute bliss at the fact that she had nowhere to be, no one to see until that night when she'd see Roxanne and Maverick for dinner, and absolutely no plan for the entire day.

Her head still felt a tad fuzzy after the bottle of wine she'd taken to bed with her, and her eyelids were sore from the late-night movie she'd indulged in right before bed. During the movie, she'd received a string of texts from William that had prompted drunken, sloppy tears (further accentuated by the end of the movie) to lull her to sleep. It was due to the grief from losing her grandfather, mixed with her bitterness over the fact that William wanted to rekindle their relationship a little too late, that she'd had a hard time falling asleep. Though, waking up without having to rush out of bed and having the luxury to feel her sheets wind around her as she curled into a tighter ball, struggling to fall back to sleep, made up for some of the previous night's distress.

Cheyenne rolled onto her stomach and stretched. The effort was a lot, but she'd feel much better when she finally roused herself out of bed. Maybe she'd go down to the kitchen and make an omelet for breakfast, or finally dig out her running shoes and go for that jog she'd been promising herself since she'd unpacked her favorite pair of leggings. The day was open for her to do whatever she wanted, a bittersweet notion that had her rolling back onto her back and tucking the blanket around her more securely.

She cracked her eyes open to try and gauge what time it was. She was sure it could have been no later than four-thirty. There was only a little bit of gray light sneaking in through her gauzy bedroom curtains, informing her that she'd been right in her tired assumptions. With a self-satisfied smile, she rolled onto her side and curled her knees toward her chest to get comfortable.

She must have dozed off again, a side effect of her internal alarm clock being conditioned for four in the morning every morning. When her eyelids fought to open again, it was to a slim beam of sunlight tracing lines over the planes of her cheeks and trying to burn itself into her retinas. The invasion of light shining into her gaze did nothing to stifle her irritation over the loud sound of the lawn mower that had woken her in the first place.

Cheyenne pulled her pillow over her head and let out a groan. Jesse was going to be left with an earful of epic proportions. It was the third time he'd woken her up that week, in his ill-conceived attempt to not be in her way while she settled into the house but still get chores done from his ever-present to-do list. She rolled onto her stomach, tangled in the sheets, and glared at her windows. He'd been great about helping her get settled, and about keeping the upkeep on the house consistent (even if she didn't know what it needed), but being woken up when she didn't have the chance to sleep in often left her blood boiling.

Cheyenne rolled out of bed and slid on her floral robe and the flip-flops she'd left dumped by the door. It was time to give him a piece of her mind.

She tore down the last flight of stairs and yanked open the front door, fully prepared to bellow at Jesse, but nearly took out a wisp of a girl on her way outside. The girl was tall, at least as tall as Cheyenne, and had light brown hair and dark brown eyes framed with enough black to keep Cheyenne in liner for a year. She seemed just as surprised to see Cheyenne as Cheyenne was to see her and let out a little whimper, stumbling backwards and dropping the armload of art supplies she'd held.

"Crap!" she sputtered as a case of pastels broke open and the nearly used-up pieces of color scattered all over the porch.

Cheyenne blinked. "Oh!" She crouched to help the girl pick up the broken pieces, shaking her head. "I'm so sorry."

"They're old. It's okay." The girl shrugged, her dark eyes a little watery at the loss of some of her supplies.

Cheyenne looked up at the girl and pursed her lips.

"We'll see what we can do about getting you some more." She smiled. "You must be Amelia." Up close, the girl looked enough like Jesse that the family resemblance was spot-on.

"Hi." Amelia shoved a handful of hair behind her ear, her cheeks a little red around their already rounding tops. "Sorry about the rainbow." She nodded at the pastel residue on Cheyenne's hands.

Cheyenne smiled and wiped her hands on the thighs of her sweatpants. "No biggie. I'm always covered in something, but I think it's time to toss these into the scrap heap."

"Dad's really big on using things until they're gone." The tween shrugged.

Cheyenne nodded. The mower's whining still filled the clearing around the house, weaving its way in between their silence. "Can I get you something?"

Amelia looked between her and the door she'd been clearly trying to enter. "I was just going to use the bathroom. If, uh, if that's okay?"

"Oh sure, sure." Cheyenne smiled and stepped to the side to the let the girl clear the threshold. "Do you want, like, a coffee or anything?" Cheyenne asked, feeling as uncomfortable as the girl did. Coffee was a good way to ease the ice between any two people, as Cheyenne recognized after years of watching first dates—and last ones—business meetings, and even a proposal or two all happen over a cup of her coffee and a pastry. Her best option was to just backtrack, leave the kid alone, and get on with her morning. The sense of propriety instilled in her by her mother's strict code of company conduct had her continuing to press to be a good hostess, though. "I have muffins?"

Amelia stopped on her way to the hall bathroom and looked over her shoulder. "What kind of muffins?"

Cheyenne felt her own cheeks turn a little pink. She was worried about the girl seeing the store of baked goods hiding under her counter for some reason, as if she wanted to seem like she had her life remotely together for the girl. "Umm… I'll check and let you know. Meet me in the kitchen when you're done."

After the plan was made, and satisfied with the little bit of less tension between Amelia's shoulders, Cheyenne passed through the archway into the dining room and hung her robe over the back of a chair on her way to the kitchen. Sunlight streamed in through the windows in the dining room and over her kitchen sink, making the use of the overhead lights unnecessary. She loved the way the warm light filled the kitchen, causing her lilac hand towels and the little ornaments she'd made sure to set up on the counters sparkle. It felt warm and homey, and it reminded her of standing on her tiptoes, watching her grandfather go through the similar motions of making coffee first thing in the morning.

Once the coffee was brewing, she crouched to open the doors to the island, which was chock-full of baked goods from her last three days: scones and cookies and muffins, a container of brownies, two plastic bags of small pretzels, and the last tub of her sugar candy. Cheyenne picked out a container of honey vanilla muffins and snagged the tub of candy, just in case the girl might want some, and left both containers open on the island for her guest. She wasn't sure if either would be to the girl's liking, but it was worth a try to get rid of some of the stress goods that she'd been working on.

Amelia made her way into the kitchen shyly and sat herself on a stool across from Cheyenne. "It smells good in here."

Cheyenne smiled and poured a half-cup of coffee for the tween. "It smells a little like my bakery, which I really like."

Amelia helped herself to some cream and sugar and sniffed at her mug. "Thank you." She ducked her head to take a tiny sip.

Cheyenne tapped her fingers against the side of her own mug, searching for something to say. "Do you go by Amelia, Amy, or Mel?"

"Everyone calls me Melia, which is cool." She shrugged. "There's, like, two other Amelia's in my grade, so it's kinda confusing."

"At least you can spell your name," Cheyenne told the girl. "When I was your age, I still had kids pick on me because my name was 'weird.' Forget being able to write out a sixteen-letter name when you're six." Cheyenne rolled her eyes over the mug's rim as she took a sip.

Amelia snorted. "Yeah, I guess." The girl seemed to be settling in and becoming comfortable in Cheyenne's presence. Comfortable enough, anyway, to take one of the muffins out of the container and take a tentative bite out of its top. Crumbs scattered all over Cheyenne's clean counter, causing her to sink a little bit on the inside, but she let it go for the time being. There would be plenty of time to reclean the kitchen, and then make it messy again, once Amelia and her father had left. "My brother can't spell his name and it's only five letters," the eleven-year-old teased, seemingly thinking this was simultaneously the dumbest and funniest thing to have ever happened to anyone.

"I'm sure he can." Cheyenne shook her head. She knew what it was like being the younger sibling and found herself vocalizing in order to keep the boy's integrity in check. "What were you drawing?"

"The garden." Amelia flipped her sketch pad over to show Cheyenne what she'd been working on. "I like to sit on the porch and doodle the flowers."

Cheyenne looked at the shadowing on the butterfly bush Amelia had been working on, amazed at how much vibrancy breathed through every stroke of pastel on the page. Of course, the lines were a little messy, and there was some room for tightening, but the girl had talent that Cheyenne envied. She wished she could draw like that—if for nothing else than to give her an even stronger hand in the cake-decorating side of her business. "My Gramps loved that bush," Cheyenne said wistfully, stroking her finger along the edge of a delicate flower. "This is really good work."

"It's okay." Amelia shrugged, her face a deep shade of pink. "The lines could be cleaner." She scoffed and took a sip of coffee. Her eyes held a little bit of sadness. "Your grandpa really liked to sit with me when I drew."

Cheyenne couldn't help the twitch in her lips. "He told me about your drawing," Cheyenne offered, the wheels clicking in place. Amelia was the little visitor her grandfather had told her about—the artist who drew life into his favorite place on Earth.

Amelia nodded. "Do you miss him?" she asked, surprising them both. She ducked her head, taking another—longer—drink of coffee.

Cheyenne blinked in surprise at the girl. She closed the cover of the sketchpad and set it delicately on the counter while trying to figure out what to say. No one had asked her in such simple terms in the month since he'd passed if she missed him. It knocked the wind out of her chest. "I do," she heard herself saying. "I can't imagine it's even real."

"What's real?"

Amelia and Cheyenne both jumped at the sound of Jesse's voice in the otherwise quiet kitchen. He walked in, barefooted, with his baseball cap in one hand and his work gloves in the other. He was covered in grass clippings, had a dirt stain on his left cheek, and he looked so good that under different circumstances Cheyenne would have fainted.

"The muffins," Cheyenne said quickly. For some reason, talking to the child about missing her grandfather and talking to the gorgeous man standing in her kitchen about missing her grandfather were two totally different worlds. She wasn't quite ready to be the resident of one of them.

12

*J*esse hadn't expected to see his daughter cuddled up with Cheyenne when he walked into the kitchen. He'd expected to find her sitting on the porch where he'd left her or at least sitting in front of the TV, although he wasn't sure how Cheyenne would react to the latter option. Instead, he found Amelia in the kitchen talking to her, drinking what looked like a cup of coffee and having an actual conversation.

He stood in the doorway of the dining room and watched the conversation for a few minutes, not meaning to eavesdrop but unable to move from the sight of his daughter talking to a complete stranger. That feeling only lifted when he saw Amelia looking at Cheyenne and actually paying attention to what she'd said. He could forgive the coffee for the openness he saw on her face.

"They look delicious," he told Cheyenne as he entered the kitchen and tugged the stool out beside Amelia. Cheyenne's muffins were sinful; they were so good that he'd found himself thinking about them, and the woman who'd baked them, nearly every night before he fell asleep.

"Coffee?" Cheyenne gave him a friendly smile and offered him a lilac-colored mug. "I'll heat you up a muffin."

"With a little butter on it?"

Cheyenne looked pained at him, but she lifted the lid off the butter by the stove and heaped two generous slices onto the insides of the muffin she'd split for him. "You and your butter."

"He eats it on everything," Amelia piped up around a mouthful of crumbs. "Butter or steak sauce."

"Do you not like the taste of your food?" Cheyenne wrinkled her nose at him, her eyes lifting in a smile.

When she made faces like that at him, he felt his stomach bottom out. "I do," he said slowly, stirring cream and sugar into his coffee cup. "I just like it better with flavor enhancements."

Cheyenne scoffed and took the muffin out of the microwave. "If it's good cooking, you don't need flavor enhancements."

Jesse laughed. "Tell that to my mother-in-law and you probably wouldn't live to see the next day."

"My moms are the same way." Cheyenne took a sip of her coffee, leaning against the island to smile at Amelia.

Jesse saw his daughter shrug back from the smile, her eyes downcast. The sadness she felt made his chest hurt. He put his hand on her back, rubbing it soothingly, at a loss for any words he could have come up with that would have eased the look on her face.

Cheyenne had caught on too, her smile shifting to

something almost nurturing. "Hey, you wanna see something cool?" she asked Amelia, her face lighting up in a childish grin. She didn't wait for an answer, just set her mug down on the island and all but tore out of the kitchen, her red hair streaming behind her.

Amelia frowned but eased off her stool and followed Cheyenne out. Jesse gulped down his coffee before he followed the two girls upstairs.

He found them standing in the doorway to the attic, looking in at the mass of furniture and other whatnots that Caleb had collected over the years. Amelia was bouncing on her toes, craning her neck to take in all the clutter. Cheyenne, who stood just behind the tween, had her hands on her hips and her head cocked to the side. She was watching his daughter, who seemed like she was bursting out of her skin.

Jesse looked over her head, trying to see what she was so excited about in the piles of old furniture, the chests filled with odds and ends, and the dressing rack of clothes.

"Go explore." Cheyenne handed Amelia her sketch pad. "If you go in the back to the left, there's a really cool end table with some carvings in it that I think you might find interesting."

Amelia stepped into the attic, her hand grasping for the sketch book without moving her head from the wonder of things around her.

Cheyenne gestured for Jesse to follow her back down to the kitchen to give the girl some peace, her eyes set in a determined, proud way as she strode past him. Jesse gave one more look over his shoulder to where his daughter had hunkered down in a corner lit by one of the two windows on the other side of the long room. Her dark hair was framing her face and her hand was already flying over the paper.

Jesse found Cheyenne on the porch, holding two fresh cups of coffee.

"I thought you didn't like kids?" Jesse asked her, taking the mug she held out when she heard him.

"It's not that I don't like them." Cheyenne shrugged the comment off. "They just don't like me."

Jesse shook his head, looking down at her from the corner of his eye. He couldn't believe that kids didn't like her. His daughter had opened up to her more in twenty minutes than she had to anyone he'd seen in weeks. Months. Even a year. Cheyenne had a knack with kids, even if she didn't see it.

He kept his opinion to himself on that one. Cheyenne didn't seem like the type of person who would budge on a steadfast opinion of anything, especially of herself.

"She's pretty."

Jesse looked over at his daughter, jarring himself from his own thoughts. "Yeah?"

Amelia had been stewing—or at least, her father thought she'd been stewing—since they'd said goodbye to Cheyenne and kept on with their busy day. It was her day to wander with him, going with him from site to site to check on his workers, having a late lunch with him in town, and then helping him pick out a few flowers for their front garden. He made an effort to spend an entire day, once a week, with each kid to give them some much needed one-on-one time. Not that he didn't spend time with his kids regularly, but a day spent alone with their father seemed to always do both of them some good.

His daughter had been silent since they got in the truck, opting to stay in its cab while he surveyed the house his crew was helping build and the two new clients he was meeting with to give estimates. He was concerned that the hour the two had spent talking to Cheyenne had made her uncomfortable, or even self-conscious. Amelia was sensitive, especially in his eyes, and he was never quite sure what would trigger the silent moments where she'd ignore him and the rest of their little family in favor of her bedroom, her shelves of books, and the art supplies she loved.

Jesse had left her be, going on with his list of tasks for the day in as good a mood as he could possibly garner. If she wanted to sit in the truck on her phone, with her bare feet propped on the dash and whatever weird music she liked at the time filling the cab, he at least knew she was out of the house.

Amelia cleared her throat, waiting for a response from her father. "She is," she insisted. "Don't you think?"

This wasn't the conversation he'd expected to have with the tween when she came out of her funk. Jesse felt blindsided, utterly confused. "Who is *she?*" Jesse asked.

"Cheyenne," Amelia chirped. "Like, the kind of pretty that doesn't need makeup."

He was at a loss for words. "Uh."

Amelia rolled her eyes at him. "And she makes good muffins." She shook the plastic container of leftover baked goods in her lap. Their little parcel included chocolate chip cookies for Miles and another vanilla-bean-and-honey muffin for Amelia.

Jesse smiled, turning the corner onto their street. The fresh attitude rolling off of Amelia—half joy at making a new friend and half admiration for the woman's abilities in the kitchens—lifted what felt like a thousand pounds off his shoulders. He couldn't remember the last time he'd seen his daughter open up so much to a stranger, especially long enough for the two of them to have a steady conversation. Especially a conversation as steady Cheyenne and Amelia had had, revolving around some sort of chairs for her new bakery and flowers Amelia had wanted to pick up for their front garden.

"She does make good muffins," Jesse agreed carefully. He could admit to himself that Amelia's good humor over Cheyenne wasn't the only thing lifting his spirits. He'd enjoyed his conversation with Cheyenne as well. He'd been enjoying her company every time he stopped by the house over the past few weeks. And Amelia was right; she was very pretty.

Jesse pulled into their driveway. Amelia unlatched her seatbelt and exited the truck before he'd even put it in park, off to hide her goodies before Miles got home and she had to relinquish her hoard. Jesse took his time following her so that he could think about the things running through his head without the distraction, or the guilt, of having the internal conversation around his daughter.

He crouched in front of their front garden, springing to life with Amelia's summer flowers and the tomato plants Miles had begged to plant, and started to tug out little green tufts of weeds. The monotonous motion was soothing, as it allowed his hands the ability to move without having to engage his mind too much. The much-needed distraction allowed his thoughts to wander freely.

With the freedom to roam, they wandered to his daughter, to the redheaded woman who had enchanted her, to the six-year-old boy who looked like him, and to the idea of being more than just a single father. A thought he'd barely entertained since his wife had passed.

Amelia was old enough for Jesse to start dating again —she had been for a while—but Miles being so young had kept him from entertaining the idea for any length of time. Whenever he'd spend even a moment thinking about it, he'd think about how Amelia had had the opportunity to form a relationship with their mother and how his son had not gotten the same chance. He wondered whether making any moves to correct that, to give Miles a maternal figure in his life, would be an insult to Miles and to Mara. Miles had been too young to form any memory, let alone a memory of the woman who'd given him life, held him for nine months, and given up everything for him.

Jess sat back on his haunches and dropped his handful of green matter into the neat compost bin Amelia had decorated the summer before. He wiped his forehead with the back of his wrist, scraping off dust, dirt clippings, and a fine sheen of sweat.

He'd always wondered if Mara would have wanted him to move on—if he wasn't respecting her memory by not moving on with his life. They'd never actually sat down and talked about the life she'd wanted for him and for their family should something happen to her (or him). At the time, they'd been young and foolish, thinking they had forever to grow their little family and expound on the future they'd both had seen so clearly. All their lives were ahead of them, with one beautiful child and one on the way, and they were young and had so many plans. And then, out of nowhere, it'd been too late to talk about any such possibilities.

Mara was too far gone, far too angry, to have any such conversations. Getting her funeral arrangements out of her had been like pulling teeth, and Jesse had been so hopeful that they'd still have time that it'd never dawned on him to push any further.

Maybe Mara would have wanted him to move on. Maybe, someday, he would find himself being inclined to do just that. He just wasn't sure, for reasons he couldn't quite put his finger on, that it would be with the red-haired woman living in the big house on the hill.

13

_____

*C*arol Heinley stood on the porch of what was, and what would forever be, Caleb Anderson's house, a basket of food hitched in the crook of her arm and her best friend, Laura Wilkers, by her side. Sabel Harris was on her way to the large farmhouse; the separate cars had been on account of all of the baskets the Ladies Auxiliary had put together. They had paid similar calls to Caleb in the past, especially after he had gotten too stiff to go into town and spend time in the VFW with Laura's husband and the other Penn Ridge residents who had served time in support of their country.

On the outside, the trip seemed like just a food run to welcome the newest member of town, even if it was a few weeks belated. Carol had her own mission: a favor to her son-in-law, who had seemed a little pink around the edges when he had asked her. Carol had agreed, out of old friendship for Caleb, adoration for her son-in-law, and her own dash of curiosity about the woman.

She readjusted her basket of food—some casseroles, as

she wasn't sure what Cheyenne liked to eat—and waited for Laura to announce their presence.

Laura rang the doorbell and fixed the hem of her best blouse (second best, in Carol's opinion), which she'd donned specifically for the purpose of visiting. Laura was more old-fashioned than Carol and insisted on dressing up. Laura loved to dress up to do just about anything, which Carol had always adored and relentlessly teased at the same time.

"You know, we're not showing up to take this young woman on a date," Carol said to her friend playfully as they waited for the young Anderson to open the door. Although she was sure her son-in-law—her son, for all intents and purposes—would like to do just that. "I hope she eats cheese. Amelia has decided she doesn't eat cheese." She sighed wistfully and hefted the basket of casseroles she was holding to rest firmly on her hip.

Cheyenne opened the door before Laura could respond, her jeans splattered with what looked like glaze and green icing, a smudge of flour on her cheek, and her hair piled on top of her head in a messy knot. She was wearing a t-shirt that read "Kiss the Baker" in red script over a hunk of bread. She had a suspicious half smile on her face. The two women had met briefly, bumping into each other in town after the funeral when Carol had been with Miles. They'd exchanged a few pleasantries and gone on their way no better, or worse, off for the interaction.

Seeing her at home, in Caleb's house, only reinforced to Carol that she was his granddaughter. Carol smarted a little, missing the older man.

Seemingly unbothered by the interruption and inspection, the young woman said, "Hi, Mrs. Heinley," while Carol appraised her.

Carol hefted up the basket of goodies, her own lips forming a placid smile. "Hello, Cheyenne. I hope you don't mind us dropping in on you like this."

"Uh. Not at all." Cheyenne stepped back, gesturing for them to enter the house. "It's a bit messy. I was trying out a new recipe."

"Cookies?" Laura barged right into the house.

"Donuts," Cheyenne offered, closing the door behind Carol.

Carol looked around the house, feeling herself relax at the familiar sight. Cheyenne hadn't put a lot of her own touch to the front entry; it still looked like a bachelor lived in it. The splash of lavender and cream in the dining room, though, proved that she was settling in. "We brought you some things to help make settling in easier. And I wanted to ask you a few questions."

"About?" Cheyenne had an expressive face. Carol could read all over it that the thought of questions was an intrusion.

"Jesse mentioned last week that you need to find an empty building for your bakery?" Carol set her basket on the dining room table, where their little progression had come to a halt.

"Oh. Yes. I'm looking to open a second bakery here in Penn Ridge, and I've been trying to get a property, but I can't seem to find one."

"Let me see what I can do." Carol smiled brightly. "I'll ask around at my Auxiliary meeting tonight."

Cheyenne nodded with a warm smile. "Thank you. I

really appreciate it. I'm going crazy just sitting in the house all day." She laughed and carried the basket into the kitchen, the two women following her. "Would you ladies like some coffee?"

"I would love a cup." Laura beamed at Cheyenne. While Carol and the young woman had been talking, her friend had wandered around the kitchen before she planted herself in front of the corkboard Cheyenne had set up by the door.

"Cream and sugar?" Cheyenne asked while she pulled down three ceramic mugs, each painted with a different type of flower over a foundation of deep purple.

Carol sent Laura a look, imploring the other woman to be quiet when she made a soft cooing sound at the look of the mugs, before she pulled out one of the island stools and settled herself on it. "Both, please."

Cheyenne filled a little blue pitcher with heavy cream and set the sugar bowl down in front of her guests. "Thank you for bringing me the food," she said as she set their mugs down in front of them. "I'm good with sugary things but not so much with the savory stuff. I've been living off of frozen pizzas and cans of soup since I moved." Cheyenne pushed her hair back from her shoulders with a shrug.

Laura beamed at the girl. Carol knew that look—it was her 'busybody' look. There was no way that Carol was going to get away from this visit without hearing about all of the different ways in which Cheyenne was going to make a good wife for someone's son. Sabel's Charlie maybe, or Margie's grandson, Nathan. Carol shook her head as she thought about all the possibilities, and then chided herself when she thought of one. Of the way Jesse's face had lit up that morning when he'd been talking to her about the woman. She was too young, Carol decided as Cheyenne led them into the kitchen and offered them coffee, way too young to be suitable for Jesse. Or, at least, to be suitable for Jesse with the kids in the picture.

"Care?" Laura was nudging her with her elbow while she stared at the girl, and she silently chastised herself for the way she was thinking. So Jesse had been spending a little extra time at the house since the girl had moved—that didn't mean he'd become interested in her.

"Huh?" Carol blinked and smiled, abashed, at the two women who were staring at her. "I was just thinking about whether or not I turned the oven off," she said smoothly and ran her hands over her tightly bound hair. "Could you repeat that, please?"

"Oh, sure." Cheyenne gave a little laugh. "I was just telling Laura that I only use heavy cream—or those flavored creams, the caramel one in particular—myself. I guess that's why I look like this," she said with a self-deprecating chuckle as she gestured at her round hips.

Laura made a snorting sound as she stirred sugar and cream into her coffee. "You're, like, twenty. You should not be complaining about your figure, girly. I wish I was that small again."

"Nora!" Carol swatted her friend's arm in a playful gesture and smiled at the girl. She looked so much like Celeste that Carol's heart swelled. "Ignore her. She has no filter."

"I do too," Laura said stoutly. "I can filter out bullshit, and I only take in good food and good wine." Her friend laughed so hard that the buttons of her blouse bobbed a little.

Cheyenne had the decency to bite back a laugh, even though her hazel eyes were wide. "I imagine I'm the same way."

They all had a chuckle before sipping their coffee, Laura and Carol making themselves comfortable on the barstools by the island while Cheyenne stood opposite them. Carol looked around the kitchen while they drank their coffee and pursed her lips at the flower-print hand towels and crockery that were starting to fill its otherwise empty counters. Caleb would have hated all of the frilly things that Cheyenne seemed to be pumping into the house—even if he would have loved the fact that his granddaughter was living in it.

"How are you settling in?" Carol asked and set her half-empty mug down. "Jesse said that you were having a bit of a rough time adjusting to the move last week."

"Not really," Cheyenne said shyly and shrugged. "There were bigger things... to adjust to, I mean."

Carol nodded and offered what she hoped was a warm, but not sympathetic, smile. Cheyenne didn't seem to be the kind of woman who wanted a lot of sympathy, or who put much stock in it. "He'd be happy you're here," Carol reassured her.

A shadow crossed Cheyenne's face that made Carol wish she'd never opened her mouth. But it disappeared quickly, replaced by forced curiosity as the young woman peeked into the basket of casseroles. "This'll keep me from having to cook for at least a month," she said after a few minutes of silence. "I really appreciate it."

Carol laughed while Nora tutted her tongue against her teeth. "Our pleasure. Do you do a lot of cooking? Your grandfather would always brag about your baking."

"I can do savory pastries. At my bakery, I sell savory croissants and quiches. But ask me to make a chicken or some stew and it doesn't turn out so well." Cheyenne laughed at herself and took a sip of coffee. Her face darkened for a moment as she thought, possibly about her other bakery and the life she had before moving to Penn Ridge, before she smiled hesitantly at Carol.

"Speaking of your bakery," Carol swirled her coffee around in its mug thoughtfully. "Did you have an idea of what kind of space you might be looking for?" She'd been going through the list of properties she knew were available in her head, but Jesse hadn't given her enough information to point the young woman in the right direction. And she owed it to Caleb, as his friend, to be as helpful as she could for Cheyenne in any area where her presence would be a help.

"I have some ideas." Cheyenne rapped her knuckles against the table. "I'm mainly looking for something that has a kitchen already in place. It's expensive trying to put one in without there being a solid foundation for it. Something with natural sunlight and, hopefully, a little space in front for some tables and chairs, and maybe some bookshelves." Cheyenne refilled her coffee mug, wrinkling her nose back at the memory of her first kitchen. "When I put the kitchen in my Albany shop, it cost more money than any of us had expected. It was a nightmare."

"Anything else?" Carol drummed her fingers on the side of her coffee mug.

Cheyenne shook her head and took a sip of coffee. "Not really. I'm willing to put the work in for anything else that I might need."

"I'll ask around and see what I can do," Carol said with a smile. "Now, tell me more about your bakery in Albany?"

14

"*W*ell… what do you think?"

Carol Heinley had come through big time. After the unexpected visit, and a rather nice conversation, the older woman had made a few phone calls and had found three properties for Cheyenne to look at by the end of the next day. On Cheyenne's third Wednesday in Penn Ridge, Carol had met Cheyenne at the store she felt was the best fit based on Cheyenne's description of her first shop, a small corner store that used to be a delicatessen. They met with another realtor, one who knew the proper lipstick-to-blush ratio, and took a tour of the front. Without realizing what was happening, and with a little bit of shock at just how short the process had been this time, Cheyenne was signing a lease—with the ability to renovate as she saw fit written in—and was hugging Carol once the realtor had driven off. The hug surprised them both and ended just as quickly as it started, but Cheyenne couldn't stop grinning.

That Friday, for the first time since she had started to

rent the property, Cheyenne stood in the empty space that would, in a short time, become A Taste of Celeste Too, watching Roxanne take in the dilapidated store front. She could already see the concept for the bakery come to life as she stood in the refractory sunlight coming in from one of the concave windows at the front of the shop. Outside the shop, the quiet bustle of Fifth Street seemed like a welcome parade. She was in love.

"It needs some work." The skepticism in Roxanne's voice only made Cheyenne grin.

She couldn't let Roxanne's skepticism get to her, which she'd learned when she was much younger. Roxanne, for all of her fanciful ideas when it came to a piece of paper, had a hard time conceptualizing things based on the space she was seeing. If only the woman could see the potential that Cheyenne did in the fifteen-hundred-square-foot gem, she was sure her best friend would be jumping for joy at the find.

The small kitchen had the space Cheyenne needed for two industrial ovens, a sound and spacious dishwasher, storage, and all the cooling racks that Cheyenne could need to start the baking business. She'd started out smaller when she first opened in Albany, and the front of this shop had more room than she had been expecting when she'd started her hunt. There was room for a drink cooler, a couple of tables and chairs, and even a bookshelf or two. Plus, the counter from the old delicatessen had a glass front for displaying food.

"Not as much work as I was expecting or had budgeted for," Cheyenne boasted as she propped herself against the solid, lightly dust-covered counter.

She could picture it. A good coat of paint would brighten the entire space; a nice shade of buttercup with white trim and white, gauzy curtains to frame the concave windows surrounding the gray front door. After the walls were painted and the dark hardwood floor, which she loved, was in prime condition, she would fill the shop with small metal tables—like the ones she'd sat at on the streets of Italy the summer before—and seats with daisy-covered cushions. A bookshelf would fill the space between the drink cooler and the wall on the other side of it from the counter. Maybe she'd buy a couple of board games—they had some worn games for A Taste of Celeste that had been proven to boost sales. There might even be enough room for Cheyenne to repurpose the two plush, deep green chairs that were left in her Gramps's basement den in the Retirement House. She couldn't remember the last time someone had sat in them and was hopeful they would get some use.

"Who are you going to hire to help you renovate?" Roxanne hoisted herself up onto the counter beside Cheyenne, her slender hip pressed to her friend's arm. "I mean, you're definitely going to need some help. Rick and I can help with the painting. I could probably ask Nick and his wife to help, too. They helped us to paint the living room last spring and it looks pretty good, doesn't it?"

"I mean, if you're into butterscotch." Cheyenne winked at her best friend and rested her head against the dark-haired woman's arm. In the full light from the large windows, cascading in in the middle of the summer afternoon, Roxanne's hair and skin glowed the same deep ambrosia shade that made Cheyenne's carrot colored hair and relatively pasty skin back down in shame. It was hard for her not to notice, especially with Roxanne's hand twirling a strand of her hair around the slender fingers that held it. She heaved a sigh and dropped her shoulders. "I was going to ask Jesse if he has the time. Carol said that he has a whole crew of men, so I figured he could spare me one or two for a few days. I mean, it's not like there's a lot of work."

Cheyenne could feel her face turning red at the mention of the man, which she was sure was much to Roxanne's satisfaction. Cheyenne tried to stifle the rush of emotion. They had spoken of Jesse on and off since Cheyenne had moved in, at first little quips about how much time he spent at the house fixing things, then long-winded conversations about how good the man looked in a pair of work jeans and boots. They'd had their fun, the most fun talking about boys since they'd been girls, but watching the smug look on Roxanne's face made Cheyenne realize just how much Jesse had been occupying her mind.

"Jesse?" Roxanne propped her foot playfully against the counter.

"Yeah. He's been around the house every couple of days to work on things and stuff. He's actually the one who asked Carol about space. He thought she'd have some suggestions and… well… she did." Cheyenne shrugged. "I'm hoping he'll take pity on me and give me a hand."

"You've been spending a lot of time with him lately, huh?" The sweet lilt in Roxanne's voice made Cheyenne's shoulders hunch.

"He works for Gra—me. He works for me. He's around the house a lot." Cheyenne shrugged, unfazed by the suggestive wink her friend shot her way. "It's nice to have the company. That damn house is so big and so quiet when it's just me."

Roxanne rolled her eyes. "It doesn't hurt that he's nice to look at either, now does it?" She elbowed Cheyenne in the ribcage, her bright eyes beaming. "I mean, he's a little too rough and dirty for my tastes, but he's got a beautiful face."

Cheyenne scrunched her eyebrows. "He does, doesn't he? A very 'Fabian' face." There was a hint of warmth creeping up from the collar of her shirt. She wouldn't admit it to Roxanne, but there'd been a few times, especially since meeting Amelia, that she'd seen Jesse around the house tinkering with something and had to force herself not to stop and stare. "He's just a really sweet guy."

"Your Gramps really liked him," Roxanne said after a moment. She'd caught on to the little smile on Cheyenne's face, the sweet upturn of her thin lips and the little glow in her hazel eyes. Cheyenne had the same face every time she met a guy she liked. The wistful, too-pale-to-hide flush of her skin and the charming sparkle to her gaze were hard to cover when she so plainly wore everything she felt on her sleeve. And there'd been a lot of guys. A lot of sparkles. "He seems really nice. We hired his company to help build the new porch and his guys had it done in a week."

"He didn't work on it?" Cheyenne frowned. She'd yet to meet any of his employees, even the two who were better at landscaping than Jesse or his partner. He was the one who was constantly showing up at the house, puttering with things, fixing things, helping her hang shelves and hooks for her kitchen stuffs. He'd even taken the time the day before to help her rearrange the furniture in her bedroom so that her bed was nowhere near the windows—just in case he got the urge to mow the yard that weekend.

"From what Mr. Carmody told me when we hired him, he and Tim don't actually work on a lot of the smaller projects. That new build they're doing down the road from us? That's more of what Jesse does. He likes to build things. I think he wanted to be an architect."

"Hm." Cheyenne didn't know what to make out of the information. If Jesse normally didn't spend this much time with other clients, then why could she not seem to get rid of him? And, better yet, why did she not want to?

"It *is* an inch shorter."

Roxanne looked up from her tablet screen at the whine in her fiancé's voice, trying not to let her lips twitch up into a soft smirk. "Yeah?"

Maverick was standing on the tails of two separate tape measures, his mouth pinched in a scowl as he angled himself to read the numbers on her left. "An inch and a half shorter," he grunted to her. "I told you. I'm not crazy."

Roxanne pushed her glasses up into her hair and hit

the lock button on the tablet to save her place in the novel she was swiping through. There were a couple hundred different quips scrolling through her head, including reminding him that he was standing practically naked in their living room and looked ridiculous. She bit her lip and resisted the urge to mock him for what she thought was clearly amusing, for fear she'd be mean about it. "It's hardly noticeable." Solemn words dripped out of her satin lips, a sweet smile budding behind the words.

"An inch and a half!" Maverick protested as he dropped down beside her on the couch and scooped her feet up from the coffee table. Roxanne readjusted while he propped them in his lap. "I'm never going to walk normally again."

Roxanne tabbed his abdomen with her toes, sporting purple and white striped socks, and gave him a loving look. "Yes, but you didn't really lose any height. You were kind of short to begin with." The couple both topped out at 5'7—Maverick could reach 5'9 when he stretched for it —and had always had the pleasure of knocking each other around about it from the time they both stopped growing in high school.

Maverick's forehead creased in a deep frown that made his dark eyes spark with dangerous mischief. "Listen, Amazon lady," he said with a grunt and tickled the instep of her foot affectionately.

"Talk to Mitch about it when you see him next week. Maybe he can help you walk a little easier?"

"It's been almost a year, Rox," Maverick grumbled, his lips forming an actual pout. "If it hasn't made any difference before, it's not going to make any difference now."

"You could get a cane." Roxanne wagged her foot at him. "Like Mitch suggested back in June."

Maverick groaned and dropped her feet onto the floor. "I am not going to watch you walk down the aisle while I have to use a cane to prop myself up," he said dramatically and tugged her to stand.

"What are you doing?" she asked with a shocked laugh, squeezing his hands as they gripped hers.

"Taking your mind off of canes and physical therapists and my missing inches." He smirked and kissed her, his hands folding around her waist. "C'mon."

15

*J*esse bumped up the drive toward the Retirement House while he listened to Amelia catch him up on what was happening with her gaggle of friends, his eyes staring expectantly toward the shadow that the house was sure to cast on the head of the driveway. While he couldn't wrap his brain around pre-teen drama, he'd found that he enjoyed his daughter's babbling years before. Amelia's voice was soft, high in pitch, and reminded him of her laughter when she'd been nothing more than a toddler amused by everything the world had to offer. The burst of chattiness was new and unexpected, but he savored the moment. As Amelia got older, these bursts of energy—of excitement— were getting fewer and farther between.

Amelia stopped, her tale coming to an end, as they made the turn into the clearing. "Do you think Cheyenne made cookies today?"

Ever since their last visit, Jesse had been hearing an awful lot about Cheyenne. Amelia had spent the first two days going on and on about the furniture in the attic, and the old chest that Cheyenne had insisted they take home with them. She'd even shown him a handful of sketches of old furniture, clothes nearing the point of vintage, and even a view of the tree line out of the attic window, all with the hopes that he'd bring her work to show the redhead on his next visit. Then she'd started to—as subtly as he was sure an eleven-year-old could manage—bring up going back to the Retirement House. Part of him thought it was for the garden, which she'd loved spending time in since he'd met Caleb, or for the cool stuff she had access to now that Cheyenne had told her she was welcome to explore in the attic whenever. But the more he listened to her talk over the last few days, the more he began to wonder if it was about the woman he couldn't stop thinking about either.

"I know she's been bringing some down to the Bean. I'm sure she has extras," Jesse said mildly, trying to hide his amusement. "But if she does, we'll have to ask her for a few for Miles."

He could practically hear his daughter rolling her eyes. "Fine." She sniffed and unlatched her seatbelt.

They found Cheyenne in the garden. She was staring at something in a patch of daisies, her hands planted on the hips of her denim cutoffs and her hair in its signature pile at the top of her head. Without turning to them, she called over her shoulder, "I think I'm gonna get a dog."

Jesse snorted quietly and tried to cover it up with a cough. "I'm not sure a dog is the best cure for a mental breakdown," he offered.

Cheyenne glared at him and puffed her right cheek

out with her tongue. Jesse was wondering if she was biting to argue back and would have welcomed the quip for the chance to see her get fired up.

Amelia interrupted the thoughts forming in Cheyenne's head with a little squeal. "Like a puppy?"

Cheyenne turned, her face mild. Jesse couldn't tell if she'd actually known who'd stepped up behind her or if she'd been expecting someone else. "I haven't decided yet." She smiled at Amelia. "What do you think I should get?"

"You could go to the shelter. My friend Ashley's sister volunteers there and she's always talking about how there's all these sad dogs who want good homes." Amelia beamed, pleased that she was being acknowledged first.

Cheyenne pursed her lips and glanced at Jesse. "It'll take you a while to do whatever it is you need to do today, right?"

Jesse rolled his eyes skyward. He'd explained to her twice the night before that he'd wanted to reinforce the fence around the garden after chasing a deer away from it the last time he'd been on the property. "Yeah. Why?"

"Well, I was planning on running into town after you got here, and I just thought Amelia might want to come with me? She can show me where the shelter is." Cheyenne made eye contact with his daughter, who was already bouncing on her toes.

"Can I, Dad? Can I?" Amelia all but squealed.

Jesse shrugged. "Don't kill Ms. Anderson." He grinned when Cheyenne flared her nostrils.

"Let me grab my shoes and my purse and we'll go," she told Amelia and shot him a dirty look.

As the two disappeared into the sliding door he could

hear his daughter, in her sweet voice, as loud as day, "Do you have any cookies left over?"

CHEYENNE HAD no idea what had come over her. The decision to get a dog had come the night before when she'd lain in bed for hours, listening to the quiet of the house and half hallucinating that she could hear someone walking around. The house's remote location had never seemed an issue when her grandfather was alive, but the fact that she was now living in the large house by herself made her anxious. So, at three in the morning, she'd made the decision that she was going to get a dog. Or a cat. Or even a hamster. Just something to keep her company and slightly lessen the emptiness, and the noiselessness, of the house around her.

Fine. They'd had dogs growing up. She'd known her grandfather had wanted one but had been worried he was too old to take care of it properly. A dog was no big deal. But to take Jesse's daughter—his eleven-year-old, apparently-comfortable-with-talking, daughter—with her to go look at dogs? Sleep deprivation apparently made you do really weird things.

However, taking Amelia wasn't actually that big of a deal. The girl did chat the entire drive into town, filling Cheyenne in on the businesses they drove past and where she and her friends liked to haunt when they were left to their own devices. She did ask a lot of questions whenever Cheyenne made an effort to respond to one, but she wasn't as annoying as Cheyenne had always thought pre-teen girls— or really, any sort of person below the age of eighteen—could be.

In fact, she was pretty smart. And fairly interesting.

Cheyenne had realized it the last time they'd spoken, but she found herself shocked by the knowledge again when they turned onto Main Street and the girl paused in her babbling to eye Cheyenne. "Are you getting a dog 'cause you miss your grandpa?"

Cheyenne frowned. "I might be," she replied. "My house is really quiet at night and it's kinda spooky."

"Is it haunted?"

"Um… it might be."

"What do you mean?"

"I used to think I was crazy when I was your age because my brothers and I used to hear weird sounds at night. But now, I hear them all the time." It was so much easier, telling the girl who looked at her with big, inquisitive eyes, than she imagined it would have been had she tried to tell Roxanne, or the guys. Well, maybe not Wes— he'd have welcomed the topic with open arms—but he was also the kind of guy who'd get in his head over a picture book.

Amelia wasn't looking at her like she was crazy. Her earnest face opened a floodgate, or a sounding board, ready for Cheyenne to bounce thoughts and feelings off of. It was a compelling face to talk to.

She swallowed, hard, before she continued, "I, like, hear my Gramps walking down the hall at night. Or hear him moving around the house. And the house just makes weird noises on its own 'cause it's big and old and weird."

"My grandma and grandpa's house makes weird noises. It's super old. Like old, old," she said solemnly. "Dad said our old house used to make noises, too."

"Oh yeah?" Cheyenne followed the vague instructions Amelia had provided, to the best of her ability, to turn onto a winding road outside of the back end of town.

"Yup. Adults are weird." Amelia shrugged. "I think your house is totally haunted."

Cheyenne laughed. "Adults are weird. And the house is probably haunted."

"So, we'll get you a dog to help with the ghosts." Amelia nodded sternly. "We're almost there."

"You are very bad at giving directions." Cheyenne chuckled.

Amelia was still giggling when they pulled into the steep incline that led to the hill where the Penn Ridge shelter was located. The shelter sat in what looked a former barn, painted a vibrant blue color to be seen from the road, and had enough space to park four cars comfortably in front of it. Cheyenne parked the Cherokee and squinted, trying to see through the aged glass into the office of the shelter.

"C'mon, c'mon, c'mon." Amelia all but bounced out of the vehicle and up the steps to the office door.

She led the way into the front lobby, the heavy glass doors shuddering closed behind them. It was a bright office, the fluorescent bulbs giving it a whitewashed feel that looked a little too sterile. Behind a glass partition sat a friendly-enough-looking older woman. Amelia stopped her bouncing and let Cheyenne take the lead, her round face looking up to her for guidance.

"Hello," the woman chirped and ducked her head in a greeting nod. "What can I do for ya today?"

Cheyenne stepped up to the glass partition and put on her best customer smile. "I was hoping to see the dogs that you have up for adoption?"

The woman squinted her eyes, the wrinkles in her face morphing into a pleased smile. "You're Caleb's grand-daughter," she breathed out.

Before Cheyenne knew what was happening, the woman had rushed out of view and was appearing through a door at the far end of the lobby. She threw her arms around Cheyenne, their heads nearly knocking into each other with the force of the embrace. "You look so much like your grandmother," the woman breathed into Cheyenne's hair before she stepped back.

Cheyenne shot Amelia a look. They exchanged confused, uncomfortable smiles before Cheyenne shook herself about. "Um, hi. Yes." She managed a light laugh. "You knew my Gram?"

The woman nodded. Her eyes, hooded slots of almond brown, lifted in a huge grin and her smile was surprisingly white for her age. "I knew Celeste from before they moved here. When they used to vacation at the lake. Back when your father was very young. You look so much like she used to."

Cheyenne felt a lump forming in the back of her throat. "My dad says the same thing," she offered, at a loss for words.

"Oh, I'm sure he does." The woman clasped one of

Cheyenne's hands in both of hers. "How are you doing, dear?"

"Well enough." Cheyenne kept her back straight. She didn't want Amelia to see her get watery or weak. "I guess a little lonely. That's why we're here looking for a dog," she said mildly.

The woman beamed at her again and peeked over her shoulder. "Hello there."

"Hi." Amelia made a polite twitch of her mouth in the other woman's direction, her eyes begging Cheyenne for a way out.

"Can we go look at some dogs?" Cheyenne interjected, taking the hint from Amelia and running with it. "We don't have that much time."

"Sure, sure. If you'll just use some of the sanitizer by the door, I can lead you back to the kennels."

Cheyenne and Amelia sanitized from fingertip to elbow and followed the older woman, who introduced herself as Anne, into the back of the converted barn. They were taken past an area dedicated to cats, most of whom were lazing in an afternoon nap. "Are you sure you don't want a cat?" Amelia asked as she shuffled behind Cheyenne.

"I think a cat would get lost in the house," Cheyenne said conspiratorially to her companion.

"Hmm. Maybe."

A chorus of barking met the trio when they entered the back of the shelter building. About two dozen kennels, nearly all filled with dogs, came alive at the sight of the three. Cheyenne and Amelia broke off from each other to poke their faces—and hands to the dogs who looked willing to sniff them—into kennel doors to assess their inhabitants. Cheyenne didn't have a game plan for the visit. The spur-of-the-moment decision had come after she'd seen the excitement in Amelia's face over the dog, so she wasn't really sure what she was looking for.

Until she found a kennel in the corner with a ball of electric fur bouncing excitedly at her. The dog couldn't have been any taller than her calf, but he was bursting to get out of his kennel and say hello, his little black tail wagging furiously and his fluffy face trying to reach her through the metal bars. Cheyenne crouched down and held her fingers out for the pup to sniff.

"Hey, Amelia!" she called out without thinking. "Come look at this pup!"

The pre-teen beamed at her. "Oh, he's cute!" She stood on her toes to read the tag at the top of his kennel. "His name is Prince."

"Hi, Prince. Hi, boy," Cheyenne crooned while the fluffy mass of hair licked at her fingers. "Does it say how old he is?"

"A year. It says he's house trained." Amelia stooped down and held her fingers out.

Cheyenne scratched the dog's head. He let out a yip and threw himself against the door in an attempt to get closer. "Hey, there. Calm down, buddy, before you hurt yourself," she murmured, trying to use her hand to protect his face from the metal bars. "We'll get you out of here real soon. Sit boy. Sit."

The dog planted his butt firmly on the ground and gave a joyful yip. Cheyenne looked over at Amelia and tilted her head. "What do you think?"

Amelia's face was bright as she looked at the small pup. "So cute!"

Cheyenne grinned in spite of herself and scratched the pup's head again. "Hear that, Prince? She thinks you're cute."

16

*J*esse was beginning to worry that maybe, just maybe, his daughter had been kidnapped when he heard the Jeep bumping its way up the driveway. He'd long since finished reinforcing the fence and had begun idly weeding the garden, although Cheyenne seemed to be doing an okay job keeping up with it. The sunny afternoon had started to turn into a warm, hazy evening. The house stood tall in front of him, its solid bones remaining strong despite the almost-constant changes happening within its walls at this point. It was looking at its first summer without its beloved owner, the middle of June fast approaching with the new mistress of the house leaving its stamp, and it still had the luck of looking grand.

He met the Jeep at the head of the driveway, ready to usher his daughter into the truck to go pick up her brother and feed them, and balked when Amelia bounded out of the front seat with a little ball of black fur in her arms.

"Look! Dad, look!" she called, flopping to the ground to let the little ball of energy dart out of her arms and into the grass. It shoved its nose into the strands and started to sniff, small tail wagging aggressively. "Isn't he so cute!"

"Cute," Jesse said dryly, meeting Cheyenne at her door. "You got a dog."

"Amelia was really fond of him." The younger woman smiled up at him, a soft pink touching her cheek bones when their eyes met.

Something stirred in him. The same force that had stirred whenever they'd made eye contact for weeks now. It was warm, and heavy, and while he liked how it felt, it startled him. The extreme sense of excitement and the slowly-dying-off sense of shame that he felt every time she was around only made it harder for him to look away from her smiling face. Until the puppy playing with his daughter yipped, interrupting his thoughts. "So, you adopted a puppy because my kid thought it was cute?"

"I adopted the dog because I wanted a dog. I never decided on whether I wanted an adult dog or a pup." Cheyenne defended, looking a little uneasy. "But Amelia has already so kindly offered to pet-sit sometimes, and I figured, why not take him home now while I have a nice strong man to carry all of his stuff inside?" She smirked and opened the back of the Cherokee.

Jesse let out a snort. "How much did you get him?" he asked before peeking into the back of the Jeep. "Geez. Do you think you got enough stuff in there?" he griped.

"I'm sure he's going to need more toys." Cheyenne gave him her dazzling smile and scooped up a bag of dog food to place in Jesse's hands. "Isn't he just the cutest thing you've ever seen?" Cheyenne's face lit up when she said it.

His stomach nearly bottomed out all over again. "If he makes you happy, then I guess he is really adorable. Melia sure looks like she's enjoying the pup."

They both looked over at the eleven-year-old, who was happily rolling around in the grass with the small dog lapping at her face. "Do you think I'll ever be able to break her away?" he asked with mock horror and grabbed a handful of pet store bags.

"You don't necessarily have to. Right now, anyway," Cheyenne offered, leading him into the house. "I have to dog-proof the house and get all of his stuff set up. And Amelia is having a really good time."

Jesse was struck, yet again, at the ease with which Cheyenne included Amelia into her day. It still amazed him that the woman didn't seem to notice how easy it was for her to include the girl. Or that, despite how she was the first one to write off her ability to connect with kids, she and his daughter already seemed to have formed a bond the girl had never had with a grown woman other than his mother-in-law. "I guess I could pick her up later."

Cheyenne had deposited her bags on the dining room table and was looking at him, pushing wisps of hair out of her face. "Why don't you bring Miles back with you and we'll have some dinner later? I have a ton of casseroles left over from the Ladies Auxiliary and I will never get them all eaten before they go bad."

"They freeze well." Jesse could have kicked himself for saying it out loud and was about to give himself a mental berating when Cheyenne let out a sweet laugh and placed her hand, lightly, on his arm. Her fingers were warm, and extremely soft, against his skin.

"I can, uh—we can have dinner here. If you're sure?" Jesse felt the urge to tug at the collar of his shirt while he spoke. He cleared his throat and shifted on the balls of his feet, trying to hide some of the thrill blooming in his gut.

Amelia tore through the open front door, chasing after the puppy, before Cheyenne could answer. "Can we have a ball?"

Cheyenne fished a bright blue tennis ball out of one of the shopping bags and tore a tag off of it. "No ball inside, please."

"Try telling Prince that!" Amelia snatched the ball and darted out of the room.

"I'm sure." Cheyenne grinned at Jesse. "Just be prepared to help me clean up after the children."

Jesse followed Cheyenne back out of the house to the Jeep, still chuckling, a flutter of excitement in his chest at the knowledge that he was going to be seeing Cheyenne again in a few hours. His daughter's delighted laughter, and the fact that she'd left her cell phone in the door of the Jeep instead of it being glued to her palm, only added to the weird bliss settling in him as he helped lug in the rest of the dog's new belongings and went on with his day.

PRINCE WAS a hit with both kids. The moment they'd pulled up beside the Cherokee and Jesse heard Miles squeal in delight at the yipping of the small dog waiting in Cheyenne's arms, and the huge grin he had for the woman, Jesse knew he was sunk. Amelia's admiration for Cheyenne was nothing compared to the love that both of his children had for the ball of fur racing around her yard. Jesse let Miles out of the truck and begged, as sternly as he could over the squealing laughter, for his six-year-old to be careful with the puppy. As soon as his small feet touched the ground, Miles ran to join his sister and the dog in the front yard.

Jesse found Cheyenne in the kitchen, her favorite spot in the house, putting a pan of something in the oven. Her hair was loose and hung down to her ribcage, a sheen of red-gold that he'd never seen loose before. The living room was a war zone, the couch pulled apart and dog toys scattered all over the floor. There was a hand towel—torn into shreds—in a corner by the island, its scraps a rainbow of shades of purple.

"Rough afternoon?" Jesse called out, pulling a stool out from the island.

"Adopting a puppy was a big mistake." Cheyenne groaned, whirling around. "An adorable. Big. Mistake." The humor in her eyes, framed by the silkiness of her red hair, made Jesse twitch.

"Was Amelia good?" Reminding himself of his daughter helped keep his mind off of the feelings Cheyenne invoked. He found himself hoping that Amelia had been pleasant the entire time he was gone.

Cheyenne nodded, pushing her hair out of her face.

"She's been great. I'm pretty sure she saved my couch cushions. Several times." She laughed at herself and reached for two glasses out of a cupboard by the sink. "Tea?"

"She was good?" Jesse perked up. "Like, behaved-herself, didn't-give-you-any-attitude good?"

"Great. She helped with Prince. She even helped me look for paint samples for the bakery and offered to help me paint and pick out furniture. She has a really good eye for color."

"She's good at color things and decorating things. I don't know where she gets it from."

"I heard that you were a design guy yourself."

"Oh yeah?"

"Yeah. Roxanne was telling me earlier this week that you usually spend your days on building houses, not tinkering around already-existing homes?"

Jesse felt his ears turn hot. He drummed his fingers on the island's countertop while she poured them some tea, searching for the right way to answer. "I enjoy working on houses. New construction with an old flare." He stopped when he saw her face and rushed through the rest of his thought. "I enjoy doing stuff around here too. I used to come by and help your grandfather out a lot. And I don't mind doing it now."

"Well, thank you for that." Cheyenne laughed, handing him a glass. "But you like to build houses?"

"Love it. It's what I wanted to do, but Penn Ridge doesn't have a need necessarily for just a home construction business all year round. So, when I met Tim, we decided we'd open kind of like a 'do-it-all' business. There were a bunch of guys—some in town, some from nearby —that were looking for year-round work. Great guys, really. Next thing I knew, we were off the ground."

"Business seems to be doing really well."

"Steady enough. Like I said, we hired great guys and that really helped."

"Sounds like it's going really well." She smiled at him with mischief in her eyes. "Well enough for you to spare a couple of days?"

He couldn't quite squelch the excited thrum in his nerve endings when she said it. It might have been the look in her eye, or the idea that she wanted him to carve out time for her, or a heady mixture of the sweetness of the tea and the proximity of her hand to his. But when she asked him if he could spare some time for her, he had to fight not to promise her more than a little bit of time. "Uh, sure." He had to coach himself to tone down his excitement. "What do you need?"

"I need to have the shop remodeled. There isn't a ton of work that needs to be done, but it definitely needs more than myself and my friends can do." Cheyenne darted out of the kitchen and came back with a giant black binder. "I was crunching numbers and I've come up with a pretty decent budget for the work I want to get done in a relatively quick manner."

Jesse leaned away when she sidled up next to him and dropped the binder onto the island. She was *so small* next to him. He was amazed by just how tiny the woman was, her own stool scooted next to his; he'd known she was short, but this was the first time they'd ever been within a foot of each other. His skin was alive. "Oh?"

"Yeah. I was really hoping that you'd be able to maybe come take a look at the space next week? I want to get started as soon as possible."

"When do you want to be open?" Jesse watched her flip through the binder, coming to a stop at what looked like a blueprint of the bakery his mother-in-law had found.

"I was hoping, probably way too optimistically, for the Fourth?" Cheyenne batted her eyelashes at him.

"You're insane." Jesse laughed. "Unless it's almost in ready-to-go condition, I can't see it being done by the Fourth."

"I figured as much." She huffed good-naturedly and flipped to the list of renovations she wanted. "I was just hopeful. The Fourth is a really good week for me business-wise, and I was really hoping to have the shop up and running."

Jesse browsed over her list, trying to find an easy way to let her down. The list wasn't long, nor was it extremely difficult, but he wasn't sure that he'd be able to pull off the majority of the work in less than a month. "I'll come look tomorrow and we'll see."

Cheyenne held her hand out, a grin fixed to her lips. "Deal. For now."

Jesse laughed and shook her hand. Later that night, he'd be sure to think about the feel of her soft, well-used hand against his. From its smallness to the sure way she'd shaken his hand and the beautiful grin that lit up her freckled face, he'd find himself thinking about it as he lay in bed. Conflicted.

17

One of the things that Jesse had come to terms with a long time ago was that there was no handbook for how to be a widower. No kitschy Hallmark movie on finding yourself after your wife died, no 'ten steps to healing once your wife moves on' booklet, and even those church basement support groups, more often than not, were older women whose husbands had passed after long, fulfilling lives. In the five years since Mara had been gone, Jesse had only come across two other men whose wives had also died young. One from a tragic car accident and one from a hiking accident; neither woman had been sick, and neither couple had kids.

Even with the help of his and Mara's parents, and the whole entirely weird little town he'd settled into when the kids were still small, there had been no easy path to figuring out any of it. A lot of thought, a lot of sacrifice, and a lot of waiting for the other shoe to drop had gone into every decision he'd made since. He'd made a lot of mistakes—a lot of decisions that could have had better outcomes had he put a little more, or a little less, thought into them. Which was why, for the past fourteen-and-a-half hours, he'd done nothing but silently obsess.

It'd started after he got Miles to bed and said his good-nights with Amelia. When the house was quiet, there was nothing good on television, but it was still a little too early for him to call it a night. He found himself making a cup of tea, something he'd never been a fan of before Mara got sick, and sitting at the kitchen table, staring into his small backyard—thinking, which was always dangerous to do after ten at night.

He didn't have an answer as to what to do about Amelia noticing and understanding how he'd been looking at Cheyenne at dinner. He wasn't ready to touch that problem with a ten-foot-pole and a hazmat suit. Instead, he sat and thought about the handbook he wished had been written for guys like him. Guys who had lost their wives when they were barely adults, it felt like, with two small kids who would, at some point, most definitely need a mother. Guys who, six years ago, hadn't had a clue how to make dinner, let alone how to get a one-year-old to stop crying in the middle of the night while the seven-year-old was sound asleep for the first time in months. Guys who could change an engine no problem but still got tripped up changing a diaper. Guys who had to move across the country just to have a hand, and still had a hard time adjusting to the fact that their children were down one parent, while the one they had left wasn't necessarily the one that was good with kids.

That first year had been hard, but not the hardest. No, the hardest had come before Mara had even died. That put him in such a sticky situation when it came to Cheyenne, who was—for all he could remember—the first woman he had looked at since Mara to whom he felt a genuine attraction. Not in the she-was-a-pretty-woman kind of way, but in the he-wanted-to-get-to-know-her kind of way. The way that had made it easy for his daughter to see it and to get what was going on.

In fact, after Mara, he'd been fairly certain that there would never be another woman whom he could look at and see something other than just a pretty face. She had left a space in his life he'd thought could never be filled, nor did he want it to ever be filled. There was enough damage there to last a lifetime. But what if?

Jesse found himself spending much of the next morning pondering those 'what ifs' while he sat, staring blankly at the windows in front of his office desk. Occasionally he'd tap on the desk with the eraser of the pencil in his hand, but the motion was more to do with muscle reflex than active thinking.

Most of his thoughts were circling that pesky 'what if' drain.

"'What if' what?"

Jesse nearly shot out of his chair when the voice interrupted his mental obsessing. The lack of sleep from the night before, paired with his inner turmoil over a few simple statements from his kid, had somehow gotten him to his office on autopilot that morning. Then he'd sat, with a cold cup of coffee and an open notebook on his desk filled with random circles he'd been drawing just to give his hand something to do, and obsessed.

He dropped his pen and rubbed at his eyeballs with the

palms of both his hands before looking up at his business partner—and friend—Tim. "What?"

"I dunno. You were talking to yourself when I came in." The other man grinned as he made his way to his own desk on the opposite side of the room from Jesse's. "You look like shit."

Jesse gulped down some cold coffee before he flared his nostrils in Tim's direction. "Didn't sleep much last night. Not that it looks like you did either."

The blond man looked rumpled—this was true. His hair, which was usually slicked back in what Jesse could only see as an older version of a boy-band style, was a disheveled mess, and the t-shirt he wore was baggy and wrinkled. He, too, had bags under his eyes, and he looked as if he hadn't shaved in three days. Still, he seemed in better spirits than Jesse. "Leah was restless all night. So, neither of us slept."

"Ah, yes, that second trimester insomnia. Mara had it really bad with Amelia." Jesse managed a tired grin before he yawned so hard that he cracked his jaw.

Tim laughed. "What's your excuse?"

"Just some stuff with Melia. Pre-teens. So much fun." Jesse tried to wrangle another grin, but his friend just raised his eyebrows. Tim had been a great friend and incredible partner since Jesse moved to Penn Ridge. Someone he could tell pretty much anything. But there were still some things, like his thoughts circling Cheyenne and the possibility of a future there, that he didn't feel comfortable sharing. Plus, it was always easier to divert conversations to topics settled around the kids.

"She get into another fight with Mitch?"

"No, she's just getting older. It's scary when they start to seem more like adults and less like kids." Jesse looked at his monitor, at the smiling picture of his kids holding each other from that summer, and felt his own face turning up. "Enjoy them while they're little, because older just seems scary."

Tim pushed off the edge of his desk, their appointment book tucked under his arm. "Okay, Gramps. Let's go grab some breakfast before you start giving me a ballad."

TIM WAITED until they were settled in their usual booth at Sadie's before he said anything else about Jesse's lackluster attitude. He made a show of opening their appointment ledger and sneaking a pen out of his pants pocket, all business as usual, even while his blue eyes focused on Jesse.

Jesse shifted around in his seat before he folded his hands in his lap. The simple act made him feel like a kid again, when his father would scold him for being too much of a handful or for not listening when his mother told him to do something. He felt unsteady, his core displaced by the uninterrupted torrent of thoughts filtering through his head. "Stop looking at me like that," he groused when Tim just continued to stare at him.

His friend grinned. "Then talk to me, Jess. You're a bad liar and we both know it, so spill."

Jesse sighed. He knew he could evade until eventually Tim let off of it. Or, in what possibly would end up being more beneficial for him, he could try to talk it out. He opted for the latter. "When Mara got sick… I didn't have a lot of time to think about it, ya know? Like what was going to happen next," Jesse said carefully, looking at the man whom, if he had to, he would consider his closest friend. A man whom he hadn't known for more than four years, but a man that he trusted with his children's lives. "After she got sick, while she still had the energy to be with the kids, I started going to this support group."

"A support group?" Tim gave their waitress, Melody, a nod when she held two white ceramic mugs and a pot of coffee out to them. "For?"

"Widows, mainly. The whole purpose of the group was to discuss your feelings, basically, about being a widow— or a widower." Jesse gave Melody a grateful grin before he dumped a healthy amount of sugar into the mug. "A lot of the women in the group who had kids—there were only two other men and they were both older—were in that stage of grief where they were accepting it. One was even dating again. And I would sit there and listen to them talk about accepting their loss and helping their kids accept it."

"Well, yeah. I mean, it's a big thing to lose a partner. I can only imagine how much harder it would be to lose the mother of my child." Tim's face darkened slightly as he ran through the possibility of losing Leah after the baby was born.

Jesse shrugged. "I remember listening to them talk about dating and moving on, moving forward. And I would think, 'How? How can you possibly sit here and talk about how you have all of these amazing memories with your husband, with your children and their father, and you're ready to see someone new?'"

Tim snorted. "What? Do you expect every person who loses their wife or husband to join a convent?"

"No. I know it makes sense to move forward, to move on. I know that no one expects that they're going to be alone forever, even if they marry someone and that person doesn't make it to forever with them. But then we had Melia and Miles, and I see so much of her in them every day. Even when she was still here but so far away, I never had a hard time seeing her in them. I never saw myself doing anything other than raising them."

Tim nodded slowly but didn't say anything. Neither man had reached for their menus and Melody, who was used to the two coming in and taking care of business dealings at the same back booth where they sat, graciously left them alone.

"Melia thinks that I find Cheyenne attractive," Jesse said finally. "We had dinner with her last night, me and the kids." The words felt weird coming out, and he had to chase them down with two long gulps of coffee.

"Well, that's definitely something." Tim waved Melody over and ordered two ham and cheese omelets with toast. "I thought you said that she didn't really like kids all that much."

"She doesn't seem to, no, but she's really good with Amelia." Jesse downed his coffee in one swig, the hot liquid sliding down his throat in an attack. He flinched and let out a dry cough. "Amelia loves her and Miles digs her. They think she's great."

"And so do you," Tim said with a raise of his eyebrow.

Jesse didn't blink at his friend when he shook his head. "She is cute," he said finally, thinking about the curve of her hips and the softness of her face. "Really cute."

Tim snorted and took a sip of his coffee. "How much did it hurt you to say that?"

Jesse shrugged at him and ran his finger along the rim of his empty coffee cup. "It's not so much that it hurts to admit. It's just weird."

"How so?"

"Do you remember the first time you looked at Leah and thought that you wanted to spend the rest of your life with her?"

"Well... yeah."

"The first time I thought that, when I met Mara at UNC, I was convinced that I was going to feel that way for the rest of my life." Jesse rubbed his temples. He looked out the window, frowning. "It's been over fifteen years since I was with anyone besides her. I have no idea what to do."

"I mean, it's only been a few weeks since she got here, right? Give it some time." Tim took a sip of his coffee. "Maybe, oh, I don't know, take her out to dinner?"

Jesse raised his eyebrows. "You just said to give it some time." He was stunned at how out of touch he felt with dating. Had it really been that long?

"You've already had dinner with her, right? So doing it again really isn't too out there?" Tim grinned at his friend. "Even if it is with the kids. Get to know her more."

"It was one dinner."

"Yeah, I got that. One dinner. But how did it go?"

"It was with the kids."

"Kids aside. How was it?"

Jesse paused. In truth, both he and the kids had had a blast having dinner with Cheyenne. He'd had a great conversation with the woman while Melia and Miles played with the dog, and when it was time to eat it'd felt… nice. Comfortable. Sitting around the table with her and his two kids, the puppy snoozing away at Cheyenne's feet, had felt normal. Almost as if it was something they'd done a thousand times before, and that they would be doing a thousand times more. "It was good. Fun. The kids had a great time."

"And are you seeing her again?" Tim raised his left eyebrow to punctuate the question.

"I've been seeing her almost every day. In fact, I'm going to see her after this."

"For work stuff. Even if the shit you do around the Retirement House isn't necessarily all work stuff, it's still in a dad-professional capacity."

"Let me go work on her bakery and then we'll see, okay?"

"Whatever gets you going, bro."

Had he been about ten years younger, Jesse would have thrown a napkin at Tim to compensate for his devilish smirk. As it was, he had to fight the urge to stick his tongue out at his friend. Melody dropped their food off and promised to come back to refill their coffees before Jesse had the chance to come up with a response to Tim. Jesse had never been so happy to see eggs in his life, even though he was under Tim's scrutiny.

18

*J*esse met Cheyenne at the bakery after his breakfast with Tim, still mulling over his friend's thoughts. Tim's input had been great food for thought, and it was only added to by the stupid grin that hit his face when she popped her head out of the back door of the bakery. "Warm today, isn't it?" she called out, shielding her face from the sun with her hand. "Hurry up and get inside. There's air conditioning!"

"Did you already turn the electric on?" Jesse grabbed his appointment book from the passenger seat of the truck and crossed over the gravel toward her.

"Electric and water are on. I've already picked out the two ovens I want. I'm afraid I'll only be able to fit two in for now. I was also thinking about bathroom fixtures this morning." She let him into the bakery and latched the door behind them.

Jesse wasn't sure what he'd been expecting; between Cheyenne's excitement and the speed with which Carol had located the storefront, he didn't have an idea of what he could have been walking into, but the interior of the kitchen was already fifty times better than what he'd been fearing. The kitchen had empty space, obviously for an industrial fridge and the two ovens she was talking about, and it had enough floor space for her to set up whatever kind of tables she'd need to work on. There was an industrial dishwasher in place already, which was one less pain in the ass he and his guys would have to deal with. The floors were a dark hardwood, and he couldn't see any visible cracks, chips, or scuffs that might cause an issue.

"You don't expect me to pull the floor up and lay down a new one, do you?" he asked, making a list in his mind of all the things he'd have to walk through with Tim when they provided her with an estimate.

"Probably not. I like the look and feel of them. I'm afraid pulling them up might ruin the vibe in here." She was already heading for the empty doorjamb that separated the kitchen and the strong front. "I want a door here, one of the swinging ones, but I need a lock on it. Do you think you guys could install it?"

"Shouldn't be an issue." Jesse eyed the doorjamb as he followed her through it. "Do you have a specific brand you were thinking of?"

"I'll see what I ordered for the Albany shop and let you know."

"Noted."

She stopped behind the counter, which was incredibly sturdy and had its own display case, and looked at him expectantly. "What do you think?"

Jesse took his time casing the shop, walking along the walls and feeling their sturdiness, stopping at each window to test its hinges and locks, and pacing the floor. "The floor's in good condition. Whoever owns the building is taking good care of it." He was impressed with the little amount of structural work that he and his guys had to do. It made Cheyenne's timeline of the Fourth a lot more feasible.

"Right? The floor definitely needs to be buffed and the bathroom needs to be updated, badly, but I think the majority of the work we'll need to do is cosmetic." She was still standing behind the counter, watching him intently. Her hazel eyes were wide, excited, and she was watching him with the same face he'd seen on his kids when they wanted something sweet. "I want to put some shelves up back here." She turned to point at the wall behind the display case. "I also want to add another counter here. And another solid shelf over there." She pointed to the left of the display case, in the general customer area. "I'll put the coffee fixings bar over there."

"You sell coffee?"

"Oh, yeah." Cheyenne grinned at him. "I do, like, a whole coffee menu, including espresso drinks and Frappuccino's. I took two beverage classes in college, and they've been a big selling point."

Jesse leaned over the display counter. "What else has to go back there?"

"I need a drinks cooler, which will go in the corner." Cheyenne pointed. "And then the rest of it will be cosmetic. Paint. Tables and chairs. I need to get a few bookshelves, at least two. Do you know if the library does any old book sales?"

"Melia might." He couldn't remember the last time he'd

been to the library. "I'll ask her tonight."

"Yeah, that'd be great." Cheyenne chewed on her lip for a moment and smiled at him. "Hey, do you think she'd be interested in helping me pick out paint swatches?"

Jesse blinked, surprised. "You want to steal my daughter so that you can look at paint?"

Cheyenne seemed a little surprised herself. At what, he wasn't sure, but she shook the glaze out of her hazel eyes and gave him a smile. "I think she'd really enjoy it. She's got an eye for colors and I could really use a touch that isn't mine."

"Why not just ask your friend?"

"She's got wedding on the brain, so all the colors she picks out are green or cream or this silver lining stuff." Cheyenne shrugged. "If it's weird for you, I don't have to ask her."

Jesse shook his head. "No, no, I'm sure it'll be okay. I'll ask her tonight and let you know." He could have kicked himself at his eagerness to try and set Amelia up with the woman. There was another one of those gray areas when it came to being a single parent and wanting to date, or even entertaining the idea of it, and that was what to do with the kids. He wasn't sure if Amelia and Cheyenne spending time together alone was the right move, but his daughter had not stopped talking about the woman since they'd met. "I just—I don't know if she'll be down for it."

"No worries. Let's finish looking at the shop?" She smiled. "I'm telling you, the bathroom needs some updating."

Jesse motioned for her to step in front of him. "Lead the way."

19

*J*esse's conflicting thoughts followed him through the rest of the day. He wasn't a master compartmentalizer, so he'd had a hard time putting aside Tim's opinions while he followed Cheyenne around the rest of the space. Anytime she came too close, he found himself stiffening, or thinking about what it would feel like to run his hands through her hair. Instead of being able to talk himself out of pursing the woman, he kept finding her more and more appealing.

He was left even more conflicted when he and Cheyenne reached for the door to leave at the same time and their hands touched on the doorknob. Jesse went stiff, his whole body going warm in a childish, unnatural flush. "Sorry," he heard himself mumbling, tugging at the collar of his t-shirt with the hand that hadn't come into contact with his.

Cheyenne only smiled up at him and took a side step so that he could open the door for her. "No worries." She seemed completely unfazed, her whole face full of warmth when she smiled up at him. "Do you think you'll have an estimate for me by tomorrow?"

"I could probably give you some rough numbers tonight," Jesse offered, stepping outside and keeping his arm extended to let her out. "Why the rush?"

"I'm just so excited to get started." Cheyenne stuffed her hands in her back pockets and rocked back on her heels to look up at the building. "I miss my routine. I miss my business. I just miss being busy." She laughed at herself. "I apparently can't sit still."

Jesse nodded. "I can see that. How's the pup?"

Cheyenne grinned and unlocked her phone to show him some new action shots of the pup that she hadn't sent to him and Amelia. "He's so smart" —she crooned—"and so messy, but he's keeping me busy."

"Sounds like having kids." Jesse chuckled, watching her flip through the pictures with pride.

Cheyenne rolled her eyes and waved him off before she unlocked her Jeep. "I'll talk to you later?" she offered with another simple grin before she hoisted herself behind the driver's seat. "Thanks!"

"Anytime." Jesse shook his head after the Jeep disappeared. It bothered him just how much he meant that every time.

JESSE HAD to put the conversation he'd had with Tim, and the thoughts about Cheyenne, out of his head after he left Cheyenne at the bakery that day. He'd have to revisit his budding feelings, and the unintentional backlash they would cause, at another time. Despite seeing her almost daily, while his crew bounced between her bakery and a couple of other small projects in town, Jesse found that it was easier to just think of her as she was. A client. A well-paying, time-oriented client who had a clear idea of what she wanted out of her time. And he was sure a widower with two young kids wasn't a part of that.

Still, as much as he'd liked to have spent the rest of the day obsessing over his thoughts and feelings, he had a laundry list of household chores to keep his mind busy and two assistants who needed watching. His kids were off from school and summertime meant a thousand and five errands, including playdates and sleepovers, the three-day-a-week camp he signed them up for every year, and little odds and ends like grocery shopping. During the school year, he could run to the grocery store once a week while the kids were still at school. Those trips were quick, in and out, with a list that he usually spent the entire day before making. It was neat, orderly, and almost calming to have to do the weekly chore.

During the summer, however, he never got away without taking Miles and Amelia with him. As soon as Amelia saw him with the grocery list paper—little packets with magnets that Carol magically found and snuck into the house—she'd grab Miles and they'd harangue Jesse until he caved and took them. It turned his thirty-minute-long chore into an hour and a half, at the minimum.

Jesse was mulling over the contemplative time he could have spent in the grocery store, thinking of all the things he'd wanted to grab but had gotten conned or whined out of buying, when he turned down the cheese aisle behind Miles and Amelia. Their cart was full, but only a fraction of it had been first round picks for the man. They had made a dent in the frozen vegetable section—they were easier to work with when he was in a rush—and had somehow also ended up with two bags of chips he didn't remember picking out. In the mix was also prepared meals, snacks, and a small collection of fruit. Amelia had even suckered in him into getting a case of Coke cans, which sat under the cart making fun of him.

Miles came to an abrupt halt, his eyes wide with excitement, as they stopped at the cheese section of the dairy aisle. It was pizza night in the Kaiser household, and that meant a mostly-homemade pizza with as much cheese as Miles wanted. Arguably, Miles found pizza night to be the best night of the month, while Amelia—who Jesse was increasingly suspicious had a dairy sensitivity—was already planning on what she wanted for dinner the night after.

"Two, Miles," Jesse warned as he walked around the cart to put a hand on his son's head. "Give poor Melia a break."

Miles jutted his lower lip out. "But… but…" Miles' fascination with cheese had always been a sweet spot for Jesse. His son had been infatuated with dairy since he was eight months old.

"Two cheeses or it's a spinach pizza tonight." Jesse chuckled and looked at his daughter.

Amelia rolled her eyes at her phone screen and continued to tap aggressively against the glass with her thumbs.

In the end, despite Jesse's best efforts, they ended up with four different cheeses for their pizza and a very annoyed Amelia. The tween didn't say a word to Jesse while they waited in line to check out, glaring at the screen of her phone and ignoring all of Miles' best efforts to make her realize the beauty of the cheeses. Jesse ignored her in return. It was moments like this where he really wished that Mara was still alive—that things could have ended differently.

The only thing that broke through Amelia's annoyance was Miles announcing, rather smugly for a six-year-old, that he was most definitely going to have the first can of soda from the case. Her head whipped up and she darted into a passionate defense of all the reasons why she should be the one who got to enjoy the first can.

"That's a lot of cheese," he heard from behind his left shoulder, his gaze jolting from Amelia and Miles to the redheaded woman standing behind him. As soon as he saw her, his heart started to pitter-patter excitedly, causing him to cough.

Cheyenne was wearing a green t-shirt with a large, vibrantly decorated mural of a butterfly on its chest and a pair of blue jean shorts. Jesse couldn't help but grin at the home-grown look the shorts and t-shirt gave her, even as they hugged the curve of her hips and waist in an extremely flattering way. "Hey," he said with about as much cool as a teenager trying to get a Friday night date.

She smiled, the corners of her eyes presenting faint wrinkles with the action. "Hey." She looked over his shoulder at the kids and gave Amelia a little wave. The preteen, so engrossed with her conversation that she barely noticed, gave a weak wave in return. "Talking quantum physics?"

Jesse glanced back at his kids with a fond grin. "Household politics."

"Ah." Cheyenne let out a knowing breath. "Between the house and the senate, I assume."

"Speaker of the house and the chairman of the left," Jesse responded, and Cheyenne snorted on a laugh.

The two adults grinned at each other. Cheyenne's entire face lit up, as it usually did, when she smiled. Her soft laugh made his face flush at the sound, from his neck to the tip of his nose, in one fluid motion.

Behind him, he could hear his daughter getting excited, her voice starting to reach the octave that meant she and Miles were about to go to war. Cheyenne looked over his shoulder and grimaced. "Sounds like they might need a moderator."

"They'll be okay. She can't do anything to him in public." Jesse chuckled dryly. "Once we get home, it'll be another issue."

Cheyenne rolled her eyes conspiratorially. "I'm on Miles' side. Just don't tell Amelia," she said in a hushed voice.

As if he'd heard her whisper his name, Miles hopped around his father to catapult himself at Cheyenne's legs. "Chey! Where's Prince? Did he come too?"

Cheyenne put her free hand on his head to stabilize them both, her basket of leafy greens swaying dangerously close to clocking his son in the head. "Hi," she snorted. "No, Prince is at home. He says hi, though."

Miles seemed satisfied. He bounced back enough to crane his head and look her in the eye, his face beaming. "We're having pizza tonight!"

"Pizza, huh? No wonder you guys took a tour of the cheese aisle." Her lips twitched at Jesse over Miles' head.

"You should come for dinner," Amelia added.

Jesse nearly started. He hadn't heard his daughter step up beside him, and her being so vocal and excited with a virtual stranger—although Cheyenne was becoming less of a stranger as time went on—still got him a little confused. He looked down at her as she smiled at Cheyenne. "I'm sure Cheyenne is busy tonight." Jesse put his hand on his daughter's shoulder affectionately while trying to give Cheyenne an out.

Cheyenne nodded slowly. "I would, kiddo, but I have to get home to Prince," she said with a quick smile.

Jesse felt a little deflated at her refusal. He hadn't realized how much he'd been hoping she'd say yes until she turned the offer down.

"You can bring him, too." Amelia bounced up on her toes. "We can play games and I finished a drawing I wanted to show you and it'll be fun! And we got Coke!"

Cheyenne smiled at the excited outburst, her hand still on Miles' head. The six-year-old had begun to bounce up and down in front of her, giving her his best 'puppy dog eye' look while his little face struggled not to split into a grin. "C'mon, Chey! Think about it! Pizza, Prince, and games!"

"Have either of you guys asked your dad if it's okay if I come over?" Cheyenne laughed, dropping her hand.

Both of his children shot him quick, excited looks. His daughter locked her fingers together, her big brown eyes doing their best to bore into his. "Can Cheyenne come over for dinner, Dad? Please?"

"Yeah! Can she come over and have pizza for dinner and play games and bring Prince and he can have pizza for dinner and play games? Please, please, please!" Miles mimicked his sister's gesture, his locked hands held under his chin.

Jesse shot Cheyenne a thankful look and scooped his son up in his arms. "If Cheyenne is okay with it, then absolutely." He didn't want it to sound like he really wanted her to come to dinner, even though he felt excited about the prospect of another meal with the redhead and her small dog.

Miles clapped his hands together, pleased that he had gotten his way, and gushed to his older sister about their impending dinner guest. Jesse gave Cheyenne a grateful smile and inched forward toward the cashier as the woman he'd been waiting behind was handed her receipt.

He had just started to unload the shopping cart onto the conveyor belt when his phone began to buzz excitedly in his pants pocket. Jesse fished the phone out to see Carol's face flashing across the screen. He sent Cheyenne a look, begging her to keep an eye on Miles, and answered. "Hey, Ma, I'm still at the store. Can I give you a call when we get back to the house?"

Carol was sniffling on the other end of the phone, soft sobbing sounds that Jesse had heard before. They made his heart plummet to the bottom of his stomach, and nausea and anxiety rolled over him in one coarse motion. "J-Jess," she sobbed.

"Ma? What's wrong?" Jesse pushed past Cheyenne to get out of the aisle, his hands trembling.

"It's… it's Mitch," she said weakly. "He—he had a heart attack."

Jesse's entire world went lopsided. "Where are you?"

"On our way to Mercy. They got him stable, but I guess Halltrap doesn't have the equipment he needs." Her voice was rough with the force of her crushing sniffles. "Jess…"

"I'm coming. I'm on my way," Jesse promised. "I'm out the door."

Jesse hit the end button on the call after receiving a torrent of sniffled instructions from Carol and turned back to the line. Cheyenne was helping Miles and Amelia load their groceries onto the conveyor belt, her eyes purposefully staying away from Jesse and on the kids. She must have heard the panic in his voice. He caught her arm in a soft grip, stopping the redhead from loading more groceries onto the belt. She turned to look up at him, her eyes asking questions that he wasn't sure how to answer.

"Mitch had a heart attack," he said quietly. If the kids heard the panic in his words, he was sure that it would be catastrophic. "I need to go to Scranton."

Cheyenne sent a look to the kids, who were busy helping the cashier bag their groceries, and nodded. She didn't say anything for a second.

"I'll take the kids home with me," Cheyenne said carefully as she fished her keys out of her purse. "I need Miles' car seat, though." She handed Jesse her keys without breaking eye contact with him. Jesse just stared, his eyes flitting between her extended keys and his two children. "Jesse," Cheyenne said softly, squeezing his arm. "You need to go. And you can't take the kids with you to a hospital, to wait for hours to find out if their grandfather is going to be okay."

He wasn't sure if it was her hand or her words that broke him out of the panic haze, but he snapped to and dug his own keys out of his back pocket. "It's not a stick," was all Jesse said before he snatched her keys and slid past her to kiss his kids on the head. "I have to go for a little bit, guys. Cheyenne is gonna keep an eye on you until I get back, okay?"

Amelia eyed him suspiciously. "Why not Grandma?"

"Just—Melia. Behave yourself, please." Jesse hugged his daughter tightly. "I love you, girly." He kissed her head again before he swung up Miles for another tight embrace. Then he was out the door of the grocery store, his mind narrowing into one pure thought: Mitch had to be all right.

20

Cheyenne managed to usher the kids, along with their now-combined grocery trips, out of the store and to Jesse's Tacoma with little trouble. Something in her father's face had made Amelia quieter than usual. The preteen had helped her get Miles into his car seat, even fielded a few of his incessant questions about where their father was and why, and helped Cheyenne load up the back of the truck with the groceries. Once the cart was returned, and after Amelia had gotten into the truck, Cheyenne had to make a quick decision as to which house she was going to bring the kids back to. She barely knew where their house was, but if it was going to be a long night of waiting, she was sure they would be more comfortable at their own home.

However, as she'd mulled it over in the check-out line, in order to settle them in in their own house for the night, they would have to make a stop at the Retirement House first. Prince was definitely not going to last the night on his own—not that Cheyenne had liked the idea of leaving him be, as much for her house's integrity as for the fact that she would miss him. Plus, she wanted to make sure she'd locked up. It wasn't the first time she'd left the house overnight. She had made a couple of trips back up to Albany to check on things, but those had always been planned out in advance with someone stopping by to check on things. Typically Jesse. In those cases, keeping the doors and windows locked wasn't as much of an issue. Plus, she'd found it soothing, standing in line watching the groceries be rung up, to make a plan of attack. The idea of someone else's grandfather being in jeopardy was hitting a little too close to home.

Cheyenne didn't say much while they drove out of town in the opposite direction of the empty farmhouse, but neither did the kids. Amelia stared quietly out her window beside Cheyenne, her slender fingers picking at the frayed hem of her purple t-shirt. The chipped purple nail polish caught the reflection off of a couple of lights they drove past, and her eyes barely blinked as they peered out of the glass. From the rearview mirror, Cheyenne could see Miles playing quietly with two Matchbox cars that he kept in the cupholders of his booster seat. She didn't turn the radio on, for fear that the town's two local stations, one country and one top forty hits, would sour the already stale mood in the truck's cabin.

"Prince is going to be so happy to see you guys," Cheyenne said, trying to break the awkward silence that had permeated their surroundings. Not that Miles probably saw it as awkward, even if Amelia could feel the same tension that Cheyenne did.

"Do you think he'll jump on Miles again?" Amelia asked, looking between Cheyenne and her little brother in the back.

"Maybe. We've been trying to work on the jumping." Cheyenne smiled a little until she saw the scowl on Amelia's face. The poor girl was trying so hard to remain calm for her little brother, but it'd become obvious to Cheyenne that she knew something was wrong.

"Why don't we make that pizza, huh?" Cheyenne asked as she turned onto her driveway. "We'll grab Prince and then go back to your house. I don't have any pizza making stuff here." She felt her voice raise as she lied.

Amelia looked over at Cheyenne. The woman wasn't sure what kind of face her young companion was making in the dim light, but she had the inkling that it wasn't pleasant. "What's going on?"

Cheyenne looked into the rearview mirror, trying to see the six-year-old in the backseat. The little boy's head was bent and he was engrossed in crashing his cars dramatically, erupting into quiet giggles every few moments. "Your grandpa had to go see the doctor," Cheyenne said carefully, doing her best to keep her voice low. "Your dad and grandma didn't want you to have to wait in the office all night," she added tactfully. "I know it's a lot to ask, and you're probably really worried, but I am going to need your help with Miles tonight."

Amelia was quiet while Cheyenne parked the Jeep in its usual spot. She unlatched her seatbelt before Cheyenne could and nodded. "I'm gonna grab Prince."

"Here." Cheyenne handed her the extra key she kept in

the glove compartment. "Can you grab the bag of puppy food and a toy or two?"

Amelia nodded solemnly. Cheyenne couldn't help but feel a twinge when she watched the girl walk into the house, her head held high despite probably feeling overwhelmed. It amazed her how strong Amelia seemed to be, despite her age and the fact that she had lost their mother when she was so young.

Cheyenne wasn't sure what the exact words were for the feeling in her chest, but the pure affection she felt for the girl was beginning to turn into something she couldn't ignore.

AMELIA WAS in a better mood when she got back in the car, puppy in tow. She sat, petting the little wriggling body while Cheyenne drove back to their house, not saying much but still existing in a more defined peace. She even made a little huff of excitement when they pulled into the paved driveway in front of the house and she could foist the dog off on the grass.

It was a nice, ranch-styled house with a yard littered with every kids' toy Cheyenne could imagine. There were flowerbeds peeking out from underneath the large windows that decorated the front of the house on either side of the white door, which was framed with butterfly bushes. Cheyenne was sure Carol took care of the little garden, and she loved the well-rounded feel it gave to the tiny house. She hopped out of the truck and helped Miles unbuckle, smiling at the little boy who babbled in intermittent rambles about making pizza and his collection of race cars and trucks.

Miles raced ahead of them to open the door—he knew where Jesse had hidden the spare key this week—while Amelia helped Cheyenne pull canvas grocery bags out of the back of the truck. "Is Grandpa gonna be okay?" Amelia asked Cheyenne quietly, her voice small and unsure of itself.

Cheyenne set her armload of shopping bags down and wrapped her arms around the little girl. "I don't know," she murmured, holding Amelia close to her body. "I honestly don't know, Amelia." She sighed and fought to keep her voice from cracking as she ran a hand, a little hesitantly, over the girl's hair. "But I do know he loves you so much, and that's something you've got to hold on to when things get scary." It was something that she held on to, almost painfully sometimes, whenever thoughts of her own grandfather caused more pain than comfort.

She felt the girl press her face into her shoulder and squeezed her tighter. Her heart ached, nearly shattering all over again at the loss of her own grandfather, but she couldn't think about her own unresolved grief at the moment. She had two kids to take care of. "C'mon," she said quietly into Amelia's hair. "We gotta keep a strong face for Miles right now. Right?"

Amelia stepped back and wiped her eyes on the backs of her hands. "Right." The eleven-year-old smiled weakly up at Cheyenne and picked her shopping bags back up. "Thank you."

The two carried handfuls of bags into the house while Miles pulled out buckets of toys and turned the tidy, if randomly decorated, family room into a war zone with the help of Prince. Amelia showed Cheyenne where she could drop the bags in the kitchen—which was on the floor, since all of the counter space was filled with toys and loose papers that Jesse hadn't cleaned up in a few days —before she sprinted back outside to carry some more in. Cheyenne appreciated the tiny, tidy kitchen as she started to stack up papers, putting the mail into one pile, the drawings Miles and Amelia gifted Jesse in another, and papers that could be put into the trash into a third.

The kitchen was well decorated and, other than the inevitable clutter of the single father caring for two kids, precisely clean. It had blue walls—light enough to reflect the light from the overhead fixture but deep enough to give the room a warm feel—and black countertops that could sustain childhood mischief and the years to come for the little family. The appliances were neat and new, the fridge organized meticulously so that the kids could find their snacks easily and so that the junk food (and two bottles of beer) was out of Miles' reach. On the fridge, a smattering of colorings done by Miles and school photos of the two kids were pinned with odds-and-ends magnets, everything from restaurants to little ladybugs. He also had a calendar, marked with playdates and appointments for both the kids and his business, which hung in the center of the left side door. Each day of June that had passed was crossed off and he'd color-coordinated the play dates—green for Miles and a deep blue for Amelia. She found that interesting and tucked away the quiet observation for a later day.

Amelia finished putting the groceries away while Cheyenne, with a little grunt as she did so, unwrapped the pre-made pizza crust and preheated the oven to the instructions on the packaging. She vowed unhappily that she'd teach the kids how to make their own crust from scratch, and Jesse too. It was more than just taste that demanded it. The homemade stuff was healthier for the kids in the long run, and teaching them how to use their hands in creative ways was good for them.

Jesse fostered Amelia's creativity, Cheyenne noted. There were drawings and paintings, all vibrant in color, hanging in frames or taped to every wall of the kitchen. The fridge had been devoted to Miles' more childish ambitions. It was sweet, the way each child's work had a diligently thought-out place and an aura of pride in each placement. Cheyenne was a little unsettled by how sweet she thought it was, but she couldn't focus on that too much. Not right then.

"Wanna go grab your brother?" she said to Amelia to distract herself from the warm thoughts that circled around the knowledge that Jesse was a good father. She'd had good fathers around her entire life—of course she'd admire another. "We'll get dinner started, and then maybe play a board game?"

21

Jesse let himself into the house at a little after six the next morning, dragging his feet every step of the way. His eyes felt like someone had dumped sand into them, and he was in desperate need of a shower, a meal, and about eight hours of uninterrupted sleep. The time on his trucks' dash before he cut the engine told him he might get two of those, if he moved quickly.

None of that mattered, not in the long run. Mitch, the grandfather of his children and the man closer to him than even his own father at this point in his life, was going to be okay. They had caught it in time. He was going to be on a strict diet and a full exercise regimen, and Carol was probably never going to let him be by himself ever again, but he was okay.

Relief shattered through the tiredness when he thought about it again as he kicked off his sneakers and hung his hat on the shelf that Amelia had made with her grandfather that winter. Just as he let go of the hat, the sound of small paws on carpet gave him a heads up before Prince's small body was pressed against his ankle.

He picked up the wriggling pup and gave him a scratch between the ears. The dog, his whole body vibrating, mimicked Jesse's yawn as he was carried into the living room. Jesse stopped yawning and looked around the living room. The entire room screamed that it'd had a long night, although it wasn't in the shambles he'd expected after an entire night with Cheyenne and the kids stuck in the house. There were toys everywhere, in neat piles that showed they were half cleaned up, and his couch had a person-sized dent in it, the little throw blankets that Carol had insisted he needed balled up in the form of a sleeping person.

Whoever had slept on the couch was gone. Jesse could hear someone puttering in the kitchen, obviously trying to be as quiet as possible in the sleeping house. He could figure who it was, and he was surprised by how much that knowledge pleased him. For the first time since he'd found himself attracted to the noise-maker, he allowed himself to bask a little in that pleasure. After the night he'd had, he deserved the little joy it could bring him.

Jesse passed through the living room to the kitchen to find Cheyenne digging through his pantry, standing on her toes to reach the shelves above her head. She'd made a pot of coffee—a full pot that brought him so much joy he nearly teared up at the sight of it—and had flour, sugar, a giant mixing bowl, and a few eggs sitting on the counter by the sink. A counter that had recently been organized.

"Hey," Jesse said quietly as he set the dog down and made for a coffee mug off of the mug tree. The tree had been another one of Mitch and Amelia's pet projects, one that Jesse found surprisingly useful.

"How is he?" Cheyenne bypassed a greeting as she dropped to the flats of her feet, triumphantly holding a half-empty bag of chocolate chips he vaguely remembered buying a few months before.

"The same as he was at one. Alive. Unconscious." Seeing Mitch so small in his hospital bed had rocked Jesse to the core. "But alive."

When he'd arrived at the hospital, it had been to find Carol all alone in an otherwise empty waiting room, balling tissues between her hands to the point that they were in shreds. He was in surgery, Carol had told Jesse when their eyes met. An emergency bypass. A surgery that, while Mitch would recover from it, had somehow managed to make the formidable man look tiny and weak. It'd nearly crushed him to see Mitch like that.

Jesse took a long swallow of the black coffee, wincing at the heat sliding down his throat and the image of his father-in-law looking like a hospital ghost, which he knew he'd never be able to get out of his head. "I was kicked out of the hospital by a nurse. Carol's going to stay for a few hours and then I told her I'd go back."

"Probably good. One of you needs to be well rested. Or, at least, get a little sleep." Cheyenne smiled at him, the soft look stirring his tired soul.

What he wouldn't give to be able to cross the floor and wrap his arms around her, taking comfort in the small feel of her body against his; to have her hair wound around his fingers as he took out the frustration, the exhaustion, and the fact that he hadn't been with a woman in so long and used it to show her exactly how much she'd been on his mind.

Jesse shook himself, trying to pull away from the lewd thoughts clouding his sleep-deprived brain. "Huh?" He rubbed at his face, looking at her. "Did you say something?"

"I asked if you were hungry." Her smile read that she'd had no idea what was running through his mind. "I'm making pancakes."

"Oh, yeah. Yeah, I'm starving." Jesse gulped down hot coffee, black, to try to shock his system away from the hunger.

"Go on and have a shower. Breakfast will be ready by the time you're out."

"Miles? Melia?" Jesse yawned again.

"Miles was just stirring when I checked on him. Amelia was out cold." Cheyenne glanced over at Jesse with a mischievous look in her eyes. "She snores."

"She does. But don't tell her I said that. She'd be so embarrassed."

"My lips are sealed."

Jesse chuckled all the way down the hall. He stopped in Miles' room to peek in through the cracked door. His son was sprawled across his bed, starting to rub the sleep from his eyes in his favorite dinosaur pajamas. Jesse eased back from the door before he was seen and poked his head into Amelia's room. His daughter was curled up in a ball on her right side, hugging her purple comforter in her arms while she lightly snored. Jesse's mouth twitched up and he eased her door closed before heading to his bedroom and its adjoining bathroom for a much-needed shower.

His children's laughter met him in the hall a half hour later, lifting his tired spirits. He hadn't heard them stirring, having spent almost the entire time under the scalding spray of his shower, obsessing over how small, and how weak, Mitch had looked in that hospital bed. How scared he was to lose the man—to lose anyone ever again. The feelings of anxiety and almost-loss had collided with his feelings for Cheyenne and left him ragged and conflicted in the shower stream.

When he'd finally stepped out of the shower and was dressed, he'd all but run down the hall toward the sound of his laughing children, the desire to hold them and just breathe in his son's sticky scent and hear his daughter's warm laugh overriding everything else he felt.

He found them crowded around the table with Cheyenne, pushing forkfuls of pancakes into their mouths in between heated, playful discussion about which character on a show they'd apparently watched the night before was better. He stood in the doorway of the kitchen and watched them, realizing for the first time that she'd grabbed one of his t-shirts and a pair of sweatpants—probably from the laundry basket he'd left in the living room the day before—and her hair was piled on top of her head in a messy knot. She looked good in his kitchen, even better laughing with his kids and eating pancakes. A man could get used to a sight like that.

"Daddy!" Miles squealed, breaking his concentration as he bulleted headfirst into his father's knees.

Jesse picked the boy up and gave his face a nuzzle, reveling in his giggles as Jesse's five o'clock shadow tickled his soft face. "Hey, kiddo."

"Where'd you go?" Miles asked with a slight lilt to his voice, his small arms wrapping around his neck.

"Grandpa's sick and I had to go help Grandma." Jesse rubbed his back reassuringly while his daughter avoided looking at him. Cheyenne had told him the night before that she'd picked up on the panic in Jesse's voice and had had a hard time settling down for the night, afraid she was going to lose Mitch like Cheyenne had lost Caleb. "He's okay," Jesse said louder, to reassure both of his kids. "Just not feeling very well. I'm gonna go back and see him later, but I think you guys are gonna go see Ms. Casey."

Amelia groaned and banged her head, quite literally, against the tabletop. Cheyenne looked at her, alarmed, her hazel eyes wide with concern. "Amelia?" she called out softly, putting her hand on the girl's arm.

"Aren't I old enough to just watch Miles? Like, c'mon." Amelia groaned, shaking off Cheyenne's hand. "Ms. Casey is lame."

"Amelia," Jesse chastised, "please don't argue with me."

Cheyenne stood to grab Jesse a plate and a fork, frowning at the children and Jesse. "Why don't they just stay with me?" She surprised all three of them. Amelia, whose face had lit up, and Jesse, who scrunched his eyebrows in a silent question, both stared at her like she'd lost her mind. Jesse watched her visibly push herself forward, shrug, and set his plate down on the table. "I have to go home and shower." She gestured down to his clothes, which she wore without a thought, and shrugged. "I need to run goods in to the Harvest Bean, even if it'll be really late, but they can hang out with me today."

Jesse took a seat by the plate she'd set out for him and settled Miles on his lap. "Well." He was doubtful, looking between his kids and Cheyenne. "I couldn't ask you to do that."

"Why not?" Cheyenne refilled their coffee cups and brought them to the table.

"Yeah, why not?" Amelia furrowed her eyebrows at her father.

"Yeah! Why not?" Miles parroted, looking up at his dad.

Outnumbered, Jesse rested his head on his free hand, exhausted, and yawned. "Okay, okay. You guys can go with Cheyenne. As long as you behave."

"We will! We can help with Prince and stuff, and we'll be super good!" Amelia jumped up and snatched Miles' hand, practically yanking him off of Jesse's lap. "Let's go grab toys!"

The adults watched as they ran out of the room, giggling to each other as if they had just won a grand prize. Cheyenne was smiling, but Jesse could see a hint of panic in her eyes.

"They won't hurt you." Jesse chuckled at Cheyenne. "I swear."

"I'm gonna hurt them," Cheyenne said weakly. "I don't

even spend this much alone time with my niece and nephews who are Miles' age."

Jesse laughed. "You won't hurt them. They do bounce back pretty easily." Jesse gave her what he hoped was a thankful grin. He was too tired to be able to determine the strength, or enthusiasm, in his face. "I appreciate you doing this."

Cheyenne put her hand on his arm and gave it a light squeeze. "Call it even for stealing your clothes last night. Now, eat your pancakes."

22

*B*y the time Jesse got to the house that evening, Cheyenne was exhausted. After a day full of errands, dragging along two kids who had ideas of their own—a real taste of what her mother and the boys' mother must have felt when she and her brothers had been growing up—she was ready for a long soak in her bathtub and a glass of wine. Or, based on the two plates Miles had broken when they were making lunch, three glasses of wine.

She was contemplating how much wine she could feasibly get away with on a Tuesday night, with a puppy who needed regular bathroom trips, when Jesse wandered around the side of the house to find her and the kids. They were making liberal use of the jungle gym her grandfather had built and taking turns keeping Prince on the slide while she nursed a glass of sweet tea and a minor headache.

Jesse looked worse for wear too as he dropped down next to her on the grass. He lay down on the sun-warmed grass, his head resting by her left hip, with his arms thrown dramatically over his face. Cheyenne took another sip of tea and looked down at her friend. "How is Mitch?"

"We've taken red meat away from him. And fries. And beer. And probably coffee too." Jesse laughed dryly and yawned. He was still tired. "But he's alive. And ready to go home."

"When are you taking them to see him?" Cheyenne nodded at the kids with a yawn herself and wrapped her arms around her shins.

"Tomorrow." Jesse propped himself up on his elbows to watch his kids chase each other around the large toy, laughing. "How were they?"

"You owe me two sandwich plates." Cheyenne chuckled into the jeans she wore before resting her chin on her knees. "Otherwise, they were really helpful."

Jesse looked up at Cheyenne with a grin. "They seem to really like you."

"I don't mind them," she said pleasantly in response, smiling down at him. The deep bags under his eyes worried her—even if she understood that they were from the minimal amount of sleep he'd been able to accrue in the last couple of days—but there was still so much love for his two kids sitting in them. It lit their dark depths up and made them glow, almost like ambrosia wine under soft lighting. "What were you planning on doing for dinner?"

"I was gonna let the kids pick which restaurant they wanted to go to. Why? Thinking about joining?"

"The kids and I made a shepherd's pie that you're going to sit and eat."

"Dinner with the kids again tonight? I figured you'd be looking forward to some child-free time."

"Oh, I am." Cheyenne smiled as she stood and wiped her hands off on the back of her jeans. "But you guys need a well-balanced meal. Did you know your son doesn't eat salad?"

"Miles doesn't like green vegetables," Jesse said automatically, his eyes never leaving his kids.

"Have him tell you what we had for lunch," Cheyenne said before she picked up her glass and went inside to set up for dinner.

However odd it felt, spending time with the kids without Jesse, Cheyenne was glad she had, and that struck a nerve as she meandered around the kitchen waiting for their dinner to finish. They'd spent the entire day together, from baking in the morning to making another trip to the grocery store and even stopping for a half-pound bag of sour dummies from the candy store on Gappler Street on their way home. Aside from the two broken plates, she'd truly enjoyed herself as they played games and colored. They'd all dozed off in the living room watching The Wizard of Oz, and Cheyenne had woken up to Miles asleep under her arm on the couch and Amelia conked out on her grandfather's recliner, burrowed into one of Cheyenne's favorite afghans. It'd been nice. So nice that Cheyenne felt a momentary sadness at the prospect of having to let the kids go, even as she watched them run around the yard and shriek as their father chased them down.

Cheyenne shook her head and grabbed a stack of plates from her dish cabinet, trying to shake the feeling from her shoulders. She didn't like kids—she didn't dislike them, but she had been adamant her entire life that she never knew how to handle them—but she found herself loving the time she spent with Amelia and Miles more than she'd ever thought she could. Watching them run around with Jesse, laughing and running and playing, her chest felt something she wasn't sure she liked.

While she waited for the timer to run out on the casserole, she tapped out a text to Roxanne, hoping for some clarity during this freak-out over Jesse and the kids. Her friend only shot back six winking smiley faces, similar to her response the night before when Cheyenne had panictexted about what to do with the kids before she suggested board games and cartoons. The closer Roxanne got to her wedding, the less helpful she was going to be, Cheyenne thought dryly.

Cheyenne texted back quickly, four angry faces and two with tears running down their cheeks, and forgot to put on mitts before yanking the oven door open. She had to backtrack and snatch them up quickly before she tripped over the open oven door.

Roxanne's response was waiting for her when she dropped the casserole dish, almost too hard, on the counter nearest the oven.

Just calm down—his kids are cute. That's all it is; you're not about to become mommy-dearest or anything.

Cheyenne rubbed her jaw thoughtfully before she peeked out the window again.

I don't even like my nieces and nephews this much.

Yeah you do—you just spend more time with them. Now stop overthinking it.

Call you later >.> They're staying for dinner.

Bye xoxo

Cheyenne stuffed her phone in her back pocket and opened the sink window. "Soup's on!" she called out loudly.

Her dinner guests shuffled diligently into the house. Prince yapped after Miles, barking at the little boy's heels and trying to gain as much of his attention as possible. Jesse scooped the pup up so that the six-year-old could wash his hands and deposited the pup on his bed in the kitchen, safely out of the dining room, before he, and his two kids, formed an awkward train into the dining room together.

Their little house didn't have a dining room—Cheyenne wasn't sure how much time they spent eating around the kitchen table—so watching Miles scramble up onto a chair to eat dinner was adorable and entertaining at the same time. The large dining room table was still set with her light purple summer tablecloth, full of daisies in little milk jugs, and had individual plates set out for the four of them—forks and butter knives out. Setting the table had been something her mother had been insistent on her entire childhood; whenever it was more than just Lisa and Cheyenne sitting down for dinner, she'd insist they'd set the table. Nights where her father was home for dinner had been grand affairs—and when all the brothers were there, they'd downright have dinner parties.

Miles stared at the tablecloth—the silverware laid out, the flowers on the table, even the cup that Cheyenne had already filled with iced tea for him—with wide eyes. "It's like a restrant!"

Jesse gave Cheyenne a pained look. "You're going to spoil them," he said with a teasing smile before he put his napkin in his lap. Miles followed suit.

Cheyenne rolled her eyes and passed Jesse the ladle for the casserole. "I don't know how you guys do it at home. My house was always serve yourself."

"Miles is six," Jesse said to her in alarm, his eyes wide.

"I got my own pizza last night!" Miles announced happily, bouncing in his seat. "Three slices!"

"Pizza's a little different, bud." Jesse scooped up a half scoop of shepherd's pie and dropped it on Miles' plate before he gave Amelia a whole scoop's worth. "You guys know there's mushrooms in this, right?" Jesse was skeptical, poking his fork through the second ladle of casserole he put on his plate.

"I chopped them," Amelia beamed, her fourth bite already on its way to her mouth.

"I ate a raw one!" Miles squealed with a giggle, licking gravy off his lower lip. "It was squishy."

Jesse gave Cheyenne an incredulous look.

"He did. He told me it tasted like dirt," Cheyenne said fondly, shooting the little boy a wink.

Miles erupted into a mess of giggles, squirming around in his seat in pleasure. "It did!"

"Did not." Amelia rolled her eyes at him.

"Did so!"

"Did not!"

Jesse started to open his mouth, to interrupt the budding argument, but stopped when he looked across the table and saw Cheyenne looking between the two kids with the biggest smile on her face that he had ever seen. The smile was beautiful, so full of affection and amusement, and it was aimed at the two most important things in his life. Whether it was the exhaustion, or the conflict brewing in his head over just what kind of role Cheyenne was going to have in their lives moving forward, Jesse made the decision right then and there.

While his kids debated whether mushrooms tasted like dirt, Jesse Kaiser found himself staring at the first woman he was going to date—or at least try to—in over ten years. And he'd be damned if that didn't do something to him.

23

*A*fter Mitch's heart attack, Cheyenne and Jesse started seeing each other more. Cheyenne became a part of Jesse's childcare routine, taking the kids for half the days that Mitch and Carol used to so that his mother-in-law could cart Mitch back and forth to physical therapy appointments and doctor's appointments. Cheyenne didn't mind the time she spent with the kids, not nearly as much as she might have if someone had asked her months before. She didn't mind seeing Jesse as much, either.

They'd become close friends in the days after that terrible night. Jesse and his men rushed to get the shop finished in time for the Fourth, and Cheyenne worked on bonding with the kids and keeping them out from underneath his feet while he coordinated projects around town. She and Amelia painted the bakery in two days, including some stenciled designs of baked goods that Amelia insisted she put on the walls. They baked in the mornings for the Harvest Bean, and both Amelia and Miles proved to be huge helps with the shop's soft open the weekend after the Fourth of July.

The feeling of not being alone—in her house or in her personal life—struck her almost every day and left her feeling unsettled. But the unsettledness had nothing to do with the storm that tore through her life the second week of July and left her world feeling a little lopsided.

The first storm of the summer tore through her house on a Saturday morning.

She'd gotten up later than usual that morning, when the early morning sunlight turned into a full-on onslaught around nine, and taken a half-hour bubble bath with her morning coffee and a new book. It'd been written by one of the women that Roxanne's publisher represented, and Cheyenne had been very excited to try it. Between the smell of the solution she used, a lavender and lemon bubble bath Roxanne had found in Memphis a few months before, and the hot coffee, Cheyenne was so relaxed she almost dozed off in the cooling water before she'd made it to the last chapter. Almost.

As she was dozing off, her eyelids struggling to stay open and her body sinking deeper underneath her bubble blanket, her bathroom door burst open. Cheyenne jerked up so hard she knocked over the little table she kept by her shoulder in the bath. Her coffee mug shattered across the floor and the water-stained novel she'd been reading dropped to soak up the remnants of creamy, cold coffee spreading across the tiled floor. Standing in the doorway, looking frantic and sweaty, was a very upset Amelia.

Her dark hair was in matted waves with tendrils of sweat-curled hair sticking to her forehead. She was in jeans and a t-shirt and was breathing so hard she couldn't speak right away. Cheyenne eased herself out of the bathtub and reached for the towel hanging beside the tub, frowning.

"Amelia?" She wrapped the fluffy purple towel around her torso.

"Hi," Amelia heaved. "I need… to ask you… a question." Her eyes were wide, and she was visibly out of breath.

"You okay, kiddo?" Cheyenne had an edge of panic in her voice, which she tried to cover with a casual cough. "Why don't you sit down?"

Amelia shook her head. "I biked all the way here. To ask."

"What's up?" Cheyenne sat on the edge of the tub to rub lotion into her legs, her concern masked by a sheen of calmness that she tried to keep in place for the frantic eleven-year-old.

"Susy Crum is having a mother-daughter picnic for her birthday tomorrow—which sounds really lame 'cause we're all in middle school but her mom had cancer so we all agreed it was a good idea—and I don't have a mom," Amelia rushed. "Grandma said she was gonna go, but with Grandpa being sick she says she can't."

"What about your father?" Cheyenne asked levelly as she stood back up and breezed past Amelia into her bedroom to get dressed. So much for her relaxing Saturday morning.

"It's a *mother*-daughter picnic. But like not really," Amelia added quickly when she caught Cheyenne's look over her shoulder. "Cat Tanner's sister is going with her. Justine is like twenty so she's basically an adult. And

Morgan and Margo Genkins are going together because they're twins."

Amelia was not going to leave the room, so Cheyenne wiggled into a pair of underwear and pants underneath the towel. "Okay," she nodded slowly.

"And Missy Nelson is taking her stepmom," Amelia finished, clapping her hands together. "So, will you pleeeaaaasseeee go with me."

Cheyenne stuck her head through her t-shirt and scowled at the girl. "Excuse me, little miss?"

While they had bonded to the brink of being almost sisters, this was territory that Cheyenne had absolutely no business being in. She and Roxanne had discussed the kids in depth, more than they had discussed how Cheyenne felt about Jesse, and they had come to a solemn agreement. She was a friend to Miles and Amelia, the kind of friend whom Amelia was increasingly turning into a confidant and who Miles adored, and the kind of friend who dropped off cookies to the kids when they weren't going to see each other that day but she'd made extra. But she wasn't the kind of friend who could take Amelia to a mother-daughter picnic. That crossed a line.

"It's only a couple of hours." Amelia's voice almost cracked. "Please." Her big brown eyes implored Cheyenne.

"What does your father say?" Cheyenne grabbed a pair of sandals out of her closet and cocked her head for Amelia to follow her out of the room.

"I didn't ask him yet." Amelia followed her back into the bathroom so Cheyenne could start picking up the mug pieces. "I wanted to ask you first."

Cheyenne dumped a handful of small ceramic pieces

into the bathroom trash can. "I'm sure it'd be okay if he took you."

Amelia let out a wild shriek at Cheyenne, as if she'd just stabbed her with a piece of glass. "I don't WANT HIM TO," Amelia screamed.

Cheyenne hadn't even gotten to her feet when Amelia darted out of the room, screaming unintelligible words at Cheyenne as she bolted. Cheyenne dumped her handful of mug pieces into the bathroom trashcan and dropped her cream-colored hand towel from the sink counter to the floor to sop up the cold, disregarded coffee. She slid her sandals on and took her time going down the stairs, grabbing two bottles of lemon seltzer and a plastic container of cookies on her way. While her grandfather's property was pretty big, there weren't a lot of places for the tween to go. Not if she was going to sit and be annoyed, which she could remember doing herself when she was the girl's age.

Cheyenne picked her way through the thick foliage which separated the yard from the creek, taking the stone path that Caleb had built when she and her brothers were still very young. She found Amelia sitting hunched over at the round table rock, tears streaking down her face as she glared out at the water. Cheyenne eased herself down on the rock next to her and offered the bottle of seltzer. "Hey," Cheyenne said quietly while Amelia used the back of her hand to dry her face.

"I'm sorry," Amelia mumbled as she cracked the seal on her seltzer. "I just…"

Cheyenne waited a beat, watching the fight start to fizzle out of Amelia. "I grew up with two moms,"

Cheyenne offered to fill the silence Amelia had left, peeling the lid off their cookie container. "I got really lucky. I had my biological mother, who loves me so very much. And I had my brother's mother, who loves me like I'm her daughter." She didn't look at the girl. Instead, she was watching the current race down the creek, tugging at loosely standing, overlong green grasses. "I have never taken that for granted, though, ya know? Because my entire childhood, two of my closest friends grew up without a mom."

Amelia rubbed her eyes against more tears. Her face was still turned toward the creek. "Yeah?" she mumbled against the skin on the back of her left hand.

"Yeah. Their names are Wesley and Connor. Their dad, Cameron Carmody, lives down the street." Cheyenne put her arm around the tween. "Have you met Mr. Carmody? He owns the hardware store on Presely with Mr. Nichols."

Amelia nodded. "Every Veterans Day he comes into school and does an assembly."

Cheyenne smiled slightly. She remembered hearing about the assemblies that Cameron would put on with help from volunteers from their chapter of the American Legion at the elementary and middle schools. Roxanne and the guys had always made a big deal about them when they were kids; they were something that she'd missed growing up in New York and not the sunny hamlet of Penn Ridge.

"That's right. He's a widower, just like your dad."

"I didn't know that."

"Mrs. Carmody passed away when the boys were young. I think Wes was six."

"I was six when Mommy died." Amelia picked at a flake of skin on her index finger. "Do you think he remembers her?"

"More than Connor, his little brother, does." Cheyenne picked up a pebble with her free hand and tossed it into the weakly moving water of the creek, just visible from under the bank. "Do you have memories of your mom?"

Amelia shrugged. "Sometimes, maybe."

"'Sometimes, maybe'?" Cheyenne frowned at the girl.

"They're all hazy. Like… I dunno." She looked closed off suddenly, staring at Cheyenne suspiciously. "You're gonna laugh at me."

Cheyenne crossed her heart earnestly, looking down at the young girl. "I'd like to hear some of them. If you'd like to share them."

"If I share my memories, will you take me to the picnic?" Amelia asked cautiously.

Cheyenne pursed her lips in thought, looking at the girl. There were a lot of things that Amelia could have asked for, especially from the random woman who was devastatingly attracted to her father in a quiet, faintly desperate way. The picnic would be awkward—especially when she had moments of complete aloneness with the mothers of the other girls (or their sisters and stepmothers)—but Amelia's burgeoning hope, in her dark eyes, had Cheyenne nodding her head skeptically. "If you share one memory, I will talk to your dad about taking you," she said after a moment. "And whenever you feel ready, you can share another. You share a memory and I'll teach you to bake something. Or we'll go to the mall. Or we'll do both, depending on how much of a memory it is." A barter system. When Richard had died, Roxanne's therapist had suggested her parents create a barter system for her in order to talk about her feelings over the accident. She'd been older than Amelia, but it had helped her come to terms with the loss of her brother.

It tingled in the back of her mind that, quite possibly, she'd need something similar soon. The weird dreams about the house being haunted, and all of the memories of her grandfather she'd been boxing with lately, were making her a little irritated.

Amelia's eyes lit up like Cheyenne had just told her she could stay up all night, on a school night, to binge watch The Vampire Diaries (Amelia's all-time favorite show). She considered the proposition for a minute, a full sixty seconds by Cheyenne's count, and held her blue-nailed hand out to Cheyenne. "You got yourself a deal, Anderson."

Cheyenne shook Amelia's hand in all seriousness and the two fished cookies out of the container. Amelia munched on a cookie while she thought up a good memory to share and Cheyenne rested her hand against the soft hair falling down the girl's back.

"She used to brush my hair every night after I'd take a bath," Amelia said quietly, looking straight ahead again. "I don't, like, remember watching her do it. Which is dumb, 'cause I guess it's not a memory."

"Keep going." Cheyenne rubbed Amelia's back affectionately. "Only if you want to."

"It's one of my favorite feelings. Like… like she would

hum and brush my hair for-ev-er. Dad doesn't do it right, but he's gotten really good at doing braids. She would brush and brush and brush and it just"—her eyes were brimmed red and her cheeks flushed—"I miss that so much."

"You don't have to share anymore, honey." Cheyenne smoothed Amelia's hair back from her dampening face. Amelia's words struck a chord in her as memories of the things she missed—the things Caleb had done for her, and with her, as a kid—came flooding in. The grief, still so raw, threatened to choke her. But Cheyenne did her best to swallow them down in order to comfort the sniffling pre-teen.

Amelia shrugged out from under Cheyenne's arm and hugged her knees to her chest. "Mommy was the best hair brusher. Ever," she concluded with a sniffle and pressed her cheek to her right knee, her head turned away from Cheyenne's.

"My mom used to brush my hair every morning before school—I got to shower in the morning and not at night 'cause my brothers liked night showers—and put them into these long, carrot-shaped braids," Cheyenne offered. "Which I loved. Until I was in second grade and we were reading Anne of Green Gables and Gilbert Blithe called Anne Shirley Cuthbert 'carrots.' And then I was carrots for, like, two years to all my classmates."

Amelia's watery giggle satisfied Cheyenne. "Did she still put your hair into braids?"

"She thought they looked cute. And insisted that I did not look like a carrot head." Cheyenne giggled herself. "But my Gramps got involved—he called us kids twice a week to talk and I told him how much it bothered me—so he helped me negotiate with Mom. We all agreed that twice a week instead of five times a week was perfectly acceptable for two braids." The negotiations had lasted for two days and had been the most adult conversation Cheyenne could remember having before the fifth grade. It was one of her favorite memories of Gramps, the man who'd always had her back when things got murky between her and her parents.

"I had lice when I was in the second grade. Dad had to shave my head." Amelia dramatically shuddered. "And Miles, who was like two, kept calling me 'brother' until it got to my ears. Brother! Yeesh!"

Cheyenne giggled with Amelia over that one, thinking about how easy it still was for Amelia to move on from one emotion to another. She couldn't remember the last time she'd been able to bounce back and forth so easily, and had to wonder if it was the charm of childhood or the precursors of adolescence, giving the girl a few more carefree moments. Her own storms as a child had been just as unpredictable, with her grandfather being the steady hand who was always able to temper them. Usually at the round table rock, just like she sat with Amelia.

"Gramps threatened to cut all my hair off one summer," Cheyenne said with a fond little chuckle. "I was about your age. Actually, I *was* your age."

Amelia looked at her in horror. "Why?"

"My mom complained to him that I wasn't taking care of it the right way when I stayed here. She was really big on the hundred strokes before bed thing—she didn't give up on me doing it until I turned fifteen." Cheyenne shuddered. "And my Gramps, well, he liked to push Mom's buttons. They got along pretty okay, but he loved to pick on her. So, she calls one night to make sure I'm brushing my hair, right? And Gramps goes 'Jeez, Lisa, if her hair is such a big concern for you then why don't we just chop it all off?' Stopped my mom mid-sentence." Her eyes were warm and she rubbed them with the back of her hand, not unsimilar to the motions Amelia had been making not long before. "No one could make Mom speechless like Gramps could."

Amelia chewed on her cheek for a moment before she spoke next. "Do you miss him?"

"Do I...? Well, yeah. I miss him like crazy." Cheyenne's voice caught. "I used to talk to him every day."

"I'm sorry he's dead." The eleven-year-old rested her head against Cheyenne's bicep. "But I'm not sorry you came here."

Cheyenne's throat felt unusually thick and hot. She swallowed down about eight responses, all to varying degrees of panic going off like a storm indicator in her brain, before she responded. "That's just because you really want to go to this picnic tomorrow," she teased. Against her arm, she could feel Amelia let out a soft giggle.

Jesse took the news of the picnic surprisingly well. Better than Cheyenne could have hoped for. The picnic itself wasn't a bad thing, especially with the light that came into Amelia's eyes when she told her father about their plans to go to it. But Jesse had a tendency to get a little tight-assed about things involving Amelia, especially things that he didn't entirely understand. For instance, he and Cheyenne had gone back and forth a couple of times about the drawing thing for school, even though Amelia had six years before she had to make a decision one way or another. In a steadfast moment, to combat Jesse's hardheadedness, Cheyenne had vowed, in front of Miles and Amelia, that she would be around in those six years to make sure Amelia got to go to school for what she felt most passionate about. Jesse had stormed out of the kitchen at that, but they had reconciled over a beer after Cheyenne helped put the kids to bed that night.

His papa-bear routine had a little to do with Mara dying when the kids were so young, Cheyenne was sure, and a lot to do with just not understanding teenage girls. Cheyenne saw a flicker of it cross his face, but he agreed to let Cheyenne take Amelia to the picnic the next day. Miles had more of an opinion on it, pouting and locking himself in his bedroom until Cheyenne promised they would have a Miles and Cheyenne only outing in the not-so-distant future.

24

The second storm that July came at the height of Penn Ridge's hot week. It was the hottest week on record in the last four summers, with temperatures dancing at around 105 for hours each day with little relief at night. The heat made everyone, especially the kids, angry. On Wednesday that week Cheyenne had the privilege of having Miles to herself for a few hours while Jesse took Amelia to a birthday party, one where he'd promised he'd stay the allotted time and help monitor the kids, as it was at an indoor waterpark. Miles had thrown a tantrum that lasted almost two days over not being able to tag along, but Jesse's understanding of Amelia needing alone time with him outmatched his desire to keep the six-year-old from finding creative ways to show his displeasure.

To counteract Miles' complete disdain for being left behind, Cheyenne had the brilliant idea that they would take advantage of the hot, sticky day to stay inside the air-conditioned house and repaint her bedroom. Jesse had advised against it, his rationale dancing between the fact that the hot day might make the paint tacky if she didn't keep the air conditioning on high and the reasoning that his son was not going to be pleasant for the task. Cheyenne had shushed him with a flirty and dismissive (even she had to admit, the words had come out of her mouth in a flirty flourish) claim that she knew what she was doing and they would be fine.

He'd tried to talk her out of it one more time before she'd left their house that morning with Miles strapped into the backseat of her Jeep. Within two hours she wished she'd listened to him.

Miles had been crabby when she'd picked him up, the early morning heat and the knowledge that he was on some lesser adventure keeping him keyed up. He'd given her a hard time when they stopped into the hardware store and she had to inform him that a candy bar was not going to cut it before noon. His tantrum was small, all quivering lips and whining that he was hungry, which she could only satiate with a stop by Sadie's and some pancakes before they made it back to the house.

His mood improved a little after he ate, enough that Cheyenne trusted him with helping her empty the things from her dresser and the little side tables. Of course, Miles could only carry a couple of small things at a time out of the room and into the hall. Still, Cheyenne made sure to give him ample praise for helping out. Miles beamed every time she thanked him, the smile on his face nearly stretching from ear to ear.

Cheyenne, enjoying the uptick in his otherwise sour mood, praised him in the way she could remember Anya and Riley praising her nieces and nephews. Warm smiles shot his way whenever he was looking at her, and even a few words of warm praise when he picked up something she wasn't sure he'd be able to carry. Miles preened whenever Cheyenne gave him a little bit of attention, which she found gratifying in a way that she wasn't sure if she liked or not.

However sunny Miles' mood was, he quickly grew bored of the task and adventured off to go do his own thing. Cheyenne left him to his own devices while she continued to paint. Luckily, Jesse had left her a small box of toys to keep Miles occupied when he was at the house, and he'd brought two handfuls of cars himself to play with.

Cheyenne spent the first hour of that hot morning painting the wall around her bedroom door, bopping to the music playing from the speaker of her phone in her back pocket. She'd been so engrossed in the work that she hadn't realized how many songs had slipped past her ears. The time on the screen of her phone, along with the title of the Arcade Fire song currently keeping her company, warned her that afternoon was fast approaching. Along with lunch time for the six-year-old who was somewhere in the house.

That was a weird thought, the six-year-old in the house. She shook her head and set the roller back into the paint tray, wiping the excess peach off on the hems of her shorts as she strode out of the room. The remainder of the house was quiet, the kind of unsettling quiet that creeps into an adult's bones when there's a child in its depths. Cheyenne's steps quickened as she peeked her head into each doorway on the second floor before darting down the stairs, her sneaker-clad feet thundering on the bare wood. She found him in the living room, gleefully watching a cartoon in the midst of chaos.

Miles looked the picture of innocence, snuggled under the caramel-colored couch blanket, two small metal cars fisted in his hands over the soft fabric, his eyes glued on the television screen. Prince was lying next to him, on his back, little paws in the air as he snored happily. Miles' dark hair stuck up at odd angles from what looked like a rough play session and his eyes were the soft, wide round-ness that made Cheyenne melt like baking chocolate. But her living room around him was less serene—the storm had shattered its orderliness in favor of a child typhoon.

Somehow, the six-year-old had managed to get into her extensive DVD collection (years of hoarding movies with her grandfather had led to a seriously dedicated stack of oldies, new releases, and blockbuster classics) and turned them into fashionable carpet accessories. Cases and loose discs were strewn all over the floor, including a ramp-looking pile situated near the glass sliding doors that peeked out at the hot afternoon and the flower garden. She could tell, even from where she stood at the doorjamb of the room, that several were beyond the point of salvaging.

Her couch cushions—she wasn't sure if the one Miles was sitting on was a part of the melee—were either upturned, on the floor, or unzipped. And the cushion for her grandfather's easy chair was pushed up at a forty-five-degree angle, held up by stacks of books, with little metal cars sitting underneath it. One of her lamps was on its side and the sliding door had smeared, sticky fingerprints across it.

"Miles," Cheyenne said as calmly as she could manage, her voice reaching several octaves above where she normally spoke.

Miles looked up at her innocently, beaming a sunny smile that caused her to check her temper before she spoke.

"Whatcha doin'?" she forced with a smile.

"Cartoons," Miles said in his 'you should know this' voice.

"Why are all my DVDS on the floor, buddy?" Cheyenne asked calmly.

"My cars needed them." He was still unbothered.

Cheyenne worked out the annoyance teeming in her throat and strode through the living room to start scooping up DVDs and inspect the damage. Miles let out a screech when Cheyenne picked up the first and flew from the couch to pound his small fists, ineffectually, against her thigh.

"Chey, stop!" he wailed, fat tears already pouring down his cheek.

"Miles, we have to clean up," Cheyenne said softly and picked up a couple more.

The six-year-old screamed again, shrieking in a full-blown tantrum that had his face turning red. He dropped onto the floor and pounded his hands against the carpet while forcing himself to continue to cry so hard he coughed. Cheyenne watched in perplexity, her eyebrows furrowing together. Temper tantrums weren't her area of expertise, even with her own nieces and nephews. Which was why she only took Kyle and Calvin for summers, and even that had begun within the last two years. Tantrums, crocodile tears, and the ever-there need for constant comfort and validation were all out of her wheelhouse.

She frowned at the child, eventually putting the collected DVDs on the side table by the couch and walking out of the room entirely. Miles' crying stopped abruptly the minute she was out of sight and she busied herself with putting together the stuff for grilled cheese sandwiches. It was too hot outside to really take much pleasure in the gooey cheese and toasted bread, but Miles' love of dairy products had had her picking up different cheeses the night before.

The small frying pan was heating up, four slices of bread were perfectly lathered on one side with mayo, and she was thinly slicing cheese when Miles walked into the kitchen. His eyes were still red and puffy from his fit, and he looked like he was worried she was going to yell at him. He was fisting a little car in each hand and gnawing on his lower lip. Her heart swelled at the anxiousness in his dark eyes, and she stopped slicing cheese, crouching so that they could be eye-to-eye. "Hey, small fry," she said with a small smile, draping her arms over her knees.

Miles rubbed at his eyes with a little hiccup. "Hey." He was miserable.

"Are we done now?" Cheyenne asked and used the back of her hand to dry the tears off of his cheeks.

Miles shook his head, his lower lip giving a little quiver in response. "I was playing with those."

"They're not toys, kiddo." Cheyenne stood up and put the first slice of bread for his sandwich on the frying pan.

"How about a grilled cheese?" If she'd learned anything from watching her sisters-in-law deal with the kids, giving in to the storm of Miles' tantrum would only perpetuate his behavior. And it wasn't behavior Cheyenne was entirely convinced she was capable of handling. So, she moved on from the tantrum all together. If she ignored it long enough, it would go away.

Miles sniffled, slowly starting to perk up. "What kinda cheese?"

"Muenster and Monterey Jack." Cheyenne offered him a slice of cheese. "Then we'll play for a bit. I guess painting's kinda boring when you can't use the roller."

He beamed and took a big bite out of his cheese slice, his tantrum seemingly forgotten.

Cheyenne was filled with a new sense of appreciation for Miles. He, like his sister, had the ability to move on from life's inconveniences in a way that she envied and adored. "How about we eat them on the couch and watch cartoons?" She ruffled his hair and finished assembling his sandwich on the frying pan.

Miles' face lit up, and Cheyenne beamed back.

25

*J*esse let himself into the farmhouse when knocking didn't garner anyone's attention. The door was locked and, despite the sun's rapid descent behind the tree line, the house was dark. Cheyenne's Jeep was parked dutifully by the front door in the same spot she parked it every day. His hackles rose, concern flashing through his mind as he unlocked the door and stepped into the house. Concern turned into relief, and some bemusement, when he found Cheyenne and Miles asleep on the living room floor with a cartoon movie playing on the TV. His son was curled up in the woman's arms, his head resting on her arm and his small arms wrapped around the purple blanket draped over them. Cheyenne's head was propped against a small throw pillow and she was taking even breaths, her hair splayed out in a river of rust-colored waves. They looked the picture of peaceful, both snoring faintly, surrounded by the remnants of a train wreck.

Miles had done a number on her living room. There

were toys everywhere and a massive pile of what looked like DVDs by the sliding glass door. He frowned and raked his hands through his hair before kneeling down to nudge Cheyenne.

She opened her eyes slowly, making a soft sound in the back of her throat that sent a flush through his body. Her nose nuzzled against Miles' head and she blinked sleepily up at Jesse. "Mmm, hi." Her voice was heady with sleep.

Jesse swallowed hard but grinned. "Hey there. I see you guys got a whole lot done today."

Cheyenne smiled shyly and laid her head back on the couch cushion. "What time is it?"

"After six." Jesse checked his watch. "How long have you been asleep?"

"I think we put the movie on at five." Cheyenne freed her arm from Miles' head and sat up. Her hair fell around her face in a tangled mess and she smiled up at Jesse. "I'm sorry I let him fall asleep so late."

"Eh. He's a good sleeper." Jesse shrugged.

Cheyenne stood up carefully and tucked the blanket around Miles before the two adults made their way into the kitchen. "Do you want some coffee?"

Jesse shook his head. "I told Melia I was just grabbing Miles and coming right back. The party was fun but"—Jesse scratched the back of his neck and yawned—"she and I are pretty beat."

"Eleven-year-olds are wild." Cheyenne smiled at him, her eyes wrinkling at the corners.

"How was he today?"

"He was… well, he was…"

"He was…?" Jesse prompted, leaning against the island.

Cheyenne gave a snort. "He was a six-year-old who did not want to paint, as his father had made really clear and as I had intended to ignore."

"How much painting did you get done?"

"Come see for yourself."

He followed her upstairs to her bedroom and nearly burst out laughing at the sight of the one pristinely painted wall and the tarps draped over all of her furniture and the majority of the hardwood floor. There was one little matchbox truck sitting on a paint tarp over her dresser, evidence that his son had, at one point, been in the room. "You got so much done," Jesse burst out, his throat making a weird, choking sound as he tried to swallow down the laughter.

Cheyenne gave him a scathing look. "I was a little busy entertaining your son."

"I… told… you." He couldn't stop the laughter.

Her dark eyes flashed at him and it was all he could do not to cry in amusement.

"I'm sorry… I'm sorry…" Jesse chuckled while Cheyenne's mouth fought to twitch up itself.

"Why're you laughin'?"

Jesse turned to see his son, hair sticking up in all directions from his nap and his cheeks flushed with sleep and hotness, looking up at him in perplexity. "I'm just picking on Cheyenne."

"Don't pick on Chey," Miles grumbled, padding over to the frowning woman.

Jesse's laughter subsided as he watched Cheyenne

reach down to run a hand over his hair affectionately and reassure him that Jesse was only messing around. Had it really only been a little over a month and a half since she'd looked at his son for the first time and turned ashen at having to interact with him? He didn't know that his son and daughter were charming the woman just as much, if not more, than he himself had been. He also didn't know, although there was a little part of the back of his brain that could nag on the thought if he let it, that Cheyenne was already holding a large space in his children's hearts that had been left vacant since Mara had disappeared from their lives.

Jesse's attention was on Cheyenne, trying to wrap his head around the way her face had lit up when she'd held Miles and how he'd slept soundly in her lap for the rest of their time at the house. He tried to help Cheyenne and Miles clean up the mess his son had made, but he wasn't paying enough attention to not just end up in the way. So he sat on the couch, with a cup of sweet tea she'd insisted he needed, and watched the redhead play and clean up with his younger child, his brain so very confused. He was still in shell shock when Miles tugged at his hand, begging him to go home and eat pizza with Amelia.

Cheyenne walked them to the truck and chatted with Miles while Jesse robotically buckled him in. He couldn't remember the last time he'd spoken—not since her bedroom, he thought—even when she waved and loudly said goodbye to him and backed toward her porch. He got into the truck to Miles chattering about all the fun he and Cheyenne had had that day and looked at his son in the rearview mirror. Miles was beaming, his dark eyes alight with joy, and he looked like the pleased little boy Jesse loved so dearly. Jesse made up his mind in that moment and grunted to his son that he'd be back before he yanked open the truck door and jumped out.

"Cheyenne!" Jesse jogged up to the porch to catch the woman before she could fully make it back into the house.

Cheyenne turned and gave him a teasing smile. "Did we decide we wanted to speak?"

"Go to dinner with me." Jesse said the words in a rush, looking almost pained.

"What?" She tilted her head to the right, her lips stunned into a soft 'o.'

"Not the kids. Just me. Go to dinner with me."

"Jesse, I…"

"Just… say yes." He looked back at the truck and then back at her, his face forming into a grin. "We've had dinner like two dozen times already. So just say yes."

She nodded yes and his grin broadened.

"I'll text you," he promised before jogging back to the truck, a little hop in his step. He couldn't remember the last time he'd felt so light, or so out of his league. But he'd be damned if he didn't grin like a moron the entire way home.

GO TO DINNER WITH ME.
    We've had dinner like two dozen times.

Not the kids. Just me.

Cheyenne replayed Jesse's sweet, shy question about fifty times in her head, standing just inside the door to the farmhouse long after the truck had driven away. She wasn't groggy from her late afternoon nap with Miles anymore, nor was she frustrated over the lack of painting she'd gotten done. Instead, she was bouncing on the balls of her feet and peeking out the window until she was beyond sure that the Tacoma was gone. Then she grabbed Prince, her keys, and her phone and all but flew to Roxanne and Maverick's.

The words tumbled out of her mouth the moment Roxanne opened the door, too big to keep a secret. Roxanne and Wesley always gave her a hard time when she got too excited, too chatty, but this was something she needed to be excited and chatty about. And, without missing a beat, Roxanne met her confusion with the same myriad of emotions on her face.

"I told you he was into her," Maverick called from the living room couch. He followed this up with a groan and the smash of his thumbs against the buttons on his PlayStation controller. "Damn it, Wes," he groaned into his headset.

She could only imagine what Wesley was saying on the other end.

Roxanne rolled her eyes at Maverick. "Children," she said.

"You're marrying him," Cheyenne said pointedly, looking down at her best friend's engagement ring. In a little less than five months, Roxanne would no longer be a Wortham but a Sterling.

"You slept with the other one," Roxanne said in a low mumble, wearing a vibrant red smirk that Cheyenne couldn't help but shrink from.

"Shh! Not too loud!" Cheyenne hissed. She could easily forget the weird fading and swaying of her relationship past, especially the one drunk indiscretion with Wesley what felt like a thousand years ago, until she got Roxanne's knowing—sometimes a little snotty—looks or comments about it in passing.

"So… you're really going to go to dinner with him?" Roxanne pulled a bottle of wine out of the fridge and reached for two glasses off of the hanging rack.

"I am." Cheyenne drummed her fingers on the island's surface. "I mean, I would be okay with going to dinner with him and the kids, but yeah… yeah, we're going by ourselves."

Roxanne's mouth pinched into a tight triangular scowl. She poured herself and Cheyenne nearly full glasses and gestured for her friend to follow her out into the backyard. The two women sat around the glass patio table, chilled glasses of wine in hand, and looked at each other. Prince waited until Cheyenne was sitting to scramble up into her lap and rest his small head in the crook of Cheyenne's arm.

Cheyenne, so used to being the meddling one, felt a prickle in the back of her neck from the look on her best friend's face. She wondered if this was how Roxanne had felt when Cheyenne had, very firmly, implanted herself into her relationship the year before. Cheyenne prided herself on being the biggest reason Maverick and Roxanne were getting married in five months, despite all of the meddling Wesley had done on Maverick's end. It felt weird sitting and waiting for Roxanne to hand back to her the same level of interference she'd given out so many times over the twenty years they'd known each other. That didn't happen often.

"Are you sure you want to do this?" Roxanne asked finally. Her bright blue eyes looked just as uncomfortable with the role reversal as Cheyenne felt. They sat deep in her lightly bronze face, narrowed at the corners in the embedded formation of the laugh lines that were starting to take shape.

Cheyenne frowned. "Why wouldn't I want to?"

Roxanne raised a perfectly shaped eyebrow. "Do I really have to state the obvious?"

"Humor me."

"The kids."

"What about them?"

Roxanne stopped mid-sip, her breath fogging the glass rim. "They exist?"

"They're good kids. You know that." Cheyenne toyed with a string on the hem of her shirt. "And I really enjoy spending time with them," she said earnestly. It hadn't taken long for the two of them to embed themselves into her daily routine in such a way that she didn't think she could clearly remember what life had been like before.

"There's no arguing Miles and Amelia are really great." Roxanne smiled reassuringly, patting Cheyenne's knee. "But dating Jesse means dating them, Chey."

Cheyenne's eyebrows knit together. "You hear how that sounds, right?"

Roxanne rolled her eyes. "You know what I mean.

You're already taking them a few days a week, making them dinner, helping out with birthday parties? You're spending so much time with them. What are they going to do when you and Jesse break up?"

"What do you mean, 'when'?"

"I mean when, you know, you inevitably… I mean when you guys just stop seeing each other."

Cheyenne bristled. She knew exactly what Roxanne meant. Her track record with relationships was a disaster zone, even with William, and they had been together for a while. Probably her longest-standing relationship since high school. "Until I mess it up?" she asked dryly.

"Chey, you know that's not what I—"

"That is what you mean." Cheyenne set her glass down.

There hadn't been a thought in her mind about her messing things up since she'd first met Jesse and the kids. No momentary pause to take into account the wreckage of her failed love life, no second thoughts on spending dinners with the kids, running errands with them, or even just hanging out with them at their houses. Messing things up just wasn't an option. Subconsciously she'd known that; she must have recognized that getting this involved meant that there was going to be no easy way out.

And, as she sat there for a second and thought about it, she didn't want a way out. Not from the kids—and, quite possibly, not from Jesse, either.

"I know that the kids make things different for me." Cheyenne looked up at Roxanne. "I love spending time with them. I mean, I'm still learning what to, like, do with them. Like today, Miles threw a complete tantrum 'cause I started to clean up this awful mess he made with my DVDs"—she chuckled, thinking about the mess all over her house—"and I just had to leave him alone."

"You what?" Concern flashed in Roxanne's eyes.

"I just let him cry on the living room floor while I started making lunch." Cheyenne shrugged. "He stopped crying."

Roxanne shook her head. "Okay, well, you like the kids. Awesome. They're great kids. But, again, what happens when you and Jesse break up?"

"If we break up. If we become anything at all. These are all ifs, Rox. Big, huge ifs. Ifs that don't even matter because he's cute and he's smart… and he," Cheyenne bit her lip, "He's an adult. Like… I don't know. I don't know if there's even anything here." She fiddled with her thumbs, staring at Roxanne. "Don't I deserve to at least find out?"

"Like you deserved to find out what Wes is like in bed?" Roxanne cocked her head to the side.

Cheyenne's face turned red. "Excuse me?" she managed to croak out, indignant.

Roxanne's face clearly read that she wished she hasn't opened her mouth even as she cleared her throat to continue the thought. "I'm just saying. Your past record with guys isn't super great, and like, especially with Wes, your friend. You bail when things get serious."

Cheyenne got to her feet, standing up hard enough to knock the chair back onto its back. "Fuck off, Roxanne," she seethed, storming into the house. "Thank you, Rox. For being there. It's nice to see how much my being at your beck and call for the last twenty years has meant to you."

Cheyenne stormed through the house, her lips curling back from her teeth in a bid to stop the frustrated tears from flowing down her cheeks. Prince ran after her, her emotions causing the little dog to yip at her ankles and try to catch her fingers to play, as if playing would solve it. Maverick stood up when she tripped over their glass patio door, his headset still on. "Hold up, Wes," he mumbled and dropped the controller and headset on the couch. "Chey!"

Cheyenne didn't stop until she made it to the Cherokee, blandly aware of Maverick's painful-looking hobble-jog as he tried to keep up with her. His leg hadn't healed entirely correctly, and the fact that he'd run after her sparked a surge of guilt in her chest.

"Go back inside," she told him as kindly as she could while ripping open the Cherokee's driver side door.

"Chey." Maverick nudged the door closed and cocked his head to the side. "What happened?"

"Your fiancée is a bitch," Cheyenne snapped.

Maverick's lips twitched. "What'd she do?" His dark eyes showed concern and a little bemusement.

Cheyenne's shoulders slumped under his steady gaze. "I don't wanna talk about it, Rick. I just wanna go home."

Maverick shook his head, his scraggly curls bouncing with the action. "Nope. Speak."

Cheyenne looked over his shoulder to where Roxanne was standing in the front door of their house, fretting with the hem of her t-shirt. Her anger, as quickly as it had risen through her, tempered down to something that bugged her like a gnat. Doubt. The obvious acknowledgement that Roxanne had spoken some truth—that the kids did change everything and that Cheyenne, if she did what she did in all relationships, could hurt everyone—sat on the tip of her tongue. "Let me cut your hair and I'll tell you."

Maverick balked. He hadn't even let her trim his hair after her grandfather had passed, and that had been something she'd desperately wanted in those first few days. It had been something to cling to. Now, as a matter of principle, she was upset enough that she was sure the only thing to make her feel better would be using scissors against his dark curls.

He looked between Cheyenne and Roxanne helplessly, throwing his hands in the air. "This better not be a conspiracy," he grumbled and shook his head, caving.

Cheyenne gave Roxanne a sour look and followed Maverick inside. The dark-haired woman at least looked guilty, even if it didn't make Cheyenne feel any better.

It only took a few minutes for Maverick to get set up with the small scissors that were a part of his shaving kit at the kitchen island. Roxanne was standing by the sink, sulking over a glass of wine while Cheyenne began to slowly trim the hair around Maverick's ears. The two women took turns filling him in on the story.

"Cheyenne isn't going to mess it up."

Cheyenne didn't stop her snipping, watching satisfactory little curls of dark hair drop onto their pale hardwood kitchen floor. "Cheyenne is well aware of that," she murmured. "Roxanne, on the other hand, doesn't seem to be."

"Roxanne is just trying to look out for your best interests," Roxanne groused. "Something you are incapable of doing yourself."

"By telling me I'm going to screw up something that could be really, really great?"

"By telling you to be careful. She's worried about you," Maverick said quickly, shooting his fiancée a warning look.

"Being a busybody doesn't look good on you, Rox," Cheyenne snorted.

The brunette snarled quietly. "Nope. It's much more your color."

Cheyenne's jaw locked. "At least I don't run away from things," she snapped, her temper boiling over.

"No. You just sleep with everyone under the sun and somehow manage to crack them," Roxanne threw back, throwing her hands in the air.

Her words halted the entire fight, sinking into the atmosphere as a look of recognition, and horror, crossed her face. Cheyenne gummed at her cheek, her fingers tight around a lock of Maverick's hair. Roxanne's words stung, but more than anything, they felt red hot in the pit of her stomach. Cheyenne knew exactly what her friend had meant and, while the harsh words weren't to be taken in all their spite, it was hard for her to move past them.

"Chey." Roxanne ran her hands over her curls as if she didn't know what to do with them.

Cheyenne shook her head, finally letting her hand drop from Maverick's uneven hair. "Too far, Rox," she said primly.

"I know. That was rotten. *I* am rotten."

"Yup."

"Do you wanna cut my hair next? I'll let you hack it all

off. Hell, I'll go get Rick's razor and you can shave my head."

Cheyenne's tips twitched. The image of Roxanne near-bald was a priceless memory, a much younger version of her friend cursed with lice in their pre-teens soothing some of the sting in her harsh words. Cheyenne shook her head at Roxanne and began to snip away at Maverick's hair again.

"I mean it."

"Where's my wine?" Cheyenne asked finally, ignoring Roxanne's words.

"Gross and warm outside. I'll get you a new glass." Roxanne scurried around the island, her shoulders still tense with guilt. Prince barked at the rushing woman from where he lay coiled around Cheyenne's left foot.

"One for me, too, please. And a little snack for Mr. Pupper." Maverick dropped his hands and craned his neck to look up at Cheyenne. "So, are you and Mr. Dad actually going on a date?"

"Yeah. Yeah, we are." Cheyenne couldn't contain the grin.

Maverick grinned back at her, upside down and huge. "Well, good. You've dated a ton of garbage. It's time for something good."

26

That night, after she'd crawled into the bed in the closest guest room to her own, Jesse texted her to set up a plan for their dinner date. His virtual company was nice, especially since she'd been having some difficulty falling asleep in the room down the hall. Luckily, she'd be done painting in the morning and could hopefully move back into her bedroom the next evening.

Jesse's schedule was tight due to the kids not being in school, and the first several dates they proposed fell short. After some negotiating, and two reminders they'd said no kids, she and Jesse agreed on the following Thursday night. Then, with nothing else to really do, the pair stayed up until after midnight.

Cheyenne couldn't remember the last time she'd felt so giddy, or so pleasant, talking to a guy into the early hours of the morning. Jesse had a sense of humor, one that she'd seen in little bursts and nods around the kids, that slipped out more and more the later it got. He'd started with well-scripted texts, ones that she was sure took too long for his large thumbs to tap out, and dissolved into quick, witty responses when long, well-thought-out answers weren't necessary. Cheyenne's favorite messages, the ones she'd end up rereading throughout the next couple days until she saw him again, were the ones about their parents.

Jesse had brought it up.

Hey, I heard that you have 2 moms? Mel was telling me 'bout it the other day.

Cheyenne was snuggled underneath her quilt, eyelids starting to droop as the clock inched toward midnight, when the abrupt change in conversation caught her attention. *Kinda. My stepmom's been really great my entire life.*

Mel thinks that's really cool.

Before Cheyenne could respond, Jesse sent a second text that had her sitting up, sleep heavy on her eyelids, and reread twice.

Not super close with my parents anymore—my dad's really cool though, and my mom's a saint.

Yeah?

You'll have to meet them sometime.

Cheyenne felt giddy through her core. She sincerely hoped that she'd meet his parents someday, and that knowledge plowed her over. Cheyenne snuggled back into her blankets, clutching her phone tightly in both her hands, smiling like a fool into the darkness.

I can't wait, she tapped out and hit 'send.'

THE NIGHT of their first date, Cheyenne thought she was going to have a heart attack.

All of a sudden, she didn't have the right clothes. Oh, sure, she had clothes. Jeans with stains of unintelligible origin and t-shirts that were worn and fading. A couple of sweatshirts with sleeves that had permanent creases from being rolled up. Three dresses, one of which she had vowed to never wear again after her grandfather's funeral and two that were too formal for the mystery night Jesse had planned. None of it would cut it for her first date with the beautiful man on his way to get her. The beautiful man with the beautiful kids who made her feel things she wasn't sure she'd ever felt before with someone else.

Roxanne had been very little help. She'd mentioned the dress Cheyenne had worn to the wake, which immediately got shot down, and then suggested that maybe Cheyenne was putting too much thought into it. Cheyenne, while logically understanding that she was, without a doubt, putting too much thought into the outfit for the evening, had shut that thought process down. She was not putting too much thought into it; her outfit was going to mean a lot to… well… everything.

When Cheyenne had explained that to Roxanne, citing the fact that Roxanne had always been a hundred percent more interested in clothes and makeup than Cheyenne had ever been, her friend had hung up the call. She'd shown up twenty minutes later with two stuffed garment bags and a tote bag full of shoes. Her bright eyes were full of amusement, and she looked pleasantly down at her friend. "Help has arrived."

Cheyenne let Roxanne in with a sigh of relief. "How do I not have any clothes?" she whined.

"Nerves." Roxanne squeezed Cheyenne's shoulder. "Now come on," she beamed at her friend.

Cheyenne let Roxanne lead her up to her bedroom and drop the two bags on the bed. "Do you know where you guys are going?" her friend asked cheerfully.

"No idea. Somewhere in Scranton, I think." Cheyenne watched Roxanne unzip the first garment bag.

It was stuffed full of dresses of different colors, some with shorter skirts than Cheyenne had ever envisioned herself in, all of which with varying degrees of plunging necklines. Cheyenne skeptically picked through them, holding up a lacy blue number that Roxanne smirked at and that Cheyenne dumped, unceremoniously, onto the foot of the bed.

"I'm not wearing that."

Roxanne huffed out a breath before she opened the other bag. "I didn't think I was going to get you into something fun." She walked to the closet, making faces at the singular peach-colored wall facing Cheyenne's bed. "How about jeans and a blouse? Are the dark wash jeans clean?"

"Which pair?" Cheyenne made a mental note to finish the wall in the coming week.

"The skinny jeans."

"They should be hanging up."

Cheyenne sifted through the shirts in the garment bag while Roxanne dug around in her hanging clothes. "Hey, did you feel this nervous when you and Rick started dating?"

"I was sixteen," Roxanne called from the back of the closet. "I'm not sure I can remember that far back."

"I actually started sweating thinking about it earlier," Cheyenne told her friend.

Roxanne wiggled her eyebrows at her friend while she tugged out a pair of fitted jeans and a pair of tan ankle boots. "Grab the green blouse with the lace sleeves," she instructed and marched over to the vanity across the room from the closet door. "What are we doing with your hair?"

Cheyenne wiggled out of her leggings and debated switching her boy shorts for something a little more date-appropriate. "I was going to pull it up in a ponytail."

"Cheyenne, this is your first date with a hot, if slightly too well-adjusted, man. You cannot just 'pull up your hair.'" Roxanne rolled her eyes at her best friend and dug through the cabinet drawer by her legs. "Where's your wand?"

"Bathroom." Cheyenne bit her lip and dug through the underwear drawer in her dresser. "What do you think?" It felt mildly ridiculous to her to be debating whether or not black or nude lace was going to go with the green top that Roxanne had picked out for her. She couldn't remember the last time she'd put this much thought into any decision regarding her wardrobe. "You know, you're so lucky you don't have to date anymore."

Roxanne nodded at one of the two options Cheyenne held up and darted into the bathroom to grab the curling wand. "I mean, everything is only a little different now."

She plugged in the styling tool by the vanity and shrugged at Cheyenne's reflection while her friend changed. "Now, when I feel like dressing up, I have to lock him out of our bedroom so he can fully appreciate the finished look." She smiled, running her thumb over the setting in her engagement ring. "And if the date goes bad, we get out of the car at the same house."

Cheyenne laughed while buttoning the jeans. They definitely complimented her legs, the full curve of her hips and the definition, from hours at a time on her feet, of her calves before ending in a sweetly folded hem above her pale ankles. The pair was a favorite of hers for all the things they did for her figure. "Yeah, but like, you're not sweating over whether or not your panties match or if you're going to be over dressed or under dressed or if your heels are going to make you walk like a fool. He's already seen you in the granny panties and without makeup and all acne-faced and in sweats and—"

Roxanne laughed. "Chey, if Jesse gave a damn about any of that stuff, you wouldn't be going to dinner with him tonight. Now stop psyching yourself out." She handed Cheyenne the blouse. "He's coming to pick you up in an hour?"

Cheyenne nodded with a huff and slid the lacy green blouse on. "You do the hair, I'll do my face." She sat down in her vanity chair and swept her long red hair behind her shoulder for Roxanne's assistance.

The woman staring back at her in the oval mirror was almost unrecognizable. There was a flush to her rounded cheeks and excitement in her hazel eyes, and the hint of expectation that kept circling through her mind.

Cheyenne couldn't remember the last time she'd felt this excited for a date—or this hopeful in the beginning of a new relationship. But as she put on the little makeup she knew how to do well and listened to Roxanne give her customary first-date speech, Cheyenne let herself bask in the excitement that promised good things to come.

*H*e had shown up, as they'd agreed, at seven on the dot with a handful of white daisies, looking so good that both women had had to take a moment and steel themselves before Cheyenne could let him in. The man wore a snug pair of jeans himself, the kind that left nothing to the imagination in regards to any part of his lower half, and a black button-down shirt—completely buttoned—underneath a sports jacket. In place of his work boots were a pair of dress shoes. He cleaned up well, really well, even if the layer of dirt and dust that usually coated his arms and face by the time Cheyenne saw him every day were part of his charm.

Roxanne shot Cheyenne an encouraging look before she disappeared into the kitchen to leave the pair alone in the entrance. Cheyenne took a deep breath to steady the waves of excitement in the pit of her stomach and opened the door, standing back to smile up at the man. Despite her heeled boots, there was still a very noticeable five-inch difference between them.

"Hey." Jesse grinned down at her and thrust the flowers outward. "These, uh, these are for you."

"They're lovely." Cheyenne beamed up at Jesse and took the bouquet, burying her nose in the soft petals.

"Melia said you'd like them," Jesse offered meekly, scratching at the back of his neck. "Are you ready to go?"

"Oh. Sure. I'll, um, let me grab my bag." Cheyenne set the daisies down on the hall table in the hopes that Roxanne would see them on her way out and put them in water.

Jesse offered her his elbow so she could navigate down the drive to the truck, which he'd had to park behind Roxanne's compact car. "Is she watching us from the window?" he whispered good-naturedly to Cheyenne when he opened her door.

Cheyenne, fairly pink in the face from the feeling of his muscular arm under her hand, glanced over her shoulder in time to see Roxanne hastily shut the front door's white gauzy curtains. "Uhhum."

Jesse snorted but didn't say anything. Instead, he helped Cheyenne into the truck and closed her door. Cheyenne crossed her ankles underneath the dash, marveling at the insane amount of leg room the cabin of his truck allowed her. Or maybe she was just that short. She smiled at Jesse when he swung into the cab of the truck and put the key in the ignition.

"She's still watching," Jesse told her with a chuckle.

Cheyenne shrugged at her date and picked at a loose string on her thigh. "We're all a little… involved."

"'Involved'?" Jesse raised an eyebrow at Cheyenne before he did a K-turn out of the top of the drive.

"In… each other's lives." Cheyenne shrugged at him and picked at the string again. "Like… involved."

"We have a bit of a drive to get where we're going." Jesse guided the truck out of the driveway. "Tell me about it."

"It's nothing really remarkable. I've known Rox and the guys—you've met Maverick and Silas, Wesley's in Bethesda and Connor's in the military—for the majority of my life. I used to spend my summers here in NEPA, I'm sure my grandfather told you about that."

"He might have mentioned it."

"Roxanne and her parents used to live in that house right there." Cheyenne nodded at the two-story house they were just passing, smiling a little in fondness at the tire swing hanging from a worn rope attached to a girthy oak tree. "The first time I met Roxanne she was on that tire swing, and I was jealous because we didn't have a tire swing at the time."

Jesse laughed.

"So, I'm almost eight and riding my bike down the street, 'cause Gramps didn't care as long as I stayed on the road. And Roxanne's on this tire swing being pushed by this annoying little boy with black hair, and they're yelling at each other and laughing, and I wanted to play."

"And you went and played?"

"Damn straight. We got so caught up playing Cops and Robbers that Gramps had to come hunt me down. It was… wonderful." Cheyenne smiled, tapping her finger against the shamrock hanging just under the hollow of her throat. "Wesley and Connor's dad still lives on Anderson Creek. I met them later on. Ever since that summer we've all just kind of been there for each other. Ya know? Maybe a little too much at times."

"I'm not sure I'm following."

Cheyenne shrugged. "It's been, like, two decades of friendship. It's just hard to not have an opinion on things and not work our way into each other's business." Her eyes rolled at her reflection in the rearview mirror as she thought about the whole debacle the year before with Roxanne's then-boyfriend, Ethan.

Jesse looked at her blankly as the truck stopped at the last light out of Penn Ridge. "Cheyenne, I have a six-year-old who's easier to follow along with."

Cheyenne laughed at herself and shrugged. "I'm kind of a busybody, so when I'm dealing with Rox or the guys it's just... multiplied. But like for all six of us. Sometimes it feels like it can be a little too much."

"Like Roxanne pushing her face against the window to watch us drive away?"

"Exactly." Or like wedging herself in the middle of the whole mess between Roxanne and Maverick last fall. Although that had been done for the greater good. "Connor's the only one who hasn't succumbed to the overtly too-personal."

"Because he doesn't have frequent contact?"

Cheyenne's phone buzzed in her pocket. She woke the home screen to see a text message from Wesley popping across the screen. *How's the date?* His timing couldn't have been better.

"Exactly." She rolled her eyes and stuffed her phone deep into the brown sack bag that sat by her feet. "What are your friends like?"

"Honey, I've got kids. The only friends I have also have kids."

"Silas has a son and he still has us."

Jesse shrugged. "I fell out of touch with most of my childhood friends when Mara got sick. I had two kids to worry about, and that meant a lot of time spent organizing playdates and doctor's appointments and lunches for school. It also meant that I spent a lot of time chasing around after two human storms."

Her heart went out to the distress she heard in his voice. "No friends at all?"

"My business partner Tim is really great. We do friend things." Jesse shrugged.

Route 6 raced past them as he navigated the winding one-lane highway, reminding her of all the times she'd driven toward Scranton with Roxanne and the guys back when her biggest worry had been whether or not she had a pimple on her nose. It made Cheyenne smile to think of all those summer days, so far gone but not that far removed. She toyed with the charm on her necklace and cocked her head toward Jesse. While there hadn't been a time when she hadn't felt lucky with her friends in her life, she suddenly had the overwhelming urge to text each of them—Silas included—and let them know it. "Now that the kids are older," she said to her date, "maybe it's time to start making new friends?"

"I made a new friend." Jesse glanced over at her with a quick, disarming grin. "Now I'm taking her out to dinner."

Cheyenne's cheeks warmed.

Conversation drifted in a more even direction as they entered the Electric City. Jesse filled her in on Miles' escapades of the day and the most recent fight he'd gotten into with Amelia, and then, in turn, Cheyenne caught him up to speed on her triumph over Maverick's hair. They were lighter topics, heartier words revolving around the family and friends they held dearest. Jesse laughed warmly at the thought of her trimming the man's hair down and Cheyenne sympathized with the eleven-year-old's newest blight.

Jesse surprised her by taking her to a nice, lowly lit restaurant in the center of the small city, the kind with one of the area's only really nice hotels as its upper floors and a valet for the truck. He tucked his arm around her shoulders and guided her into the restaurant. While he didn't look like he quite belonged in the space, Jesse was definitely the most attractive person there.

Attractive and uneasy. He sat across from her at the small table they were guided to and made small talk with the waiter while Cheyenne leafed through the drink menu. She ordered a mojito and beamed at him, expecting him to relax his shoulders once their waiter had walked away. Instead, his shoulders stayed hunched in on themselves and he kept his gaze diverted at the menu. It dawned on her, in a way that she felt kind of stupid for not noticing it sooner, that the man was uncomfortable. He wasn't nervous, per se—no, he wouldn't be nervous when they had, as he had pointed out, had dinner together dozens of times by then. But the poor man was out of his element in the restaurant, in his nice shirt with the sleeves buttoned all the way down to his wrists. And, for all his dressed-up glory, the man was wearing a tie. He hadn't even worn a tie to her grandfather's will reading, and they'd been good friends. Jesse was so out of his element that this couldn't possibly count as a first date—she'd be lucky if she got the man to say two words to her while they sat and ate.

She put her menu down. "It's a little stuffy in here," she declared, looking up into his dark eyes with a smile. "Do you mind if we go somewhere less... formal?" With her left hand, she made a quick gesture around the restaurant, at all of the people in their nice clothes, and then at the two of them.

Jesse's face showed pure relief. "Please," he agreed with a nod.

The pair stood up and Jesse dropped two twenties on the table for their poor waiter, who hadn't even gotten back with their drink order. He then put his hand on the small of Cheyenne's back and the two of them walked out of the restaurant and into the still warm July night air. Cheyenne tried not to shiver, enjoying the solid heat the flat of his hand made pressed against her through the blouse's thin fabric, and was instantly grateful it was so hot outside still. That way, Jesse wouldn't be able to guess that the flush in her cheeks was from his touch and the thoughts running through her mind.

"I know a great little burger place." He grinned down at her. "It's in walking distance, and it's nice enough out that I think the walk'd be nice, but I think we might be a little overdressed." He dropped his hand from her back to gesture down to her ankle boots.

She wasn't having any of that. Cheyenne stuck her left hand in his right, squeezed its rough, calloused, deliciously masculine muscle lightly, and grinned. "Fuck it. Let's go."

She let Jesse lead, walking a half step ahead of her and entirely too slowly to match the pace of her in her shoes. He chatted, casually swinging their entwined hands gently, as if he didn't notice he was doing it. Cheyenne wasn't sure what it was about the simple act—the relaxation in his muscles, or the fact that he looked so pleased to be walking with her—yet she enjoyed every second of it. Even just touching him wasn't like what it had been with her previous affairs, including with William.

The burger place Jesse was taking her to was a little stand with a few outside tables and a line wrapping around the corner. It advertised the 'Best Walking Burger in NEPA' in neon yellow lettering backed by vibrant red over the ordering window. On top of the best burger, it boasted spectacular milkshakes and fries that would make a person weep. She and Jesse were the oldest two people in line waiting to order, with the man towering over the heads of all the kids in line before them, enjoying the last few days of their summer vacation.

"Do you take the kids here a lot?" Cheyenne looked up at Jesse, who had dropped her hand to place his arm around her shoulders again.

"Amelia and I come here sometimes when I've got to run pickups and stuff out here. Miles is a little too young to handle the drive and behave."

"It's cute."

"Mara told me about this place when she and I first started dating. Mitch used to take her here every Friday night in the summer."

"Gramps wasn't a big fan of Scranton. He always said it reminded him of what used to be."

"What does that even mean?"

Cheyenne shrugged while they stepped forward with the rest of the line. "With Gramps? Who knows."

"Mara got that way about the area sometimes too," Jesse said thoughtfully. "I don't understand it."

Cheyenne tried to keep her smile big. Of course, he was going to talk about his late wife; she wasn't sure why she'd expected anything less. It did smart her—bugged the hell out of her, actually—but she wasn't going to let the hurt get in the way of their pleasant evening.

Still simmering a little with jealousy, Cheyenne forced a smile on her face and continued on with their conversation. "I guess it's a NEPA thing. Wes is really bad about it, Rick and Connor not so much. And Roxanne's always been really… well… Roxanne-ish."

Jesse let out a snort. He'd met Roxanne and had a fair understanding of how the woman worked. Cheyenne smiled, a little broader, at the sound and inclined her head in his direction.

They ordered two burgers, a pile of fries, and two fountain sodas that were more syrup than carbonation. With their food in hand, Jesse led her to a small pocket park two blocks from the stand, nestled between two large gray stone buildings worn with age. She followed him toward the back corner and let him guide her around a sand pit where two little boys played in the end-of-day light with their parents nestled close by on a picnic blanket.

Jesse nestled his cup in a patch of grass and handed

her the container of fries before he shed his jacket, shifting his burger from one hand to the other in the process. Once the jacket was off and his burger was checked, Jesse draped his outer layer over the ground and settled down on a third of it.

"What are you doing?" Cheyenne laughed.

"We didn't bring a blanket." He patted the mostly vacant fabric next to him. "C'mon. Your burger's gonna get cold."

Cheyenne passed him the food in her hands and lowered herself, as gracefully as possible, onto the ground beside him. She made it, with only a little bit of contact from his arm to hers—a closeness she instantly wished she could have more of—and offered him a cheeky smile. Jesse's response was a cocked eyebrow and a monstrous bite of his burger.

They ate in a companionable silence while the little city breathed in the late summer evening all around them. Jesse made quick work of his burger, eating in the way that only men could, and seemed completely content to just be beside her. It briefly crossed her mind that his own thoughts could be wandering to any number of things, including Mara, but she let it go when she caught him smiling at her. His dark eyes glazed over in contentment and Cheyenne realized that they were in this moment together. Somehow, despite all of the baggage that had guided the two of them together, he was enjoying their quiet moment. That knowledge filled her with something warm and fairly fulfilling.

All around them, Scranton carried on its quiet evening routine. Teenagers walked past in shorts and flip-flops, laughing too loud and soaking up the sun, reminding her of summers spent crimping her hair while Roxanne tried to flatten hers and making the freckles her pale complexion warranted vibrant in her round face. Families scooted along, toddlers exploring the uneven sidewalks and pre-teens haranguing their parents for sleepovers or ice cream money. She wondered if Jesse missed his kids, seeing so many out with their parents in moments of what could only be described as white-collar bliss.

One family in particular passed by that reminded her so much of the life Jesse could have had that her heart ached. They were a young family—a mother, three blonde-haired children, and a husband tall enough to combat Wesley for height. The baby was young, less than a year, with her arms wrapped around her mother's neck and a content, drowsy smile on her cherubic face. A pre-teen, probably around Amelia's age, was bickering with the middle girl in a way that only sisters could manage. And the father, when he wasn't busy refereeing the argument between his two older children, gazed at their mother like the Earth rotated and stopped at her whim.

Cheyenne watched them meander past, then looked at Jesse, unsure of what she was expecting in his open face. She saw nothing but contemplation in his dark eyes. "What's up?" She adjusted the wrapper on her burger to take another bite.

"This is the first date I've been on since Mara," Jesse said after a moment, leaning back on his long arms, the inside of his right brushing dangerously close to her side. "That just kind of hit me."

Cheyenne raised an eyebrow, the image of the family that had just passed stuck in her mind.

Jesse frowned at her, his face briefly registering what she must be thinking. "No, don't get me wrong, I'm not sitting here thinking about my dead wife and eating dinner with you." He laughed nervously, shaking his head quickly. "I guess I just feel a little out of practice."

"Hm?"

"Like… when we're with the kids we never have a dull moment, but…" Jesse shrugged and inclined his head toward her. "I guess I've just forgotten what it's like to have an adult conversation with a beautiful woman that doesn't revolve around the weather, the kids, or the business." His grin was disarming.

Cheyenne found herself grinning back at him, her own face lighting up with pleasure at the simple compliment. "Well, you're lucky I do a lot of talking." She grinned and offered him the remaining quarter of her burger. It was hard to palate when he was looking at her like that.

"You're not hungry?" His brow furrowed. Usually, as they both knew, Cheyenne was capable of eating. Sweets, savory, salty, crunchy—she was a fan of it. But her food sat, largely untouched.

"I'm a little nervous," Cheyenne admitted with a laugh and leaned back on her arms, tilting her head back to catch a few rays of golden sun.

Jesse frowned down at her but didn't say anything.

When she opened her eyes, her own smile slipped into a frown. "What's up?" she asked, cocking her head to the side.

"Do you think we rely too much on the kids for

conversation?" Jesse asked her with a chuckle as he reached out to push a few stray hairs out of her glossed lips and behind her ears.

"Nah, I don't think so." Cheyenne shrugged. "They just make things more interesting sometimes." His palm brushed the tip of her nose when he retracted his hand, and the gesture coiled something in the bottom of her stomach.

Jesse shrugged and laid back in the grass completely, crossing his ankles. Cheyenne eased onto her back as well and the two of them looked up at the orange and pink sky. Jesse laid his hand over Cheyenne's until it entirely engulfed hers. "I need you to understand something," he said after a moment.

Anxiety pricked at the back of her neck. She felt like a child who had done something wrong and wasn't sure what to do. She turned her face to look at the side of his and arched an eyebrow. "What's up?"

"Whatever this is." Jesse squeezed her hand. "Whatever is happening right now. I am into it."

Cheyenne and Jesse made eye contact and he grinned. "Whatever we're kind of… or could possibly be. I'm in it, Cheyenne. And I need to know if you're into it, too."

A little flutter picked up in Cheyenne's stomach. The swell of emotions running up her throat caught her breath and paused her for a moment. "I'm here, aren't I?" Cheyenne looked back up at the sky, trying to play it cool.

Jesse sat up. "Me being in it means the kids are in it too. You know?"

"I know." She smiled up at him, the anxious pricks at

the back of her neck soothing themselves. "I love the kids."

Jesse leaned down, keeping eye contact with her until his breath touched her face. "They love you, too," he said, assured, before he pressed his lips to hers.

28

_____

*M*iles woke Amelia up by crashing through her bedroom door and body-slamming her into the mattress. Amelia woke up with a scream and nearly kicked her brother off of the bed. If she'd been any more awake she would have, with a clear conscience, thrown the boy off the bed just for the chance to do it without getting in trouble. However, in her sleep-ridden state she wrapped her arms around him to keep him safe and groaned.

"Miles," she grunted, rolling them onto their sides.

Her little brother wiggled out of her arms and sat upright, his hair sticking up in all directions and the sleeve of his striped pajamas twisted around his arm. "Chey is here!" Miles informed her excitedly.

Amelia made a little noise in the back of her throat and rolled away from Miles. "Is she taking you some-where?" She yawned against her pillow and tried to squeeze her eyes shut. There was barely any sunlight coming through her white curtains, meaning that it was not the time to be awake during summer vacation.

"She's in Daddy's room." Miles shrugged. "They're sleeping."

Amelia bolted upright and pushed her blanket off. "Nu-uh."

Miles waited impatiently while she slid her feet into her monkey slippers. "C'mon, c'mon, c'mon." He grabbed her hand and tried his hardest to drag her out of the bedroom.

Amelia let him guide her down the hallway, his hands gripping her fingers. They both peered through the crack in their dad's open door. Sure enough, Cheyenne was asleep next to their father on his bed, wrapped in his blankets. Amelia stepped back from the door, her eyebrows furrowing and her heart doing some sort of weird beating in its cavity.

"What does this mean?" she asked Miles, even though, at six years old, there was no way he would be able to answer.

When Molly's mom got remarried, Arthur, her step-dad, had started sleeping in her mother's room. But Cheyenne had told her that they were 'taking it one day at a time,' whatever that was supposed to mean. Amelia scratched her head and pushed past Miles into the bedroom.

Jesse, a heavy sleeper, didn't so much as budge, but Cheyenne slowly opened her eyes. "Mmm?" She sat up and rubbed her eyes. Amelia was grateful that her friend —Cheyenne had become her best friend in the last couple of months—was fully dressed. Her eyes, which were a pretty color that Amelia was unjustifiably envious of, widened when she saw the kids standing in the doorway, staring at her. "Oh!"

"Hi," Amelia said carefully. She was angry—she couldn't place why she was angry, but she was angry. So angry that her eyes felt hot and wet.

"Hey…" Cheyenne didn't look guilty, maybe just a little confused. She carefully got out of bed, so as not to disturb their dad, and offered her hand to Amelia. "Hey, let's go make some breakfast?" She didn't use the 'sad-kid' voice that she took on with Miles, but it still didn't sound like she was talking to Amelia on the adult level.

Amelia rolled her eyes at the woman. Cheyenne was unkempt, her hair a mess and her clothes wrinkled, and she looked… different. Amelia couldn't put her finger on what exactly was different, but something was. And she didn't like it.

The two stared at each other, Cheyenne waiting for a response and Amelia fighting the urge to break into tears, an odd sense of betrayal siting in her stomach. It struck her, so hard she almost gasped, that Cheyenne was probably just hanging out with her and Miles to get to Jesse. Or worse, that Jesse would ruin the friendship she had struck up with Cheyenne. Neither option was good—and both felt to her like they could be very real in that moment. "I'm not hungry," she muttered and turned to head back to her bedroom.

"Melia." Cheyenne didn't raise her voice, but she did adjust the pitch.

Amelia looked over her shoulder at the woman who

she'd thought was her friend but now wasn't entirely sure about. "What?"

"Please." Cheyenne looked so small. She'd hunched her shoulders in and was looking at Amelia much in the same way that Amelia had seen Miles do on occasion when he knew he'd done something wrong.

It put Amelia off-kilter to see the woman look so guilty. Still... she could find some reassurance in the fact that Cheyenne did in fact look guilty. Amelia found herself shrugging and, at a loss for what to do with her hands, crossing her arms over her chest. "Whatever," she muttered and followed Cheyenne and Miles down the hall toward the kitchen.

CHEYENNE HADN'T MEANT to stay the night.

After they got home from dinner to Carol, who had had dinner with the kids and then passed them back to Jesse and Cheyenne with a skeptical smile at the hand-holding adults, she'd stayed for some coffee and board games with the kids. An hour stay turned into a three-hour Monopoly game that was postponed rather than won when Miles fell asleep on the table. And then, after both kids had been tucked into bed, she and Jesse had sat in the den talking over a bottle of wine and a little laughter.

Their conversation had drifted from heavy topics, like

when to tell the kids that things were more than just friendship between them, to lighter things, like how Jesse had learned to fish when he was drunk with his friends or how Cheyenne had had to make cookies with a melon baller for six months before she landed the perfect size. Jesse hadn't acted like the simple fact that Cheyenne's anecdotes revolved around baking bothered him—in fact, he'd pressed for questions about her favorite recipes and the things she had the hardest time making—and Cheyenne found that, when he talked about the business, his whole face lit up.

A bottle of wine and some soft, staid conversation later, Cheyenne had fallen asleep on the comfort of the couch. Where she'd slept when Mitch had had his heart attack. Where she felt comfortable sleeping in the house.

And somehow she had woken up in his bed. With his two kids staring at her, Amelia looking like she'd had her heart broken or her favorite toy taken away from her in one instant. It hurt—it felt like a blow to the chest to see the betrayal on the eleven-year-old's face. Cheyenne had been honest with Amelia when she'd asked her what was happening between her and their father, but she hadn't realized how hard the child would take things.

In the end, the kids got guilt pancakes, stuffed so full of chocolate they were almost fifty-fifty batter and baker's milk chocolate. In addition to the pancakes, they got fresh-squeezed orange juice—done by hand—and whipped cream in place of the low-sugar syrup that she knew Jesse usually used for them.

Miles was in sweets heaven, his eyes all but glazed over and excited the entire time they ate. Amelia hardly did more than stab the pancakes with her fork, her eyes never leaving Cheyenne's face. Cheyenne felt that the stabs were intended for her.

"Amelia, look," Cheyenne started, after she'd poured her second cup of coffee of the morning.

She sat down next to Amelia at the table and sent Miles off to play.

Once they were alone, the eleven-year-old looked at her with expectant eyes. Cheyenne had never realized it before but the darkness in them, the deep brown that mixed with a light hazel, looked so much more grown up than Cheyenne thought her own face, or Roxanne's, had ever looked at eleven.

"Your dad and I went on a date last night," Cheyenne started and took a long swallow of coffee. "And we're gonna be doing that a lot more often."

"I knew you were going on a date," Amelia scoffed. "Dad sat me down and asked me if that would be okay."

"Is it okay?"

Amelia frowned at her pancakes. "Are you gonna leave if you and Dad don't wanna date anymore?" she asked after a few moments of thought.

Cheyenne shook her head and put her hand on Amelia's wrist. "Honey." She squeezed the girl. "I would never just leave. No matter what happens between me and your dad now, I am not going anywhere." When Amelia looked up at her, she smiled as warmly as she could manage and gave the girl's arm another squeeze. "You are stuck with me for the rest of your life, Amelia Grace."

Amelia held out her pinky. "So, we just take things one day at a time?"

Cheyenne hooked their pinkies. "No. Your dad and I take things one day at a time. You and me, kid? We've got a bakery to finish decorating."

Amelia looked at her skeptically but took a bite of pancake and nodded.

29

*J*esse stood on the steps of Carol and Mitch's farmhouse, feeling the same knot of apprehension in his gut as he had the first time Mara had brought him home for the holidays. Miles held his hand tightly and kept looking between his father and the front door expectantly. It was Tuesday, which Miles marked as the day that he and his grandmother usually made jam.

"Are you okay, Daddy?" Miles squeezed his fingers.

"Yeah, buddy, why wouldn't I be?" Jesse looked down at his son with an affectionate, tense smile.

"We gotta go inside," Miles told him firmly.

Jesse scratched the back of his head with his free hand before he sighed and bent to untie his boots. "Shoes off," he instructed.

Miles unvelcroed his running shoes and kicked them off. Jesse opened the door to let him in and then neatly set their shoes off to the side of the frame. Inside, his son screamed a hello at his grandmother and audibly launched himself at her legs. Jesse forced a smile onto his face, feeling a sinking feeling in the pit of his stomach when he passed Mara's picture on the wall. He stopped, as he always did, and touched the bottom of the frame with his fingertips, hoping that she, of all people, would understand what he was about to tell her mother.

Carol was listening to Miles talk about his day and measuring coffee grinds into a filter when Jesse finally made his way into the kitchen. The guilt sat in the bottom of his stomach and only curdled when his mother-in-law turned to smile at him.

"Hey." Jesse stooped to kiss her cheek. "Where's Mitch?"

"Outside in the garage." After looking at Jesse, she gave Miles a nudge toward the back of the kitchen. "Can you go get your grandpa?"

Miles ran toward the back door, stopping only to put on his mud boots, before he slammed the door behind him. Once they were alone, Carol dumped water into the coffee maker, flipped its switch, and dropped down into a kitchen table chair. Without a word, Jesse took the cue from her and sat down as well.

"What's on your mind, Jess?" Carol asked, resting her chin on her palm.

"I'd rather wait for Mitch to get here too." Jesse tapped his finger on the table surface and jiggled his foot simultaneously.

Carol's lips twitched in a motherly smile. Seeing the man anxious, in all his burly sense of self, only reminded Carol of the young man he'd been when Mara had first brought him into their lives. "Does it have to do with Cheyenne?"

Jesse raised an eyebrow but didn't say anything right away. Carol's mother's intuition had always been strong, and it had decidedly chosen to encompass Jesse as well after he and Mara had started dating. "It does," he finally answered uneasily.

"I heard." Carol got up to pour cups of coffee. Her voice was flat.

Jesse's stomach curdled again, bile racing up from his stomach. "I… heard…?" He shook his head and forced his hands through his hair. It was getting long. Needed a cut. Probably wouldn't worry about it for a few weeks—especially since the business always got swamped with work in July. Cheyenne was also taking up time that he could have allotted toward getting his hair cut. Maybe she'd offer to do it. Her fingers through his hair had his pulse racing in his ears, only slightly faster than it had been resting.

Carol's face was smiling when she turned back to him, even it was a little forced at the edges. "She's been attending Ladies Auxiliary meetings with me," Carol said and set a mug down in front of him. "The hens in the Auxiliary adore her. So naturally… when Hester's husband saw the two of you kissing in Scranton last week after you took her for a 'thank you' meal… well, we kind of put two and two together." Carol's teasing voice did nothing to alleviate the knot at the base of Jesse's stomach. It didn't help that he could see, behind the mask of happiness, the hesitation and the hurt lingering in her gaze.

Jesse took a long swallow of hot coffee, the bitterness of the black beans burning their way down his sternum. He winced and set the mug on the table. It didn't sit well with him, the idea that she would fake a smile for him, fake happiness for him getting on with her life, when she was still grieving the loss of her daughter. Jesse didn't want her to think for a second that he was trying to replace Mara, but this was neither the time nor the place for that particular conversation.

Mitch let himself into the house with Miles hanging off of his arm, kicking his feet when Mitch raised it enough so that he hung like a little monkey. "Why does the boy look like he's going to hurl?" Mitch asked Carol and planted a kiss on his wife's head.

"He's trying to tell us that he's got a girlfriend." Carol held her mug out to Mitch and took Miles into a hug.

Mitch gave Jesse a knowing look and sat down in the chair at the head of the table. "It's about time," he said without any of the sadness lurking in his wife's eyes. "Don't you think, Miles?" he asked his grandson with a chuck under the chin.

"Yes," Miles said, unconcerned, eyeing the cookie jar by the sink.

30

There was something refreshing about being on the open road. Cheyenne found solace in the open lanes of highway stretching from Penn Ridge to Albany, periodically broken up by little towns and the occasional mill from the area's industrial past. On her trips back and forth that summer, she'd found that the alone time it provided her was somehow more refreshing than the time she spent alone in the Retirement House. Maybe it was the fact that she was used to being alone in the car rather than the large farmhouse. Or maybe it was because, on every other trip she'd taken back, the empty road and monotony of keeping her hands firm on the steering wheel had provided her with the perfect excuse to think about Jesse. And all of the things she felt awkward thinking about when she was within driving distance of him.

This trip was different, though. There was nothing to obsess over, nothing to wonder over, nothing to worry herself over. She and Jesse had gone there—gone past where she could have thought, could have *hoped*, the relationship would go—and it kind of sucked leaving him behind. Even though she was only going to be away for the night, the idea of not seeing him, and not seeing the kids, had given her reason to pout when she first got into the Cherokee.

Jesse had seen her off. He'd arrived at the house a little after seven that morning and had inevitably delayed her departure, for reasons that put a blush on her face, for over an hour. When she finally wiggled her way out of his embrace, lips a little swollen, and climbed into the Jeep, her blood was coursing and she couldn't quite wipe the smile off of her face. Mornings with Jesse, she was quickly learning, were just as amazing as nights with him.

"Are you sure you don't want company?" He'd leaned through her window to try and steal a kiss, a mischievous grin on his face.

"You can't go with me," Cheyenne had laughed. "Besides, if you come, then who's going to watch Prince?"

The little dog was staring at her with his big brown eyes from the little dog run that Jesse had set up for him in the side yard. She wasn't a fan of tying him up outside, but that morning he'd been a terror and had tried, several times, to best his small stature and jump into the vehicle. He was indignant, his head cocked to the side and his tail still for the longest she'd ever seen. The sight was enough to tug at her heartstrings.

"Carol and Mitch wouldn't mind." Jesse's voice tugged her attention away from her little dog. "And he loves Mitch."

She'd laughed, leaned through the window, and given

him a lingering kiss. "Uh-huh. Do not feed my dog any human food, Jesse Kaiser."

His returning kiss, and the wave he'd given her—Prince in his arms—when she backed the Jeep into a K-turn kept her company for the drive.

Cheyenne was still smiling over it when she pulled into one of the three staff parking spots behind A Taste of Celeste at a little after eleven. She parked beside Margo's orange Audi and leaned her head back against the seat. So much had changed since her last visit to the shop—her entire world taking on a new spin in the span of two weeks. The small (or what she'd thought was small) crush she'd been harboring had blossomed into a full-on relationship. The moody teenager she'd found fascinating was quickly becoming an astounding confidant and a fixture in her life. The little boy that perplexed her was warming up to her, and she to him. The life she'd left in Albany only a few months before was so far from the life that she was now living, the woman in her rearview mirror so different from the woman who had first opened the bakery.

Margo met her at the back door with a squeal and a hug when she finally dragged herself out of the Jeep. "Hello!"

"Hey," Cheyenne laughed and returned the hug. "It smells delicious in there."

"Doesn't it? I'm trying that apple crumpet recipe you sent over." Margo stepped back and ushered Cheyenne inside. "How is the new place looking?"

"Good. Jesse and his guys are doing an amazing job. And Amelia found this really funky color for the walls in the bathroom that I'm kind of in love with." Cheyenne looked around the familiar kitchen, the pride of her young life's work, with a sense of satisfaction. Not a single thing was out of place; nothing that Cheyenne had painstakingly installed, purchased, and loved looked off. Returning to the kitchen was like returning home. "It feels amazing to be back."

"It's amazing to have you back." Margo beamed at her boss. "Do you want to look at the books or do you want to have a cup of coffee first?"

"Coffee, please." Cheyenne left Margo to fix their coffees and let herself into the tiny back office of the bakery.

Margo had made the place a little more homelike for herself, including putting two framed pictures of her and Rob, her fiancé, on the corner desk by the computer screen. Cheyenne's usual mess of papers and folders had been neatly rearranged and joined by a giant yellow binder. Despite her additions, Margo had left Cheyenne's personal touches in place, including the wall of pictures Cheyenne had collected over the years in front of the desk. Among them sat one she'd never thought too much about, having seen it nearly every day (because one doesn't really have days off when they own their own business) for years. It sat proudly over the computer monitor in a turquoise frame and beamed back at her with the proud faces of herself and her grandfather.

Cheyenne dropped her purse on the desk and leaned forward to inspect the picture, a pulse of sadness thumping in her chest. In the picture, Caleb had his arm around Cheyenne's shoulders while she held a neon sign reading 'Now Open' with an earsplitting grin on her face. The picture had been taken on the day she'd opened A Taste of Celeste, and it had been the first one she'd put up in her cozy little office. It was the only copy of the picture she had.

Cheyenne took the picture off the wall and sat at the desk chair, staring at her grandfather's proud smile. All the joy she'd felt that morning came to a shuddering halt around her, outweighed by the pressure of missing the man who'd inspired the woman she had become. "Ah, Gramps," she muttered, stowing the picture, frame and all, in her purse to take back with her. The space on the wall looked weirdly empty, unsettled by the disturbance its missing placeholder caused, until Cheyenne took one of the pictures Margo had put out and used the nail in the wall to support it.

"It looks weird," Margo said from the doorway. "I can take the pictures out if you want."

Cheyenne looked over her shoulder and shook her head. "Nah. I told you to make yourself comfortable. Besides, it's nice… knowing that you're making this space your own."

"Just until you come back." Margo dragged one of the kitchen stools into the office before she passed Cheyenne a mug of coffee.

"Ah." Cheyenne wrapped her fingers around the lavender-colored mug and inhaled the steam rolling off of it. "I'm probably not going to be coming back. Not permanently, anyway," she said with a sense of certainty that had felt so elusive in weeks past.

"The house?" Margo took a sip from her mug and

lifted a ledger out of the bottom drawer of the filing cabinet next to the desk.

"Mhmm. Among other things."

Margo had caught the little hitch in Cheyenne's voice over 'things' and paused before she opened the ledger. "The handyman?"

Cheyenne bristled at the teasing. "His name is Jesse." Her defensiveness gave way to the warm, almost unsettling feeling Jesse gave her. "And... possibly. At least, partially."

"'Cause that makes sense."

"Mhmm. Let me see that ledger."

"Are you seeing the handyman now?"

"Jesse."

"Are you seeing Jesse now?"

"May I please see the ledger."

"Can you answer my question, please?"

"Yes. Now, ledger."

Margo smiled but didn't say a word. She held the ledger out to her. "We've had a busy couple of weeks. Lots of fruit tarts."

"I saw on the spreadsheet. Do you think you need more help?"

"Maybe one more part-time person. We're not usually busy during the day, but more so once the schools start to let out for the day."

Cheyenne nodded and grabbed a pen from the desk drawer. "Thinking a college student or an older high schooler, then?"

"Whatever you think would be best." Margo sipped her coffee and crossed one of her legs over the other.

Cheyenne smiled and shook her head. "No, Margo, this isn't one of those 'whatever Cheyenne thinks is best' situations. This is your bakery now... well... in a round-about way. You get to have some say in who gets to work here. Especially since they'll be working for you—even if I'm the one who signs their paychecks."

"I'd prefer a college student, then. More flexibility in their schedules."

"Sounds good. I'll write up a job posting and put it on a couple of those job-hunting sites."

"How are your brothers and the kids doing?"

"They're doing... okay. Chester's new baby is almost due, so he's on edge. And CJ's just himself. The kids and I send each other Snapchats that let me see what they've been up to, so that's pretty cool."

"Do they have a name yet?"

"Nope. They're just going to wait and see what it looks like when it comes out."

Margo nodded slowly. "Okay. Well, whatever makes them happy."

Cheyenne snorted. "Now. How is Jonathan doing?"

"Drama boy, as always."

The two women shared a laugh and a clink of coffee cups before they dove into Jonathan's love life and the shop's ledger. The conversation was nice, normal. One of the first conversations that she'd had since her grandfather's passing that didn't revolve around the house, the wedding, or her new relationship. Cheyenne savored it, as much as she savored the company of her friend and the familiarity of her first business.

I CAN'T WAIT to see you tomorrow.

Cheyenne couldn't fight the smile that Jesse's text had caused as she shuffled out of the bakery a couple of hours later, after helping Margo close down, on her way to find dinner. While she'd planned on spending the night with Margo and Rob, she hadn't been included in their cozy dinner reservations—not that she'd necessarily wanted to be. That had given her two hours to explore the small city a little bit and find a place to have a bite. Her old city, which she found that she didn't miss as much as she thought she would when she'd left.

Some of that might have had to do with the sexy man texting her, telling her that he missed her.

Cheyenne was tapping a message out to him, echoing his excitement, when she all but crashed into another person on the sidewalk. "Oh! I'm so sorry."

"It's okay. Are you o—Cheyenne?"

Her head jerked up and she found herself staring into William's big brown eyes. He was wearing glasses, thick black frames that obscured his sharp cheekbones and prominent brow, and he was dressed for work. "William?"

"Hey. It's good to see that you're, ya know, alive." He grinned. "Did you get any of my texts? Or my calls?"

"Mhmm. You bet I got them all." Cheyenne stuffed her phone in her bag, text message half finished, and pushed a sweep of red hair behind her shoulder. "Good to see you. Now, if you'll excuse me." She stepped around him, determined to not fidget with the hem of her shirt or the strap of her purse in an effort to not show him her nerves.

"What are you doing back in town? Are you back?" William whirled around to get back in her path.

Cheyenne shook her head. "No, I'm not back. I come up every couple of weeks to check on the bakery and Margo and Jonathan." She had no idea why she was standing on the sidewalk, wasting time talking to him.

"Ah. Well. How long are you in town for?"

"Tonight. Now, if you'll excuse me." Cheyenne stepped around him again, this time making a push to get a few steps away from him.

"Let me take you to dinner," he called after her.

"Excuse me?" She whirled around, her hair flying around her face.

"Dinner. Ya know. Food. We'll go to City Line. Have a drink, have a bite. Catch up?"

"And why would I go to dinner with you, William?"

"Because, at the very least, we were friends at one point."

"We're way past that now, aren't we?"

"Look, I know how I treated you wasn't fair. How I reacted wasn't fair. Let me just… let me take you to dinner."

Cheyenne shook her head. "I can't." She fiddled with the strap of her purse before pulling out her cell phone, unconsciously checking to see if she had any missed texts. "I'm… well… I'm seeing someone." Just thinking of Jesse put a little flutter in her chest.

William raised an eyebrow. He stuck his tongue in his cheek, as if he was trying to say something, before he clapped his hands together. "That's… fine. Dinner between friends."

Cheyenne chewed on her lower lip. "I mean. I'll buy my own dinner. But I don't see why not." She finished her text message to Jesse and, for the sake of not feeling guilty later, added that she was going to dinner with a friend. She didn't think Jesse would make her feel bad for having dinner with William, but she knew herself and knew how twisted her dating history was. "I'll meet you there?"

"Sure. Sure."

As Cheyenne climbed in to the Jeep, she kicked herself for not just saying no to the invitation and leaving it at that. She didn't owe William anything; he was the one who had ended their relationship, for crying out loud! It wasn't as if she needed closure, and she and William hadn't ever been the best conversationalists when together. But Cheyenne had never been good on the spot.

She cranked the key in the ignition and gave herself another mental scolding before pulling out of the parking spot.

CITY LINE HAD ALWAYS BEEN one of her favorite restaurants. The ambience was always nice, soothing without being overly gentle, and it had a way of easing her nerves after a long week. She and William were seated at a table in the front of the restaurant, surrounded by the rush of people having quiet dinners. Cheyenne was thankful for the conversation around them, because she and William had done nothing but stare at each other over their menus and do a lot of not-talking.

Their waitress had only broken the uncomfortable silence long enough to take their drink orders and drop off their cocktails. Cheyenne couldn't blame her. The scowl on William's face mixed with her own unease was enough to ward anyone away.

Cheyenne set her menu down with a flop and scowled at William, crossing her arms over her chest. She needed to say something to break the silence before she got up and walked out. "You know it was your idea to have dinner, right?"

"I'm still digesting," William snorted.

"'Digesting'? What do you have to digest?" Cheyenne rolled her eyes.

William shrugged. "I just think it's weird."

"What is?"

"That you went to Pennsylvania to take care of your grandfather's house and have ended up in a relationship already."

Cheyenne bristled. "You chose to end our relationship, William. Do you not remember that?"

"Yeah. Because you were about to have a lot on your plate. Your grandfather had just died. I didn't expect you to have the time for a relationship."

"I didn't. I don't, really. I'm opening a new business and I'm still coming to terms with the lot of it. But these things just... happen." Cheyenne shook her head at herself. She wasn't ashamed of her relationship with Jesse;

she was on the far side of shame, and she wasn't going to let William make her feel that way. "Jesse is… well, he's amazing. And he treats me like, well, like I'm amazing too. And he's been there while I've been going through all of this. And he has these two amazing kids." Cheyenne felt herself smiling. "They're amazing."

"'Kids'?" William took a long drink of his cocktail to cover the snort. "Cheyenne, in case you forgot, you don't like kids."

"I don't dislike kids. They don't like me. And I've just never had a lot of time with them. Amelia and Miles make it so easy to be with them. They're… they're great." Cheyenne fished her phone out of her purse and swiped through until she found a smiling picture of both kids.

They were sitting on her porch, each with an arm around Prince, and laughing at some cheesy joke Jesse had just yelled out from the bed of her grandfather's truck. She showed him the picture with a proud smile on her face. "I adopted a puppy, too. His name is Prince."

William leaned over the table to examine the picture. "You've become an entirely different person," he marveled.

Cheyenne's smile dropped. "Is that a bad thing?" She was indignant. "I'm happy and I'm settl-"

"Shh, shh. I'm not saying it's a bad thing. You just… you didn't smile this much before. And now you have this big smile and this weird new family and a dog. It's… weird. It's like you've been abducted by an alien and they replaced you with this happier version of yourself."

"I was happy before."

"You were never this happy with me."

Cheyenne sat back in her chair and frowned at him, thinking over what he was saying. Of course, she'd noticed a change in herself over the last few weeks, but she'd put that down to losing her grandfather. To the move. To all of the new things in her life. Even, to some extent, to Jesse. But to think that he'd given her so much to smile over, so much to change for. Talking to William, she was starting to see all of the positive little changes that he was pointing out. And she couldn't fight the smile on her face—even if it was crazy, and a little irrational, that she'd only known Jesse for a few months and he was already turning her life upside down.

"I... no. I don't think I was," she said finally, honestly, running a hand through her hair. "And that's nothing against you, William. We just... we didn't click."

"Not like I had hoped we would." He sighed and patted her hand resting on the table.

"I can go if this is too... I don't know... painful or annoying." Cheyenne started to gather her purse, ready to leave.

"No, no. Sit. I really do want to catch up. Even if it means hearing about your new... friend." William gave her a more relaxed smile and picked his menu back up. "But we should probably order first."

31

*C*heyenne's life fell into the kind of peace that she'd always wondered about. She'd read about it in books, watched it on the screen, had even gotten to witness it with several of her best friends in the entire world. She'd designed cakes for it, helped be a part of days that were monuments to it, and had even gotten to watch both of her brothers find it. The peace that she'd been sure would elude her for the rest of her life—a side effect of her not knowing whether or not she actually wanted a life with kids, or a life she shared with another person— had crept up on her and entirely changed her life.

Summer was drawing to a close, and with it was fast approaching the end of Cheyenne's first summer in the Retirement House without her grandfather. In that time, she'd managed to fall in love with two wonderful children, start seeing an amazing man, and work through some of the feelings that had conflicted her since Caleb had passed away.

Amelia had played a big part in that. She and

Cheyenne spent a lot of time together that summer. Whether it was working in the bakery, which Amelia gladly did almost every weekday, or hanging out in the house with both kids and Jesse, Cheyenne was willing to talk about missing her grandfather, and about all of the changes she wanted to make to his house to make it feel more like her own. Her father had encouraged her to do more than paint the bedroom and put knickknacks up, insistent that changing some features in the house would make it feel like home and, as weird as it sounded to Cheyenne, help his father find some peace. She also found that talking to Amelia about missing Mara and Caleb had helped a lot with the process—and had made her more willing to open up to CJ and Chester about their shared loss.

Amelia's perspective on the world was so refreshing, especially when she and Cheyenne set their heads together and talked about those loved ones they missed. The tween gave Cheyenne a new perspective on a lot of things, including her own grief.

Cheyenne still felt like Caleb lingered around the house sometimes, especially on the nights when Jesse and the kids didn't stay over. But she had an easier time talking about him. And her anger had started to ebb, slowly, into acceptance. It didn't hurt that she was able to spend the time that she'd have spent with him that summer with her little tribe.

And, to top off the couple of weeks of existence that had surrounded her and Jesse and the kids, Cheyenne thought that she might be falling in love.

That realization had bowled her over like a ton of

bricks, knocking her nearly onto her back in surprise, in the most unexpected way.

Cheyenne had made the decision to add more space to the garden in the beginning of August. The inkling hit her when she and Amelia were in Penn Ridge's only home improvement store looking for some screws for Jesse and wandered across some rose bushes. Amelia was delighted by the colorful petals and had puppy-dog-eyed Cheyenne until she agreed to bring some home and plant them. Neither home was specifically named, but the look of understanding she exchanged with Amelia made it clear that they meant the Retirement House.

To make room for Amelia's roses, though, Cheyenne needed to expand the fenced-in area that was her grandmother's garden and uproot some of the ground. It was more than a one-person job, but luckily her new boyfriend was surprisingly good with his hands.

Jesse came over the second Friday in August after dropping the kids off at around eight in the morning to Cheyenne standing on the porch already with two bags of fertilizer, three of the rose bushes that Amelia had picked out, and enough extra wood to expand the fence. She couldn't fight the grin that spread across her when she saw his truck pulling up next to her Cherokee, or the little laugh of delight when he held her latte up in triumph.

"Good morning," she called out, pushing her sleeves back over her wrists. "Is that for me?"

Jesse grinned, carrying two cardboard cups with him to the porch. "No. They're both for me." He leaned down to give her a kiss, his prickly five o'clock shadow tickling her lips. "I decided I really enjoy caramel lattes."

Cheyenne rolled her eyes and snatched the cup out of his hand. "Are you ready to get started?"

"Can I enjoy my coffee first?" Jesse laughed, locking his arm around her lower back. "And maybe another five seconds with you before you put me to work."

Cheyenne leaned into him and took a long swallow of her latte. "No, 'cause this is gonna be a long job and I don't wanna be out here all day. It's supposed to be muggy."

"It's the north tip of Pennsylvania in the summer. Of course it's going to be muggy." Jesse dropped his arm from around Cheyenne and propped his cup on the porch railing. "C'mon, you."

Cheyenne had very little planting experience. Even when she was a kid, working with her grandfather in the beautiful garden almost every day of every summer, her green thumb stretched as far as being able to weed without pulling out vital parts of the flowers. Caleb had used to make fun of her for her inability to bring new life out of dirt—especially after it became clear that she did have talent in other ways.

Luckily, Jesse had enough green in his thumb for both of them. He instructed Cheyenne on how to turn the dirt to aerate it and helped her settle the roots of each bush, using the calm and gentle voice that reminded Cheyenne of her grandfather. Jesse also labored over expanding the fence around the garden, a nitpicky request from Cheyenne because she'd insisted Amelia's bushes be a part of the main garden. Jesse's patience was astounding—he was able to explain the process to her without losing his cool or getting frustrated, something that Cheyenne appreciated—but the main draw for her was the way she'd catch him smiling at her. Whenever he thought she wasn't looking, he'd steal a glance her way, like a schoolboy with his first crush. Every time Cheyenne caught him, she'd feel a flutter in her chest and laugh at herself.

Cheyenne paused, in the middle of burying the roots of the third rose bush, to admire the sweat rolling down Jesse's face as the midmorning sun toasted her plot of land and gave him a wicked grin. "We should paint the fence," she called out as she hunched back over to finish moving dirt over the roots.

"What do you mean 'we' should?" Jesse stopped tapping in the last stake of the fence.

"I don't remember the last time Gramps had this painted." Cheyenne smiled fondly at the memory of her grandfather admonishing her efforts to paint the fence. He had much preferred to work with the flowers than their perimeter. "I mean, I think I have some white paint in the basement." She coughed at the swell of sadness in her throat, and at the image of Caleb standing where Jesse was staring at her. It still struck her as alarming, how the waves of sadness, of grief, still crashed into her when she least expected them. Cheyenne straightened up and pushed her hands into her lower back. "I'm gonna go grab it." She grinned at him and made her way to the porch.

"Nu-uh. You want this painted, you can do it yourself," he called after her, but she was already disappearing into the house.

It only took a few minutes of digging around in the basement, which was slowly becoming a mix of Amelia's project space and Cheyenne's overflow from her minor house improvements, for her to procure the almost-full can of white paint and two brushes. The simple white would help her summer flowers pop and would make the garden look all the more appealing. Especially when Amelia's roses began to bloom.

Cheyenne carried the bucket and brushes outside, beaming in triumph. The find, and the mental image of the roses in bloom against the white backdrop, lifted her frustrated spirits. She didn't like that there was dirt underneath her fingernails instead of flour, or that she'd have to spend another hour outside at the least when the recipe for the cinnamon rice cake she'd found that morning was digging at her mind. But she really wanted the white fence.

Jesse hadn't moved from where she'd left him. He was standing by the recently expanded fence, his arms folded over his chest.

Cheyenne did her best to not skip over to him, holding her find out proudly. "Ready?"

"I told you, you can do it yourself," Jesse groused.

Cheyenne rolled her eyes at his grumpiness and set the can of paint down by the fence. "Can you at least open the can for me?"

"You know this is interior paint, right?" Jesse fished his truck keys out of his pocket and used one to pry the lid off the can of paint.

Cheyenne shrugged. "Paint is paint." She dipped the tip of her paintbrush in the can.

Jesse let himself out of the garden and dropped onto the grass. Cheyenne busied herself with painting a small section of the fence, humming to herself while he lay and stared up at the clouds.

They passed the mid-morning in the companionable silence. Jesse wasn't in a rush to get on to any other projects, the idea of his girl doing a passion project nearby keeping him satiated. Cheyenne continued to work, her thoughts alternating between the rice cake recipe and the fact that she and Jesse had completed a project together. It was a nice feeling, to know that he wasn't that far off from where she was and that if she needed his help he'd be right there. She briefly wondered if Roxanne ever felt that way, then had to kick herself mentally to stop it. Comparing her relationship to her best friend's wasn't fair to anyone, and the circumstances revolving around them were entirely different.

Cheyenne worked her away around the fence, applying only a light coat of white paint in order to make the can last. She only got done a third of the one side, the older, fading white coming alive with the fresh coat over it. With her can almost empty, and a satisfied cramp forming in her lower back from the work, Cheyenne made her way out of the garden to where Jesse was dozing.

At some point, Jesse had pulled his hat down over his face to hide it from the sun and had crossed his arms behind his head. With the light from the almost-noon sun hanging over his long, taut body, and the grass nestling around him, he looked so much like a magazine cover—or the cover of an evocative novel—that it left Cheyenne breathless. She paused a few feet away, looking down at him in awe.

Something settled over her, warm and kind of gooey on the inside, that left her feeling solid through and through. Cheyenne took it in for a moment, thinking about the man lying in front of her and the way she'd read characters feeling in books for most of her life, and had to giggle.

"I'm turning into a ball of mush," Cheyenne laughed at herself and eased down onto the grass beside Jesse.

"You are a ball of mush," Jesse mumbled without moving.

Cheyenne, completely forgetting about the paintbrush in her hand, rested her head against his shoulder and propped her hand on his abdomen. Paintbrush and all.

Jesse didn't move at first, seeming to enjoy her body pressed against his, until the dampness from the leftover paint on the brush seeped through his shirt. Then he sprang up, dumping Cheyenne into the ground face first, and held his shirt out in front of him. The white spot on his shirt stood out on the dark fabric.

Cheyenne sat up and giggled so hard she snorted. "I'm so sorry," she hiccupped out, covering her face with both of her hands.

Jesse fought a grin as he crouched down so that Cheyenne and he were face-to-face. "You will be." He picked the paintbrush up out of the grass and ran the tip of it down Cheyenne's face, from her forehead to the tip of her chin.

Cheyenne shrieked out a laugh and scrambled to get away from him. Jesse snatched her waist and pulled her back onto him and onto the grass.

They lay in the grass, laughing, white paint smears spreading between them. Laughter that turned into soft kisses and a warm feeling tingling in Cheyenne from the top of her head to her toes.

Eventually, Jesse had to get up to leave. Cheyenne stayed in the grass and watched him collect his things, twirling a stand of her hair around her index finger.

Jesse stooped to kiss her goodbye. "We'll see you tonight," he said against her warm lips. "I love you."

Cheyenne balked at him, her eyes nearly bulging out of her head. Jesse just grinned and gave her forehead a kiss. "It's okay, you don't have to say anything. I'll give you a call when I pick the kids up from Carol and Mitch's."

He got up, not prompting any sort of response from the wide-eyed woman lying in the grass beneath him, and grinned.

And it took Cheyenne almost an hour to get back her feet. Partially because the warm sun felt really good on her skin and partially because she loved him, too.

32

Cheyenne was fitting into his life in an amazing way.

Jesse was amazed at how easily she'd fallen into the folds of his life, into the folds of his kids' lives, and into her own new life. He was amazed at how easily he'd fallen in love with her, and how easily that love had felt right. There were still moments where he had to stop and ask himself if the new relationship was something Mara would have resented or if he was doing the right thing for his children, but he was working through that. It didn't hurt that Cheyenne had gone out of her way to make his kids feel loved and welcome in her life.

Carol and Mitch had taken the relationship in stride, which had also made the transition easier for him and the kids. They had started inviting her to Sunday night family dinners and had gone out of their way to stop by the bakery at least once or twice a week to exchange the kids or chat with Cheyenne and the assistants she'd hired to help her. Mitch was also pulling Jesse aside every once in a while to check in and see how he was handling the change in his life.

Jesse thought that the almost bi-weekly check ins with his father-in-law weren't necessary, but he did find himself wondering about the adaptation. He'd gone nearly six years sleeping by himself, the bed empty beside him and the room perfectly quiet. Now he was spending half his week sleeping next to another warm, restless body that fell asleep every night watching TV at his place or listening to audiobooks at hers. Where he'd been used to enjoying weeknights without the kids once in a while with a beer and a book, he was now spending his childless nights hanging out with groups of people younger than him in loud, crowded places. Jesse had reprogrammed himself as a single dad without any real warning, and then he had thrown himself into the weird position of being a single dad in a new relationship with a woman he was crazy about.

More than just his personal life had changed with Cheyenne wandering into it. His kids were thriving, both of them adjusting to the new person in their lives, the new constant, and to having someone else they could lean on. It didn't hurt that, with Cheyenne, they had somehow ended up with five other adults to attend to their every whim. Especially her friend Wesley. He'd come up for a week and spent the entire time talking art school with his daughter and rolling around on the ground, and in the dirt, with his son.

Jesse was still amazed at it all. And found himself feeling more amazed every once in a while for what felt like no reason.

The most profound moment came not too long after the first time he'd told Cheyenne he loved her. They were sitting around Tim and Leah's dining room table, three-fourths of the party entertaining bottles of beer while the very pregnant Leah good-naturedly shot dirty glares around the table. Tim's very pregnant wife had been dying to spend one-on-one time with Cheyenne, but Jesse had been unable to oblige until now, especially when his goddaughter had nearly kicked out Leah's back while she was pitching the idea to him and Tim.

Cheyenne was entertaining Leah and Tim with a story about her bakery in Albany, reliving some highlights of memorable customers while Jesse finished his second beer of the night. Her hazel eyes beamed at him from across the table while she talked and waved her hands with emphasis. Leah was holding on to every word while Tim rubbed her belly. It was nice.

"I'm not sure why you ever let them back into the bakery," Leah giggled when Cheyenne was finished.

"They were good for business," Cheyenne giggled with her, shrugging her shoulders. "I learned shortly after I opened the bakery that it was customers like the Humphreys that were going to keep me in business. Especially where A Taste of Celeste was set up."

"We have a few of those." Tim shot Jesse a look. "Last year, we were working on this house off of Maple—the Adams'—the husband was remodeling the entire house for his wife for their tenth anniversary. Nice enough guy. Wife's a little high maintenance. We send a crew over there, Jesse does his on-site rounds because he's more the inside-the-house guy, and it's all good for the first two days."

Jesse let out a snort when Tim began his story, choosing to open the top on a third beer and let his friend take the lead. For now.

"Then, Mrs. Adams decides she doesn't like the specs that Jesse drew up for their new en suite bathroom. Which there was no room for, actually. Mr. Adams had discussed turning the guest bedroom next door into this giant bathroom so this woman didn't have to share with her kids, and we get the all clear and Jesse and the guys are already demolishing the wall between the two rooms, right? And this woman starts freaking out because we're taking away a bedroom." Tim rolled his eyes and reached for another beer from the center of the table. "Talking about resale value and getting rid of the house and all of this crap."

"Mind you, when this started, I'm standing in the middle of the wall between the bedroom and the soon-to-be bathroom," Jesse added. "I believe I was in the process of making the hole I was standing in bigger when she stormed in."

"What did you do?" Cheyenne asked him, her attention turned fully to him.

"Well, I put down my sledgehammer and I asked her what the matter was. And she starts going on and on and on about resale value. Like really giving me a hard time about how dare I demolish this bedroom that they don't use and do I know how much I'm ruining her house. It was an absolute headache."

Tim chuckled. "And then Mr. Adams calls me, telling

me that Jess is giving his wife a hard time and how dare we not know that his wife had her heart set on reselling the house even though he was having the house redone for her for their anniversary. Like, how are we supposed to know that you're paying all this money to completely renovate your house just so that you and your wife could sell it? Didn't tell us."

"And, by the end of the project, she loved the house so much they didn't end up reselling it at all. They still live there and we do their yard every other week in the summer." Jesse rubbed his face with both of his hands.

Cheyenne laughed. "I love that."

Leah rolled her eyes with a giggle. "You didn't have to deal with them while they were going through it. Trust me, you wouldn't have loved it."

Cheyenne rested her hand on top of Jesse's where it had landed on the table and smiled up at him, still giggling at his misfortune. "It's not as bad as having a bride change her wedding cake ten times the week before the wedding, but it's definitely not a fun time."

Jesse turned his hand over so that he could hold hers. "No, luckily if they change their mind the week before the renovation's done it usually means we get a contract extension." He grinned and leaned over the corner of the table to kiss her. "You can't really extend a wedding date."

"Nope. But you can shell out enough money for a wedding cake that the extras can be donated without it hurting the baker too much." Cheyenne smiled into his kiss.

It was one of the best feelings he'd ever known. It didn't equate to holding Amelia and Miles for the first time—which would forever be the best two moments of his entire life—but the soft smile that touched his lips could have buried him.

"How did you get into the baking business?" Tim broke in, taking the spotlight of their moment off of Jesse.

Jesse sent his friend a dirty look. Cheyenne squeezed his fingers, having caught the look, and smiled at Tim and his wife.

"When I was a kid, I used to spend every summer here with my grandfather. Actually, I did it every summer until I turned fourteen." Cheyenne smiled sadly. "When I was eleven, he found one of my grandmother's cookbooks in his attic. All handwritten recipes. And he gave it to me." Her smile softened and she reached for the pendent around her neck. She played with it whenever she was upset, a tell that Jesse was grateful for. He squeezed her fingers and she smiled at him. "He'd gotten me an Easy Bake Oven the year before for Christmas and I already played with that. But having her recipe book, all of her recipe books actually, there was a dozen of them, really solidified that I liked being in the kitchen.

"I'm not as good with savory food—I can make savory food, I can work my way around a saltshaker and a spice rack—but I really love baking. I love making sweet things that put a smile on people's faces." Cheyenne shrugged. "Gramps helped me go to culinary school so I could master my skills, and then I opened A Taste of Celeste."

"That's so sweet," Leah cooed, rubbing the side of her belly.

"My Gram was a sweet lady, from what they've told

me. I named my bakeries after her." Cheyenne opened her second beer of the night and settled back in her seat.

"That is so entirely adorable." Leah's face lit up. "I can only hope that my baby's babies love me as much." She cupped her swollen stomach with both of her hands.

"They will." Tim gazed at his wife with open adoration and kissed her on the cheek. "Our babies' babies will love you more than anything else in this entire world."

Jesse grinned and squeezed Cheyenne's hand again. The way he'd seen Tim look at his wife over the last four and a half years that they'd known each other often amazed him—but what amazed him right then and there was that the way Cheyenne was looking at him was similar to the open-eyed admiration Leah gave Tim. In that moment he was buried. Completely lost without a doubt.

Leah let out a hard yawn, her hand cupping her swollen belly from top to bottom. "I don't know about the three of you, but I could use a cup of coffee." She struggled to get up and gave her husband a dirty look when he opened his mouth to speak. "Decaf. I promise."

Cheyenne slid out of her chair, giving Jesse's hand a squeeze. "I could use some decaf," she said and followed Leah out of the room.

Tim waited until the girls left the room to lean across the table and wriggle his eyebrows at Jesse. "Leah loves her."

"I'd have to agree with Leah there," Jesse said happily, leaning back in his chair and crossing his ankles. "She's one great girl."

Tim raised his beer to Jesse. "I'll drink to that."

Jesse clinked his bottle against his friend's, completely bowled over. From the kitchen, he could hear Cheyenne and Leah laughing, and the beer was just enough to give a slight buzz to sweeten the evening. He was a lucky, lucky man.

33

*I*t was a dreary Thursday. Fat drops of rain had been falling steadily from the dark sky since dawn, splattering the earth with wetness and a certain melancholy that storms in the area were famous for provoking. Carol didn't mind the wetness, or the bleak way the sky loomed over her from the front seat of her car. Mornings like this reminded her of when she brought her daughter home from the hospital, lazy Sunday mornings with Mitch and Mara and coffee in bed, long afternoons in her kitchen, and cozy evenings with a book in her hands. When Mara had been growing up, Carol had reveled in rainy days because they meant her spitfire daughter was calm—calmer, anyway. They were a pause from her usual routine, from the constant running and planning and general existing that had come with her tenure as a stay-at-home mom.

Carol still didn't mind wet afternoons while being a grandmother. She loved the idea of a rainy day, where she and the kids would stay inside playing board games and catching up on the newest episodes of the kids' cartoons. Miles had never been a big fan of the rain. When he'd been a baby, no more than a year, Jesse had tried to get him to play in the mud while it drizzled outside. The child had screamed bloody murder for nearly an hour while Jesse, stricken with grief over hurting the kid, had hovered over him and Carol had watched. And laughed.

Miles stood on the porch of his friend Andrew's house now, wearing yellow rain boots and clutching his Tonka umbrella tightly in both hands. Carol smiled endearingly at the child, tapping her finger against the hollow of her throat as she sat in the car. Miles turned toward the driveway and caught sight of Carol in the van. His whole face lit up when he saw his grandma.

Carol couldn't help but beam back at the boy. She got out of the van and tugged her hood up. She met the child at the steps and looped an arm around him, giving his head a kiss. "Did you have a good time?" she cooed at her grandson with a squeeze before she straightened up to smile at Andrew's mother. "He was good?"

"As always." Kaylee smiled at Miles.

Miles beamed back up at Kaylee and wrapped his arms around his grandmother's leg. "Can we go home now?" He looked gravely at Andrew. "My stepmom is making lasagna for dinner tonight!" he boasted.

Carol stiffened, her fingers pausing through his dark hair. "Who is making lasagna?" she asked in her nicest voice.

"Chey!" Miles beamed up at her. "She's making lasagna for dinner for me and Daddy and Melia. We're gonna eat it in the dinner room 'cause Roxy and Rick are comin'."

Carol laughed weakly. "Kids," she said to Kaylee with a shrug and ruffled her grandson's hair.

She hadn't missed the look on Kaylee's face when Miles had said 'stepmom.' Carol knew that all of the moms in Jesse's circle thought it was a shame he was single—she'd heard the tsking at Auxiliary meetings and had seen the longing looks from the single moms who fraternized with Jesse at town events. Her son-in-law was attractive and smart, and she'd been beyond pleased when Mara had brought him home in her freshman year of college. But then her daughter had died and, as Carol knew, it'd changed his life forever.

When Carol roused herself from her thoughts, it was to make eye contact with Miles, who was staring up at her and giving her a skeptical frown. His big brown eyes showed a hint of worry, as they always did when his grandmother wasn't feeling well, and he nuzzled her cheek with his when he saw her looking at him. "I'd better get this little guy home," she said to Kaylee with a pleasant smile.

"Sure, sure." Kaylee's young face lit up in a smile itself, even as her eyes shone with curiosity. Carol was sure that, as soon as they left, Kaylee was going to let the news out that Jesse was pretty serious about Caleb Anderson's granddaughter. If Carol didn't douse the flames on that one fast, then all of Penn Ridge would be planning a wedding that was most definitely not going to happen.

"Are we still on for next Tuesday?" Kaylee was asking, oblivious to the concern in Carol's mind.

Carol's upper lip relaxed. "Of course. I'm going to need every hand possible to help get ready for the fair."

"We're gonna make pies!" Miles told Andrew proudly.

Andrew bounced up and down in his light-up sneakers, clapping his small hands together. "I love pies!"

The two little boys said goodbye to each other, making grand bows playfully and then rolling around with giggles erupting out of them. Carol collected her grandson and said a final goodbye to the young mother and her little guy before loading him into the van, thankful that the rain had let up enough that Miles wouldn't make a big deal out of it on his way from the porch to the vehicle.

Carol thought about what Miles had said to Kaylee the entire drive back to her house. Miles had no actual concept of what a stepmother was—he couldn't know the weight of the words he had used or see that there was no possible way for him to think about it that way. Miles chattered while she drove, talking about the lasagna he was supposed to have for dinner—which was a novelty, as Carol didn't cook with pasta often—and about the day of fun he'd had with his friend. The babble was easy for Carol to tune out in favor of the paranoid mantra running through her head.

She'd made up her mind to talk to Jesse about what Miles had said by the time she pulled the van into the driveway, parking it beside Jesse's truck. The man was standing in her front yard talking to her husband, his head thrown back in a laugh that proved he didn't see the enormity of their current situation.

Dating the girl had done good things for him—of course Carol, and everyone she knew, had been able to see that. He had color in his face, not just from the sun or the long hours he put in but color that animated him, made his dark eyes shine. He'd put on a little weight, too. Not the wrought muscle that Carol knew the young women in town admired, but the girth that Mitch had started to put on after Mara had been born. For the first time since Mara died, Jesse looked young again. Happy again. And that was wonderful. It was all she'd wanted for him for five years, to see him look as carefree as he did in the damp evening, standing with the love of her life and talking about something pointless to her but meaningful to them.

Yet, while she unbuckled her grandson, her eyes left on the young man, she was ashamed of the fact that there was no joy running through her. No maternal love at seeing him laugh with her husband, seeing him light up at the sight of his son tearing through the soggy grass, momentarily forgetting about his aversion to the wet, to throw himself around his father's legs. And not a single ounce of concern for anything but her daughter's memory as she tore across the yard and all but snapped at her little grandson to go inside. Miles looked at his grandmother in shock, his little face peeking out from around the leg of Jesse's jeans. "But—"

Jesse, frowning at Carol, ran his hand over the boy's head. "Go on, kiddo. Go get your bag and your yellow truck."

Miles squeezed a hard hug into Jesse's arm and ran to the house. The little brown head of hair skidded to a stop right before stepping into the threshold and kicking off his sneakers, remembering at the last second that he couldn't wear his shoes inside. He ran inside the house, the screen slapping shut with a loud clang.

"Jesse, I need to talk to you," Carol said tartly, running her thumb over the stone of her wedding ring.

"I got that. What's up, Ma?" He pushed his hand back over his head, knocking his hat loose.

Carol looked at her husband, silently hoping that he'd see her side and back her up. "You'll never guess what Miles said to Andrew and Kaylee today when I picked him up."

Jesse raised an eyebrow. Behind him, her husband crossed his arms across his chest with a look on his face that clearly read 'here we go.' At that moment, both of the men in her life made her so angry she saw a little bit of red at the corners.

"He told them that his 'stepmom' was making him dinner tonight," she said tartly.

Jesse's lips twitched and his shoulders gave a steady shake as he choked back a laugh. "Christ, Ma. I thought he said something bad."

"That is something bad." Carol jabbed her fingertip into his sternum. "He called Cheyenne his stepmother."

"He's six, Carol, he doesn't know what stepmother means," Mitch called out.

"Well, then, how could he have heard the word if he doesn't know what that means?" Carol pointed out, feeling a surge of annoyance and triumph. "Don't you think it's a little too soon for you to be telling my grandkids that this woman is going to be their stepmother?"

Jesse raised both his eyebrows at her. "Uh… I never told them any such thing? And I thought you liked Cheyenne."

Carol rolled her eyes. "It doesn't matter whether or not we like the girl. She's not their mother, Jesse."

"I know, Ma, I know," Jesse said placatingly at the escalation in her voice. "I'll talk to them about it. I swear."

"Do you know, Jesse?"

Jesse looked stricken. "Of course I know, Carol!"

Carol furrowed her eyebrows at her son-in-law and worked to remind herself that yes, it was normal for Jesse to be dating again and yes it was wonderful that her grandkids enjoyed the woman he was seeing. *She* enjoyed the woman he was seeing. But she looked at her son-in-law and could still see the woman who had come out of her womb and had given her two beautiful grandchildren.

"Jesse, I'm… that's not what I meant." Carol put her hand on Jesse's arm.

Jesse shrugged out from under her hand with a shake of his head. "Carol, I get it. Cheyenne isn't Mara. But don't I deserve to be happy again? Don't I get that?"

"Jesse," Carol sighed. "We like Cheyenne, we do. And you do deserve to be happy, but my grandson is calling her his stepmother."

"Without any concept of what that means."

"But still." Carol could feel the dirty look her husband was giving her. She was in for it later. She had a stubborn streak in her, the same one that her daughter had inherited and passed along to her own children. And while she did like Cheyenne, she did like the happiness she'd given Jesse and her grandkids, the idea of them looking at Cheyenne the way they did, their attachment to her, it was a recipe for disaster. It also lent itself to a lot of future pain when—if—Cheyenne decided she didn't want to be in their lives anymore. "Jesse, I'm not trying to hurt you. I'm trying to look out for you… and for the kids."

Jesse rolled his eyes. She could see the control he was exercising in not arguing with her more than he already had been. But she could also see the hurt in his eyes, and that broke her.

Miles darted out of the house before she or Jesse could say anything else to each other. "C'mon! We're gonna miss Roxy and Rick," Miles announced. "Can we go, please?"

Jesse scooped his son up and took his backpack from Carol. "We have dinner plans." Jesse stooped to kiss Carol on the cheek out of habit and stalked to the truck with a wave to Mitch.

Carol looked to her husband, who stood shaking his head at his wife. Before she could say anything to him, he turned on the heel of his work boot and walked into the house, leaving her to stand in the grass alone. She looked up at the sky, searching for some guidance. All she got was a heavy drizzle starting to sputter out of the clouds overhead, aimed for her face.

34

*J*esse didn't return to the conversation he had had with Carol for a while. August was on the horizon; the summer heat had started to die off into autumn's warm, if slightly damper, embrace.

It wasn't that Jesse was putting off the questions that Carol's unnecessary anger had raised. It was just that he was busy. He had two kids to chase after, a young and sometimes overly zealous girlfriend to keep up with, and a business that was in the middle of its busiest season. There was too much on his plate for him to sit and reassess the damage that he might be causing.

He couldn't see a problem with the relationship—not that he was looking too hard, feigning ignorance to his mother-in-law's microaggressions and the nagging in the back of his mind. Carol's words had hit a nerve, strapped deep into the center of his chest, and he was having a hard time moving past them. He convinced himself that if he ignored them—and the discomfort they caused his conscience—long enough, the feelings would go away.

Jesse could hope, and he could even pray, that he'd get through the little bit of doubt Carol had shoved into his mind with as few casualties as possible.

But then his son or his daughter would mention Cheyenne's name, their face lighting up with some soft childhood emotion, and he would be left to wonder what he was doing and if he was going to end up hurting them all in the process. That idea nagged at him, too, that to end things with Cheyenne before they became too serious, he would end up hurting his kids and the woman he found himself loving without being able to put a finger as to why. On the other hand, if he didn't break up with her but continued on with their relationship, he was bound to hurt the man and woman that had taken care of him and his kids after Mara had died.

He spent a week in turmoil, biting back harsh words at the kids when they got on his nerves over Cheyenne— whether it was their desire to see her or their desire to talk about her—and faking laughter and fond memories with Cheyenne herself. Whenever he could find a moment alone he'd wallow, silently beg for his late wife to tell him what to do, or even pray that a resolution would come that might not hurt anyone in the process. If only there was a blueprint, or that pesky how-to-be-a-widower pamphlet that he found himself hoping for more often than not. Some answer to help him figure out what happened next, or what to do when it felt like the walls were closing in around him.

The answer came one night, after Cheyenne had left for home and he was putting his children to bed. Cheyenne had stayed for dinner after dropping Amelia off and participated in a few rounds of one of the kids' favorite board games. She'd laughed and let Miles win and shot Jesse secret smiles and gentle looks all night—much to his chagrin and the satisfaction of his daughter.

After Cheyenne left and Jesse had put Miles to bed, he found Amelia waiting for him in the den. She was curled up on her side of their couch, a book on her lap and a cup of water in her hand—he'd seen Cheyenne curl up in a similar position, usually with tea, after a long day when she was putting together her supply order. Amelia had even piled all the hair she could manage on the top of her head in a small knot, in a similar fashion to the way Cheyenne normally wore her hair.

"How's the book?" Jesse asked, lowering himself onto his side of the couch.

"It's good." Amelia smiled at him and set her cup on the little end table beside her.

"Can I ask you a question, kiddo?" He turned the TV off and shrouded the room in silence.

Amelia gave him a suspicious look but stuck a bookmark in to mark her page. "What's up, Dad?"

"What do you think of Cheyenne?" Jesse ran his hands over the back of his head, leaning against his arm of the couch so that he could look at his daughter. "I mean, I know you guys are pals and everything, but like."

Amelia frowned at him, her thin eyebrows bunching together over the bridge of her nose. "If you know we're friends, then?"

Jesse shrugged. "I mean. Like, how do you feel about me and Cheyenne dating each other?"

"I like it." Amelia's face lit up. "You're all smiley and she makes us dinner and does stuff with us. Mary's stepmom doesn't do all that stuff with her and her sisters all the time, but Chey takes us to the store and she bakes with us and plays games and it's really cool."

Jesse frowned at his daughter. "A lot of your friends have stepparents, don't they?"

Amelia shrugged. "Not a lot of us have only one parent." Her face lit up again. "It would be cool if you and Chey got married."

Jesse nearly choked on air. "What do you mean?" he sputtered, his hands freezing over his eyes. He couldn't believe the words that had just come out of his daughter's mouth.

"I mean, if you and Cheyenne got married then she'd actually be my stepmom and she could do things like pick me up from school and take Miles and I to the doctor so Grandma doesn't have to do it." Amelia's face was split into a grin. "Do you think we could live in the Retirement House? I really like the big gable room on the third floor, the one that she let me sleep over in last week."

"Whoa, whoa." Jesse put his hands up as if the motion could actually stop his daughter from spiraling further down the rabbit hole. "Melia, Cheyenne and I are probably not going to get married," he said carefully, picking his words as slowly as possible.

Amelia's face twitched. Her eyebrows scrunched together, the clear confusion bleak on her face. "What... what do you mean? You love her, don't you?"

Jesse's chest ached. He wished that, even if for just a moment, he could see the world through his daughter's eyes. Seeing the beginnings of a new love in its purest form and understanding it on the complex level that kids did might have changed his mind. Could have changed his mind. "I do," Jesse said cautiously. "But… well… you'll understand it when you get older." He hated that line. He'd always thought 'when you get older' was a loaded sentence that never came to fruition.

"That doesn't make any sense." Amelia frowned. "If you love her, then why won't you get married?"

"I just… it's complicated, kiddo." Jesse floundered. What could he say to his eleven-year-old that would make sense? That he was afraid—afraid of what? Of the woman they'd both come to love leaving them, or of the fact that she might change their entire lives permanently. And what of the consequences? Amelia was young. She didn't need to worry about consequences of the magnitude he was going over relentlessly in his mind. Not yet.

"It's not complicated," Amelia sniffled, on the verge of tears. "You love her and she loves you. She loves us."

"Melia." Jesse scooted over to sit next to his daughter. "Sometimes that just… isn't enough." His mind was made up, looking into the tears and the sadness in his daughter's face. He'd protect all of them from the inevitable heartbreak of Cheyenne leaving them—he'd protect his babies, and himself, from that kind of loss again. The seed that Carol had planted had bloomed and the decision, as much as it crushed him, couldn't match the weight of Amelia bolting off the couch and down the hall to her bedroom, slamming her door.

35

As much as that summer had once felt impossible, like the entire world was coming to an end around her, Cheyenne found herself falling into her new rhythm, her new life, with an ease that had the end of August creeping up on her. It'd become apparent to Cheyenne, long before that last Tuesday of the month, that her life was never going to be the same again. That it'd been changed for the better. And that having Jesse and the kids in her life was the best blessing she could ever hope for. But even good things, even good seasons, had storms they had to weather.

The storm that had been brewing silently for weeks, sitting untouched and unspoken in the air of the Retirement House when Cheyenne found herself alone for too long, caught up with her at the end of a long, busy day. She'd just gotten back from dropping Amelia off at Jesse's —and staying to enjoy some barbequed chicken and corn that Jesse and Miles had prepared in their absence—her shoulders stiff from the long day they'd spent filling orders and restocking on the half hour, every half hour. Her eyes stung from the smoke from the fire Jesse had built for the kids and her reserved energy was spent wrangling Prince from the Cherokee and getting him to do his business before they trudged into the Retirement House for the night.

On top of the day she'd had, there was laundry to be folded and a new book burning a hole in her nightstand. She also wanted to make a cup of tea, to soothe the smoke burn in the back of her throat and help her unwind. Cheyenne let herself and Prince into the house and slid her shoes off by the front door. Prince raced ahead of her toward the living room. After a few minutes of mental juggling, debating whether she should let him do his damage or follow him into the living room, Cheyenne took her time retracing Prince's path. A few minutes on the couch weren't going to kill her, and she'd left an episode of one of her cooking shows half-finished.

She'd just stepped into the living room, forgoing turning on the overhead lights for the lamp waiting for her by her grandfather's easy chair, when it happened. A sharp pain radiating from the sole of her foot up through her calf, courtesy of a little plastic brick left in the center of the floor. Cheyenne yowled in pain and caught her foot in both of her hands, hopping to the easy chair to avoid walking on the tender spot. Prince ran over and yapped at her. She sank down into the leather and yanked on the chain to light the lamp, scowling in the direction of her injury.

Sitting in the middle of the hardwood floor, left completely abandoned, was the little brick. A shiny new yellow Lego that had come as a part of the set Roxanne had picked out for Miles the week before. It must have been left behind from his last adventure into the playroom, which'd been Sunday, when they'd been stuck inside on account of the rain. Cheyenne sat and stared at the piece of plastic, torn between annoyance that the toy hadn't been put away and amazement that her only concern was the fact that the Lego hadn't been picked up and put in its chest.

Not that it was sitting in the middle of her floor, a remnant of a child's presence in the house, but the fact that said child had been careless enough to not pick up his toys when he was finished with them like she'd asked him to do what felt like a hundred times before. A hundred times. She'd scolded Miles over something so trivial at least a hundred times in the span of two full months.

How the tides had turned.

Cheyenne frowned at the piece of plastic. It was so much bigger than the tiny square of space it took up—so much more important than the foundation of a children's playset. The little Lego, which had been a gift from her best friend to the son of the man she was seeing, was absolutely so much more than a tiny piece of forgotten plastic. The fact that it existed, that it belonged to someone small whom she'd grown to love so much in the span of such a short time, spoke more about the life she was living in Penn Ridge than she could have put into words.

"Is this what you'd hoped I'd find?" she asked the house skeptically. Leave it to her grandfather to set her up to do something as stupid as falling in love, as to becoming a part of a family. He'd never been judgmental over her lack of commitment, or the fact that she'd clearly never intended to have kids, but somehow her grandfather had been the catalyst of her falling into a relationship that felt like it could be something real. And into the lives of two kids whom she adored more than she'd ever felt possible.

Prince, thinking she was addressing him, let out a little bark and flopped down, his tail wagging.

Cheyenne leaned down to scratch his head. "I'm surprised you didn't gobble this up."

The pup tilted his head to look at her, his big eyes glossy with expectation and love. Cheyenne laughed and scooped up the little pup, nestling him on her lap. He burrowed down while she scratched his ears and flipped on her show. The background noise helped her mull through the realization that she wasn't even mad about the Lego, or about the fact that her grandfather had more or less trapped her into owning a home she hadn't been sure she wanted a few months ago. And into a life that she never could have expected.

Still, his memory smarted, leaving her a little angry that he was gone. It wasn't the intense anger or the sadness she'd felt when she first lost him, but it still burned in her chest. In its place was the knowledge that she could thank him for doing what he did because it'd somehow created a better her.

Even if that her was completely wrapped around the fingers of two kids.

CHEYENNE DIDN'T SLEEP well that night. A feeling that something was off was sitting in her stomach. Not the latent anxiety she'd expected when she'd finally torn herself from the easy chair and put the Lego where it belonged, but the kind of uneasiness that usually preceded something bad. Roxanne, had Cheyenne put it into words for her friend, would have told her that it was similar to the feeling she'd had the night before Maverick's accident. Those kinds of feelings were the stuff of fantasies—something that Roxanne entirely believed in and Cheyenne didn't. But the uneasiness in her gut, the heavy feeling that something on the horizon was going to wreck her bubble of bliss, stayed with her.

Her restlessness had left Prince restless, the poor pup readjusting himself several times while they tried to sleep. Several times, the two of them made eye contact in the dark room before she patted his head and tried to settle back down to sleep. The feeling wouldn't go away, no matter how hard she tried to squelch it.

And she didn't like that.

Still, she slid out of bed when her alarm went off at four and stumbled into the bedroom rubbing her eyes. There was no text from Jesse from the night before on her phone, which she was saddened by, but she'd woken up to almost an entire novella from Riley about the escapades of her unborn niece to entertain her through her morning routine.

By the time she made it to the bakery at quarter to five, there was still no word from Jesse, even though he should have been awake. Cheyenne checked her phone a handful of times on her drive into town, her shoulders hunched in on herself at the despondent feeling in her gut. They'd seemed to be on good terms when she'd left the house the night before. Really good, based on the kiss he'd given her at the Jeep.

Elena had already opened up shop and was putting out the first round of muffins when Cheyenne made it into the bakery. Her new assistant, the tall willowy saint whom Carol had helped Cheyenne find to work in the shop, beamed a greeting when Cheyenne let herself into the building.

"Morning, boss," she chirped from the other side of the display counter, her round face peeking out through the glass. "You look like hell."

Cheyenne rolled her eyes, ducking behind the counter to stow her purse under the register. "Couldn't sleep."

Elena tilted her head to the side, pursing her lips. "There's coffee in the back and I made breakfast burritos last night. There's a cheese and beef one in the back fridge with your name on it." She wiggled her eyebrows, her left piercing winking at Cheyenne. "And if you need to talk about it, I'm all ears."

"Very large ones." Cheyenne forced a laugh. "Let me go heat up my burrito and we'll get started. We have quiches to make."

JESSE SAT in front of A Taste of Celeste Too for what felt like an eternity. The street moved around him—the daily thrum of people in their natural routines passing him by while he sat, feeling an almost immovable surge of panic come in waves. At the top of the tide, when it churned desperately in his gut, Jesse could tune out the kids playing hockey in the street, their laughter penetrating his truck's closed windows and metal frame. At the bottom of the tide, when the anxiety slowed to a gentle sloshing in his chest and his brain, their childish mirth soothed him.

He sat, his head laid back against the headrest and his eyes squeezed tight, mulling over the words forming on the tip of his tongue. He thought of the stricken look on Carol's face when she'd spat 'stepmother' at him, and the calm way Mitch had placed a hand on his shoulder to reassure him that he'd actually done nothing wrong before they'd left the house. In his mind's eye, Miles' transgression felt like more than just a betrayal of his mother's memory (not that he'd seen the slip-up as a transgression, at least not in the same way that Carol did). Rather, he saw the word 'stepmother' framed by Cheyenne's hazel eyes and the way she lit up the room when the kids were around. Its weight was in the blossom of Amelia's being—his quiet, sullen girl had started to crack her shell around the red-haired woman and, as much as he hated to admit it even to himself, she'd needed a woman's touch. Not the touch of her grandmother, but the touch of a woman figure who could grow with her, learn to be a mother in the same ways Amelia was learning to be a woman. Its worth was in Miles' growing interest in science, and school as a whole, and his pure joy whenever the woman was around.

Somehow, in the course of only a few weeks, Cheyenne had slipped—against both their wills—into the role of 'stepmother.' She'd become a maternal figure to his kids and a major part of his life in ways that no one had come even close to filling since Mara had changed after her diagnosis. If things kept up the way they were, then by the time the kids got back to school in a little over a month, he'd be down on one knee asking her to fill the role permanently. And it wasn't something she would want. Even if she said yes, Cheyenne most definitely would not want to fill the role of 'stepmother' to his children. Cheyenne didn't like children. She didn't know what to do with them—she'd told him so herself.

So how could he sit in his vehicle and see her so clearly as his partner, as the person he'd spend the rest of his life learning to love every day in new and exciting ways? Jesse rubbed his eyelids with his fingertips and exhaled sharply at the thought of asking her to be his partner. Of the initial response, more than likely positive, followed by weeks, if not years, of resentment. He couldn't face that again. Not with all he'd learned from the first time around—and not with his children hanging so perilously in the balance.

Jesse got out of the truck after his long tenure of thought, his mind made up. There was only one thing that he could do to protect his kids, and himself, from the future heartbreak they were destined to experience. Even if it meant that he'd have to hurt himself and the woman he loved in the meantime.

Cheyenne was behind the counter, concentrating on the order ledger, when Jesse walked into the bakery. The bell over the door sounded when he pushed it open—the bell he'd helped Amelia install, preening in joy when she beamed up at him. The redhead looked up when it sounded, her customer face on like a mask until she registered who had just walked into the quiet shop.

"Hey." Cheyenne beamed at him. "Is it seven already?"

Jesse rubbed the back of his neck, his own mouth fighting to smile at her in return. "No."

"Oh. Good." Her eyes dropped back to the ledger in front of her. "I've got some stuff to straighten out still. There's fresh coffee in the back."

Jesse nodded without offering a response and let himself around the counter. Cheyenne scooted closer to the door and pushed her neck toward him at a drastic angle for a kiss. A kiss that Jesse couldn't deny providing. The feel of her soft skin against his lips was something he hoped he'd hold on to for the rest of his days. Tucked safely in the back of his mind, with his coveted memories of his wife, to look back on when he was old and alone and the kids were no longer his to worry about. At least, not as worried as he'd been while they were young.

Cheyenne tucked a stray lock of hair behind her ear and smiled up at him. Her hazel eyes were searching, asking what was wrong with him with their warmth and their gentle nosiness. "Could you get me a cup of coffee too?" she asked instead.

Jesse grunted and walked into the back room. She'd made the coffee nice and strong, the way he liked it, and the smell permeated the musk of yeast, sugar, and heat that filled the small kitchen. On one of the long metal tables sat a half-decorated cake, covered in teal fondant and several sugar skulls that he'd seen Amelia sketching a few days before.

Would she still let Amelia come and sit in the bakery for hours? Was he taking his daughter's outlet away from her in his own selfishness?

Was it really selfish?

Jesse shook the questions away and dumped a generous amount of cream into both of their cups.

"Have you had any customers?" Jesse handed her a cup.

"Not in the last hour." Cheyenne took a sip. Her eyelids fluttered at the taste of the coffee.

That was going into his memory bank too.

"Can you lock up, then?" Jesse asked over the rim of his mug.

Cheyenne frowned. "I... sure. Is everything okay?" Cheyenne slipped around the counter and snapped the deadbolt on the door. She flipped the "Open" sign over and proceeded to draw the blinds on the store front's windows.

"Can you... can you sit?" Jesse took a deep breath, gesturing to one of the small metal tables in the center of the shop.

Cheyenne's frown deepened. She waited until Jesse was seated, bouncing his leg rapidly so the fabric of his jeans rubbed against the edge of the table, making noise, before she sat across from him. Her slender fingers wrapped around her cup and she looked at him, waiting.

"We've... we've been having fun." Jesse had no idea how to start. How did you tell someone that you loved that this was the end of that love? Jesse had never had to do so before; had never once uttered the words he was about to spit out. The thought of doing it made the acid in his stomach creep up his esophagus.

"We have," Cheyenne agreed cautiously.

Her hazel eyes surveyed him, searching for answers to questions he'd rather she didn't ask. It would be easier, at least for him, if the words came out of his mouth without any prompting from her.

Jesse put his hand out, his palm up, to invite her touch. Just one more thing for him to put in his memory bank. Cheyenne rested her hand in his, her touch hesitant. "I... I adore you. My kids adore you. You've breathed life into us... into us in ways that I didn't know we were missing. Didn't know I was missing." He rubbed his thumb over the knuckles of her hand. She had a dye stain on her middle finger, and her nails had flour caked under them. He was going to miss that. Just as much, he realized with a sad start, he was going to miss the flour handprints on her pants and the way she'd throw her hair up just to keep it out of her way.

"I... wow..." Cheyenne pulled her hand away from his as understanding dawned on her features.

"Look." Jesse licked his lips. "It's not... it's not you," he started.

Cheyenne's face turned red, almost as red as her hair, and she stood up abruptly, knocking her chair over in the process. "I know damn well it's 'not me'," she said dryly, tugging at her necklace. "You best believe that this is one hundred percent you, Jesse Kaiser."

He blanched. He'd never been very good at confrontation. Or at finding words when they were needed. He stared up at Cheyenne, his face turning its own shade of red. There were so many words trying to break out from his frustrated throat, a mixture of apologies and half-baked explanations that even he knew wouldn't have withstood the hurt, the anger, and the pure distrust he saw in her eyes. Still, he heard himself begging, without even realizing it. "Cheyenne, please sit down. Let me explain."

"No. No. You don't need to explain." She shook her head in disgust. "You can see yourself out, Jesse."

Jesse stood up and caught her hand when she started for the back room. "Cheyenne. Please."

When she looked up at him, it was with eyes full of tears and a mouth hard set to fight him. "I have some things to figure out with my flour order." Her words were cold—not angry, but steeped in hurt. She jerked her arm away from him, keeping her spine as straight as possible, and made a sweeping gesture toward the door. "Please see yourself out."

36

"I'll kill him."

Cheyenne lifted the pillow from her face and peered out at her best friend, who was pacing the length of her bedroom. Roxanne was fired up. Her face had taken on a red color, which still looked odd to Cheyenne under the surface of her skin, and she had balled her hands to her sides so tightly her arms were shaking. Maverick was sitting in the sleeper chair in the corner, his left leg stretched out while the right was hitched over his knee. He'd been taking in the scene more calmly, although there was the stubborn set in his jaw that told Cheyenne that if he dwelled on it too hard he'd be looking for a fight.

"I'm not sure murder is the right way to go," Maverick offered for the third time, lifting his beer to his lips. "I'm pretty sure all of our deposits are non-refundable at this point."

Roxanne threw her hands in the air at him. This was a new quip, the last one having had to do with Roxanne breaking one of the nails she'd been meticulously working on getting healthy and strong for the wedding. The one before had had to do with how bad Roxanne would look if she had an earring ripped out of her earlobe. Neither of the previous responses had been met with any sort of kindness. "He broke Cheyenne's heart!"

"He wouldn't be the first one," Maverick offered and got a shoe thrown at him.

Roxanne smirked when the flip-flop made contact with his arm. "He was a good one!"

Cheyenne pushed the pillow back onto her face, the fabric squishing over her mouth and nose. Jesse was supposed to be a good one. That's what bit her. Made her furious. Had dampened the underside of her pillow while she held it over her face and sulked. "Rox, let it go," she grunted from under the cushioning.

"I can't let it go, Chey. He's a creep. And a jerk. And we really, really thought that this one was going to stick and it didn't." Roxanne sounded like she was on the verge of tears.

Cheyenne lifted her pillow again to see bright blue eyes looking down at her, not a hint watery but filled with temper. "Yeah. And it sucks. But it's not the end of the world. I'm not seventeen years old anymore, so I'm going to lay here and wallow for a hot minute, and then I'm going to get my shit together and figure out how to use the lawn mower."

Roxanne made a little 'hurumph' sound in the back of her throat and flopped back onto the bed beside her. "Where are the tears? The heartbreak? Chey, you were really into this guy!"

"I was dating a guy with two kids who is in another decade than I am. I should have seen this one coming." Cheyenne rolled onto her stomach and pressed her face into the mattress. She wasn't sure why she'd called them over—Roxanne was prone to drama and Maverick was going to be a hothead about it—but having Roxanne next to her was a comfort. Her friend smelled like lilies from her new perfume, and when she laid an arm over Cheyenne's lower back, the redhead found herself on the verge of tears. She tilted her head, just enough to take in some air, and lay as still as possible.

Maverick stood, rubbing at his left knee. "Wes is here," he announced to the room after stuffing his phone in his back pocket.

Cheyenne picked her head up. "You called Wes?"

Maverick leaned down to give Roxanne's head a kiss. "We needed backup," he said simply and walked out of the room.

Roxanne smiled over at Cheyenne. "Did you see that his limp is getting better?"

"Mhmm." Cheyenne dropped her face back into the bed.

The two women lay side by side, Roxanne's arm still over Cheyenne's lower back, for what felt like an eternity and a heartbeat all wrapped into one. In the simple way that being next to your best friend does, Cheyenne felt herself coming down from the extreme rush of emotion that had been building inside of her since Jesse had left the bakery the day before. She hadn't let herself cry over the breakup, hadn't given herself a second to mourn the fact that he'd ended everything that had been between them.

"What if I never get to see the kids again?" she asked, half hoping that the comforter would muffle her voice.

Roxanne pushed herself up again. "I'm sure if you really want to see the kids that he'll let you. The man's not a monster."

"I didn't think I'd ever date a guy whose kids I was going to miss about as much, if not more, than I was going to miss the sex," Cheyenne provided grumpily. "But I think I'm going to miss the sex a bit, too."

"Only just a bit, huh?" Roxanne snorted and then winced when Cheyenne threw a pillow at her.

"Have we threatened to kill him yet?" Wes asked as he plodded into the room and dropped down onto the bed beside Cheyenne. "Like, in earnest, threatened to crack his skull open? Or maybe lay him in a hole and pour concrete over him?"

"Wes," Cheyenne whined and burrowed her face into Wesley's shoulder.

His long arms wrapped around her and he placed a friendly, platonic kiss on the top of her head. "He's a jerk, babe," Wesley announced for the whole room to hear.

Maverick had settled back into Cheyenne's sitting chair and was rubbing his knee, shaking his head at the scene on the bed. "Did he give you a reason?" he asked, now that their small assembly was present.

"No," Cheyenne sniffed against the fabric of Wesley's t-shirt. "And I don't think I need one, either." Her eyes burned, even if she still didn't want to cry. Having Wesley's familiar warmth around her helped the sadness, even if she wasn't ready to admit that she was sad. "I just. Don't think I want to know."

Roxanne ran her fingers through Cheyenne's hair while Wesley held her closer and Maverick made a soft 'hurumph' from his seat. With her friends around her Cheyenne knew that she would eventually be okay, even if there was a gigantic grown-man-and-two-children-sized hole in her heart.

37

SEPTEMBER 2017

*J*esse was in a foul mood.

He'd been in a foul mood since he'd broken up with Cheyenne and had had to spend two weeks hiding his sulking for the sake of his kids. He wasn't talking to Carol at the moment, nor was he speaking to Tim, who had voiced his opinions on Jesse's decision in an overt, disgruntled statement of the facts. Jesse felt that he had the right to be angry—at himself, at the world, at the dead woman who had broken his trust in people and relationships and had made it hard for him to trust again.

Angry or not, hurt or not, he had to pick his head up for Amelia and Miles and plow on through. Even if his children weren't exactly speaking to him either.

Amelia had taken to ignoring Jesse whenever he walked into the room. At first, he had figured it would blow over like any of her other tantrums, lost in the wave of her needing his help, or just a hug, within a few hours. Instead, she'd spent two weeks using Miles or Mitch as a channel to answer Jesse's questions or inform him of her hard facts. She spent a lot of nights out, sleeping over at this friend's or that's, and when she couldn't make plans amongst her cohort of other eleven-year-olds, she would scamper back to her grandparents' or lock herself in her bedroom.

Miles didn't seem to be angry, except that Prince and Cheyenne were gone. It'd taken him a couple of days to realize that the woman, and her pup, weren't coming over with the same frequency that they had been before. And another few days to realize that they might not be coming back. He was old enough to be asking questions, persistently following Jesse around and constantly asking for Cheyenne and the pup to come over. Nothing Jesse could say, or do, could convince the child that Cheyenne was not coming back.

He'd broken his children's hearts in order to preserve them, and that sucked. But what sucked most of all was the feeling he had every night as he lay in bed and felt the sheets beside him where she would have been. Jesse couldn't close his eyes at night without the feeling that he was missing a big part of himself. A part that he hadn't realized he needed until it was too late.

Carol had caught on to his anger and must have figured out that some of his decision had stemmed from her freak-out over Miles calling the woman his stepmother. She walked on eggshells around him, or as much as she could without opening her mouth. Mitch, on the other hand, voiced his opinions loudly and with some disappointment.

"You were happy, Jess," the conversation had started.

They were standing in the barn the week after Jesse had broken up with Cheyenne, nursing cold sodas in glass bottles while Carol made Sunday night dinner. The sugary drinks (well, diet for Mitch) were a substitute to the beers they used to share prior to Mitch's heart attack that Jesse went along with willingly and that Mitch turned his nose up at every time they were busted out of the basement cooler. "Mitch," Jesse grumbled over the rim of his bottle.

"I'm just saying." The older man wiped a bit of grease from his tractor off on the side of his jeans. "You were happy."

"Carol wasn't. And the kids—" Jesse started, leaning against the toolbox.

"The kids love that woman," Mitch snapped. "You broke their hearts, you broke that girl's heart, and for what, Jess? A little cold feet? My foolish wife sticking her nose into places?" Mitch snorted, the lines in his face contorting.

Jesse flinched. "It just wasn't working out."

Mitch snorted and leaned over the tractor. "You're a fool, Jess."

Jesse rubbed his face, the condensation from his bottle dampening his skin. "It is what it is, Mitch."

"It's stupid, is what it is."

"I don't need a lecture."

"No. You need a punch in the face. Or a trip to a mental institution. You had something really great here, Jess—and I mean really great—and you tossed it out the window because you got a little nervous. This girl was the best thing that's happened to you since Mara died. At least for yourself. And you just let it go."

"Amelia asked me if I was going to marry her."

"And you very well should have. Or at least let it run its natural course. Or done something other than tuck your tail between your legs and run when things got a little scary."

Jesse didn't have anything to say to the disappointment in his father-in-law's face.

Mitch didn't force him to use his words, though. The man shook his head at Jesse. "When Mara brought you home from college, Carol and I weren't unsurprised. Or unhappy. Mara was happy, she had found someone to keep pace with her, you can't ask for more than that as a father. Especially when your daughter is a firecracker." Mitch laughed dryly and reached for his diet soda. "But then we got something neither of us had seen coming. We got a son. Someone else to be proud of, someone else to hold in our hearts. And you and Mara gave us two beautiful grandbabies. And we love you, more than either of us ever thought we could love the man who married our baby girl."

"I love you guys too, and I'm thankful for everything you've done for myself and the kids." Jesse handed Mitch his soda. "You know that."

"We know. That's not my point here, Jess. My point is, we love you and we just want you to be happy. And Carol, even with her busybody nose and her irritating habit of getting into the middle of things, would have loved Cheyenne eventually because she made you happy." Mitch shook his head.

"It wasn't just what Carol had said. Things were moving fast, too fast for the kids."

"Too fast for you."

"Mitch—"

"Mara hurt you. And then she died and you never got over that hurt. We know, more than you know we know," Mitch reassured Jesse when he saw the confusion in his face. "And we have never loved you any less for all the thoughts that Mara had—and the mess she put herself in by the end of it all. This was your chance to move past that. To move on with your life."

"And you think I blew it."

"I know you did."

Jesse rubbed the back of his neck. Mitch wasn't wrong. It'd been two weeks since he'd last seen Cheyenne, and he knew that Mitch wasn't wrong. His anger, his own self-inflicted hurt. They were all a side effect of him getting cold feet.

"I blew it," he said aloud, kicking himself for the fallout of the relationship. "I really blew it."

38

Wesley stayed for two weeks and spent the majority of that time hovering over Cheyenne, acting as if she were going to break at any moment. He hovered when she tried to accomplish simple tasks and grumbled about the pounds he'd put on since he'd come to stay.

Cheyenne got over heartache, or at least tried to convince herself that she was getting over it, by trying out new recipes. She'd started making new savory crepe combinations for the bakery's lunch rush—she saw more lunch business at A Taste of Celeste Too than they saw in Albany, and Wesley found himself in the unfortunate position of trying each and every combination she came up with.

They spent a significant amount of their time in the kitchen of the Retirement House or in the bakery, usually with Wesley's face stuffed with pieces of crepe and muffin. He took the time that he was in Pennsylvania to design a website for the new bakery, including a full shoot of the full bakery on a busy Saturday, her and Elena doing various things in the back kitchen, and her beautiful new display case. The case that Jesse had surprised her with—he'd taken the original case that'd been there, completely torn it apart, and built her a new one. The front glass was framed with lavender-painted wood, with delicate curves and design work, and the inside now held four rows to display instead of two.

Cheyenne tried her hardest to put on a good face for Wesley; his hovering, his constant questioning whether or not she was okay, his overly cheery demeanor which was digging at the back of her mind in the worst way. She loved Wes—he was her best friend, second only to Roxanne, and he had been the biggest help since the breakup. But Cheyenne had spent an immeasurable amount of time, at least in her eyes, with other people around her, and she desperately just wanted to be left alone.

The first few days had arguably been the hardest. Every morning she found herself waking up next to Wesley in bed, snuggled up next to his side while the man slept, her head aching and her throat dry. She'd found her way through several different bottles of wine, and even some tequila, and had finally managed to cry about Jesse in the shower the first night after Roxanne and Maverick left.

Wesley had found her curled up in the tub, hugging her knees to her chest and sniffling away the remnants of her tears. Instead of asking questions, Wesley had kicked off his shoes and climbed into the tub beside her. They'd sat across from each other, Wesley's knees nearly touching his ears as he squished into the porcelain, Cheyenne sniveling to get the rest of the tears under control. He didn't judge, he didn't ask questions.

The only thing Wesley had said to her that night was "He doesn't know what he's missing, Chey." And then she'd burst into tears once more.

After that first night, Cheyenne didn't allow herself to cry again. She had a business to run, a house that needed some finishing touches to it, and a puppy who adored her and needed her attention. She threw herself into baking, into Prince, into long nights with Wesley and Roxanne and Maverick, into getting her life back together.

Even if that meant that there was something missing from it that she might never find again.

Two weeks post-breakup, Wesley informed her that he was going back to Bethesda.

Cheyenne was sitting at the kitchen table, sifting through a catalogue of supplies for the bakery and working on a bowl of cereal, when Wesley walked downstairs from his second-floor room. His overgrown, sand-colored hair was damp and sticking to his forehead and the back of his neck, and he was sporting a worn-out blue t-shirt and jeans. Wesley was tall and lanky, with a quick grin for her in the mid-morning atmosphere, and he kissed her on the top of her head like she was always meant to be there with him.

In the moment, Cheyenne could only picture Wesley as the twenty-year-old man he'd been the night they'd made the biggest indiscretion you could make in a friend group. Wesley had come to visit Cheyenne while she was at the Culinary Institute and spent the weekend with her and her roommates. After a couple hours of drinking and partying with the kids in her class, they'd found themselves on the roof of the house she rented with three other girls.

In the moonlight, Wesley and Cheyenne had passed a bottle of rum back and forth and talked about all of the changes in their lives. They weren't kids any longer, they weren't quite adults yet, and they were the only two of their circle that had no clue about what the rest of their lives were going to look like. Those anxieties, that conversation, led them to Cheyenne's bedroom and a promise in the early hours of the next day to never speak a word of it to anyone if they could avoid it. And Cheyenne hadn't, except for when she'd told Roxanne over a bottle of wine a couple of years before.

Cheyenne lifted her head as Wesley stepped back from the kiss he planted on it, debating whether or not a repeat performance would help heal the numbness that was still in her stomach.

Wesley must've seen the look in her eyes because he smiled his patient, all-knowing smile and got himself a cup of coffee. "Don't go there, Cheyenne," he warned and grabbed a muffin from the basket on the island.

"I'm not going anywhere," Cheyenne shrugged at him. "I was just thinking."

"Well, don't think." Wesley laughed and sat down next to her.

"You're going home tomorrow." Cheyenne giggled and took a sip of her coffee.

"I am."

"Are you excited?"

Wesley gave her a mischievous grin. "I am very excited."

Cheyenne rolled her eyes. "Am I that bad of a hostess?"

Wesley's laugh was light and warm. "No, I just have something waiting for me back in Maryland."

"Oh, yeah? Is that why I'm not going anywhere?"

"Yeah, she is."

Cheyenne rested her head against Wesley's arm, her stomach getting that aching feeling in it again. It stunned her, and brought her unparalleled joy, to know that Wesley had found something worth defying her for. Even if he wasn't ready to tell any of them about this new person, or the new life he'd discovered. "I'm happy for you, Wes," she said affectionately.

"I'm worried about you, Chey," he countered and gave her head a pat.

"I'll get over it eventually. I've had enough practice with getting broken up with that this shouldn't be anything new."

"That's the way to be." Wesley hopped up from his stool, his muffin untouched. "Shall we go to the bakery?"

"I guess." Cheyenne slid off her stool and tucked her catalogue under her arm. "I'm thinking we're gonna make some fruit tarts this afternoon."

"Oooh, that sounds delicious."

WESLEY WAS SITTING in the front corner of A Taste of Celeste Too, sending rapid-fire texts back and forth with the woman he found himself having a hard time not focusing on, when the bell rang for the first time in over an hour that afternoon. He looked up, a grin still plastered on his face. What he saw surprised him, made his eyebrows lift toward the hair resting against his forehead.

Jesse's older child, his daughter, was standing in the entry of the bakery. She was holding on to her bookbag's straps, her face crestfallen, and she looked so small that Wesley found himself getting to his feet to check on her. It wasn't that Amelia looked out of sorts—she was wearing jeans and a t-shirt and reminded him a lot of the kids he'd gone to school with. Her thick hair was in a messy bun, akin to the bun on the head of the woman she was staring at with wide eyes, and she looked like if she held onto the straps of her bag any tighter she'd lose feeling in her fingers. Wesley stopped himself from interjecting in the moment when he saw the determination on her face, the look of assuredness that she was going to do something. Anything. He couldn't take the moment away from her because he wasn't sure when she'd seen the woman last, or if she'd ever see her again.

Cheyenne stopped talking to the customer in front of her at the same time Wesley stood up, her hazel eyes narrowing a little at the newcomer before recognition cleared the way for a loving, pleased smile to spread across her face.

The pre-teen squeezed the straps of her bookbag again, but she smiled back at the older woman. Wesley sat back down at his table and took his phone out of his pocket to busy himself. While he wanted to be a fly on the wall for this conversation, he could also respect the boundaries of the people closest to him.

39

*H*ad she ever felt so small?

Amelia knocked her knees together once, more out of frustration with herself than with anxiety, as she looked up at the storefront of A Taste of Celeste Too. She scolded herself, trying to remind her hesitant brain that only a few weeks before she could have run right into the bakery, and into Cheyenne's embrace, without any hesitation, and it would have been fine. Welcomed, even, because Cheyenne had done a wonderful job of making Amelia feel wanted. And that was what she needed the most right now.

Amelia took a deep breath and pushed open the door of the bakery, the bell jingling overhead. The large, open space smelled exactly like she'd remembered it. A little spicy, utterly sweet, with the savory lick of coffee running over the back of her throat and filling her senses. Her dad hadn't let her have coffee since he and Cheyenne broke up, convinced that the caffeine was going to stunt her growth. He didn't know that Cheyenne would always make her decaffeinated coffee, mostly milk instead of water, or that it was their thing. That they would sit while they were busy painting A Taste of Celeste Too and just drink cups of coffee and talk about Amelia's dreams. And how much she missed her mom—even if she didn't remember her. And how much Cheyenne missed her gramps—she'd had so many memories of the man to share. And they'd talk about Miles and about Jesse and about everything else. And Amelia missed that so very much.

She didn't understand why the woman had left them, or why she'd broken all of her promises. She also didn't understand why she'd lied to the bus driver when she put Miles on the bus and said that she was going to a friend's house before she'd walked down the hill from the middle school and through Main Street to end up outside the bakery. Amelia looked around the bakery, which she'd put so much of herself into decorating, and her stomach finally started to not ache. It'd hurt the entire walk from school to the bakery, but her eyes landed on Cheyenne and the pain subsided.

Cheyenne was standing behind the register, talking to a customer with her 'customer service' smile plastered on her face. She was wearing a purple t-shirt and had her red hair in a knot on the top of her head, and she looked every bit as wonderful as Amelia had hoped she would.

Cheyenne stopped talking briefly to glance at the shop's new arrival, her forced smile cracking into a genuine grin that added some sweetness to her voice. "Have a great evening." She handed the customer a brown paper bag and closed the till.

Amelia stepped up to the register hesitantly, still gripping the straps of her bag. "Hi."

Cheyenne lifted the counter and stepped around the register, hesitating for only a second before she drew the eleven-year-old into her arms and pressed a kiss to the side of the girl's head. "Hi." Cheyenne squeezed Amelia, hard. "Are you okay?" she whispered to her, stepping back far enough to thoroughly inspect her.

Amelia nodded, wiping tears away from her cheeks. "I am. I'm okay." She sniffled. "I just…"

Cheyenne smoothed a few loose strands of hair away from her face, taking some of the dampness with her. "Do you want a snack? I made some oatmeal chocolate chip cookies a little bit ago. They should be cool."

Amelia's lower lip trembled. "Is it… is it okay if I have some cookies?"

"Of course, baby," Cheyenne said quickly with a smile. "C'mon. Let's go sit in the back?"

"But…" Amelia looked around the bakery, still feeling a little jittery.

"Wes can watch the front." Cheyenne shot the tall man a look before she put her arm around Amelia's shoulders. "Let's go have some cookies, kiddo."

Amelia let the older woman lead her into the back of the bakery, trying to gather all of her courage. It hadn't dawned on her until she'd seen Cheyenne again that all she really wanted to know was why Cheyenne had left them. That was why she'd made the walk from the school to the bakery, why her stomach had been rolling for the last half hour, and why she wasn't entirely sure how to feel—other than watery—when she saw Cheyenne.

They walked into the back room and to the little corner that Cheyenne used for her working office. The metal table had the stools Amelia had spent a few days decorating with butterflies flying up from the base of each leg to the seat. She settled onto one of the stools and set her bag by the base of her stool while Cheyenne made them some hot chocolate and brought over a plate of cookies.

"How's school been?" Cheyenne sat across from her and found herself fidgeting with her fingers. "You've been back for a few weeks now, right?"

Amelia nodded and wrapped her fingers around her coffee mug. "It's okay. I have a really cool math teacher. And my reading teacher is really funny."

"That's good. I always liked reading when I was your age." Cheyenne took a sip of her coffee. "Are you taking an art class?"

"Yup. It's kind of a mishmash of art stuff right now. Next year I get to pick what kind of art I can take." Amelia looked down at her cup, biting her lower lip.

Cheyenne nodded. "That's really cool."

"Yup." Amelia popped her 'p' and looked up at Cheyenne. Now was as good a time as any for the reason she'd come. "You lied to me," she said simply, frowning at Cheyenne.

Cheyenne tilted her head to the side but gestured for Amelia to keep talking.

"You told me that you were gonna stay with us. That we were like a family." Amelia rubbed at her eyes, smearing her makeup. "And then you left us."

"Melia." Cheyenne put her hand on Amelia's. "Things

are really complicated. Being an adult is complicated. And when you are an adult and you're seeing another adult, it becomes super complicated."

Amelia frowned. "So, it's okay to walk away from promises when you're an adult?" That didn't make a whole lot of sense, but she was willing to listen to what Cheyenne had to say. "It's okay to make people you love sad when you're an adult?"

Cheyenne flinched. "Sometimes adults make decisions that might seem complicated... or decisions that even we don't understand."

"Dad is so sad. Miles is so sad. We miss you," Amelia insisted, pushing her loose hairs back from her face. "That's not complicated."

As Amelia watched, Cheyenne's face switched between a couple of emotions that she couldn't put her finger on. While Cheyenne searched for an answer, Amelia took a sip of her hot chocolate and helped herself to a cookie. The sweetness of the drink and the buttery softness of the cookie put her in a rush of heaven that she'd never thought she'd experience again. Even if she still wasn't entirely sure why Cheyenne had left them, sitting there with the woman again felt like the way things used to be, and that made her very happy.

"I will make more of an effort to be there for you and Miles," Cheyenne said finally.

Amelia nodded reluctantly. "Are you going to get back together with my dad?" she asked, hope spilling into every word.

"I don't think so, darling." Cheyenne squeezed her arm lightly. "But I will be there for you and Miles. I'm so sorry

I haven't been there for the last few days, but I will make an effort to be there from now on. I promise."

"You made promises before and you didn't keep them," Amelia said quietly. It hurt her more than she could explain, thinking about how Cheyenne had promised her things in the past that she'd given up on.

Cheyenne pursed her lips. "Fair enough. I'll do my best to show you, though, you and Miles both. Okay?"

"Okay," Amelia mumbled.

Cheyenne ran her fingers over her red hair. "Now, tell me more about this math teacher of yours."

Amelia tried not to smile. It felt good, even if she wasn't sure Cheyenne wasn't going to disappear again, to get to sit and tell her about her new teachers and her last few weeks at school. Amelia took another cookie off the plate and snapped it in half while she delved into the story of her new school year and her math teacher with the funny name. And, while she talked, Cheyenne sat and listened, and things felt normal for a little while.

40

The blessing of living in a small town was that Jesse didn't look manic or panicked when he met Cheyenne and Amelia on the front porch of his house. His facial expression wasn't entirely calm, but he didn't look like he was about to call the police. Cheyenne had spent the latter half of that evening, including the entire drive to Jesse's house, wondering if she was about to be arrested for kidnapping Amelia. Of course, the chances of that happening were very slim, but she was worried nonetheless until he opened the door and smiled, first for his daughter and then for her.

"Melia," he breathed out in relief and reached his hand out to gather his daughter into his arms. "Next time you decide to go on a field trip after school, let me know. You know you're supposed to tell me if you're not coming directly home." Jesse's tone had 'scalding' down to a T, and he looked down at his daughter with both disapproval and love.

"Sorry, Dad." Amelia shuffled her feet and passed off her backpack.

Jesse slung the pack over his shoulder and pressed his lips to his daughter's head. "Go on inside and wash your hands, kiddo. Dinner's almost done."

Amelia turned and flung her arms around Cheyenne, burying her face in her shoulder. "Thank you," she whispered against the fabric of Cheyenne's t-shirt before she slipped around her father and into the house, leaving Cheyenne and Jesse alone.

It was the first time they'd seen each other since the breakup. Cheyenne wasn't sure how she felt about it, but she forced herself to look him in the eye. Jesse gave her a soft grin. "Hey," he said quietly.

"Hi. Sorry for not having her call… she just needed some girl time." Cheyenne shrugged and stuffed her hands into her back pocket. "Won't happen again."

"I didn't tell them they couldn't see you. I just… neither of them have said anything about wanting to see you, ya know?"

"They're always welcome to see me. I can even come grab them for an afternoon this weekend, maybe?"

"I don't know if that's the best idea."

"Jesse, you broke up with me. I didn't break up with them, and they need to know that I didn't abandon them. Amelia walked into the bakery and was in tears, Jess. They're both hurting because of this." Cheyenne gestured between the two of them. "I know you don't want to hurt them. I don't either. So, if they ever want to see me, the door is always open. I wasn't the one who tried to close it."

Jesse ground his teeth together thoughtfully before he gave in with a reluctant nod. "I'll see if they want to come over this weekend."

"Let me know." Cheyenne turned.

"Cheyenne," Jesse called after her, making her pause mid-step. "I'm sorry."

Cheyenne rolled her eyes skyward, her back still to Jesse. "Let me know if the kids want to come over this weekend. I'll come get them if they do." She walked back to the Cherokee without turning to look at him. Seeing him, for even those few moments, had made her chest feel tight and gross and her eyes feel dry. It hurt almost as much as it had hurt to hold Amelia in her arms earlier and hear the girl she'd come to love, the girl she'd made up her mind to raise, sniffle because she'd been missed. Cheyenne had thought she missed Jesse, and she still might deep down, but she'd realized she'd never be able to forgive him for the pain he'd inflicted on herself and on his children. Her parents had always put their best interests first, and, for the first time since the breakup, Cheyenne questioned whether or not Jesse had actually put the kids first—or if his decision had been driven purely on his own best interests.

SEEING CHEYENNE, and the way she'd so protectively insisted on being in his kids' lives, had put it all into perspective for Jesse.

That night, once he'd gotten over the relief of having Amelia home safely and had done his due diligence as a father to remind her to never put him through the wringer like that again, he'd had dinner with his kids and settled them down for the night. All the while, he couldn't have gotten Cheyenne out of his head if he'd tried.

They'd only been apart for sixteen days—sixteen whole days without her. When Mara had died, Jesse had been convinced that time had stopped. The world had stopped spinning. The clocks had all stopped ticking. The kids had stopped growing. But with Cheyenne, being away from her, it wasn't as if time had actually stopped. It was like Jesse had stopped and everything around him had kept moving. The couple of months he'd spent trying to woo her, falling in love with her, and then inevitably losing her had all slipped away. His kids kept living and Jesse had stopped.

Seeing her had been like a breath of fresh air. Seeing her had also been like Jesse had been punched in the chest. Jesse sat in the dimly lit den, his face resting in his hands, thinking about the woman he'd let slip through his fingers because he'd been foolish enough to think that leaving her was what was best for his children. In reality, leaving her was probably only the best move for himself, and even that had been a lie.

He missed her. He hated the way Tim would randomly bring it up when they were in the office and rub it in his face that he'd made a huge mistake. He hated the way his son asked for her and Prince. And he hated the way his daughter had held onto her when they said goodbye. But above all else, he hated that he'd let her go because he'd gotten cold feet and run. Instead of being his normal, levelheaded self, he'd run away.

Jesse was going to make things right. He leaned back on the couch, rubbing his hand from his chin to the back of his head. Jesse made a decision in that moment that he was going to get her back.

41

———

The little bell above the door jingled, letting Cheyenne know that a late-afternoon customer had wandered their way into the bakery. For a September day business had been slow, slow enough that she'd let her apprentice go home early to get ahead on some of her coursework. Cheyenne liked being in the bakery alone when it got later in the day. After the lunch rush was usually the best time to do some thinking and some soul searching. Both of which had felt like second nature to her after Jesse had ended their relationship.

All of the extra time needing to keep her hands, and mind, busy had resulted in new recipes and a brand-new coat of paint in her dining room. But business was good, and wedding plans had slowly started to take over her life as well as Roxanne's.

"I'll be right with you," Cheyenne called out without turning around from the coffee bar. She and Roxanne had been up late the night before working on formal invitations and she was lagging. "Okay, what can I get for you—"

Jesse was standing on the other side of her counter, his baseball cap in his left hand and the right rubbing over the back of his head. "Hey," he offered with a meek smile, the left corner of his lip quirked upright. "Do you have a minute?"

"I'm busy." Cheyenne set down her coffee cup, hard enough that the contents sloshed over her fingers. The hot liquid scalded the skin and she had to wring her hand to keep from yowling. "Do you want to buy something?"

"You gave Amelia some cookies last week."

"Amelia missed me."

"She's not the only one."

Cheyenne fought back the urge to yell. She swallowed down the majority of her fury in one hard gulp and squeezed the bridge of her nose between her thumb and forefinger. "Jesse, I really do not have the time for this." She reached behind the counter to the prepackaged bags of cookies she kept for customers and dropped one on the counter. "For the kids. Now get out."

"Cheyenne, c'mon. Give me a few minutes." She started to head for the back of the shop and Jesse nearly lunged over the counter. "Chey."

Cheyenne looked down at the hand wrapped around her upper arm, and the man standing on his toes over the counter. He looked tired, his dark eyes sunken in and the skin around them bruised. He'd let his hair grow out—the dark wave of it was starting to curl around his suntanned ears and reach toward his eyebrows. She didn't realize how long it had been since they'd seen each other until they were looking at each other, and she wondered if she looked as tired as he did.

"Let me at least lock the door. It would be bad for business if someone walked in on me crushing your head with one of my rolling pins," she snapped and yanked her arm away from him.

Jesse smiled. It was a weak attempt at a smile, but the corners of his mouth were turned upright. "I'll make sure to lay down on the floor so no one can see the attack."

"You can sit in a chair." Cheyenne rolled her eyes at him and let herself around the counter.

Jesse pulled a chair out at the nearest table for her before he sat down himself.

She crossed her legs and propped her head in her hands.

"So…" Jesse rubbed his hands together underneath the table. "How have you been?"

Cheyenne noticed how hard he was trying to avoid making eye contact and snorted.

In a perfect world, she might have flipped the table between them in a show of irritation, cracked him across the face with the steaming emotion running through her head, or a combination of the two actions. In a lesser, but still perfect, world she might have crumpled, a mess of tears and sadness. She might have begged him to find out why he'd ended their relationship when things had felt so good, so natural. In Cheyenne's head, in between conflicting thoughts of falling to his feet and forcing him out of the bakery, she pondered just turning and walking into the back room, closing the door behind her.

Instead, with a deep breath and a calm voice that

didn't feel like her own, Cheyenne leaned back in her seat and crossed one leg over the other. "Is that what you came here for? Because, Mr. Kaiser, I do not have the time for small talk."

His mouth twitched. "I came to talk to you." His dark eyes smiled, amused at her little outburst, and a sadness steeped into them. "I miss you, Chey."

Her anger came to a crashing halt around her. "You... you're the one who broke up with me," she accused.

"I did." Jesse nodded. "And I did so without giving you the explanation you deserve. And for that, I am so sorry."

There were no words. Cheyenne opened her mouth, twice, and closed it, having all but lost her ability to speak. His words had plowed her over. She didn't think she necessarily deserved an explanation, just the ability to be left alone. And to still get to hang out with Amelia and Miles. Her days felt empty, and sad, without them.

"When Mara got sick," Jesse started, taking her silence as an invitation to keep going. "Well. Okay. Maybe I should backtrack. I didn't know that Mara was sick when she first got sick. I'm not even sure when exactly she found out. Sometime after we found out that she was pregnant with Miles. I was working with an architecture firm in South Carolina at the time, working crazy hours. Sometimes I would come home just in time to read Melia a bedtime story and then be out the door the next morning before she even got up."

Cheyenne shifted in her seat and crossed her legs. The tension in the air, all of it radiating off of Jesse, had her interest piqued. When he'd spoken about Mara before, it had always been with the reverence you saved for the dead. That was gone, replaced with a bitterness in his voice that Cheyenne had never heard before. As much as she didn't want him to drag himself through his paces just to make peace—if that was even really why he'd come—Cheyenne couldn't help but feel some satisfaction with the fact that he was going to tell her his side of the story. The story that plagued him in bed at night, in every aspect of their relationship, in every day of his life. The story that had come between them.

"So, Mara was on me about having another kid. I wanted to wait, thinking I could make partner with this firm and hopefully have less hours at the office or on project sites. If we could have just waited another year, another two years, then I would have been able to dedicate more time to them. The time that I've been able to give them since moving out here.

"Anyway. Mara got pregnant. She was ecstatic, but I was feeling pretty reserved about the baby. But we were expecting a second baby, and Amelia was all excited about being a big sister. We tried making it work. Started going to a therapist because we were having some issues, and I was able to scale back my hours a little bit to make more time for her and the kids. I thought everything was going really well. Mara was about five months along when it happened." Jesse stopped to take a deep, unsteady breath.

Cheyenne raised both eyebrows. "When what happened?"

"We were in the kitchen making dinner one night—talking about baby names. Melia was in the living room watching cartoons. And I turned around to get something out of the fridge for Mara, my back was turned for less than a minute, and when I looked back Mara was on the ground. She'd collapsed."

Cheyenne stood up, unsure of what she was listening to, and got him a cup of water from the filter by her bookcase. She set the plastic cup down in front of him.

Jesse took a drink of water before he continued. "I found out in the hospital room, holding my five-year-old daughter while she slept, that my wife had breast cancer. And that she'd known for almost three months and had chosen not to receive treatment for it."

Cheyenne covered her mouth, her eyes wide. "Why didn't she get treated?"

"The doctors told her that if she started the chemo and the radiation, she was going to have to give up on the pregnancy."

"She didn't tell you she was sick? Like at all? You didn't notice?"

"She didn't tell me, and I was working a lot. I just chalked up the tiredness to the pregnancy, and to being at home with Melia all day." He rubbed his face with his hand. "By then it was too late. We had a name; we had a room painted. And she kept refusing to even talk about getting help. Or about what would happen after Miles was born. Every time I brought it up, she would pick a fight or leave the room. The further along she became, the more she started to blame us. Blame me. Blame the kids. Blame Miles. For existing. For getting sick. For being so tired and for losing herself. We learned after she passed away that she'd been sick for a while, that the tumors had metastasized from her breast tissue to her brain. The woman she'd become... the woman that I'd been living with for months, for possibly a few years, was not the woman I had met in college and fallen in love with. The tumors had changed her. Drastically. It explained some of the issues we'd been having, which didn't seem to be getting better with therapy and had started to sprout up out of nowhere.

"Anyway, she hung on for almost a year after Miles was born. But she was angry and bitter, and she wouldn't pick Miles up or feed him, wouldn't play with Melia or hold her. She was so angry. And while I could understand, to some extent, her being mad at the situation, I couldn't understand her anger with the kids. It wasn't their fault. Maybe mine. But not theirs."

Cheyenne shook her head, otherwise at a loss for words. Jesse's story was halting, a little all over the place. His scattered thoughts filling the space between them tragically.

"I'm sorry. I know that's a lot of words for you to digest. And probably doesn't make a lot of sense in the greater context of the conversation. But… I owed you… I needed to tell you."

"You don't owe me anything, Jesse."

"I do. I should have told you about this trash with Mara when we first started dating, but I had thought—had hoped—that I was far enough removed that I was over it."

"You were married for seven years." Cheyenne reached across the table and put her hand lightly on his.

He was still forcing himself to make eye contact with her, his dark eyes filled with emotion. It was hard for Cheyenne to look away, but she had to, for the both of them. For her, because her eyes were dry, and for him, because he looked like he was a minute away from bursting into tears.

"Watching the woman I loved change before my eyes, turn into this person that I didn't recognize, that didn't want our future, or our family, it hurt. I didn't have time to really feel that hurt, either. I went to a couple of dead-spouse support groups after the funeral, before Carol and Mitch convinced me that moving the kids here would be better for all of us in the long run. A lot of the guys there, there were more widows than widowers, but none of those men had lost their wives to illness, and a lot of them had lost their wives a long time ago. I mean, they had older kids, but their kids lost their mothers. They lost life partners while I lost the person I was just getting to live a life with. A life where I wasn't even there to see I was losing her until it was too late." Jesse laughed, the wry sound coming choked and crackly out of his throat.

"I can't imagine."

"I'm not telling you this to feel pity for me. I'm trying to get to the point. Sorry. There was a lot of stuff to get through before I get to the bottom of the explanation."

"I think that's explanation enough, Jesse."

"Just let me finish, please, Chey."

"Sure. Do you want coffee first?" A break could do the two of them both some good. "Maybe I'll even give you that cookie."

"I could go for a cup of coffee if you have any made."

"Yeah, sure." Cheyenne got up to make them cups of coffee, thankful for the reprieve from the look on his face. She wasn't sure how to handle the situation, or the word dump he'd just provided. She wasn't looking forward to telling Roxanne that she and Maverick had been right, that his late wife had been the divide between them, but she was grateful that the explanation for their breakup seemed to have very little to do with her.

When she turned to look over her shoulder, to check on him before dishing up a plate of cookies for the man, she found him looking at her. The sadness wasn't in his face anymore. It had been replaced by a look of contemplation, and a small smile, neither of which she found unwelcome.

"You don't have to continue if you don't want to," Cheyenne said as she carried back a tray with their two cups of coffee and the cookies.

"I need to. I didn't get to the you part." Jesse smiled wider. "But I also need one of those cookies."

Cheyenne felt herself grinning back as she set the plate in front of him. Oh, how she had missed him. "Okay. I'm ready."

"Fast forward to meeting you. And asking you out. And watching you and the kids. For someone who doesn't like kids, or at least tells people they don't like kids, watching you with Miles and Melia has been amazing. They both just opened up to you. My daughter stopped wearing black and started talking about college already and what she wants to do with the rest of her life? And my son is in love. Whether that's with you or the cookies I'm still not entirely sure." Jesse chuckled and took a sip of his coffee.

Cheyenne felt herself giggle and hid it behind a swallow of coffee. "I think it's the cookies."

"It probably is. But he loves them, and he's been asking about you every day." His smile fell through. "He misses you a lot."

"I miss him."

"He called you his stepmother to his friend Kyle's mom. And Carol freaked out. And then I got freaked out," Jesse segued. "I kept thinking about whether you loved them, too. Or if you would eventually decide you didn't really like them. Or that you didn't really like me and were only with me for the kids. And that one was weird."

"So, you ended things?"

"To protect my kids. And, probably more importantly, to protect myself."

"Hm."

The two of them sat there for a long moment, looking at each other over the little metal table and the two cups of cooling coffee, wearing similar expressions of disappointment. Jesse busied himself with crunching on a cookie to keep from having to say anything else.

Cheyenne felt like she was going to burst. The silence wasn't helping the questions running through her mind, including the one begging to find out where they went from there. Or where she even wanted them to go from there. The stomach-rolling feeling, the same one she'd felt the night before he'd broken up with her, was back. Only this time it rumbled as if she were excited, not as if she were about to get some bad news.

She shifted around in her seat, making a mental note to invest in new seat cushions, and forced herself to voice out loud the words burning underneath the skin. "Well, the kids were never going to lose me, regardless of what happened between you and me. I hope that they realize that by now." It had pained her to think that she'd never see the kids again—and pained her even more to return Amelia after her not-so-secret visits to the shop.

"Amelia does. Miles is still really confused, and I can't blame the kid. I'm a little confused still myself."

"Confused about us?"

"Confused about what I should do. About what's best for me. And the kids. And you. Moving forward."

"Jesse, I'm a big girl. I can make my own decisions."

"And what decision do you think you need to make?"

"I don't think jack right now. I know that I want to be with you. I know that I have missed you and the kids so much over the last couple weeks. I know that I'm very mad I missed their first day of school—not that I understand why I'm so mad about it—and I know that I have spent more time in the past month thinking about you and not being mad than I have at any man who has ever broken up with me before. And, as you know, there have been a few."

"Cheyenne, I can't make any promises right now. About the future. About us."

"Jesse, you told me on our first date that you were all in." Cheyenne reached for his hand again, this time wrapping both of her small hands around his long fingers. "You told me that whatever we were, you were all in. And I didn't have an answer for you as to whether or not I was in it too. Or if I could be in it too." She squeezed his fingers, trying to keep herself calm about the words that were about to come out of her mouth.

Jesse squeezed her fingers in return. "Please... please

say that you want to be in it. Please tell me that you want to try to at least be in it. With me. Not just in the kids' lives but in my life. With... uh... with me?"

Cheyenne hesitated. "I am in it. I'm in it with you and in it with the kids. And, not for nothing, I might be in it more for the kids than you."

"Cheyenne." Jesse squeezed her hands in his and shook his head. "I'm not sure what you're getting at. I mean, I think I am, but."

"But you messed things up really bad, and we have to rebuild. We're adults, and we can't just rush back in before we aren't ready. And I think you should start seeing someone, a therapist or something. Someone who can help you work on whatever is going on in your head." Cheyenne shook her head at him and held up her free hand to stop his protests when the corners of his eyes scrunched up and he began to argue. "Now you have Carol and Mitch, and me and the whole damn village that comes with me, to help you with the kids. You need to get help for yourself, too." Cheyenne kissed his hand, her eyes damp. "Can you do that for yourself? For me? For us?"

He didn't say anything for a few moments, and she could see the gears turning in his head. They both knew that he was going to have to commit, and be willing to put the work in, for it to mean anything. Cheyenne could only guess that Jesse was taking the time to think; to decide if he could—if he wanted to—put that work in.

His pause wasn't long, and when he spoke, there was a confidence in his eyes that made her heart swell. "I'll do absolutely anything I can for you." Jesse put his free hand over hers, squeezing her fingers between his.

"I'm gonna have to start holding you to that. On a whole 'nother level." Cheyenne's face nearly split open at the strength of her smile.

Jesse stood up and pulled her to her feet, wrapping her in his arms. "You'd better," he told her before he leaned down, closed the gap to her upturned face, and kissed her so thoroughly that her lips would be numb for a solid two minutes after they parted.

Cheyenne wrapped her arms around his middle, pitched herself up on her toes to make sure that he didn't strain himself too hard, and fell into the kiss. She hadn't realized how much she'd missed his touch until she was surrounded by it. Surrounded by him.

She was the one to break the kiss, stepping back and placing her hands firmly on his chest to keep him from coming in for more. "I think you're forgetting something."

"'Forgetting something'?" Jesse cocked his eyebrow in a question.

"We should probably go tell the kids." Cheyenne laughed. "Don't you think?"

"Ahh. Probably a good idea. Melia's going to be so excited."

"Her and me both."

THAT NIGHT, before she went to bed, Cheyenne wandered out to the garden. In the early autumn moonlight, the garden had taken on a magical glow that made each thriving flower seem even more alive. As she took the small path, slow footstep by slow footstep, a soft breeze blew through and rustled the flora around her.

Cheyenne tugged at the sleeves of her sweatshirt and wrapped her arms around herself to ward off some of the chill. She took a seat on the stone bench, crossed one leg over the other, and looked up at the angel fountain. There was so much on her mind, aside from the pure happiness that being reunited with Jesse—and the kids—provided. So much that she wished she could say to her grandfather, to walk through with his guidance. Which was the reason she found herself taking a midnight stroll.

Cheyenne stilled herself with a deep breath. "Hi, Gramps." Her voice sounded small but strong as it settled among the plants. "I… uh… I guess, if you're out there, if you can hear me, I miss you." She did miss him. Somehow, though, the pain from missing him was starting to ebb. Not fading—no, she was sure there would never come a day where Gramps being gone didn't hurt—but starting to lessen. It was becoming more of a dull sensation than the throbbing echoes it had been a few months prior. "I'm sure you know by now that Jesse and me… well… we're going to try to make it work. Make an honest effort at it."

An owl hooted in the distance, providing a little noise in the serene night air. Even the road outside the property was dead, not a single car bumping along its cracking pavement and hairpin turns. It was the kind of night that, as a kid, she'd have spent outside with her grandfather talking over hot cups of tea and cookies.

Cheyenne took some peace in the calmness and the

barely interrupted quiet. She shifted around on the cold bench and propped her hands on her knees. "I know what you thought of him, and you were right. He is… he's really great. And the kids. The kids are amazing."

She didn't quite know what to do with her hands, with herself. It'd made sense at first. If she wanted to talk to her grandfather, the garden was the right place to do it. With the house aglow with light behind her, settled on their bench, this was as close to him as she could get without making the journey to the cemetery. She was possibly even closer to him—to his essence, anyway—than she would be sitting at his headstone.

Despite the closeness, there was no way she could expect an answer from him. Roxanne had told her she sometimes got comfort from talking to RJ's grave, but Cheyenne didn't really see the point. There was a difference between a tipsy goodnight called out to the possible ghosts inside the house and sitting in the yard by herself, waiting for an answer.

She trudged on, however, for the sake of trying. "I don't know what I'm getting at." She laughed, imagining him telling her to take her time and think before speaking. Of all the things she wanted to say to him, she felt that none of them would come out right. "I guess I just wanted to say thank you. For leaving me the house and for getting me out of my rut. I never would have guessed that coming to the Ridge—that living here—would be exactly what I needed to get it together. So… thank you."

Cheyenne dried the small bit of moisture collecting under her eyes and started to stand up, her peace made, when a small lightning bug zipped past. She stopped and watched it circle the head of the angel statue once, twice, three times, before it seemed to stop and blink at her.

She smiled despite herself and pressed her fingers to her lips. Cheyenne blew the lightning bug a kiss. "I love you, Gramps."

EPILOGUE

SEPTEMBER 2018

*C*heyenne hung up with her fruit supplier and rubbed at the tension in her temples, thankful that their day was almost over. She still missed how much easier it'd been to get fresh tropical fruit in Albany, but her clients in the Ridge were definitely a step up. So was her shop help.

On the other side of the long kitchen, Amelia stood, concentrating on smoothing down the white buttercream sides of a sheet cake. Her tongue was poking out of the corner of her mouth and her long, slender fingers were clenched around the handle of a metal spatula. Cheyenne had fishtailed her hair back from her face that morning and the braid still stuck in place, with only a few wisps of her light brown hair hanging loose around her round face. The tween looked happy, concentrating intensely on the task at hand.

"You're getting really good at that," Cheyenne observed, closing her order book and sticking the cap on her pen.

Amelia turned the cake on her lazy Susan, her tongue retreating so that she could smile. "It's still a little bumpy on the sides."

Cheyenne got up from her corner desk and strode over to inspect the work. Amelia was right, the sides were a little uneven, but the fact that she could point it out to Cheyenne promised that she was learning. And that she was enjoying it. The twelve-year-old was learning steadily, and she was proving to be a big help with both the business and its customers.

Amelia set her spatula down and beamed at Cheyenne, pushing her loose hairs behind her ears to show off the four studs that Cheyenne had gotten her for her birthday. The second hole had been a long-term battle that she and Amelia had won against Jesse and that had given the girl a sense of transitioning from childhood to adulthood. The studs, the new hair, and the subtle sharpening of her cheekbones helped Amelia look so much older than the first time they'd met. Cheyenne found it amazing to watch her grow into a woman, almost as fascinating as she found watching Miles grow up. In a little over a year he'd changed so much—and had almost doubled in height.

"I like doing it, ya know?" Amelia said, almost shyly, while she crouched down to check out the levelness of her top.

Cheyenne nodded with a proud smile. She knew. Knew enough to have a little orange-bound notebook waiting for Amelia's thirteenth birthday. Every day, she took twenty minutes to write a recipe in it for her—from cakes and cookies to the dinners that Amelia enjoyed the most. She threw in extra recipes when she had the time, or when she and Amelia made something so good that even Miles threw aside his hatred of all things green and crunchy. They had bonded over their shared love, and eyes for detail, when it came to food. That bond had really helped the rest of it fall into place over the last fifteen months.

"I get it." Cheyenne winked at her as she set down the baby-shoe-shaped cookie she'd been icing. "That's exactly how I felt when I was your age."

Amelia beamed. "I'm just about ready for the lettering. Can we do the basketweave tip for the words?"

"I think they would like that." Cheyenne picked up an empty piping bag and started to stuff it with the admiral-blue frosting that Amelia had whipped up earlier. "Okay. You do the big lettering for the rest of it, I'll write the name when you're done." Cheyenne handed her the piping bag and laid out their practice card.

Amelia looked at her with wide eyes, a little nervous. "Are you sure?"

"Of course. She'll be over the moon."

Amelia hunkered down to concentrate, looping the letters slowly over the creamy white backdrop. Out in the shop, Cheyenne's new baker's apprentice, Maia, was chatting with customers and moving orders along, her pleasant lilt floating back to them weakly through the open door. She'd proved to be a great hire, despite her age —great enough that Cheyenne had consented to hiring two more high schoolers part-time in the evenings.

The shop was picking up, almost beating out the Albany shop in daily sales despite catering to a much more exclusive client base. Maia was almost good enough to leave alone for more than the three hours it took Cheyenne and Jesse to take the kids to church and then Carol's for brunch on Sunday. It had taken a lot off of Cheyenne's shoulders to leave the day-to-day operations to Nadia and Maia. She was making fewer trips to Albany, too, which helped with how things were changing.

Cheyenne wiped down the metal countertop while Amelia piped icing, then dried her hands on her apron. Harsh rays of early fall sunlight snuck through the windows over the sink and lit up the room, shining over the sugary perfection that Amelia was working on so intently. Aside from the counter they were working on, which sported all sorts of baby shower goodies, the kitchen was clean. Ready-to-be-closed-for-the-day clean. The kind of clean that made Cheyenne a little sad because it meant that she was leaving behind another day.

Amelia's triumphant laugh drew Cheyenne's attention away from the clean kitchen and to the tween, who was beaming down at the blue lettering with a sense of fulfilled purpose Cheyenne completely adored. "What do you think?" Amelia asked when they made eye contact, bouncing on the toes of her scuffed and well-worn tennis shoes.

Cheyenne walked over and took the blue piping bag from Amelia to quickly write herself. Once she finished the small lettering, she looped her arm around the girl's shoulders and stepped back so that they could admire the cake. "Baby Boy Sterling - December 2018" was spelled out across the top of the cake, announcing the happy, if still shocking, news to the world. "You did an amazing job, Melia." Cheyenne squeezed her shoulders. "Help me put the garnish on so we can stuff it in the fridge?"

Amelia grabbed the metal tub of candy racecars they'd made the day before. "Dad said I can stay at your house tonight so you can help me get ready in the morning. Is that okay?" she asked as she stuffed her hands in plastic gloves and started to pick out the little colored cars.

"I have our dresses hanging in my bathroom." Cheyenne nodded while she carefully laid out the black and yellow lines of the racetrack in a neat figure eight around the words on the cake. "He and Miles are going to meet us at Rox and Rick's house."

They worked on the cake in silence for a few minutes, moving in a kind of synchronized way that Cheyenne had never experienced before with any of her other assistants. When she'd mentioned it to her mother, she'd been given some sort of vague lecture about the bond of mother— even stepmother—and child and how Cheyenne would learn, and come to love, it. As usual, Cheyenne had nearly vomited at the 's' word and had rerouted the conversation to Roxanne's impending motherhood. What a pregnancy that had been.

Roxanne was sick all the time, her iron levels were plummeting, she had gained like fifty pounds, and they were already talking about having another one. Cheyenne still didn't get the appeal of having a baby. But Roxanne and Maverick had sat her down and asked her to be the baby's godmother, which she found only slightly less terrifying than the idea of having a baby herself. Of course, she'd be in the baby's life regardless of her role in relation to him, simply because of Roxanne. But now there was an expectation that she'd have a role to play, especially should something happen to her friends. Cheyenne had almost said no out of sheer panic; after all, she was still getting used to raising Miles and Amelia. Still… being involved in the baby's life came with the territory of being the mother's best friend, and Cheyenne was sure Amelia and Miles would be plenty of experience should she ever have to take over the parenting responsibilities.

Cheyenne had agreed, with some nausea at the idea, and had taken up Amelia's help in planning a baby shower. Which had led to the racecar cake and the dozens of baby-shoe and racecar-shaped cookies they'd made in the past three days.

"Can you believe we're having a party for this kid who isn't even going to be here for another three months?" Amelia asked finally when she'd placed the last candied stop sign on the cake.

"Hey, I don't get it either. According to Rhea, it's a way to con people out of more stuff for the kid than they were already going to buy him." Cheyenne grinned at Amelia, loving how they were on the same page for the umpteenth time that week. "Did you see the new sonogram?"

The tween nodded and opened the blast fridge door for Cheyenne to put the cake in. "He has a big nose."

"He has his father's nose." Cheyenne laughed and slid the cake onto its empty shelf. "And do not say a word about it to either of them."

"My lips are sealed!" Amelia mock-zipped her lips shut.

Cheyenne shook her head, tossed the tween a towel to

wipe down the counter, and pulled out a plastic tub to start stacking cookies in. "Wanna grab burgers on our way home? There's a new episode of that show you like, the one with the redhead, on my DVR. It always goes better with burgers."

"And onion rings?"

"And milkshakes."

"Sweet!"

Once they had finished cleaning up their workstation Cheyenne tasked Amelia with picking up their coats and bags from her office. She dried her hands on her legs and picked up her watch and the silver-and-diamond band off the ledge of the sink. She held the ring up to a ray of sunlight and watched it wink back at her, full of promises. Promises to be loyal, to love her forever, to help her be the best not-mom mom she could be. The whole list had made her head spin when he'd gotten on his knee, while the sky overhead had exploded with Fourth of July heat and color, and asked her to spend the rest of their natural lifespans together.

She'd almost said no. With Amelia and Miles, Roxanne and Maverick, Wesley and Connor, Carol and Mitch, and her parents all staring at them she'd almost said no. From panic, not from the fact that she didn't want to marry him. It had been too public, and she wasn't sure she was ready.

Cheyenne had braced herself for the 'no,' or for the stall, staring into his dark earnest eyes with dread in her belly. Thinking back on it, she couldn't place exactly what, or when, but the idea of putting it off, of begging for more time, disappeared with something in that steady gaze. She could see it, see her and Jesse and the kids together, and it just made more sense that her place in his life, by his side, be a little more permanent. So, much to the surprise of both herself and those around her, Cheyenne had heard herself uttering a dreamy 'yes' before she rushed him, wrapping her arms around his neck and knocking him over in the process.

She slid the ring on, her lips twisting into a small smile at the way it fit on her hand. It still amazed her how well the ring fit, just like she fit into the glue that had been the life Jesse had built for Amelia and Miles. Cheyenne often felt like the ingredient that no one had known was missing—like the soup had been delicious but had been missing a couple pinches of cumin. Once she'd been added to the pot, and stirred in thoroughly, no one realized that the old recipe hadn't called for her. Sometimes she even felt like the kids forgot the life they'd had before her; they were young, though, and there was plenty of room for those old memories to get added to by the new ones she and Jesse made for them. Together.

"It's a nice hand."

Cheyenne turned to see Jesse standing on the other side of the island, smiling contently as he watched her stare at her hand. "It's a nice ring." She cleared her throat against the warmth that had started to build in it. A recipe that sometimes clung to her vocal cords and made it hard for her to think straight. "What are you doing here?"

"I figured I'd take my girls for some burgers, since I won't get to see them for the rest of the night." Jesse rounded the island and kissed her, putting his arms around her.

"We were just headed for Sadie's," Cheyenne said with a laugh and kissed his cheek, his beard tickling the soft skin of her lips. "Where's the little man?"

"He's in the truck. When I told him he couldn't have a cupcake before dinner and he so kindly told me you'd give him one anyway. Knowing that he was probably telling me the truth, I told him he had to wait for us in there." Jesse rubbed his face against hers, his prickly facial hair making her giggle a little. "Melia in your office?"

"Yup." Cheyenne squeezed him around the waist before she stepped back and hit the light switch, dimming the kitchen lights. "Let's go grab her."

They laced their fingers together. His hand fit so well around hers that she sometimes wondered how she had ever doubted they belonged together. Or that she had doubted how much she could do for Amelia and Miles when the tween grinned up at them from her desk, ready for dinner.

They walked as a unit out to the parking lot of the bakery, where her grandfather's truck sat in its prime. She hadn't sold it—not like she'd initially thought she would. Rather, Jesse and Mitch had managed to breathe new life into the vehicle, and she now alternated driving it and her beloved Cherokee all over town. The truck was more suitable for her alone, or for the days when Amelia put in time at the bakery, while the Cherokee was turning into quite the dependable family car. The car for the family Cheyenne had never thought she'd have—that she never thought she'd wanted—but that her grandfather, who she still believed still played a hand in everything in her life, had given her the pieces to build.

She'd somehow put her perfect family together herself, piece by piece. It amazed her, even when Amelia and Jesse dragged her out of the bakery to the truck where Miles shouted her name happily from the open windows, that they belonged to her. That this was her family, her perfect recipe. That it all belonged to her. And she to it.

ACKNOWLEDGMENTS

Writing this book has been one of the most phenomenal, and painful, things I have ever done in my life. Cheyenne's story is close to my heart—and to the people around me who have helped shape these characters into who they are. I couldn't have brought them to life without the support, and the hard work, of GenZ Publishing and their fantastic team. I will forever be grateful for all of the time, guidance, and help that the team put in to make *The Family Recipe* a reality. Thank you—for everything!

THANK YOU FOR READING

Please consider leaving a review so that other readers can find this title. Who knows? It might just be their next favorite book!

Discover more titles from other GenZ authors at www.Genzpublishing.org

OTHER GENZ PUBLISHING ROMANCES

All You Hold On To by K.T. Egan

Take My Whole Life Too by Justine Ruff

Escaping to the County by E.A. Stripling

Made in the USA
Middletown, DE
24 June 2023